Trust

APRILLE CANNIFF

Copyright © 2019 Aprille Canniff
All rights reserved
First Edition

PAGE PUBLISHING, INC.
Conneaut Lake, PA

First originally published by Page Publishing 2019

ISBN 978-1-64584-758-8 (pbk)
ISBN 978-1-64584-759-5 (digital)

Printed in the United States of America

To my wife,

Thank you for showing me that together we can accomplish anything "Against all odds."

Prologue

Two months earlier

"We've been hit, we've been hit! Prepare for emergency landing and assume crash positions," the pilots screamed after a lucky shot from an AK-47 took out the tail rotor of the Black Hawk they were in.

"We're going to come in hard, brace for impact!"

They all grabbed their weapons, placed them on their laps, and braced themselves as best they could. The helicopter hit the ground so hard that the landing gear was forced into the belly of the helicopter and crushed, but with the main rotor still having power to it, when the fuselage leaned to the right after impact, the rotors caught the ground flipping the cabin and its passengers four times before finally coming to a stop. A cloud of sand, dust, and smoke surrounded the helicopter, giving them a small bit of cover but leaving them blind as well.

"Sitrep!" Sarge called as her team crawled out of the cabin dizzy, winded, slightly disoriented, and trying to regain their bearings.

"All green, Sarge, with the exception of the pilots. Preparing to extricate now," airman Stiller said.

"Johnson, Brooks! I need a 5/25 then post for lookout. Stiller, Williams, Miller! Get them out now!"

They were running out of time, and she knew it. They were in a valley between two sets of mountains just outside of Torkham, Pakistan, a known stronghold for insurgents because of the ease of access across the border and the plethora of caves hidden throughout the range. They were not supposed to be there in the first place, and now they were sitting ducks. They were wide open; the helicopter was their only option for cover, but it meant that the insurgents had to be exposed as well.

Johnson took up position at what was left of the tail section of the helicopter, and Brooks took nose fuselage. As soon as the dust began to clear, Johnson called out, "We've got four potential hostiles at one o'clock, fifty meters out minimal cover, Sarge!"

"Aircrew is clear, Sarge. Pilots are both amber. Both appear to have broken legs and multiple lacerations," Stiller reported as he put the second pilot on the ground and returned to the sarge's side, weapon aimed downrange.

Pop-pop-pop! was all they heard before the dirt started to fly.

"Defensive posture, hold your fire until we have a clear shot! Brooks, I need a confirmation on the number of hostiles. Can you identify and confirm?"

"Stand by, Sarge." Brooks half stood up and leaned around the nose to get better eyes on the hostiles, leaving himself wide open and exposed.

"Brooks, get down!"

The sarge went flying through the air at Brooks, catching him around the ribs and tackling him to the ground as the insurgents opened fire. Scrambling to return to cover, she grabbed Brooks by his vest and pulled him back behind the downed helicopter.

"Return fire!"

Without hesitation, the five of them lit up their targets. Having almost no cover, the four hostiles were neutralized in less than thirty seconds. Sarge went out to verify the situation, approaching at a forty-five-degree angle to allow cover from her team if needed. The team kept close watch on the targets, prepared to engage should one of them make even the slightest of movements. When the sarge reached the men who were the cause of their crash, she looked them over, attempting to verify that each one was either neutralized or, in fact, dead. As she placed her fingers on the neck of the last man she came to, he jumped. Kicking out her legs, she landed hard on her back, and as soon as she hit the ground, he was on her, wrapping his hands around her throat and squeezing. She balled her hands together and hit his forearms from the side, rolling out from under him at the same time. He turned and took a swing at her, screaming profanities in his native tongue, Farsi. She caught his fist in mid-air and used his own momentum against him, dropping him to the ground. She kneeled on his back and, with one swift movement, took his head in her hands, twisted it, and broke his neck. Standing up, she dusted herself off and then looked at the insurgents one more time before searching them, looking for any possible documents that might be useful to the paper pushers back at the base. The only thing she found was a picture of one of the men with whom she assumed to be his son, who appeared to be approximately fourteen years old and lying dead next to him.

"Son of a bitch."

Keeping her eyes on the surrounding mountains, the sarge returned to the helicopter.

"What the hell happened?" was all that she could say when she saw Williams and Stiller performing CPR on Brooks. His vest was off, shirt cut, and there was blood seeping out of a small hole just under his armpit. The sarge stood watch while they tried to save their comrade, but after two minutes of chest compressions, it was obvious to them all that he was gone. For a moment, they all sat silent. Looking at her team, she saw the shock and pain in their eyes and she knew she needed to bring them back.

"Williams and Johnson, get to work on the pilots, splint their legs. And, Miller, find a way to fabricate two litters. I'll keep watch." She watched as they all moved to accomplish what she had ordered, working on autopilot, training having taken over completely.

Thirty minutes later, both pilots' legs were splinted, and the two litters made from pieces of the helicopter and their shirts were ready to go. Noticing that the sarge was holding her left arm close to her chest, Williams asked, "Sarge, are you okay?"

"Fine. Are we ready to go?" she said through clenched teeth. She was the least of their problems.

Williams looked at his sergeant. "Sarge, if you don't let me take a look at that, we aren't going anywhere," he said, nodding to her blood-soaked arm.

Without even looking, she shrugged out of her ABU top. She had been shot through the upper arm, but it looked like a through and through. Knowing how the sarge was, Williams put a dressing on it and let it go for now.

"Sarge, what do you want to do now?"

Turning, she looked at her men. All the water had been removed from the helicopter, and the individual locator beacons had been activated.

"Williams and Stiller, take one litter. Miller and Johnson, take the other, and I'll get Brooks." Both pilots protested, giving her direct orders to leave Brooks behind.

"We can send someone back to get him. We can't take the chance of him slowing us down. We need to get out of here now! Leave him, Sergeant Thomas, that's a direct order."

Bending over to lift Brooks onto her shoulders so she could fireman's carry him, Sarge turned to the pilots, looked at them, and informed them in a cold, clear, and calculated voice, "We don't leave anyone behind." And with that said, she started to walk.

Even with stopping every half hour to get their wind back and stay hydrated, the sun and wind were wearing on the team.

Where is our rescue chopper? It should have been here by now, she thought. She was tired, her arm was throbbing, and she was beginning to wonder how much longer she could keep herself going, let alone her team. She needed to get them across the border. Once she did that, then maybe they could find a secure spot to rest and wait for the rescue team to find them.

Two clicks later, they were finally crossing back into Afghanistan. Tired and in shock, they climbed halfway up and down the surrounding mountains, loose rock sliding out from under their feet, caves everywhere they looked, and the sun beating down on their already worn-out bodies. The wind was beginning to pick up, making it more difficult to maintain their balance over the loose rock, and stirring up the powdery sand that seemed to be everywhere, it was difficult to see with the sand blowing and the sun shining overhead as bright and hot as a spotlight. The sarge once described what it was like to see out here to a friend of hers back home. "Put a box over your head, cut a hole directly in front of you, and put a flashlight through it and turn it on. Then put the finest grain sand and baby powder inside and have a fan blowing it around the inside of that same box, and that should give you a good idea as to what it is like."

As they entered into yet another valley, they came onto one of the main supply roads, but before she could get an idea as to their exact location, they came under fire again. Posting behind a rock formation and securing the pilots as well as they could, they returned fire. Trying to get an idea as to what they were facing, the sarge took a quick 5/25. There were approximately fifteen to twenty hostiles with AK-47s, and they were closing in on their position. *God, I hope the rescue team gets here soon*, she thought as she engaged in suppression fire. The firefight continued on until the sarge yelled for another magazine and was told they were out. For the first time since coming to Afghanistan ten months ago, she was afraid. She looked around for a possible escape route, and that's when she saw an American convoy in the distance running toward the east. She couldn't believe her luck. Firing off a flare and signaling for their assistance, two Humvees and a deuce and a half responded, the Humvees firing off with their fifty caliber and 240s, while the deuce and a half pulled up for the evacuation. With speed and precision, they loaded their wounded, dead, and tired personnel and headed back to Bagram Air Base in complete silence.

Chapter 1

Alex got on the plane with an anticipation and excitement that had been building for a year now. She was finally on her way home, and in just over twenty-three hours, she would be able to sleep in her own bed, take a shower for more than three minutes at a time, and not have to wear a hundred pounds of gear every day. She thought about the first letter she got while she was gone, and the hurt returned. She thought she was over her, but that "Dear Jane" letter still hurt the same as it did the day that she first got it. Was she still in love with Amanda? No, but she didn't know if she could ever open up to another woman again. Looking back on the relationship they had, she had to wonder if she was ever truly in love, or if she was in love with the thought that someone cared enough to say that they would wait for her. She had not made love to a woman in over a year and she didn't think that she would again anytime soon.

Being in a war zone changes a person. Alex knew better than most that war is five percent combat and ninety-five percent boredom. The trick to survival eluded most, and for that, she watched many of her friends pay a steep price. At one point during her tour, the commander of her unit finally decided to let her lead a mission to recover sensitive material and rescue any potential detainees, a mission that no one expected her to be able to complete given the lack of intel and terrain that would have to be traversed. Nevertheless, she took the mission without thinking twice, organized a team, and formulated a plan in less than ten hours. When she and her team returned the next day in the helicopter with three rescued detainees and the sensitive materials that were requested, she was given the respect that she knew she deserved, as well as a step promotion and many more missions. Unfortunately, not all missions went according to plan. People were wounded and/or killed, but as her commander told her after the last, "We can't win them all Thomas, but we try to save as many as we can along the way."

The only comfort Alex attained from the commander's little speech was when he said, "Dismissed."

It was time to evaluate who she was, what was important, and what she wanted. She realized that she had found herself and her strength in her independence and self-reliance. She didn't need anyone, and didn't want to either. At one time, she was called the hopeless romantic, telling everyone that the magic is in the eyes. What she didn't tell anyone was that she didn't think that she would ever find anyone that would love her for who she is. She lives a life that few would be willing to put up with. Constantly being at risk, on the run, and "doing the right thing" is not an easy thing to deal with when you are the one at home waiting. This was her life and she liked it. She was good at what she did, and the last thing that she needed was the distraction of a woman. It was time to focus on the next mission in line and nothing more. All she was told was to expect resistance and isolation because she was to be spearheading a new team. She sat back in her seat and resigned herself to the fact that she would have to endure roadblocks with whatever this new assignment was, but she was happy in the fact that she had to answer to no one. She was on her own to ensure success with the team that she would be given, and this time she swore to herself that she was not going to lose another person. Not if she could help it. That was the other reason why she did not want another woman in her life; there was too much to do, and she had to focus on the task at hand, whatever it may be. Not long after the plane took off, she fell asleep wondering, against everything else who, if anyone, would be there waiting for her when she landed.

***

She was tired. Tonight was the night from hell, and Jen could not figure out what was wrong with people. The night started off with lights and sirens as she headed to a domestic assault call. When she got there, the husband had already done significant damage to his wife's face, and it didn't look like he was done. After taking him to the ground, handcuffing him, reading him his rights, and taking him to booking, it just got worse. Assault and battery, armed robbery, carjacking, and it felt like the night would never end. Now as she unlocked the door to her apartment, all she could think was that the world was going to hell. She knew that it wasn't, of course, but sometimes the job got to you. All she saw day in and day out was the worst side of people, and soon you started to see it off the job too. Trust was the hardest thing for her to give. In fact, aside from her old partner, she didn't know if there was anyone that she did trust.

She took her duty belt off, put it on the chair next to her bed, and hung her shirt on the back. A hot shower was what she needed to relax away the knots in her back…and her mind. Stepping in, she thought about Emily and how nice it was to come home to her. How on nights like tonight all she had to do was look into her eyes, and the world righted itself again. She would try to slip into the bed as softly and quietly as possible, but no matter how hard she tried, Emily always woke up. She would wrap her in her arms and hold her, breathing in her scent; it was like a spring meadow, and then she would slowly fall asleep with Emily's scent to guide the way. That was until a stray bullet from a drug dealer's gun had found its way into the heart of the woman who held hers so dearly. She did everything she could to track down the man who took away her life, and when she finally found him, a fourteen-year-old kid, it took everything in her to keep from hurting him the way he had hurt her. He was a kid, and Emily would have told her that he needs guidance, not jail, and it was because of Emily and what she believed that she did not fight when he was tried as a juvenile. He was set to be released in a year, and still not a day went by when she didn't wonder if she would ever find it in herself to forgive him like she knew Emily would have wanted her to.

Turning off the water, she silently cursed herself for allowing this melancholy to invade her heart and mind. It had been six years since Emily had died, and although she had indulged in a few one-night stands here and there, she never could give herself to anyone. No one had been able to capture her attention for more than a night. She knew from watching everyone else that she worked with how quickly marriages broke up all because of the job. She got lucky with Emily, but she knew in her heart that she would never again feel the warmth of another woman like her. No one understood the job or wanted to wait for that call to come in the middle of the night, informing them that their loved one had been killed in the line of duty. She herself could not understand it, how anyone would be willing to live with the constant knowledge that at any moment, the person you loved could be taken from you…over a job. That was why she knew that she would spend the rest of her life alone. Not only would she not put anyone in that situation, but she doubted if there was anyone that could look at her and really see her for who she was.

***

The plane landed at Hanscom Air Force Base at 0730 Saturday morning, and standing on the tarmac waiting for Alex was Colonel Jacobson, commander of the 557 Military Police Squadron on base. Everyone knew his reputation—hard ass, barked orders, never gave a compliment, and an all-around jarhead. He looked like the stereotypical G.I. Joe from his high and tight haircut and perfectly trimmed mustache to his perfectly polished, mirror-shined boots. He was the type that worked out five days a week for the sole purpose of being able to intimidate those smaller than he was. His first four years of service was in the Army, but he got smart and transferred to the Air Force. Unfortunately, he did not leave the Army mentality behind. Alex did not know who was supposed to be picking her up, but she knew that it wouldn't be a full bird colonel, so she scanned the tarmac. She was looking for her ride when he approached her.

"Master Sergeant Thomas, do you have any other bags?"

Snapping to attention, Alex quickly responded, "No, sir. All I have is my carry-on. I shipped the rest of my things directly to my apartment prior to leaving, sir."

"Follow me then," the colonel said before he turned and walked away.

As the colonel walked toward the car that was waiting for them, his mind was finalizing his initial assessment of the so-called "best there is." She stood approximately five-foot-six inches, one hundred twenty-five pounds, blond hair, and blue eyes. Coming off the plane, she walked with a purpose and had the air of control. If she hadn't been so breathtakingly beautiful, the look on her face and in her eyes would have been enough to warn anyone to back off. He was impressed that when he approached her, she never flinched. Most people who saw him coming tried to find a way to clear out, but Master Sergeant Thomas looked him straight in the eyes, unknowingly telling him that it would take more than a reputation to rattle her.

Sliding into the back seat of the Suburban, Alex closed the door, and the driver slowly headed out. She sat straight-backed and looked out of the tinted windows as they drove off the flight line and headed toward the colonel's office. She wondered why Colonel Jacobson had come to pick her up and knew that whatever the reason, it couldn't be good. Flashes of the last mission went through her mind—helicopter crashing, the retrieval, and then the small arms fire when they thought they were almost home. No, she had to clear her mind and focus. If the colonel was here because of what had happened, then she would take whatever disciplinary actions they gave her because good or bad, what happened was on her. It was her team and her responsibility, and therefore any and all consequences should fall on her, and she was ready for it.

***

Jen woke up agitated and unrefreshed, so she decided that since there was no way that she was going to be able to go back to sleep, she might as well go for a run. Trading her boxers for black running shorts and T-shirt for a running bra, she headed out the door. Jogging always helped Jen to clear her mind, and she loved how her heart felt when she pushed herself. There were days when she would get so lost in her thoughts that by the time she realized she was still running, she had gone a good four miles out from her normal route.

She woke up this morning holding onto the extra pillow and curled up on her side. She knew why, of course, but admitting it, even to herself, would do nothing to help. Her mind was made up, and she had built her life around her decision. Whenever an extra shift came open, she jumped on it, and if she wasn't working, she was working out in the gym or at the gun range. Being completely and totally focused on the job was the way she was able to suppress the loneliness that was growing in her.

It was a beautiful day. The sun was shining, the wind was gently blowing, and the trees were beginning to bloom. The colors that exploded from everything in the spring never ceased to amaze her; blues, reds, greens, purples, and lavenders combined with the warm sweet smells emanating from each blossom, and Jen was in heaven. There was nothing more beautiful than Boston in the spring, and today was the perfect example as to why. As she was rounding the corner and coming up on the garment district, she heard the *whoop-whoop* of sirens right behind her. Recognizing her old partner, she headed back to see what was up and was surprised into a complete stop when he got out of the car and walked up to her. Chris never had a serious look on his face, not even when they tag-teamed that arsonist right before he was about to light up the old mill warehouse and got a face full of gas.

"What's going on, Chris?" she asked. When he put his hands in his pockets and looked at the ground, she knew that it had to be bad. "Chris, what's up?"

He looked up at her. "Jen, the captain wants you in his office now. He sent me to come and get you."

Without hesitation, she slid into her old spot on the passenger's side of the cruiser and went over the many reasons why the captain would send someone to come and find her. Nothing like this had ever happened to her before, and for the life of her, she couldn't figure out what was going on. Seeing the concern in her ex-partner's eyes had her scared. When they pulled up in front of the precinct, Chris turned and looked at her.

"Listen, I don't know what you did, but I have your back, so call me when this is over, and I'll help you figure out how to deal with whatever they throw at you."

She got out of the car, and when she realized that Chris was not behind her, she leaned into the window to look at him.

"Chris, what the hell is going on? You didn't say a damn word the entire ride here, and now you are just dropping me off and telling me that you have my back! What do you know that I don't?"

Looking at Jen, he saw the fire in her eyes, the same look that always got to him. He sighed. "Jen, I don't know what's going on. The captain called me and told me to bring you to him ASAP. When I asked him what it was about, he just told me to mind my own business and get you," he said, sighing. "Call me when you are done," and with that, he pulled away, leaving his old partner to stand on her own, alone.

**

The car pulled up in front of an old but pristine building that was tucked away behind blossoming oak trees and evergreens, a place that, unless you knew its location, you were sure to miss. She followed the colonel into the one-story brick building and past several standard offices to what appeared to be the colonel's office in the back. Once in, Colonel Jacobson ordered her to close the door as he situated himself behind a large mahogany desk that was clear of everything except a desk blotter and a file folder. Behind him were pictures of an old farmhouse with its surrounding farm and barn but nothing else. He eyed her as she came to the position of attention in front of his desk. Without acknowledging her, Colonel Jacobson opened the folder and began to skim through it. It was not necessary. He knew her file and career by heart, but he needed a moment to center himself. She had been under his command for three years, but until now, he had never had to bother talking to her face-to-face. Taking a deep breath, Colonel Jacobson looked at Master Sergeant Thomas and began the line of questioning that he enjoyed so much.

"File says you have never been in trouble. Is that correct?"

"Yes, sir," she answered.

"It also says that you were the noncommissioned officer in charge of approximately thirty airmen, and you were well regarded by your troops. Is that also correct?"

Without hesitation, she responded with the truth. "Sir, I was in charge of approximately that number of airmen. However, whether or not I was well regarded by them, well, that is a question better answered by my men, sir."

The colonel was taken aback by her answer. The standard answer to that question was "Yes, sir," so why would she not try to capitalize on a positive accolade like that? "Were you or were you not well regarded by your troops, Master Sergeant?" He was determined to get a direct answer from this "female" that everyone had been talking so highly about.

"Sir, with all due respect, my answer is a matter of opinion. You asked me for a fact, and the only way to get the correct and accurate answer for you is to ask my troops, sir."

She maintained eye contact with him, refusing to back down. She didn't even blink. Finally, he stood up and walked around his desk until he was facing Master Sergeant Thomas nose to nose, so close that he could smell the shampoo in her hair, but saw not a single trace of fear. "Then answer me this, Sergeant. Why is it that everyone tells me that you are the best at what you do?"

Calm and relaxed as if she were speaking with her peers, she looked the colonel directly in the eyes. "Because I am, sir."

He took a step back and was slightly surprised by her confidence. He paused for only a moment before reaching into his desk and pulling out a large manila envelope. "Well, I hope that you are as good as you claim to be because you have been assigned to liaison with local law enforcement and assist in training, interrogations, apprehension, and investigations. It turns out that Homeland Security, CIA, FBI, and however many other alphabet agencies are out there are too busy looking for terrorists, so the DoD decided that they would instate a new program of cooperation between the military and local law enforcement. They decided that the best way to be effective is to cooperate and share information across the board in a joint training operation. You will have the lead, and the team that is assigned will be yours to do with as you see fit, but you will cooperate fully. Is that understood?"

Alex took every word the colonel said in and processed it just as fast, and the red flags were flying high. "Sir, how many military personnel will I have on my team?"

"It will be just you, Sergeant. DoD wants to see how well this experimental team works before assigning any more of its assets. And just to be clear, you are there as the training liaison only. Nothing more, which means no field work. That will be on them. Clear?"

This is going to be a cluster fuck, she thought. How could the DoD expect an operation like this to work with only civilians on the team? They had no concept of discipline and therefore did not always feel the need to follow orders when given, and that in and of itself could get people killed. "Then I have only one question left, sir. When do I begin?"

Jacobson handed her the sealed manila envelope, contents unknown to him, with her orders, guidelines, and personnel roster with jackets. "At 0700 Monday morning. You will not be given reconstitution time due to time constraints per General Scott. Dismissed."

"Yes, sir," was all she said before she did a perfect facing movement and left the room.

Jacobson prided himself on his ability to intimidate just about everyone around him with his sheer presence, and the fact that Thomas, one of his troops, did not seem to care who he was infuriated him. She was arrogant, bold, and entirely too small to do all of the things CENTAF claimed she had done. She was a woman for God's sake! It was then that he swore to himself that if she so much as breathed in the wrong direction and he heard of it, she would be off the assignment and peeling potatoes in the kitchen for the remainder of her career. Now all he had to do was find out who it was that chose her for this assignment and how it was possible for him to be circumvented when it came to authorizing the redistribution of his personnel.

***

Jen knocked on the captain's door, whom everyone kindly referred to as Barney Frank, and when she heard him bark what sounded like "Come," she walked in and realized that whatever it was that she did this time, it was probably a career ender. Standing beside the captain was the Chief of Police Mike Collins, a formidable man in his late fifties who held the air of someone who had done more and seen more than anyone else ever would. They were both looking at her like she was about to be released from duty at any moment and were waiting for the right time to tell her. Feeling slightly uncomfortable in her workout gear standing in front of her captain and the chief, she did what she always did…she spoke her mind. "Okay, what did I do now? Whatever it is, I am sorry, and it will not happen again."

"Officer Miceli, do you really believe that I would ruin a perfectly good Saturday morning to be here when I could be out golfing right now for a disciplinary matter?" The chief looked as if she was a child trying to talk her way out of a punishment.

"I am here because your captain was asked to give me the name of his best officer, one who has shown initiative and confidence in every aspect of their career. Someone who does not back down, is not afraid of a fight, and is willing to participate in a groundbreaking joint task force operation. Your captain gave me your name."

Jen looked at her captain in utter astonishment. She was always in his office because of something she did wrong, anywhere from the way she spoke to John Q. Public to her not waiting for backup to arrive before going headfirst into a bad situation.

"Officer Miceli, although we have had to have discussions on some minor details from time to time, you have a knack at finding what needs to be found. You have good instincts, and you follow them. Because of that, you stand apart from the rest of your brethren. The question now is, do you want the chance to prove just how good you are, or do you want to be walking a beat for the rest of your career?" The captain leaned back in his chair, waiting for her response and hoping that she could keep her mouth closed long enough to think about what was being offered. She had the potential to be a great cop, and this just might be the opportunity to help her to do just that.

Having never heard a compliment come to her from the captain before, Jen stood straight up and looked the chief in the eye. "Yes, sir, I am ready to come on board."

At that, the chief handed her a white envelope and told her to report to the address listed inside at 0700 on Monday morning. "You are not to tell anyone that we spoke, where you are going, what your assignment is, or anything that I have just told you." He took one last long look at Miceli to drive his point home, and then the chief turned and walked out without another word, leaving the two of them to their own conjecture.

"Captain," Jen said after the chief left the office, and she dropped down in the chair, "what the hell did I just sign up for?"

"I don't know, and the chief won't tell me anything. I was telling you the truth. You are good and you do have the potential to be great. This might be your chance to prove it no matter what the job is. But do yourself a favor, Miceli, keep your mouth shut!" He dismissed her for the weekend, knowing that whatever task his officer was just assigned to would be difficult but confident that she was the right choice for whatever this turned out to be.

Chapter 2

Walking into her apartment later that night, Alex dropped her bag in the living room and stopped for a moment to take a look around. The apartment was clean, dusted, and aired out. The plants were green and healthy, and a new arrangement was sitting on the living room table with a note on it:

> Alex, Welcome home!!! I took the liberty of putting some food in the refrigerator for you. I put the boxes you sent into the spare room for you to sort through later. Come over when you can so we can catch up. I've missed you, girl!!! Love, Tina.

Smiling as she smelled the flowers, Alex walked down the hall to the bathroom, stripped out of her uniform, and jumped into the shower. Turning it up as hot as she could take it, she let the water beat on her neck, back, and face. As simple a pleasure as it was to some, a hot shower with no time limit was something that Alex always cherished. It was the only time that she felt that she could let go of everything from her mind and breathe without having to deal with expectations or schedules or whatever else might jump up. Placing her hands on the wall, she tried to let the past year slowly get washed away by the hot water, but Brooks continued to jump back in her mind.

Wrapping up in her softest bathrobe and slipping into her favorite Smurf slippers, Alex went to the kitchen and made a cup of chamomile tea. When it came to the military, she was hard, consistent, and on point. Everything had its place and a specific order in which to be accomplished, but when it came to her personal life, she wanted to be able to relax. Her home was soft peaches, bright yellows, and mint greens. Priding herself in the fact that she embraced the innocence of her childhood, her Smurf slippers always made her feel at home and good. Her furniture had the light floral design of roses, the couch and chairs were overstuffed and comfortable. Potted plants surrounded her walls at perfect intervals, allowing her to enjoy the scent of the flowers and the varieties of color they provided. She placed her cup on the end table, sat on the couch, and opened the manila envelope. She read the mission details over and over until she had them memorized, and yet something in them did not sit right with her. She read the jackets on her new trainees, wondered first where their pictures were, and then, after a short review, was mildly impressed with some of the things the officers had done. It did not mean any of them would make her cut or could even handle working for her. In fact, they all seemed like loners. There were eight officers in all assigned to her, and to no one's surprise, they were all men except for one—and lucky her. The female officer appeared to have a problem with following the basic procedures when dealing with the public and seemed to be indifferent to standard operating procedures. It appeared to Alex that Officer Miceli had no problem with heading into dangerous situations but didn't care at all about the way she handled the public or victims when in a tight spot. "She won't last."

Putting the personnel folders down, she began reviewing the aerial photos, area and building layout, and training equipment that she had to work with. The building was an old warehouse that had been gutted in preparation to be turned into a storage area and offices before red tape stopped it from being completed. One side of the building sat on the water, one opened to a spacious parking lot, and the other two sides were cluttered with boxes, crates, garbage cans, fence pieces, and every other type of debris that normally accumulates around buildings at the docks. Placed in the corner of the warehouse were eight treadmills, a free weight set, four hundred feet of rope, workout mats, two thousand Simunition rounds and the hardware for the weapons' conversions to Simunition barrels, eight bulletproof dragon skin vests, and a few other odds and ends that she could work with.

The way her mission statement read, she would have two months to work on getting these officers up to speed on the way that the military handled both hostile and hostage situations. She was to be the one who set the schedule for training, and if she felt that one of the officers could not complete the training, she was authorized to release them from the program. As nice and detailed as all of this was, there was one bit of information missing from the plethora of paperwork sitting in front of her—why did she have to teach these officers interrogation techniques? She read her orders again and realized one other small fact that sent up red flags: Why was she to report to a one-star general via phone, and why was it that neither she nor any other member of her team was authorized to discuss the training or missions that they were on except to General Scott? She picked up her phone and called the number that was given with her orders. After a brief conversation with General Scott, Alex hung up the phone happy in the fact that she was able to get extra supplies upon request but uneasy with the lack of information being handed out. The general was guarded in what he said, and she found it strange when he told her that there was to be no further contact until notified otherwise. Something was going on, and Alex was not sure if she was going to like it. Sifting through all the information and pictures, she started making notes, but the comfort of her couch, the taste of her tea, and the softness of her robe overtook her, and she fell asleep lying down on her couch with paperwork surrounding her.

***

When Jen finally got home, she ripped the envelope open and was agitated to see nothing more than the address to a warehouse out by the docks and orders telling her not to inform anyone as to her current assignment or the duty location. The uniform of the day would be PT clothes, and her service weapon was to be carried in an unmarked bag or container.

What the hell is this? was all she could think as she looked over the instructions for the second time. Having always been the curious type, the short but to-the-point letter piqued her interest. She was faintly aware of the location but decided to look it up on the computer. After three hours of surfing the Internet, she sat back and tried to tie together what she had been able to pull up. The building was a warehouse situated on the docks in the middle of the district. As all of the cops knew, the district was notorious for trafficking everything from drugs to antiques. The only problem was that whenever they came in to grab a possible suspect, word of mouth wet out, and the bad guy was gone before they even left the parking lot of the precinct. All she was able to come up with was that she was possibly going in to conduct a surveillance operation, but if that was the case, then why all of the secrecy?

Jen paced back and forth across her small living room going over the information from the envelope the chief gave her and what she had found out on the Internet. Finally, she raked her fingers through her hair and realized that she was not going to be able to rest until she found out more about what this was, so she decided to go for a drive out to the docks. Before leaving, she had changed into an old pair of baggy jeans, oversized black hoodie sweatshirt, and her old running shoes so that she could hide as many of her features as possible. She parked a half a mile from the address she had for the warehouse and slowly walked toward the building, taking special care to keep her head down and eyes open for anyone or anything suspicious.

As she approached the building that she would be reporting to, she did a quick scan of the area. Nothing around except the usual district junk piled on the sides of the building, but the parking lot was clear. Rather than walking directly to the building, she came around the north side using the debris as cover and tried to get a good look into the windows but instead found that all of the windows on the first floor had been blacked out. She walked east around the building, noting that there was only five feet from the building to the water, and with the combination of wind and high tide, the spray from the waves came at her from every direction, effectively soaking her by the time she had walked ten feet. She tried to open a heavy steel door that had a cipher lock on it halfway down, but it was to no avail. Continuing on, she was making mental notes, and warning flags kept popping up. So far, she had not seen any broken windows or pried-open doors, but what she did notice was that the windows were not your standard single-pane glass that most of the buildings in the district tended to have. Not one window was broken or cracked, which was so often the norm for warehouses in New England. Her gut started to tell her something was off about this place. As she turned the corner to the south side of the building, she was not surprised to find that the windows were blacked out on this side as well, but there was a fire escape.

The ladder stopped about ten feet from the ground, so she looked around for something that she could use to climb on. Using four pallets and two long metal rods that she found in the trash surrounding the area, she stacked the pallets on top of each other and used the rods to hold them in place against the building. Jen climbed the pallets, not caring if anyone was watching, up to the fire escape and to the second floor. She tried opening the door to no avail but was able to look through the small window in the door. There was a long hallway with what appeared to be offices on either side, a fire extinguisher hung on the wall to the right, and what looked to be a metal fire door set at the end of the hall. With nothing more to see, she climbed back down the ladder and dropped the rest of the way down rather than trying to use her makeshift ladder, landing perfectly on her feet. She replaced the rods and pallets and made a slow but calculated return to her car.

On her way home, she called Chris to let him know that everything was all right. Wanting details, he tried everything that he could think of to get her to tell him something, but she was locked up tight. All that Jen would, and could, tell him was that on Monday, she was starting a new assignment and she would know more then. When Chris finally realized that he was not going to get any more details from his old partner, he told her good luck and made her promise to meet him Wednesday night for a beer at Mickey's, which she was more than happy to accept. She hung up the phone, stopped by Jim's pizza to pick up a meatball sub, and then went home to think.

Sitting on her bed with her laptop in front of her, Mountain Dew on the nightstand, and sub in her hand, Jen ate while going back and forth between what she saw, had read online, and was told. She didn't know of any undercover operations in that area, but she did know that this had to be something big, or the chief would not have hand-delivered her the orders. She didn't know if she was the only one reporting or if there were more, and she could not tie in anything at all with that warehouse or its location. As she began to dig deeper and look for leases and ownership turnovers in the last ten years, fatigue got the best of her, and she fell asleep with her laptop beside her, confusion and frustration on her mind.

***

Alex slept until nine the next morning, seemingly dreamless, until she jumped up, screaming, "Get down!" Taking deep breaths to steady herself, it took her a minute to remember where she was and what she was going to be doing. She picked up the pictures, paperwork, and notes that had scattered everywhere when she jumped up slid them back into the envelope and locked them in a desk that she kept in the spare room. Looking around the room was like looking into the past. Pictures were hung next to awards and decorations that she had received over the years, and although most people would call it the "I love me room," to her, it was a chronological record of her career. Eighteen years go by so fast when you love what you do, and she loved her life in the military, or at least she did. Sitting in one of the boxes that Tina was nice enough to bring in and put against the wall were two more decorations, and she had no intentions of adding them—not now, not ever. There are times when you do things not for yourself, not for your country but because something deep inside of you moves your body without thought or hesitation. Times when you don't know what you are doing until you are actually doing it, and although someone higher up decided that she should be decorated for her actions two months ago, it did not mean that she agreed with them. In fact, when the base commander informed her that she would be receiving the awards, she tried to politely decline them, but he made it abundantly clear that she would accept them with a smile on her face, and after that, she could do whatever it was she wanted with them. She meant to throw them away, but in the rush to finish all of her overdue paperwork and the short notice to pack and get everything home, she just threw them into a box without giving them a second thought.

She had to get out of the house. She couldn't deal with the memories that those boxes contained. She went to her room, changed, and ran out of the apartment like she was running from a ghost, which was, in fact, exactly what she was doing.

***

Jen woke up slowly, stretching out her body the length of the bed and throwing the pillow that she had been holding on to so tightly during the night onto the floor. She dreamed of warehouses and waves as she went looking for something but not knowing what it was. She took a deep breath and let it out slowly, still trying to figure out what she was going to be doing on Monday. She had an entire weekend off for the first time in months, and for the life of her, she had no idea what she was going to do. She decided to make herself breakfast, and just as she slid the eggs out of the pan, her phone rang. Recognizing Chris's phone number, she hit Ignore and put some bacon in the pan to fry up. When all was done, she sat down to eat the first real breakfast she had had in a long time and decided to check the message Chris left her. "I am going to be there in an hour. And like it or not, you are going to tell me what the hell happened yesterday."

"Damn it!" Chris was hardheaded, and not knowing something always drove him up the wall. She threw her breakfast in the trash, grabbed her gym bag, and left the apartment before overprotective Chris showed up and began his relentless rounds of questioning.

***

FWO was a gym designed for women only and was where Jen had started going six months ago when she had things on her mind that she needed to sort through or if she just needed to blow off some steam. It was not an overpriced flashy pickup joint that people went to show off their bodies or to try and hook up with whoever might be looking. The layout was designed to be convenient to the customer so that if they wanted to work their upper bodies, all they had to do was start at the first machine on the left wall and work their way to the end of the row. That was how the whole gym was set up, convenient for the user and geared toward women and their particular needs. Every day they had classes which varied from a light aerobics class to a boot camp where just about everyone dropped by the end of the session.

Changing in the locker room, Jen grabbed a towel and began her routine starting with abs exercises. She pushed through her normal routine but added ten pounds of weight to each station, trying to work off everything that was on her mind. The gym wasn't busy today, most likely because it was the perfect beach day, so when Jen switched over to begin her leg workout, she was able to see clearly through to the cardio area. There were women of all shapes and sizes who came here, but everyone eventually ended up doing cardio at some point, and today was no exception. Looking around, for no reason other than to keep her mind busy, she looked to see if there was anyone that she knew, hoping maybe for someone to go to lunch with after she was done. Switching from calves to quads, she set herself up, selected the appropriate weight setting, sat back, and began her routine when "she" walked by. Jen couldn't help but stare as the most breathtakingly beautiful woman walked right past her and into the cardio area. Jen watched as the woman got on the treadmill and keyed it up. Most people who got on the treadmills went at a fast walk or a light jog, but not this one. The second it started going, she pushed it faster and faster until she was at a full-out run. Not realizing that she had completely stopped her workout, she watched this woman. It was as if she was trying to outrun something or someone. The look on her face was that of total determination as her breathing quickened and sweat began to run down the side of her face and glisten on her arms and neck.

Realizing that she was staring, Jen quickly shook her head and moved to the leg press and began her movements, but within a minute, her gaze drifted back to the mystery woman. She had an air around her that told people to stay clear, but the more Jen really looked, the more she realized that what she saw was pain in her eyes. "No," she said, shaking her head and bringing herself back to the here and now. She quickly got up and headed to the showers. Feeling the need to cool off, she turned the water as cold as she could take it until her body began to shiver before turning the temperature back up so that the entire shower area was filled with steam.

***

Other than making sure that she had a place to come home to before she left, Alex also made sure that her membership to the gym remained up to date. She kept a locker with some basics in it, and today she was glad she did. She needed to run and work up a sweat; she needed to clear her mind of the past and focus on the future, and this was her way of doing just that. When she ran, she was able to focus and sort through everything that was running through her mind. When the world turned upside down, decisions had to be made, and a phone call had to be placed. She ran until she had a plan and was ready to deal with the tasks and whatever repercussions that were sure to follow. Today she ran to escape the past, and nothing else could help her to do that. She was going to run until she couldn't run anymore, or she finally was able to forget the past and leave it behind her. At least for today.

She went straight for the treadmill, all of her attention focused on getting on, getting it up to speed, and clearing her mind. Getting on the first one she came to, she set the speed control, turned up the music on her iPod, and ran. Within the first two minutes of running, her mind began to replay the most recent events that happened while she was overseas, the ones that she came here to forget. Frustrated, she turned the music up, increased the speed, and went for broke.

All or nothing was her motto, so when she felt her heart pounding in her chest, sweat soaking through her shirt, and her legs starting to give in, she finally looked up and took her first real look around the room. It always bothered her to see how so many people spend money for a membership, come once or twice, and never show up again. So when she looked around at the women in the gym today, she was not surprised to see most of them trying to look like they were attempting to work out when in fact they were doing little more than sitting on equipment and taking up space. Then just as she was shaking her head in disgust and began to slow her pace for her cool down, a woman walked by that actually made her miss a step and almost fall off the machine. She quickly regained her footing without anyone noticing, but she was taken aback by the woman headed for the locker room. She was sweating lightly, her ponytail was loose from her workout, and she looked like something had shaken her. Not knowing why she noticed these things about a total stranger walking by, she completed her cool down and headed for the shower.

Stopping long enough to strip off her sweaty clothes, grab her towel, shampoo, and soap, Alex headed for the showers, trying to see through the steam so as not to bump into anyone. She got under a hot stream of water and, after lathering up, took a cautious look around to see how many other people were in there with her. There she was…the woman who walked by and caught her so off guard. She was absolutely beautiful. Seeing her profile through the steam made her heart speed up and her stomach do a little flip. She was tall, maybe five foot ten; her back was strong and toned, and she had a tribal tattoo on her lower back just above the hips. Her hair was light brown and came down just past her shoulders. The way she was standing as she rinsed the shampoo out of her hair perfectly outlined her tight form, strong legs, rounded breasts, and tight ass. She was perfection. She was so completely absorbed in the moment that when Jen turned around and saw Alex appraising her, it took her a minute to realize what she was doing. It wasn't until Jen made eye contact with her that she realized what she was doing, and completely embarrassed, she turned around and felt her skin turn eight shades of red. She was not only embarrassed at being caught staring at someone whom she didn't know in the shower, but she was shaken by how this woman was able to stop her flat in her tracks. What was wrong with her? She never eyed someone up and down, let alone without their permission. She tried to finish her shower as quickly as possible so she could get out of there, get her mind on track, and really start planning for Monday.

***

She should have known better than to think that Chris would give up when he realized that she wasn't at home when he got there. As she came up the walk to her apartment, there he was, sitting on the step, waiting for her like he had done so many times in the past when he knew something was off with her. To the outsider, he looked like the stereotypical Guido sitting there in his tight black shirt, blue jeans, and gold cross around his neck. "What's up, Chris?" she asked as she walked past him and up the stairs, as if she was truly surprised to see him there.

With full animation that she always called Chris-isms, he began his round of questioning. "What happened? Are you in trouble? Did you get transferred? What is going on? You have always talked to me, and now you want to get all secretive and expect me to just go with it?" He was exasperated.

After her wasted trip out to the docks, skipping breakfast, and ruining her workout because she couldn't stop staring at some woman, Jen was not in the mood to be interrogated. "I am going to change, Chris, and when I am done, if you would like, you can join me for lunch, but you need to stop questioning me like I am some suspect you just brought in!" With that, she went to her room and slammed the door, knowing that he would be there when she came out.

She was still worked up over everything when she came out of her room, so when she saw Chris patiently waiting for her on the couch, she let out a deep sigh and said as she walked past him, "You're buying. Let's go," and walked out the door with him close on her heels.

As they were coming down the steps, Chris went for his keys but quickly put them back in his pocket when he saw Jen walk right past his car. "Hey, Jen, where are we going?" he asked as he ran to catch up with her.

"I figured that since you are here now, we might as well hit Mickey's. Why wait until Wednesday? And before you ask any more questions—one, yes, its five blocks away, but I feel like walking. And two, I am not talking about the meeting." Knowing how Chris was, she knew that she had bought herself a little time, but how much was the question as he quickly got himself in step with her.

They took their time getting to Mickey's, the local hole in the wall bar, talking about Chris's wife Melissa and their six-month-old daughter, Megan. Megan was on the road to becoming the most spoiled girl in all of Boston, and Melissa wanted Jen to calm down on the baby stuff. "Sorry, Chris, you're just going to have to tell Melissa that the moment I became her godmother, I was granted the right to spoil that child any way I see fit." Laughing at the pained look on his face, she patted him on the back knowing that no matter what, at least she had a friend that she could count on.

Chris stopped just outside of the door to the bar, blocking her entrance, and gave her his serious look. "Don't make me tell all the guys at the precinct that you are wrapped around that little girl's finger, cooing and awing every chance you get." He smiled and ran inside before she could thump him upside his head.

"Seriously, Jen, what is the big deal?" he said. They sat in the corner booth on the left-hand side of the bar, talking as the waitress brought their food to them. "I mean, believe it or not, you are a girl, and girls do show emotions and do girl things from time to time, so why does it bug you when I say I am going to tell the guys that you love your goddaughter and treat her well?" He was genuinely curious, and after all these years, she thought that by now, he would have figured it out. Chris was a great cop, a good husband, a great dad, and a loyal friend, but sometimes he was thick.

"Let's just put it this way, my friend—I don't want to ruin my reputation." She smiled and took a big bite out of her cheeseburger, chasing it down with a bottle of Bud. In reality, she never forgot the looks everyone gave her after Emily died or how everyone tried to "comfort" her. She was so frustrated with everyone's sympathy that she decided to take a week of leave, hoping that they would just stop looking at her.

"Chris, I love you like a brother, but you have to understand, it's who I am. Look at me. Do I look like the foo-foo femme type to you?" She put her arms out to make her point, showing off her white T-shirt and low-cut blue jeans.

"Okay," he said as he finished off the last of his fries and pushed the plate aside. "Then answer me this, when in the hell are you going to go out and get yourself a life, stop working so much, and maybe even find yourself a little hottie to play with? When are you going to realize that you are supposed to work so you can live, not live to work?" His eyes were penetrating.

Jen thought of the woman from the gym that morning, remembering the sweat and how it made her skin shine, the strength of her legs while she was running, the tan bandanna that covered her strawberry blond hair, and, most of all, her troubled but beautiful doe eyes. When she turned around to finally get out of the shower at the gym, she saw the mystery woman staring at her. They made full eye contact, and Jen felt her breath catch in her chest. She was overwhelmed and didn't know why. She wanted to walk up to her, gently place her hands on her soft face, and fix whatever it was that she was running from earlier, and when she realized that, she all but ran out of the shower.

"I have a life," she said, shifting her eyes down, avoiding his stare, knowing that it wasn't true but refusing to admit it all the same.

***

Alex was still mentally kicking herself for losing her composure like she did when she walked into her apartment. She was completely and totally embarrassed by her behavior and was trying to figure out if she should switch gyms when there was a knock on her door.

"Oh my god, I missed you! You have to tell me everything that you did, and then I will catch you up on what's been going on here!"

Tina said with everything that is Tina as she walked in and sat down on the couch waiting for Alex to join her.

Alex shook her head and smiled as she sat down next to her best friend. Throughout the years, people would always assume that they were sisters because of all of the physical similarities they shared. Tina was an inch shorter than she was, and her hair was straight with no body to it, but those were the only real physical differences between them. Personality was where they were opposites. Where Tina was outgoing, Alex was quiet. Tina was the life of the party wherever she went and a true people person who could talk to anyone she just met like they were best friends, and Alex admired and at times envied that in her. In reality, Tina was not only her best friend, but Alex also saw her as the little sister that she never had. "Well, hi to you too, hon! Tina, thanks so much for watching my place while I was gone. I really don't know what I would have done without you." She meant every word. Tina had taken care of paying all her bills over the past year and, when she needed it, listened to her rant and rave or just almost cry over the phone.

Tina took her hands, and her face became serious, which was very rare for her, and she looked at Alex. "Alex, I know that you can't tell me everything that happened over there or everything that you did, but you know that if you want or need to talk to someone, I am here for you, right? You know that I won't tell a soul if you don't want me to, but I am worried about you." She heard Alex yell this morning, and shortly thereafter, she watched her run out of the house like her hair was on fire. Nothing spooked Alex, and because of that, Tina swore that she was going to be there for her best friend, one way or the other.

Still holding Tina's hands, Alex looked right back at her friend. "First of all, you pretty much know everything that happened while I was gone, and the parts you don't know I can't tell you. Secondly, I know that you are here for me. You have been since we were in elementary school, and some things never change. And thirdly, I am fine, kind of." She blushed and pulled her hands back.

"Kind of? What do you mean kind of? And why in the world are you blushing? I haven't seen you blush in years! What did I miss?"

Alex never blushed unless something really embarrassing happened to her, and now Tina was interested, and she just had to know what happened.

"I think that I have been gone too long that's all. I think that I am overreacting and I don't even know why I brought it up, so why don't we just drop it." Sitting up straight, she tried to close herself off in the hopes that Tina would drop the subject. "So how is work treating you? Are they still running you around like a dog?" Tina was with the police department, and when Alex left, she was still considered a rookie.

"Nope. They finally gave me my own car and they let me use the big girl cuffs when I am good! You are so not getting out of this one. Spill it, woman!" She knew her too well to fall for her distraction techniques. "You are three shades of red right now, and if you don't tell me, I will arrest you for disturbing the peace!"

"I am not disturbing the peace, and since when do you abuse your authority and use it for blackmail? And here I thought that you were a professional on all levels. You probably flaunt your badge when you go to the clubs too, don't you? A way to pick up new girls perhaps?" It took everything in her not to start laughing on the spot, but she kept her composure and tried to look offended.

"Not going to work this time, hon. You have been gone for too long, and I am totally focused, so spill it."

She knew that look. Alex knew that she wouldn't be able to get out of this one, so she looked around and then looked back at Tina with a smile on her face "How about we go for a drink and I will tell you on the way?"

"Sweet!" Tina was so excited that she was almost jumping out of her skin.

After putting on a little makeup, changing into a pair of tan Capri's, leather flip-flops, and a thin white cotton button-down shirt, and then running a brush through her hair, they were out the door. As they walked to the new bar that Tina had been introduced to by a few of her cop friends, Alex began to tell her what had happened at the gym. She left out nothing, as embarrassing as it may have been, because sometimes you just have to tell someone. With Tina, she was able to relax and be herself, and that included acting like a girl sometimes, so these rare outings she considered to be a blessing.

It was a nice place. Plenty of open booths to sit in, the music was not too loud, and the lights were not too dim. The walls, floor, and bar were all made of a dark grain oak, giving the feel of relaxation and privacy. The bartender was perhaps in his fifties, his hair more salt than pepper. He was cleaning out a glass as he stood watching the Red Sox on a television that was bolted to the ceiling in the corner of the bar. They walked directly to a table to the right of the bar, and each ordered a screwdriver. Sitting back and enjoying her first drink in thirteen months, she waited for Tina to tease her about her little episode at the gym.

"Here is my opinion on your whole situation with that girl at the gym. Are you ready?"

Drinking down the last of her screwdriver, she motioned to the bartender to bring another one, sat back, and indicated that she was ready to hear judgment. Tina was blatantly honest, never holding anything back, and it was a quality that Alex loved and, on occasions like this, feared.

Looking Alex in the eyes with love and understanding, she began, "I think that it is perfectly natural and I would be shocked if you hadn't looked. Alex, you have to remember that you haven't really been around any women for how long now, six, seven months? And you haven't been laid in over a year. I don't know how you are able to do it, and I hate to be the one to break it to ya, but everybody needs sex or at least some form of companionship. Like it or not, you are human, and therefore you have human needs and tendencies." Tina leaned back and took a deep breath before slowly allowing a smile to rest on her face. "So, did you try to get her name or phone number, because damn girl, she sounds hot!" Seeing the look of utter shock that came across Alex's face was priceless and had her laughing like she hadn't laughed in years. It was a minute before she could compose herself enough to wipe the tears from her eyes, and still all she could manage to say in a squeaky, trying-to-control-herself voice was, "Sorry, sorry, but you know it's true."

Chapter 3

After having ordered their second beer, Chris tried another tactic on Jen. "So, what has you so distracted? When you got back to your place earlier, you looked like you were miles away. So where did you go?" As he was asking the question, he saw her eyes dart up for a second, but it was enough to confirm that there was something going on that she was trying to hide or figure out.

She looked at the bottle she was holding like it had some hidden secrets to share, and then she finally admitted to him what was on her mind. "When I was at the gym today, I saw this woman running on the treadmill. She was running her ass off. Chris, I couldn't stop looking at her, and then when I decided enough was enough and was taking my shower, she ends up in there too. When I saw her in the shower, I was caught off guard, Chris. I looked right at her. For some reason, I just had to get out of there. I ran, Chris, I ran." There was no way she was going to tell him all of the details, but seeing the look on his face told her that she might have said too much already.

"Jen, I love you like a sister, and I am going to tell you something that I have wanted to say for years now." Shifting in his seat, he leaned forward so she knew how serious he was, and if she got pissed, oh well, she would get over it sooner or later. "You need to stop hiding and start letting people in again. You locked yourself up after Emily died and only let a few of us back in, but, Jen, it's time to move on. You ran because you felt something for her. There is more to the story than you are telling me, but something about her got to you. If you see her again, you need to ask her out."

She sat still for a few minutes before looking up or answering him. He was right, of course, and she hated it when he was right. "I know what you are saying is true, but damn it, Chris, it's easier said than done." Taking in a calming breath, she continued, "I'll tell you what, the next time I see her, I promise you that I will at least talk to her. Is that good enough for now?"

He leaned back in his seat with hands behind his head and looked up at the ceiling, carefully formulating his words before answering. After a minute, he looked at her again and said, "I will back off if you give me your word that you will talk to her the next time that you see her *and* promise me that you will not try to sabotage it. You have to be yourself, deal?"

"Deal," Jen said, knowing that she was probably going to avoid going to the gym for a while. She didn't know what she would say to her if she did see her again without sounding like an idiot, but if she did see her, the one thing she would have to do would be to look in her eyes and see if the torment was gone.

***

"Okay, I have to head to the bathroom," Alex said after downing her third screwdriver and feeling the buzz already. "Do not get me any more, okay?" And she meant it. It had been too long since she had had a drink, and the last thing she needed was a hangover in the morning.

Just as the door to the women's room shut behind Alex, Tina, who was curiously looking around the bar, saw Chris. She missed him before because Alex was sitting with her back to him and directly in her line of sight, but now having seen him, she thought that it might be a good idea to have a little company. She didn't know Chris well, only in passing since they were in different precincts, but he had always been nice enough to her. Tina caught his eye almost instantly and walked over to his table. "Hey, Chris, I don't know if you and your friend would be interested, but I would love it if you two would join us at our table. My friend just got back from Afghanistan, and this is her first night out. I just thought it would be nice if she didn't have to suffer with just me all night." Mentally she had her fingers crossed, hoping that he would say yes. Alex needed a pick-me-up, and hopefully if they agreed to come over, it would be just what she needed.

Chris looked at his friend, and after getting some kind of silent consent, they stood up, grabbed their beers, and joined Tina at her table. As soon as they sat down, the waitress came over, checking in to see if anybody needed any refills. Looking at the empty glass on the table, Chris ordered another screwdriver for Tina and her friend and two more beers.

Watching as the waitress put another screwdriver down at the spot where Alex was sitting, all Tina could think of was that Alex was going to kill her when she saw another drink waiting for her. Looking at Chris's friend, Tina decided to introduce herself. "Hi, I'm Tina, pleasure to meet you," she said with all the sincerity in the world. This woman was beautiful, and all she could think was "Is she or is she not gay?" Realizing that she was starting to stare, Tina asked, "Do you two work together?"

"It's nice to meet you too, and yes, Chris used to be my partner before I wised up and got rid of him." Jen laughed because she knew that saying that made poor Chris wonder if it was true no matter how many times she told him that she was just messing with him.

"Ha-ha, you are not funny. Just can't stop being mean to me today, can you?" If she wanted to play, he would play because it might just give him a means to finding out what happened with the captain. One way or the other, he was going to find out what happened in the captain's office yesterday, and if that meant setting her up or getting her drunk, so be it. Normally, he would never have sunk so low as to consider the things that he was, but something was going on, and in his mind, she would always be his partner, so if something was wrong, he needed to know about it.

The banter and laughing between the three of them continued until Alex came walking out of the bathroom and stopped short when she saw the new addition sitting with Tina at the table. The man appeared to be in his mid-thirties and, by the way he held himself, a cop, and the woman who had her back to her also had the air of a cop. She saw another drink waiting for her, and although she was not happy about it, for now she was going to let it go. *Leave it to Tina to find company*, she thought as she chuckled and continued on her way back to the table.

The shock was mutual. When Alex came around the table and went to pull out her chair, the recognition was instantaneous for the both of them. Within a matter of three seconds, Alex had turned five shades of red, and Jen, who had been talking, had stopped speaking in midsentence and stared at Alex open-mouthed. Noticing the reactions of their friends, Chris and Tina looked at each other in puzzlement.

She didn't understand why Alex was acting so strangely, so Tina did the only thing that she could think of to do and introduced them. "Jen, Chris, this is my friend Alex. Alex, this is Chris and Jen. They are with the fifth precinct." *What is going on with her?*

Chris stood up, shook her hand, and told her what a pleasure it was to meet her, but when Jen went to shake Alex's hand, Alex dropped eye contact and, as impossible as it sounded, turned another shade redder. Jen just stared at her. With her hair down and wearing a white button-down shirt that was open just enough to keep you wondering, she was breathtaking. She looked so soft and shy, and for reasons that she could not explain, even to herself, Jen wanted to protect her. She wanted to wrap Alex in her arms and keep her safe. "It's nice to meet you," was all she could manage to say before excusing herself to get another drink.

Chris followed Jen to the bar and, after ordering two more beers, looked at his friend. "What in the hell was that? Are you okay, because I almost didn't recognize you back there? Do you know her from somewhere?" All Jen had to do was look at him. "Oh my god, are you telling me that that is the woman from the gym! Okay, you made me a promise, and you are going to deliver. Damn, you said she was beautiful, but I thought you were exaggerating. She's hot!"

Something deep inside of her woke up while Chris was talking, and she quickly pushed it back down. There was no way she could be upset with what he was saying, but in the same respect, she wanted him to shut up and stop looking at Alex as if she were a piece of meat.

After Jen and Chris went to the bar, Tina looked at Alex, appraising her appearance. "I know that you aren't drunk yet, so would you mind explaining to me what just happened. And why are you blushing? My God, you are as red as an apple. I know she is hot, but I've never seen you like this before."

"Tina, can we please go?" was all she could get out of her mouth in a quiet whisper. She could feel her color coming back, and rather than feeling embarrassed, she just wanted to leave and never go back to that gym or bar again.

"Why? What is going on? I am not going anywhere until you tell me…" And that is when it hit her. "That's the girl from the gym! Oh my god. Now I know why you couldn't stop staring, and girl, I don't blame you one little bit. Umm, umm, umm."

"Really, Tina, you don't have to go there. I mean seriously, do you have to stare at her like she is a piece of meat?" Where that came from and why she sounded angry, she didn't know. She and Tina used to sit back and check women out all of the time, and it never bothered her before. She tried to tell herself that it was just the embarrassment from this morning, but she didn't believe it.

"No way are we going anywhere for a while, so just sit there and play nice because here they come." When they sat back down at the table again, Tina watched as Alex tried to make the transformation from just Alex to damn G.I. Jane. Her back got straighter, her shoulders pulled back some, and her eyes somehow blocked anyone from truly seeing her. *That's it*, she thought to herself, *defenses are up and everyone is locked out. Ladies and gentlemen, Sergeant Thomas has arrived. Damn it!* And with that, she downed the rest of her drink. As soon as her glass hit the table, something happened that Tina thought never could, and as she watched it, she was shocked, astonished, and, for the first time in a long time, excited for her best friend. Although Alex may not have known it yet, it was obvious to Tina…she was hooked on this girl.

"So, Alex, Tina said you just came back from a tour overseas. How long were you there for?" Chris said, trying to break the ice.

"I did a year in Afghanistan, no big deal, really." Alex shrugged her shoulders and looked down at her glass, running her finger along the rim.

"What did you do, or can't you tell us?" he asked with a playful laugh that seemed to lighten the mood marginally.

"I suppose you could say that I was in re-acclimation and recovery. Nothing interesting, really," she said, trying to downplay her job. She was not supposed to discuss her missions, and the nature of her assignments were "sensitive," to say the least. Tina, of course, had pieced together most of what she did and knew that what she was saying was a gross understatement, as well as intentionally misleading.

"Alex, stop downplaying yourself. You were named the best in your field. Hell, the things that you did…" and there she stopped dead. She knew the look that she just got, and it was clear. Shut up.

"I did what everyone else in my field does, and I just happened to be the one to get recognized. Like I said before, nothing interesting." *Oh, please don't ask any more questions about what I do*, she thought to herself, and when she saw Chris getting ready to ask yet another question, she saw Jen touch his arm and stop him with a simple shake of the head. Looking at Jen, she thought she saw understanding in her eyes, and for that one moment, she was grateful that Jen was there.

***

Jen watched Alex slowly get more and more uncomfortable as Chris asked about her job. Finally, she stopped him and shook him off. She couldn't watch Alex struggle to avoid and talk around something she didn't want to discuss. Looking at Alex, she said, "Given the fact that she just got back, I doubt that she really wants to talk about everything she had to do. With that being said, are you going to be taking leave, or do you have to go right back to work?" That's when she saw Alex relax. It was not in anything she did, but it was like the color of her eyes turned a deeper blue. She never saw anything like it before, and she was completely mesmerized by it.

Appreciating how Jen turned the topic of conversation to something easier to discuss, Alex was finally able to look her in the eyes as she answered, "I wish that I could take leave, but I just got handed a new assignment that I have to start on Monday. The good thing is that I get to stay here at home this time." With that, Tina picked up and carried the conversation everywhere else.

After a couple of hours talking and laughing, Tina noticed that Alex had started leaning closer and closer to Jen, and when they were talking to each other, it was as if they were tuning the rest of the world out. Happier than she had been in a long time for her friend, Tina leaned over to Chris as she stood up and asked him if he wanted another drink, and picking up on her cue, he offered to join her. As they were waiting in line at the bar, Chris looked at Tina. "I haven't seen Jen smile this much in years. All she does is drown herself in her work, and every time that I try to get her out, she stonewalls me. Please don't get upset with me for saying this, but I hope like hell your friend Alex can help bring her back to civilization." The hope in his eyes was heartbreaking.

"I know what you mean. Alex pretty much sealed herself off at the beginning of this deployment when she got 'the letter,' and after that, it was like talking to a robot. She was so matter of fact and removed from all emotions that I didn't know what to do. That on top of whatever it was that she did over there…God, I was scared that I had lost her. I hope that they can bring each other back." And with all of her heart, she really truly did.

"So," Chris said as he and Tina sat back down. The two of them took their time at the bar, hoping to give their friends a little alone time to get to know each other and hopefully connect. Chris smiled at Alex. "Alex, maybe you can help me out with something that has been bothering me."

Seeing what she thought was a bit of mischief in his eyes and figuring that he was about to mess with Jen a little, Alex was interested to know just what he needed help with. Watching Jen from the corner of her eye, she saw the look of warning, but Chris paid her no attention. After Jen bailed her out from Chris's questions, though, Alex proceeded with caution, saying, "Well, it depends on what it is," and gave Jen a knowing smile that radiated in the air around them.

If they were any closer, they would be in each other's laps, Chris thought as he looked at the two of them. They made a good-looking couple, and Chris knew that Tina saw it too. Seeing how comfortable they were with each other, he figured that this might work. If he could get Alex on his side, then he didn't think that Jen would stand a chance. "Well, Jen starts a new duty assignment tomorrow morning, and she won't tell me what it is or what she is going to be doing."

"I told you I am not allowed to say anything about it to anyone, Chris, so why don't you just back off." The look of pure frustration on Jen's face was obvious. Knowing that Jen wanted to escape Chris's questions for whatever reasons, Alex stood up and asked Jen if she would go with her to the bathroom.

Jen readily accepted her invitation, grateful for the bailout. When they walked into the women's restroom, Jen lightly touched Alex's arm. It felt as though she could feel little sparks of electricity where she touched her. She caught her breath and calmed her stomach before she looked at Alex. "Thank you. I am sorry, but when Chris…" and it was at that moment that Alex wrapped her arms around her neck and slowly stepped into her. Their bodies were a perfect fit; it was as if they were made for each other. Jen felt Alex pull her down to meet her face-to-face. She watched as Alex slowly closed her eyes and paused just before their lips touched, as if waiting for permission, and when Jen responded by wrapping her arms around Alex's waist, Alex pressed her lips to Jen's. Softly and slowly, Alex kissed her, and when Alex parted Jen's lips with her tongue, her body melted. Alex probed Jen's mouth with her tongue, slowly at first, but soon lost herself in the heat that was consuming them. The kiss turned from soft and sensual to possessive and greedy. Jen pulled Alex tighter against her body, positioning her so that Alex straddled her thigh, and at the same time, Alex's kiss grew hungrier with need. Alex, feeling Jen's leg pressed against her, pressed her hips even harder against Jen's thigh and let out a small moan as she realized just how wet she had become. With her legs shaking, Alex held on tighter to Jen, making sure that her legs didn't give out on her, but that was one thing she did not have to worry about. Feeling the heat on her thigh and hearing the moan that escaped Alex's lips set her into overdrive. Jen moved her mouth down Alex's neck and attached her lips to the spot where her shoulder and neck meet, as if she were feeding off her essence, and at the same time grabbed her hips and slowly rocked them back and forth. Jen was possessed, and a primal urge was beginning to take over. All she knew was that she needed this woman, and she wanted to take her right here. Alex threw her head back, and Jen attached her lips to her neck, overwhelmed by the power and need that had built up between them, and as her hands began to trace their way to the curve of Alex's breasts, the door flung open. Startled and a bit embarrassed at getting caught by a stranger, who walked directly to a stall, avoiding eye contact, Alex tried to jump back and away from Jen, but the hold that Jen still had on her kept her right where she was.

"Sorry," Jen said, her voice hoarse and her eyes clouded with desire, but with a smile as she bent down and gave Alex a small but telling kiss. "Are you ready to go back out there now and help me deal with Chris?" Alex was lost in her eyes. Even though Jen was trying to pass herself off as calm and collected, her normally emerald green eyes were dark, her voice was rough, and her breathing was still heavy. There was something in her eyes that made Alex want to stay right where she was. Shaking herself back to the present, she looked up at Jen, and with a new sparkle in her eyes and smile on her face, they turned and went back to join their friends.

When they got back to the table, the only thing that Alex was thinking was when she would be able to see Jen again. It was a minute before she noticed Tina eyeing her with the knowing look of a longtime friend, a look that only she had. No doubt she knew that something happened, and there would be a heavy questioning session when they left. So to ease her friend's mind, she gave her the award-winning smile that they reserved to confirm to each other the accuracy of suspicions when they were in the company of others.

Without missing a beat, Chris looked at Jen and said, "Jen, if the chief of police came to me on a Saturday and told me that I was on some secret squirrel type of operation, I would be considerate enough to at least let my best friend know what I was going to be doing or where I was supposed to be reporting so that he didn't worry. I know that they said they needed the best of the best because that is what Connery from first precinct said they told him. Just give me a little something, please." True to form, Chris placed his hand over his heart to show the pain he was feeling. Jen, however, just shook her head and laughed. After what just happened and the connection that she was feeling, like an uncontrollable pull, nothing he could say right now could set her off. She was on cloud nine.

"Wait a minute," Alex interjected. She looked at Jen and grew serious and laser-focused instantly. "Did you get offered a job working for the chief, or are you going on an op? And did he really tell you that he needed the best of the best?" *Please say no, please say no*, was all she could think as she held her breath, waiting for Jen's answer.

"Look, I am not supposed to talk about it, and if Connery wants to open his ignorant mouth, that is on him, but some of us know how to keep our mouths shut, wouldn't you agree, Alex?" Jen looked at Alex with a smile, expecting her to agree and get them past the subject, but she didn't.

She stood up quicker than intended and inadvertently knocked over her chair as a result. Alex looked around her, trying to calm herself before speaking. "I need to go. I am sorry. It was nice meeting you all. Have a good night." She turned and was out the door, all but running down the street with Tina fast on her trail.

"What the hell was that about?" Chris looked at Jen as if she could answer his question. "What happened in the bathroom that got her so upset?"

Jen looked at Chris in utter shock. "Do you really think that something happened in the bathroom if we came out smiling, sat down, and continued on with the conversation? Did you ever stop to think that maybe it was something that you said?" She was furious. She didn't know how, but she knew that something Chris said spooked her, and she hoped like hell that she would be able to see her again.

Chris watched Jen just stare at the door, like she was waiting for them to come back in. "What did happen in the bathroom?" That got her attention. "And don't try telling me nothing happened because it's written all over your face."

"I don't know, Chris. We went in and I was thanking her for getting me away from you. And the next thing that I know, she was kissing me. It started to get hot and heavy, but someone came in and snapped us out of it. When we came back out here, she was nothing but smiles." She really didn't know what happened, but she realized that she needed to see her again. Alex woke something up in her, and now that it was back, she didn't want to let it go. For the first time in years, Jen felt alive.

***

Tina waited until they got back to Alex's apartment before she rounded on her. "What the hell was all that about? I thought everything was going good, and then out of the blue, you decide to up and leave like someone lit a fire under your ass or something. You need to start talking!" And it was then, when Alex looked up at her, that she realized that her best friend was on the verge of tears. "Alex, what's wrong? What did Chris say, or did Jen do something? Talk to me, girl." Jen had only known of Alex crying twice in her life, once when her father died and once on the phone a couple of months ago. Something big happened, and she needed to find out what it was.

"Nothing, it's no big deal. I'll handle it," was all that she could manage to get out before two traitor tears escaped and trailed down her cheeks. She didn't even know why she was crying; it's not like she really knew Jen. So what if they kissed? It's not like it was that big of a deal. Only deep down she knew that she was lying to herself.

"Alex, honey," Jen said as she walked her over to the couch. "What happened when the two of you went into the bathroom?"

Her eyes betrayed her as she looked at Tina and said in almost a whisper, "We kissed, or I kissed her, and she kissed me back. I don't even know why I kissed her. It was like I had no control over my own body. Tina, I liked it so much that I wanted more, and I was ready to take her right there in the bathroom!" She covered her face with her hands and put her elbows on her knees to try and steady herself. She could still feel the soft pulse of heat and desire that spread throughout her body the instant their lips met.

"Hun, that doesn't exactly sound like a bad thing. I mean, when the two of you came back, you both looked pretty happy and you looked like you could fly. Did she say something that got you this upset?" It was then that the answer had dawned on her; she thought she knew what had happened, but she wanted to be sure. "Talk to me, Alex. You know I am here."

Alex rubbed her face as if to clear away the pain and steady herself. She turned to look at Tina and, in a calm and composed voice, asked, "Tina, what is my number one rule?"

"You never date people that you work with. I know this and it's nothing new." *Oh God, I was right!* "Alex, are you going to be working with her? Is that what her new assignment is? Is that your new assignment?" Alex didn't say anything, nor did she have to. Tina knew her all too well. Taking a deep breath and wrapping her arms around her best friend, she said, "So you finally found someone who woke you up, and now you are just going to cut her out? Sweetie, sometimes we have to break our own rules."

Alex backed out of Tina's arms and composed herself as best she could. "But sometimes the ones we want to break the most are the ones that are the most important." With that, she gathered herself up and went to bed, leaving Tina on the couch, wondering if her friend would ever find happiness.

Chapter 4

It was 0645 and Alex stood on the second floor of the warehouse waiting for her new trainees to arrive. When she got there at 0500, she conducted a walk-around of the outside, taking mental notes of the area, obstacles, and training aids that could be of use over the next two months. Once she had completed her initial sweep, she proceeded inside to see what she could use to set the officers up for a challenging first day.

She had eight officers assigned to her, but she didn't think even half of them would be capable of handling the standards and training that she was going to try to instill in and put them through. Last night was a wake-up call for her, and she was grateful for it. She was reminded of what happens when you allow yourself to drop your guard, and that was one mistake that she was not going to make again. Complacency is what gets people killed, and when you are walking into an unknown situation, the last thing that you need is to have anyone on your team who is complacent, least of all the team leader.

She was dressed in her form-fitting black Nike running pants, black Under Armour T shirt that clung to her body like it was painted on, black running shoes, and had her hair tied up into a tight knot. The way you dressed was key in any situation, and she was ready for the day ahead. The first day of training was always the most difficult for any new trainee, but the key to a successful first day was the element of surprise. Don't do what everyone expects because nothing ever happens according to plan, and if you can't adapt quickly and instantaneously, then the mission could be compromised and lives could be lost. She was sure that by the end of their first day, every one of the officers was going to think that she was over the top, slightly crazy, and a world-class bitch. She couldn't wait.

She smiled as she watched seven cars stagger into the parking lot. She watched the drivers standing around their cars talking to each other as if they didn't have a care in the world. Finally, at 0657, the officers began to make their way to the front door, and with a small ping of disappointment, she noticed that Officer Miceli was not among them. As she moved from the window to position herself at the top of the catwalk, Alex wondered how much of last night had kept Jen from showing up today. She had a feeling that if they had not met last night and she had not lost all control, practically jumping her in the bathroom, Jen would have been one of the first ones here.

She gave herself a quick mental shake and then positioned herself on the Northwest side of the catwalk; it was the darkest spot to be found in the building. She had a perfect bird's eye view of the entire warehouse, with the added benefit of being completely hidden from sight. To her utter amazement, Miceli was the first one through the door, followed by the rest of the officers who seemed to be enjoying themselves immensely. While the male officers talked, laughed, and traded stories, Miceli positioned herself just outside of their little circle. After twenty minutes had passed, one of the male officers, the biggest one of the group, walked over to Miceli, exchanged a few words with her, and then positioned himself just to her right. The two of them looked as though they were on watch in a prison recreational yard and did not make any attempts to rejoin with the others, even after repeated requests had been made to them.

Alex stood there waiting and watching, and as the first hour passed by, she watched as the six officers who were carrying on when they first came in slowly quieted down and started to become restless. Officer Miceli and her new friend had made several slow circles around the bottom floor, apparently taking in their surroundings. Looking at her watch, Alex smiled, leaned back against the wall, and got herself ready for the beginning of a long day.

***

Miceli was at the docks at 0600. There was no way that she was going to park her car in front of a building, which she might be working in indefinitely, down here at the docks. There was too much going on in the area, and the last thing that she wanted was to bring any type of attention to who she was, what she had, or what she did. She parked her Corolla half a mile down the road from the building and started her walk. She wore bulky clothes again for the same reasons she had on Saturday but couldn't explain why she felt the need. Whenever she had a feeling about something, she went with it, and because of that, she was able to get out of a few situations that could have turned out bad. She went around the back of the freight warehouse that sat beside the building she was to report to, came up on the east side, and then skirted around to the north end of the building. Leaning against the wall next to the front door, she waited for the others to arrive.

While she waited, she replayed the previous night through her mind for the hundredth time. She couldn't figure out what had happened that made Alex leave so quickly, and the more that she thought about it, the less she understood. There was one thing that she did know, however; after work today, she was going to get with Tina and see if she would give her Alex's number. If Tina wouldn't give it to her, then she was going to swing by the precinct and do a search on Alex. One way or the other, she had to find her.

As people started to show up, she realized that she only recognized two of them. One of them was Tony Connery, the guy who couldn't keep his dick in his pants or his mouth shut, and Troy James, one of the SWAT guys. He was known as the silent chocolate giant throughout the Boston PD because although he stood six feet six inches tall, had biceps bigger than her thigh, and never missed a shot, he was rarely heard joking and cutting up like everyone else. When he spoke, there was a reason for it. Jen had spoken with James only once before, and that was at the gun range when she was getting rid of some built-up frustration. He had been watching her fire off round after round before finally coming up and tapping her on the shoulder. Not knowing what to expect, Jen had put her weapon down and got ready for some type of lecture or snide remark like she had heard many times over, but instead, in his baritone voice, he said to her, "If you pull your left leg back an inch or two, I think that it might help," and then walked away. The funny part was that he was right.

She knew that it was time to go in when everyone had started to walk toward the door, so when they walked up, she pulled the door open and was the first through the door. She took a good look around and was slightly amazed at how much room there was. It was almost cavernous. While she stood there waiting for the instructor to show, she scanned the building, trying to form a mental map.

There was a large pile of wood along the far wall, all of the windows were blacked out, and there was a catwalk that went around the entire building and led to what she thought were the offices that she had seen yesterday. The lighting in the building was average for a warehouse; she noted the halogen lights suspended from the rafters and how they lit up most of the building's area, except for the overhangs and corners. On the ground level, directly under the office area, there appeared to be two restrooms, and if she was correct in assuming, it had showers as well. To the right of the restrooms was a workout area with treadmills, weights, etc. There was a set of lockers to her left placed up against the wall, with a folding table positioned just to the right and a set of stairs to access the catwalk to the left. After a little while, James came over to where she was standing. "So what do you think we are supposed to be doing?" he asked.

Still scanning the area, Miceli thought about it for a moment before she replied, "I don't know, but considering how hush-hush this is supposed to be and the fact that the chief is the only one who knows what's going on, I am not letting my guard down for anything."

After giving a small nod of agreement, James stood next to Miceli, as if showing with whom he was aligning himself with, and began to scan the building with her, waiting for whatever it was that was going to come.

The two of them began to circle the area, trying to get a better feel for the place and to see what, if anything, there was hidden away from sight. They came to the only set of stairs in the building and were about to check out the second floor when they found the small chain strung across the railing with a sign reading "Do not cross." Deciding to continue on with their investigating circle, they continued on past the stairs and back to where the others were still standing around having mini conversations.

As they once again approached the group, she and James could hear the others begin to complain about how they were wasting their time waiting for someone who obviously wasn't going to show. The two of them just continued on walking past the others for the fourth time, and as they came around the southwest corner, Jen looked at her watch. It was 0843. Something was going on, and she would be damned if she was going to wait for it to slap her in the face. With James beside her, she headed to the stairs, and as she started to slide under the chain, she felt him grab her arm. With a look that told her to be careful, James let go of her and took up position at the bottom of the steps, as if he was her lookout. Quietly she climbed the stairs one at a time and, by the time she came to the top, was lying flat on them. She looked right and saw nothing, but when she looked left, she thought she saw the shadow of a person. She knew it. They were being watched like they were some kind of lab rats. She turned and looked back down the stairs, and when James made eye contact with her, she used hand signals to let him know what it was that she had seen and what she was going to do. With a small nod, James backed up a few inches, quietly unhooked the chain, and climbed up the stairs to join her. After a minute or two of silent discussion, they were ready to go.

***

Where did Miceli and the big boy go? Alex asked herself. She began to take a step forward in an attempt to get a better look down below when she caught movement out of the corner of her eye. *Well, well, I might have underestimated some of these officers,* she thought as she positioned herself against the railing, her back to the stairs, smiling inwardly as she prepared herself for the big boy to come at her. She saw the shine off his cleanly shaven head, a perfect giveaway, but she had to admit…she was impressed. She didn't know how long it would take before someone decide if and when to cross the chain. She didn't know if any of them would, but Big Boy did, and taking him down would be the perfect way to introduce herself to her new trainees.

Appearing as though she was following what was going on below her, Alex positioned herself, listened, and waited for his approach. *Three, two, one!* She spun around on her right heel, grabbed his right arm with her left, took the back of his neck with her right, and in one motion used his own momentum to pull him forward and down, and at the same time, she lifted her knee to connect with his sternum. He went down hard, but what she was not planning for was Jen, who had come up using Big Boy as cover. Before she knew it, she was being tackled, tripping over Big Boy, slammed into the wall, and pinned. It was pitch black, so they could not see each other's faces, but it didn't matter; Alex knew what to do. Raising her arms over her head, she used the smoothness of her clothes and the bagginess of Jen's to slip out of the hold that Jen had on her and then grabbed Jen's sweatshirt in an attempt to drop her. Jen felt the pull on her sweatshirt and allowed it to slip off over her head. As soon as Alex had a handful of empty sweatshirt, Jen had squatted down, swung her leg out, and dropped Alex where she was standing. The second that Jen went to grab her, Alex took her hands, pulled her forward, and kicked up with her legs, propelling Jen's body over her own, landing Jen on her back as she followed to stop on top, straddling Jen's chest with her knees, and pinning her hands to the ground. It was at that moment that Jen was finally able to see clearly that her opponent was Alex.

All of the muscles in her body relaxed the moment she realized that Alex was on top of her. "What are you doing here?" she asked in an almost whisper. She felt the strength of Alex's legs as they tightened around her before finally standing up. She couldn't move, what was going on here?

In a voice that carried throughout the entire building, Alex called out, "I want everybody in a line in the middle of the floor.

Now!" Looking down at Jen, she asked, "Is there a problem, Miceli, or are you going to join your team?"

Seeing a flash that looked like pain in Jen's eyes before quickly recovering and replacing it with anger, Jen pulled her sweatshirt back on and headed down the stairs. Alex, for the first time in her military career, felt the backlash of the pain she had caused someone else.

As she walked the line in front of her new trainees, Sergeant Thomas felt every pair of eyes following her, sizing her up. She enjoyed this part of the training; this was where she figured out what kind of people she would be working with and who had what strengths. Stopping at the center of the line, she stood at the parade rest position with her hands behind her back and legs shoulder-width apart, and addressed the group.

"My name is Master Sergeant Thomas. You may call me Master Sergeant or Sarge. I am here to train you, so have no doubts. I have no friends, I have no family, and I have no life, which means that you will not have a life. I don't care if I hurt your feelings and I don't care if you hate me. I only care about two things, so pay attention. First, I will train you to the utmost of my abilities. I will work until I drop to bring the best out of every one of you, even if it kills you. You will always get my best, and as such, I expect to always get your best in return. Second, I believe in integrity, or the truth to those of you who may not understand the concept of the word. Trust is the key to any productive and successful team, and without being able to trust your team members absolutely, you don't have a team. Lie to me once and you are gone. Am I understood?"

In unison, they all answered with "Yes, ma'am."

"On your faces!" As they all dropped, she had to admit that she was surprised they were following orders already; maybe this wasn't going to be as bad as she thought.

"Obviously not a single one of you was listening. If I am going to be working with anyone, they had better be damn well able to listen and understand what I say. Now down! Keep your bodies three inches from the floor and don't move." No group has ever been able to figure out what it was that they did wrong, so that usually gives her time to see who the quitters are.

"Up!" she said as she began to walk around the line, watching as some of them were already showing signs that they were beginning to struggle and observing the looks on their faces. Determination was key, and she needed to find out which one of these officers had it the most and then use it.

"Down!" She took one last look across the line and asked, "By a show of hands, who thinks they know why you are on your faces? And don't you dare stand up or fall on your face." Watching them struggle, she was about to move them again when she saw a hand come up.

She took her time as she walked over to the officer whose arm was now up in the air, and when she looked down, she took a minute before asking him, "What's your name?"

"Officer Shawn O'Malley, Master Sergeant Thomas," he responded as he quickly put his hand back down on the floor.

Oh, this one might be on a roll. Looking down at the officer in front of her, she took a quick assessment. Approximately five and feet ten inches tall, strawberry blond hair, freckles, and a hint of an accent. "Are you a second-generation Irishman, O'Malley?"

"Yes, I am, Master Sergeant Thomas," he said as his face began to turn red, the first sign of weakness.

"Up! Now what in the world would a little Irishman have to say on the subject at hand?"

"Master Sergeant Thomas, we are on our faces because we addressed you by ma'am instead of Master Sergeant. Master Sergeant Thomas."

"On your feet and get your hands in the air." *Well, this one obviously has the brains in the group. Now let's see what the others have to offer.* "After being told that you were required to be here, how many of you told anyone about any aspect of the conversation you had with your captains or chief? Step forward if you did."

They all stepped forward, arms still up in the air. "Now how many of you said anything other than you were given a new assignment that began on Monday? Step forward." She looked at them and not a single person moved. Walking up and down the line, she made eye contact with each one, and when she got to the end of the line, when she got to Miceli and when she looked in her eyes, she saw anger. Well, she needed to get over it because regardless of what Miceli wanted, she was going to prove a point today. There was always one person that you dropped the first day; it was the only way to get the rest of the group's attention.

"There are combinations taped to each of the lockers to your left. Get your weapons and stow them and your cell phones in the locker that has your name on it and then get back here. Move!" They all ran for the lockers, but with four on top and four on the bottom, there was a log jam as soon as they got there. She watched as three of the officers dropped to their knees immediately to get at their locker but still allow for others to gain access to the upper set. One of the officers thought that it would be funny to drop one of the others' combinations to the floor before he could reach it, and another was nothing more than a bully forcing his way through.

As they lined back up in front of her, Sergeant Thomas stepped forward and addressed the man in front of her. "What is your name?"

"Officer Jonathan Weaver, Master Sergeant Thomas."

"Officer Weaver, do you think that you are good enough to be here?" she asked him.

Smiling down at her, he said, "Yes, I do, Sarge." He thought it was cute watching her try to be a tough guy.

"Uh-huh." She turned and walked two people down and stopped. "What is your name, Officer?"

"Officer William Jacobs, Master Sergeant Thomas."

"And do you think that you are good enough to be in the company of the rest of your peers?" She enjoyed this part.

He looked bored as he answered, "Yes, Master Sergeant Thomas, I do."

"Outstanding then. Officers Jacobs and Weaver, would the two of you please step up by me." They both stepped forward, and once they were positioned beside her, she said, "I want the two of you to run, recover your weapons and cell phones, and then get back here as fast as you can, positioning yourselves in front of the rest of the team. Go!" And off they went. While all eyes followed the two officers to their respective lockers, Miceli looked directly at the sarge. Feeling the weight of someone staring at her, she looked up and made eye contact. *God, she is beautiful.* And for a second, her guard dropped, and in that second, Miceli saw it. Mentally shaking herself, she brought herself back to the matter at hand and waited for the two officers to rejoin her.

At a full sprint, Officers Weaver and Jacobs came to a sliding halt eight feet in front of the rest of the team. Weapons and cell phones in hand, they were both ready to prove themselves when Thomas slowly moved and positioned herself between them and the rest of the team. Then she looked directly at Weaver.

"Officer Weaver, it is clear to me that you are a strong man who, when he sees something that he wants, goes for it." Then turning her attention to Jacobs, she said, "Officer Jacobs, a lot of the same can be said for you. You have a goal and come hell or high water you will reach it."

She took one step back so that she could focus on both men before continuing. "I *trust* that the two of you will do whatever it takes to achieve whatever tasks are placed in front of you." She paused and looked at the two officers who now had smug looks on their faces and then continued on. "And I also *trust* that the two of you will not consider the welfare of your fellow teammates. I *trust* that you will always put yourselves first over that of your team, and as such, I have no need for your services. Please report back to your respective captains and inform them that your services will not be needed. But before you leave, gentlemen, I have one final thing to say. Although you are no longer on the team, you are not to inform anyone of the fact that there is training being conducted in this building, or at all. Dismissed."

Outright shock was painted in their expressions, and just as Weaver was about to get into her face, she turned and looked him square in the eyes. There was something about the way she looked at him, cold and absent of fear, that sent a clear warning. Instead of arguing, the two furious officers walked out of the warehouse, dismissed from the team. Turning around slowly to face what was left of the group in front of her, the sarge took in their expressions—shock, enjoyment, complete acceptance, and fear. It was a good way to start training, but she was far from done.

"The rest of you, on my command, will go to your lockers, retrieve your weapon, and begin searching for the hardware for the conversion of your weapons that will allow them to be capable of firing Simunition rounds. Once you have converted your weapons, place your original hardware back into your lockers and return to the exact spot that you are in now. Do I make myself clear?"

In unison, she was answered with "Yes, Master Sergeant Thomas."

"Go."

She went back up the stairs, to the same spot that she had been occupying earlier, to watch them as they began searching for the conversion kits. Four from the group shot off in opposite directions as soon as they retrieved their weapons, but Big Boy and Miceli were not so quick to jump. She watched as the two of them systematically went through the first floor, conducting a clean and detailed search of the area. She watched as Miceli conferred with Big Boy, whom Alex now considered to be her partner, as to what was next to be searched. Smiling inwardly, she leaned back and turned the dial for the heaters up to ninety-five degrees, leaned on the railing, watched as they began their task, and began to think.

Why didn't I call out Connery? That was the first thing that I should have done, and I have never failed to call out a liar, so what the hell happened? That was easy—Jen. Seeing the look in her eyes when she knew that Connery was about to be called out stopped her in her tracks. She knew if she did, Jen would see it as a betrayal of trust. It would hurt her, and she just couldn't bring herself to do that. Clearing those thoughts from her head, Alex regrouped herself. *There is a reason that you don't get personally involved with people you work with—you start bending rules or changing what you know works and making exceptions. That in itself could get people hurt or killed,* and that is why from here on out, she resolved herself to make sure that she treated Miceli the same as the others. Whether she got her feelings hurt or not was not her concern; creating an effective team was. Happy with herself and her new resolve, she continued watching as Miceli searched with Big Boy, taking special note on how fluid her movements were and how she almost….

***

Miceli and James searched and searched but came up with nothing. The temperature was rising, and the two of them were in perfect agreement that the sarge had something to do with it. This was another test, unorthodox as it was, but a test nonetheless. Refusing to give up like Connery had and just lay on the floor trying to keep cool, Miceli took off her sweatshirt and the sweat-soaked shirt beneath it and continued to look around. Tapping James on the arm to get his attention, the two of them briefly exchanged words and then headed for the stairs. The chain was down, so the two of them went up with no hesitation, but when they reached the top of the stairs, Master Sergeant Thomas was staring at them with her arms crossed over her chest and blocking their way onto the catwalk.

Jen could have sworn that she saw Alex catch her breath when she saw her coming up the stairs, but she wasn't sure and, at this point, didn't care. She was not surprised to find her waiting for them up here, so without missing a beat, Miceli looked at her. "Excuse us, please, Sarge."

There was a moment where the two of them stared each other down, waiting to see who would back down first. Slowly Sergeant Thomas backed up enough to allow them passage and watched them head for the offices on the north side of the building. She followed behind them and watched as they each took a side of the catwalk to search as they went. Jen's body was covered in sweat, and stray hairs that had fallen from her ponytail were plastered to her face and neck. Every muscle in her body worked in unison it seemed, and every movement had a ripple effect. She wasn't overly muscular, but when she would bend over, twist, or reach for something, the definition of her muscles stood out. She had the perfect athlete's body.

After bending over to look under a part of the catwalk's railing that had a lip to it, Jen looked behind her and caught Alex staring. Granted, Alex maintained her composure and did a quick scan of the building, but she could not erase the fact that Jen had caught her watching. Heading to the fire door and the offices that she knew were behind it, Jen tried to figure out just what was going on. Obviously Alex had realized that she was going to be her trainer when Chris started running his mouth, but why did she run like that and what happened to that shy girl that she met in the bar? What the hell was going on?

After searching the first two rooms and coming up with nothing, they headed for the next in line. As soon as they walked through the door, they saw what they were looking for. "Hot damn! I'll go tell the others," Miceli said, but as she turned to leave, she found her exit blocked by Master Sergeant Thomas, arms crossed in front of her chest again and completely void of all expression. The only plus to the situation now was the fact that the air conditioner in the room was running and the air that was coming from it felt like heaven. "Excuse me, Sarge."

"No. Have a seat, Miceli. And what is your name?" She was looking directly at James.

"Officer Troy James, Sarge." As much as he didn't want to admit it, this woman scared him. Big guys are easy to figure out and easy to take down, but the little ones were the ones to watch, and he was going to watch her.

Inadvertently noticing how the air conditioner was making Miceli's nipples poke through the fabric of her sports bra, Alex cleared her throat and asked, "Why did the two of you pair up?"

Miceli answered quickly, "Because two sets of eyes are better than one and because there is strength in numbers, Sarge."

The carefree tone in Miceli's voice hit a nerve inside her. "And why did you think that you had the right to come up here to look for the hardware?"

"Because at no point should any area be overlooked during a search however big, small, or inconvenient, Master Sergeant Thomas," Miceli replied with a faint smile on her face. They found what she didn't think would be found, and as a result, the sarge was aggravated, and that pleased Miceli.

"I want the two of you to stay in here until your fellow officers figure out where to go as well. Do not leave this office." And with that, Sergeant Thomas closed the door and walked back to her spot on the catwalk, condemning herself for her lack of control.

***

James looked at Miceli when the sarge left the room and, as they both took a seat at the table, asked her, "Do you have any idea as to what we got ourselves into?"

"Not a clue. You?"

"No, but whatever it is has got to be big. I did six years in the Army, and this is worse than the things they put us through, and it's only the first day. The first day is when they weed out the weak, but they normally do that with push-ups and physical stuff, you know?" James shook his head and sat back. "I'll admit one thing, though. When she was sizing us up the first time, I couldn't stop looking at her ass. It's tight as hell," he added with a smile.

"I can't believe that you were checking her out! Are you serious?" Jen, upset at the fact that James was checking Alex out and making comments like that about her, felt a surge of protectiveness that she couldn't explain run through her. It's not like they were together, and in fact, Alex ran out on her.

"Miceli, you can't tell me that you were not looking at her while she was walking back and forth in front of us or when she was hovering over you or when she was blocking our route when we were coming up the stairs because you were. I saw it, you looked like you were hungry for her."

She couldn't argue with James because she was watching the sarge closely. Her entire outfit had to have been planned; everything she had on was form-fitting, and with a body like hers, you couldn't help but look.

"Yeah, I was...a little, but it's not like I was drooling or anything. I was sizing her up, more or less." She couldn't believe that this was the same woman that let her wrap her arms around her last night and today slipped through them like she was butter. She didn't know what was happening; after all, they only talked for, what, a few hours. Why couldn't she stop thinking about last night? All she could think about was how soft her lips had been when they kissed and the pull that they had on each other. How could she go from hot to cold like that? It was as if last night never even happened.

"You know that they will never come up here, don't you?" James said after a few silent minutes, pulling her out of her thoughts.

"Yeah, I think she scares them more than they let on." How she could scare anyone was beyond her. Alex's eyes gave her away; all you had to do was look. "We need to find a way to let them know that we are up here."

"Well," James said after taking a deep breath. Leaning forward with a small smile on his face, he said, "She said that we couldn't leave the room, right?"

"Right." Where was he going with this?

"But she never said we can't signal for them."

Looking around, it became obvious that there was only one way to get their attention. The only problem was that it was sure to get the sergeant's attention too. They positioned the small table and the two chairs against the far wall, and then they each climbed on a chair. Looking at each other and hoping that this was going to work, they jumped off the chairs and landed on the floor at the same time, making a bang that had to have been heard downstairs. Quickly they got up and did it again and again and didn't stop until the first of four officers came through the door.

Douglas, the first through the door, looked at them in complete puzzlement. His brown hair was soaking wet, and his shirt was plastered to his chest.

"What the hell are you two doing? Why are you jumping off chairs and making all that noise?" he asked. Before either of them could answer, the sarge walked through the door.

"Because I told them they could not leave until their fellow officers figured out where to look for the conversion hardware as well. My question is this, why did it take this long and them jumping up and down like fools for you to realize that they were gone?" She stared each one of them down, hoping that one of them would be stupid enough to speak. When no one did, she looked at Miceli and James and said, "Pass out the hardware and get your asses downstairs. Now." And with that, she walked out of the room.

Running like there was no tomorrow, the six remaining officers grabbed the hardware for their weapons and ran down the stairs two at a time before coming to a halt directly in front of their new sergeant in exactly the same spots that they left from. They were sweating profusely, and with the exception of Miceli, everyone's shirts were plastered to their skin. She walked the line again, looking at them, and started to see what she was aiming for. Confusion. They needed to be shaken up and have their worlds turned upside down before she could really teach them anything. She had to undo all of the training that they have been through already so that when she started her training, there would be no conflicts between what she was teaching and the training they had already received through the police department. Everything had to be done her way. With her not knowing exactly what the mission called for, she decided that this was going to be a crash course in everything, so she had no time to lose.

"I thought I made it clear that you are a team. In my opinion, a team works together as a unit, never leaves anyone behind, and is productive in nature. Put the Simunition hardware on the floor." As everyone placed their pieces and parts down, she moved into position in front of the center of the group and stood at parade rest. "Connery, step forward."

Connery, who was standing to the left and at the end of the line, took one step forward and stopped.

"Are you a team player, Connery?"

"Yes, Master Sergeant Thomas."

"Do you think that *I* would consider you a team player?"

He turned his head and looked her right in the eyes. "Yes, Master Sergeant Thomas, I do."

"Then not only do you know how to abandon your team but you also lie so well that you even have yourself fooled. Tell your captain that your services will not be needed. You are dismissed."

Turning on the spot so that he was facing her, Connery, in a forced but controlled voice, asked, "What in the hell did I do? How did I abandon my team and how am I lying?" Connery was furious. He has never been dismissed from anything before. He was always at the top of his class, the favorite at any sport, and the best in his precinct. He was not about to let this chick screw up his perfect record.

Raising one eyebrow at him, Sergeant Thomas was just waiting for the inevitable. "You are not the best of the best. I think that your captain made a mistake in sending you here. You are dismissed." She stared him down while in the parade rest position, calculating whether he was the swinging type or the mouthy type. She got her answer almost immediately.

Turning red with rage, Connery's voice began to rise until he was shouting. "I am the best in my precinct, my captain said so! If it wasn't true, then the guys at the station wouldn't have agreed when I told them on Saturday!"

Bingo. With a smile that was so cold it made him take a step back, she turned her body and faced him. "Exactly."

She began to take slow steps forward. "You did tell people what your captain briefed you in his office, and it was more than you just having to be somewhere on Monday. When you lie, Mr. Connery, it shows. I knew the moment I asked the question, and you didn't step forward that you had said more about this to others. You left your team to look for the hardware to the weapons while you had lain on your back because you were getting hot." She stopped directly in front of him. "You quit on them, and that, sir, is unacceptable. You are dismissed." She turned her back to him, returned to her spot at the center front of the team, and watched the reaction of the remaining members.

Furious but clearly defeated, Connery walked past the remainder of the group without looking at a single one of them. Once the door closed behind him, she told everyone to grab two bottles of water, directing them with a nod of her head to the southeast corner of the building. Running at full speed, they got the water and returned to their respective places, waiting to see what was next.

When everyone returned, she began, "When we sweat, we dehydrate. I will not allow anyone to fall out because they didn't want to drink enough water. Now drink." She watched as the remaining five officers drank their water down, standing stock-still where they were and never taking their eyes off her.

"For now, I will leave the fact that Antonelli, Douglas, and O'Malley were acting as individuals with no concern for the team as a whole. I will also leave the fact that Miceli and James made no attempt to inform any members of their team as to their plans to leave the group as a whole." She walked the line with her hands behind her back, stalling, making them wait on her next move. Stopping in front of Douglas, she said, "Douglas, with everything that has happened so far, can you name one thing that you observed that is out of the ordinary?"

Looking confused, Douglas said, "No, Master Sergeant, I can't."

Continuing her walk, she stopped in front of O'Malley. "Can you tell me if there has been anything out of the ordinary so far today?"

O'Malley was struggling to recall anything from the morning's events so far that was different, but disappointed, he came up with nothing. "No, Master Sergeant Thomas. I can't either."

Smiling and shaking her head, she looked at the bunch. "Is there anyone who can tell me the one thing that any of you may have observed today that is out of the ordinary?" The answer was right in front of their eyes.

Stepping forward, Miceli said, "I can, Sarge." She had a minute smile on her face.

Is she cocky, or is she that good? Thinking that she knew how to drop her down a notch or two, Master Sergeant Thomas walked up to Miceli, stopping within six inches of her, and asked, "Are you sure? Because if you are wrong, everyone will pay for your mistake."

Miceli looked down at Master Sergeant Thomas with a look that told her game on and said, "You are not sweating, Sarge." She took a step back and rejoined her team, smiling, knowing that she was right. Surprised that Miceli picked up on it but refusing to let any of them know, she pushed forward.

"Well, Miceli, you are correct. Exposure to the elements is the number one cause of injuries and the key to avoiding them is knowing the symptoms. I am not suffering from a heat-related injury. I am just used to the heat and I know how to dress for work. From here on out, you will be working long and sporadic hours. You will not know what time your day will end until it is over, so do not make any plans. We begin our day at 0700 on the dot every day unless otherwise notified. I want every one of your phone numbers, home and cell, so that if I need to recall you, I can get you. At 0700, I expect your service weapon to be ready for use with Simunition rounds. If your barrel is not ready at 0700, you and the rest of your team will pay for it. At no time are any live rounds authorized in this building unless I issue them to you." She surveyed the group and, noting that they looked like statues, continued.

"From now on, I don't want to see any cars parked in my parking lot, and you had better be ready to go through hell. If you are not prepared to give me what I ask for, then remove yourself now." She waited ten seconds before finishing with, "It's time to begin."

Walking toward the back of the building, the sarge indicated for the group to follow her. Stopping two-thirds of the way in the back center of the building, she looked around and said, "This building is large and spacious, and it would be a waste to not utilize as much of it as we can. To your right are hammers, nails, and several types of wood. I want a three-foot wall, a six-foot wall, and the framework and walls for a small two-bedroom home, including closets, and no one leaves until it is done. Go."

As she walked away, she looked at her watch, noting the time: 0956. *They are better than I expected so far.* She headed for her office upstairs to begin loading up ammunition and getting ready for tomorrow, but as for today, it was going to be a long one.

***

Week 1

No one spoke a word until they were sure that the sarge was out of earshot. They walked back to their lockers, stowed their weapons, grabbed some extra water, and stood at the pile of wood. O'Malley looked around and, when he was sure that the sarge was gone, addressed the group.

"Everything that we do is a test, you guys do realize that, right? With that being said, we need to figure out what her game is." James turned to look at O'Malley and laughed. He knew what O'Malley was getting at and he knew it wasn't going to work.

"O'Malley, we have known each other for seven years now, and you know that when I say something, it is a fact, not opinion, and I am telling you now that that woman has no game. This is her reality, and she is going to make us a part of it. I have seen her type before and I am telling you all right now, you will not be able to anticipate her next move. The only thing that you can do is go with it and know that there is a reason for everything that she does."

"Man, I hope you are right because if I am going to bust my ass, it better be for a good goddamn reason," he said to James but was addressing the group as a whole. "Miceli, how did you know the answer to her question? Never in a million years would I have guessed it."

The group looked at her. She knew that while being overseas, Alex had been exposed to some serious heat and was probably used to it, but to tell the group didn't seem right.

"She looks at the facts in hand. So far, everything she has had us figure out has been right in front of our faces. When I looked around and saw how caked with sweat we all were and then looked back at her, it surprised me at how comfortable she looked. With her, I think that the obvious answer will always be the right answer."

Then they all felt it. The air conditioner had been turned on, and the group gave a collective sigh of relief as O'Malley brought them back to the task at hand.

"Okay, so who knows how to build a house?"

***

Slowly they began to get a feel as to what it was they had to do, and by one o'clock, they had finished the three- and six-foot walls and had the outline for the "small house" that the sarge wanted. They all were taking a step back to look at the outline to make sure that everything was right when Douglas spoke up. "So is anyone going to ask the sarge what we are going to do for food, or are we going to just starve ourselves?"

Watching everybody shift and avoid eye contact with one another, Miceli, annoyed with the tepidness of the group, responded, "I'll go ask. We need to eat, and I don't see how she could deny us food. I mean what's the worst that could happen? She yells at me or makes me do push-ups, big deal." As soon as the last word was out of her mouth, she saw the looks on everyone's faces. The sarge was right behind her, she knew it.

Dropping the box that she brought for the group on the floor, Master Sergeant Thomas eyed Miceli, but instead of backing down, she just eyed her back. A war of the wills had begun, and it was going to be an interesting ride.

"Who here has ever been in the military?" Sarge addressed the group but continued to look directly at Miceli. James stepped forward, snapped to the position of attention, and replied, "I served six years in the Army, Master Sergeant Thomas."

"Well, good then. Perhaps you could explain to the rest of your team how we eat our food in the field. And fair thee warning, one MRE, which is what you will all be dining on today, is designed to be able to feed one individual for a day. Enjoy your lunch and dinner. Also, a little word of advice…now is the time to get to know one another. Strengths, weaknesses, likes, and dislikes are good to know when you are required to work as a team." She turned and walked away back to her office upstairs.

"Okay, Miceli, I thought that you were done for. If you could have seen the look on her face when you asked 'What was the worst she could do?' I thought you were a goner." O'Malley put an arm around her shoulder, and they all shared a collective laugh at Miceli's expense.

"So, James, what's up with the food?" Antonelli asked, but it wasn't long after they all sat down and found out that there are some foods that should not be heated, let alone eaten.

"Did you guys seriously have to eat this garbage?" Douglas asked James as he pushed his "granola bar," or brick as he felt it really was, back into the bag.

"They are not bad if you eat fast and try not to taste them." James laughed. "But in all fairness, there are some good ones out there. You just have to fight to get them."

"I don't know if I would ever fight for this crap," O'Malley said as he stood back up. "How much longer do you guys—no offense, Miceli—think it's going to take to finish this up?"

They all knew that it was going to be an all-night affair, but no one wanted to say it out loud. Looking around, Miceli stood up.

"It's going to take forever, so allow me to recommend that you guys go and move your cars because I don't see us leaving here tonight."

She told them where she had parked her car and was about to start on some of the framing when she heard her name being called from the catwalk.

"Miceli, up here. Now."

Chapter 5

Great. What now? was all she could think as she ran up the stairs and into the sarge's office. "You called for me, Sarge?" she asked when Alex didn't acknowledge her entrance to the office.

"Off the record, Miceli," Alex said as she closed the door and essentially isolated them from everyone else. "I am sorry about last night. I had been drinking and I normally don't allow myself to lose control, and for that, I want to apologize. However, I want you to know that I will not look at you any differently than any other member of your team, and I ask that what happened last night stay between the two of us."

That was a well thought-out speech, but as always, Jen's mouth had a way of doing its own thing without consulting with her brain first. "First, I had no intention of informing anyone about what happened last night. That was between the two of us, and I am not one to kiss and tell. Second, I never expected you to treat me any differently. And third, since we are off the record, I have a question for you." She waited for a moment to see if there would be any kind of reaction, which there wasn't.

"You said that you never lie, so answer me this—if I was not one of your trainees, would you have walked out on me last night, or would you have considered going on a date with me?"

She didn't know what she wanted to hear, but she held her breath anyway, never once giving away her feelings.

Alex looked at her. Why did she have to ask that? Well, the right thing may not always be the easiest, but it is the right thing. "No, I would not have walked out on you, Jen. Yes, I would have gone on a date with you, but there is one rule that I have never broken, and it is that you never fool around with the people that you work with.

Knowing that I am working with you puts you completely out of my mind as anything other than a trainee. Now get back to work."

Walking back down the stairs, Jen felt a mixture of emotions. She was glad to know that Alex felt the connection last night, too, angry that she walked out on her like she did, and confused at the transformation from last night to today that she saw in Alex. How much self-control does it take to completely shut yourself off like that? Overall, though, she was happy with the fact that she knew where she stood with Alex, and there would be no more questioning her intentions. But still, why did it bother her so much?

***

Two o'clock in the morning and they were still hammering away. They were tired, worn out, hungry, and still had several hours to go before they would be done.

"Do you think she is even awake up there?" Douglas looked to the offices with a bit of frustration in his voice.

"Yeah, I think that she is and I am willing to bet that she has been watching us more than we think," James said matter-of-factly. "There is a reason that we are building these things, and I don't think that it is for any of the obvious reasons."

O'Malley looked at James, brushed his fingers through his hair, and gave a half laugh. "I wish I knew what it was because I am tired as hell, and don't forget we still have to change our weapons over."

"I'll change them over now so we don't forget. Get me your weapons." One by one, they unlocked their respective lockers and handed their weapons over to Miceli, and when she was handed the last one, she went to a table by their lockers and got to work on the conversions.

"Hey, Antonelli, did you notice how Miceli looks at the sarge, almost like she is trying not to laugh? It's almost like she has something on her, or am I wrong?"

Looking at O'Malley, Antonelli considered the question before answering him for a minute. "I think that Miceli's defense mechanism is sarcasm, and with what we were put through this morning,

I am not surprised at her reaction." Antonelli did notice how Miceli only called her Sarge and not Master Sergeant Thomas, and it was like the sarge didn't scare her at all. Antonelli was going to be watching the exchange between the two of them during this whole op. Growing up in an old-school Italian family, he learned quickly that the women were the most dangerous and formidable opponents and never to cross them. Growing up as a good-looking Italian kid with the perfect jet-black hair and olive complexion, he always had girls chasing after him, but contrary to popular belief, he was never one to "play the field." His mother and grandmother taught him at an early age to respect women, and his father always showed nothing but respect and at times a little fear for women. When he turned thirteen, his father pulled him aside and told him, "Son, never underestimate a woman. You may think that she is small and weak, but remember this, there is nothing more dangerous than a woman who is protecting her home, her heart, or her young." There was going to be a battle of the wills, and they had front-row seats.

***

At 0655 Tuesday morning, Master Sergeant Thomas put five fifteen-round magazines loaded with Simunition rounds on the table next to the weapons lockers, while the potential team was passed out in the new "training house." She watched them work until 0502 when it appeared that they had finally finished with the last piece of plywood and gave each other high-fives before passing out where they dropped. They talked all through the night about everything—from the Red Sox to what was for breakfast. They were beginning to assume individual roles within the team, and the morale throughout the entire night was actually quite high, all things considered. She knew all of this because unbeknownst to them, there was an intercom box situated on the wall near where the "house" was being built.

At 0700, shots were fired and the team jumped up. Looking around them and running to take cover behind the walls of the makeshift house in what was supposed to be the back bedroom, the team attempted to assess the situation. Not one of them had a weapon.

TRUST

Two more shots were fired and they sounded close. "We need to get to our weapons," O'Malley whispered to the others.

"If we leave out from this cover, we are sitting ducks. Anyone have any ideas?" Douglas was plastered to the wall but remained calm.

"Who can run?" James asked the group. "I'm slow as hell."

The team looked at one another before Miceli finally spoke up. "I can. Is there any way that you can give me some type of cover? All I need is two seconds to get going, and then I might just be out of the line of sight judging from where the reports are coming."

"I've got you, Miceli. Don't worry about the cover, I have the perfect distraction," James said as he turned and began to low crawl to the "first bedroom" where they had eaten their dinner. After about two minutes, James came back and looked at Miceli.

"Get ready. I don't know how long I can stall for you, but I am good for three shots. I hope you are fast."

Looking at the rest of the group, James said in a whisper, "There is going to be one hell of a boom that should echo off the walls if I did this right, so be prepared." Handing a water bottle and packet of powder to O'Malley and Douglas, James instructed them as to what they had to do. After everybody was in position, James emptied his packet of powder into his quarter-full water bottle, screwed the cap on, shook it up, threw it, and counted down.

Boom! Dropping to the floor of the catwalk, the sarge looked around, trying to figure out what the hell just blew up. Seeing no signs of smoke, she set her sights back on the "house" and got ready for the next wave of shots. Watching them jump and scramble around was priceless, and it is the one thing that she never got tired of. She was just about to zero in on Big Boy's leg when another explosion erupted just to the left side of the house. Looking in the direction of the explosion, she began to understand what was happening and, to some extent, was impressed. She scanned the area for bodies; they obviously scattered with the first explosion, so where were they? *Got one behind the three-foot wall but no clear shot and four in the "house." Have eyes on Big Boy's leg but only a calf by the front door, waste of time. Have sights on Antonelli's shirt sleeve but only the elbow at the kitchen,*

Douglas is at the doorway of the bathroom, but again only a small piece of his shoulder showing. Boom! Another explosion, but this time it was to her right on the catwalk and it was close. She refocused and set to hit Big Boy's leg, not happy that she couldn't find Miceli. She attained sight picture and sight alignment, controlled her breathing, exhaled, and just as she began to pull the trigger, she felt a sharp pain in her ribs on her left side just a second before hearing the rapport from the weapon that fired it.

"Good morning, Sarge," Miceli said with a smug smile on her face as she looked down at her. "Did we pass?"

Standing up and refusing to show how much that shot to her ribs was hurting her, she looked down and saw the group emerging from their cover and weapons being distributed. "I'm impressed. How did you recover all of the weapons that fast?"

"With all due respect, Sarge, if I told you that, then the next time, it wouldn't work. Some things we are better off keeping to ourselves, wouldn't you agree?" Throwing that little stab of double meaning that only Alex would understand, Miceli stared her down. Last night, she had time to think about their "private conversation," and the more she thought about it, the more upset she became. She decided that if Alex wanted a war, then that was exactly what she was going to get, not realizing that her line of thinking was because she had been hurt. Jen was satisfied with her plan.

Nodding and smiling the coldest smile she could pull out, Master Sergeant Thomas looked at Miceli and in her coolest voice said, "Downstairs and line it up."

***

She walked the line and looked each one of them over. They looked like hell and smelled worse. Last night, she had changed in her office into her combat boots, black military grade cargo pants, and tight-fitting black T-shirt that now had yellow paint on it, indicating exactly where she had been hit. "I am impressed at the coordination on the retaliatory attack. Your response time was excellent. You made excellent use of your cover, and the improvisation on James's part to make MRE bombs was well executed." The pride radiating from their eyes was welcomed but needed to be put out. She was coming to the part in the training that she disliked the most. "Put your weapons on the table and follow me." With that, she walked to the rear of the building and out the back door.

There was a slight breeze outside, but it was warm, bright, and sunny. The waves against the barrier wall were only at a foot, and the smell of the ocean energized Alex, as it always did. Leaning against the building, she spoke in a soft voice and painted on the fake smile that was required for certain aspects of the training. "Line it up facing me."

There was not a lot of room in the small area behind the warehouse, and when the sarge told them to line it up, they ended up having to stand right on the edge of the walkway and close enough to the water that if a strong gust of wind came, they could very well lose balance and fall into the cold water behind them. On the small gray walkway that they were standing on, the concrete was worn by weather, and the edge closest to the water was wet from the light mist of the lapping waves. There was no wall or lip to create a barrier between land and sea, its only purpose being a place for the warehouse to sit on. The water was Atlantic black, as every New Englander referred to the color, and much deeper than one would expect at the water's edge. O'Malley stole a quick look down the line and saw Antonelli, sweating and looking scared as hell. *What's going on here?*

Still leaning against the wall of the building, the sarge asked the group, "Did you all have a nice night?" Cool and calculated.

Confused but in unison, they responded, "Yes, Master Sergeant Thomas."

She pushed off the wall and walked the line with her hands behind her back like she was on a Sunday stroll. "Did you do everything that I told you to do?"

What was she getting at? "Yes, Master Sergeant Thomas, we did," O'Malley answered for the group.

Alex stopped dead in front of Antonelli and raised an eyebrow. "Really?" she said with a smile so cold they could feel a chill wash over them from it.

"Yes, Master Sergeant Thomas," O'Malley said again.

"I doubt it." She extended her left arm so fast that they almost didn't see it as she connected her hand square with Antonelli's chest right before he went into the water with a scream.

Just as Antonelli hit the water, she looked at the group and said, "Did you know that he can't swim?" and walked back inside.

***

O'Malley and Miceli hit the water fast and hard, while Douglas and James stood by to lift. The water was cold and black and so deep that neither one of them could find the bottom. "Miceli, O'Malley, he just went under five feet behind you!" Douglas shouted when the two came up looking around, unable to find Antonelli on the first dive.

They both took deep breaths, trying to fill their lungs for the dive. Down they went in the direction that Douglas indicated, and after what seemed to be the longest minute of their lives, they finally came up, each one gripping their teammate's arm. "We've got you, Antonelli. Hold on, man, we'll get you out," Miceli said and together they swam to the voices of encouragement on the wall.

James and Douglas pulled Antonelli out of the water followed by Miceli and then O'Malley. "Thanks, Douglas, thanks, James," Antonelli said between coughs and gasps for air.

Antonelli was on his hands and knees coughing up the remnants of water that he both breathed in and swallowed. When he finally got enough of the salty water out, he looked at the group as he stood up and started to pace. "That's it, there is nothing that is going to make me quit. It's personal now."

"Damn it!" Miceli shouted. "She told us yesterday." She was frustrated at the fact that she never picked up on it. *"Also, a little word of advice…now is the time to get to know one another. Strengths, weaknesses, likes, and dislikes are good to know when you are working as a team."* She planned this all out. "She's taking this too far! He could have died." She was fuming.

"No, I wouldn't have," Antonelli said as he stopped dead in his tracks with a look of total understanding. She saw us last night and she saw us this morning. We are already working as a functional team/unit, which means that we take care of our own. She knew it. I don't think she would have done it if she had any doubts." Shaking his head and collecting himself, Antonelli opened the door and walked back inside. James, Miceli, O'Malley, and Douglas all looked at one another for a minute before giving a collective nod of acknowledgment. War has begun, and in their minds, this was their battlefield. Game on.

***

Falling into their respective spots on the floor, the five of them stood at the position of attention and waited for instructions—three soaking wet, two damp, and every one of them pissed off and determined. "So are you ready to quit yet? There is no shame if you do, but you need to know this, today was the easiest day you will have." Not a single word. Not a single movement. This could be good. "Upstairs to the conference room. Now!"

The group ran up the stairs and down the catwalk to the conference room. Once in, they positioned themselves along the wall and waited for the sarge. Miceli did a quick scan of the room. It was approximately ten-by-twenty feet in size with the fake wood laminate flooring. Eight cushioned leather chairs were positioned around an oval oak table, and aside from that, the room was empty. After twenty minutes of standing there, waiting for the sarge to join them was beginning to wear on the group, fatigue was beginning to set in, and they were swaying on their feet. Miceli bumped her shoulder against James, who looked like he was about to fall asleep leaning against the wall just as the sarge walked in.

"Sit." Alex waited for them to all take a seat. Once they were all situated, she placed her hands on the head of the table, leaned forward, and looked at each one of them in turn. "I need to know that each and every one of you is in on what you have been chosen to do. I need to know that you are in this for the long haul and will not quit on me or your team. I need to know that at this point, you are fully alert and aware of what is being asked of you. Are you all fully alert?"

"Yes, Master Sergeant Thomas," they responded in unison.

Looking at Alex, Miceli saw an inner debate going on. She was stalling, and Miceli wanted to know why. She wondered if anyone else saw it too. "Sarge?"

"Yes, Miceli."

"I am in this to the end and I have no hesitations when it comes to doing whatever it is I have to do to do my job. I will always be there for my team."

"And your point, Miceli?"

"Sarge, what is it that we are training for?"

"Last chance. This is the point of no return." Alex waited a minute, scanning the group and making eye contact with each one before continuing on. They needed to know that this was no game and that this could end up ugly. "You were picked by your captains because they thought all around you were the best. They did not know why they were asked to give you up, nor will they. From this moment on, everything said in this room is considered classified. Is that understood?"

"Yes, Master Sergeant Thomas." They all replied as they moved closer to the edges of their seats. They all wanted to know why this hard-ass military person was on their turf and treating them like they were pieces of garbage that she could just throw away.

"No one is to know what you are doing or where you are training, not even spouses. If anyone from your respective precincts asks what your new assignment is, you tell them that you are learning how to be an effective trainer. It is not a lie. Essentially by the time training is complete, you will be proficient enough to train almost anyone. The only people who know what is going on are the chief of police and Brigadier General Scott. I answer to General Scott and you answer to me, that's it. If something happens to me, information goes to no one but the general. Is that clear?" The team nodded their understanding. "The chief of police is out of the information loop on this one, with the exception of what the general informs him of himself. We are now on an information blackout." She paused for a moment to let the information sink in. "Does anyone here have any personal issues that could compromise the effectiveness of the mission, whatever it may be?" She waited for a moment before continuing on. "I need complete and total professionalism at all times. If I give out an order, it must be followed without hesitation or question, and personal conflicts can interfere with that, I won't allow it." It was as though she was looking at five statues. Not a single movement between any of them with all eyes on her, but when she looked at Miceli, it was as if she had put up a wall, like she was trying to hide something. She didn't know how she knew; Miceli was sitting as still as the others, but it was something about her eyes. She needed to be watched.

Miceli leaned in as she started to see part of the picture beginning to form. When Chris was grilling Alex at the bar about her job, she was deflecting and downplaying what she did. *What in the hell did she do over there?*

"You are the first team assembled by request of the DoD. It seems that there has been an increase in drug trafficking in and on military bases, and they want a team that can find out how the drugs are getting on to the base, who is selling them, and stop it from continuing."

"Excuse me, Sarge," Miceli spoke up again, "but it seems like overkill. That is something that the base police can handle and have been for years. The training that you plan on giving us, although we don't know what it is yet, appears to me to be over the top. I have a feeling that you are holding something back. What is it, Sarge?" The sarge was keeping something from them, and she knew it. *It is in her eyes, and no matter how good she thinks she is, she can't hide it from me,* she thought.

"Why do you think I am holding something back, Miceli?" *She's good, I'll give her that,* she thought to herself, but there was something in Miceli's expression that wasn't sitting right with her. She looked excited, more than would be expected.

"Call it intuition, Sarge." This was no game, and they were not here to play. Looking around the table, Miceli realized that no one else picked up on how she was holding back information. How could they miss it when it was so obvious?

"If I answer that question, I would only be making assumptions. Do you want to hear them?"

"Yes, Sarge," Miceli answered for the group.

"DoD never gets involved in something as petty as drugs. The level of information blackout that is being put in place is not standard. In fact, I think that there are things going on that are so sensitive that it is probably a wise move to inform us of as little as possible. I think that we are going to find things on our own that are going to rock someone's world. Answering only to a general, giving up police officers without informing anyone as to the reasons, and choosing me to train you means that we will be getting into some serious shit. Now I don't mean that we are going to war or anything of the sort, but you need to realize that sometimes there are things that can be a whole lot worse." She watched as they considered the information that she just dropped into their laps. She had their full attention, and they all seemed resolved and ready to push forward, with the exception of one.

"Miceli, is there something that is confusing you?" She looked puzzled.

Taking a deep breath and pulling the courage she needed to push forward, Miceli looked up and into Sergeant Thomas's eyes. "Sarge, what is it that you really do? You said that if you were chosen to train us, then it is bad. What have you done, or what is it that you do?" She felt like she was calling her out, but if it was going to be as bad as she was implying, then Miceli thought that they had the right to know.

"I am not at liberty to tell any of you the details of any of my past assignments or missions. However, what I can tell you is that I am a specialist in training, interrogations, apprehension, and investigations of hostile situations as well as black market fencing interception. I have done three tours in Iraq and two in Afghanistan and I have come home each time on my own two feet. I have led several teams in the past, and my qualifications are unique. I don't do things half-assed and I get the job done, come hell or high water. Ultimately, however, I am considered military police." Looking at the officers sitting around the table, she hoped that things didn't turn as bad as they did a couple of months ago because if they did, well, she didn't know if she would be able to handle it.

"There will not be any paperwork generated or documentation created for this training. From here on out, we are our own self-contained unit. We will eat together, train together, and know each other better than we have known anyone before. You will learn how to read each other's minds and anticipate each other's actions. First names will not be used…period. Last names or call signs only. I want to make one thing perfectly clear to every one of you—no one in this room is your friend. You are teammates, you are a team, and you are a unit. Nothing more, nothing less."

"No shit?" Douglas slipped.

"No, Douglas, no shit."

O'Malley looked around the table at his teammates, trying to get a feed on their intentions, and, once he felt he could, stood up, looked the sarge directly in her eyes, and said, "So what are we waiting for, Sarge? Let's get to work."

***

Alex pulled the chair at the head of the table out and sat down. She was tired and worn out from the lack of sleep. When she got back to her apartment on Sunday and finally lay down, she couldn't get her mind to turn off. Every time she closed her eyes, she saw Jen and her emerald green eyes staring back at her. She knew that she did the right thing, but it didn't make it any easier. There was something about Jen that captured her attention and emptied her mind all at the same time. Lying there, she thought that she could still smell the hint of jasmine in her hair, her hands wrapped around her, and her lips on her skin. Sleep did not come.

"Everyone here has had some type of formal training, some more than others, but training nonetheless. With that being said,

I feel that after seeing your performance today under less than ideal circumstances, we can push through the boring stuff and get right down to the necessities. There will be times that I will join in on the training with you. I will be doing that not only to keep myself proficient but also to work with my new team and to form some type of cohesion. There will be times that you will wonder why I am subjecting you to certain tasks, and how they are pertinent to our mission, I am not always going to explain. Just know that at no point am I going to waste my time or yours on needless taskings." She surveyed the group sitting in front of her. They were dirty, sweaty, sore, and overly tired, but they were completely alert and on point with what she was telling them. Standing back up, Alex outwardly appeared to be at the top of her game and ready for round two, but she doubted if she would last another two hours.

"You will have at the ready every day three sets of black cargo pants, three pairs of black T-shirts, two pairs of black boots, three sets of PT gear with sneakers, one towel, a toiletry set, one duffel bag, and your weapon. All of these items, with the exception of your weapons, will be stored in the lockers that have been placed in the latrines downstairs so that they can be accessible at any time. Do not bother bringing a lock. If you can't trust each other, then we might as well quit now. As I am sure that you have noticed already, both bathrooms are equipped with gang showers and are fully functional. In the event of an emergency and you need to be contacted, tell whoever it is that you have to that they need to contact the chief of police, and he will relay to General Scott who will then relay to me. The use of cell phones will not be permitted while you are training." There were definitely a couple of them that didn't like the idea of not having access to their phones.

Alex looked at her watch. "It is 1027. All of the items that I told you to have on hand will be here with you at 0700 tomorrow morning. You will be ready to go in a pair of your cargo pants and black T-shirt. You will bring food for lunch and possibly dinner every day, you will not be going out to eat, we do not get a lunch hour, and you will eat when the opportunity presents itself. Today I am releasing you early so as to get whatever it is that you don't have, but it will be the last time you go early. I have one suggestion for those of you who might have nosy friends or coworkers." She looked directly at Miceli. "Don't call them today, don't answer your phone, and don't try to relay information to them. You don't have time to waste deflecting questions and you need to get yourselves prepared for tomorrow and the next two months. The code to the cipher lock on the front door is 11-5-55 and then hit Enter. Dismissed."

Watching as they silently went downstairs, retrieved their weapons, and swapped out the hardware, Alex began to ask herself for the hundredth time, what exactly did they need to be trained for? She was an expert at getting men trained and ready for combat overseas against known enemies, but they were not overseas. They didn't know who the enemy was, and worst of all, she didn't know what the real mission was. She had limited time to train them in the unknown and she prayed that she did not fail them.

Chapter 6

They walked as a group to their cars in silence, everyone replaying what they were just told and letting the facts sink in. When they arrived in the parking lot, Antonelli stopped and looked at everyone. "Okay, before I drop here from exhaustion, does anyone know where we can get all this stuff?"

"Go to the Tactical Outfitters on Commonwealth Avenue. They should have everything that she wants. Hey, does anyone know why she was wearing that skintight shirt?" Douglas asked with a hint of a smile forming at the corner of his mouth.

Jen answered almost instantly, "So that it doesn't get caught on anything. It's cool and it's slippery as hell. Everything is pertinent, remember? Her clothes are functional but tactically advantageous." *And she looks damn hot in them too*, Miceli added to herself.

"So is everyone going to be getting the same shirts then?" Douglas asked

The round robin all agreed; if they were going to do this, might as well go all the way, and right now, all the way was the Sarge's way.

O'Malley asked the group something that he just couldn't understand. "Why did she say that stuff about us being a team, a unit, and stuff but in the same breath said that we are not friends? I mean, won't it lead to that eventually?"

"She is saying that to protect us. If something happens to one of us and all we are is a group of coworkers, we can deal with it, but if we are friends, use each other's first names or in other words get on a personal level, then if something happens to one of us, it could devastate the whole team. It is meant to save us potential pain in the future," James said with a knowing and haunted look in his eye that no one questioned.

They all split up and headed out in different directions, but before she did anything else, Miceli decided that her first priority was going to be getting something to eat. She swung into the drive-through of Dunkin' Donuts and ordered two chocolate crullers and a large iced coffee and ate them on the way to pick up her new "uniforms," as she thought of them. The woman liked black; she would give her that much.

After finally getting the last of her uniform items packed up in her duffel bag, Jen looked up and saw that it was almost two o'clock. "Damn, how long have I been up for now?" she asked herself. After a quick shower, she thought that she would check the news before heading to bed, so she sat on the couch, turned on the TV, and fell asleep almost instantly.

At five o'clock, her phone rang. Still lying down on the couch, face buried in the cushion, she reached out for the phone. "Hello?"

"Hey, girl, how was it yesterday? What are you doing? Fill me in," Chris said in an all too energetic voice.

"I'll call you later and fill you in. I have to get some sleep, Chris."

"Jen, it's only five. Are you okay?"

"We pulled a twenty-seven-and-a-half-hour shift. I need sleep. I'll call you later." And without waiting for a response, she hung up and passed back out, falling into a dream that was so realistic she didn't know she was dreaming.

***

Alex waited for everyone to leave before locking up the building and heading out herself. She was determined to stay awake at least until eight because she hated messing with her sleep schedule, and the best way to stay awake was to keep occupied. Stopping at Market Basket, Alex shopped for groceries, trying to anticipate what she would want to eat for the next two weeks and what she could make that she could eat on the fly. Having been gone as long as she had, everything looked appetizing, so she found it difficult picking out food. Finally, after settling for two loaves of bread, peanut butter, jelly, turkey, ham, cheese, a variety bag of chips, a box of granola bars, Gatorade, and two cases of Mountain Dew, she headed home.

Before unpacking her groceries, Alex called the China Blossom and ordered a sweet-and-sour chicken combination and a General Tso's combination plate. She unpacked and put away her groceries while singing along to a mix of The Celtic Woman, Jewel, and Beyoncé. Turning the music up louder so she could still hear it, Alex jumped into the shower, did a quick power scrub, and changed into her baggy BC sweatpants and Patriots T-shirt. Ten minutes later, there was the expected knock on her door.

"So where in the hell have you been?" Tina said as she walked past Alex into the apartment and sat on the couch, smiling all the way. "Did we go and have ourselves a little fun last night? Curious minds want to know."

"How did you know that I was home and how did you know that I didn't come home last night? Are you checking up on me?" Alex smiled, almost closing the door on the delivery guy. "Oh, I am so sorry," she said as she took the food from the man and handed him twenty dollars. "Keep the change."

"Um, what's in the bag?" Tina eyed the bag from where she sat with potent curiosity.

Laughing and shaking her head, Alex walked over to the couch, opened the bag, and handed her the General Tso's, enjoying the shock on Tina's face.

"How did you know I was going to come over? I swear it's scary the way you know things," she said, shaking her head as she took a bite of her chicken.

"You are nothing, if not predictable, hon. You always have been. And you didn't answer my question—are you checking up on me?" Alex asked while relishing her sweet-and-sour chicken.

"Mmm, God, you never know how much you take for granted until you can't have what you want when you want it."

"Yeah, I know what you mean. I wanted this little hottie at the club the other night, but I guess it just wasn't in the cards," Tina said as they both laughed and then just sat eating in silence, enjoying each other's company.

"So, Alex, how is the writing coming?" Tina asked without lifting her head. She knew that Alex hadn't written anything in over a year, but she was hoping just the same.

"T, you know that I haven't written anything, and it's not like my writing is that good either. I mean, really, what would I write about? I haven't had a reason to write, and even when I did, I couldn't bring myself to do it." A trace of sadness crossed her face for a second, and if it had been anyone other than Tina, it would have gone unnoticed.

Tina pushed her food to the side for a moment and took Alex's hand. "Sweetie, first off, you write what's in your heart, so it is always good. Second, you have plenty to write about. I just don't think that you want to think or deal with the things that you have locked up inside right now, but one thing is for sure—when you write, you find the answers to the questions you're afraid to ask. You always have. Sooner or later, you are going to start writing again, and when you do, I have a feeling that you are going to either surprise yourself or scare yourself to death. So do me a favor and call me when it happens… I want to be there to see the look on your face!" She jumped back as Alex tried to hit her with one of the pillows on the couch, laughing.

"Honestly, I don't know why I put up with you sometimes," Alex said, laughing as she picked her chicken back up.

"Oh, that's easy because you love me, silly. No wonder I am your best friend. I mean, who else would remind you of things like that?"

The two of them sat on the couch talking until Tina had to leave to get ready for work. When she finally left, Alex headed for the kitchen and pulled out the necessary ingredients that she needed for her lunch and dinner the next day and prepared it. Next, she packed her black duffel bag with her clothes and the extras that she liked to have handy for the "just in case" factor, put her lunch and dinner in it, and put it next to the door. Finally she went into her room and laid out her clothes for the next day on the bench at the end of the bed, set her alarm clock, and picked up her journal in hopes that she could get a few things off her mind.

APRILLE CANNIFF

Dear Journal,

I don't know what is wrong with me. I think that I might be losing my edge. I met a woman the other day, and we hit it off pretty well. By pretty well, I mean that I practically jumped her in the bar after talking to her for only a couple of hours. I have never done anything like that before, and you know that. There was something about her that I just couldn't pull myself away from. Every ounce of my being wanted to be next to her. I couldn't get enough of her, and the more we talked, the more I wanted to know. I'll admit that she is beautiful, but that isn't what got my attention... It was her eyes! Oh my god, her eyes! When we first began talking, they were a light green with a hazel tinge around them, but after about an hour, they turned to the deepest emerald green I have ever seen. I kissed her! I practically took her clothes off in the bathroom and made love to her right there. All of my reasoning is out the door when it comes to her. It's like my mind forgets to function when she is around and my hormones take over.

But I can't date her now because I found out Sunday night that she is one of my trainees, and you know my policy. I ran out of the bar without so much as an explanation. In the past, I have been able to turn off my feelings and emotions at the drop of a hat when it comes to work, but for some reason, I am having a hard time doing that right now. When we touch, I feel like we are sharing the same current of electricity that is powering the both of us. I feel a pull that I have never felt before, and it is killing me. Today I began round one of "bitch," and she felt it like a slap in the face. At one point, I had to get her in a takedown move, and it put me straddling her waist. I got so excited I had to practically jump off her. As the day went on, I watched as she got more and more mad at me, and it hurt—it actually hurt! By the end of the week, she is going to hate me, and although right now it hurts knowing all of the things that I am going to do to her, I know that it is for the best, and it will hopefully help me to get my perspective back. Here is to hoping that I can stop my heart from racing, my mind from wandering, and my hormones in check, because if not, it is going to be a long couple of months.

Well, I am tired, so I am going to close for now. I will write more later.

Alex

Closing her journal, she slipped it into the nightstand and thought about what she had just written. The more she thought about Jen, the more she could picture the depth of her eyes, the heat of her body, and the safety she felt in her arms, and it was these things she thought about as she slowly fell asleep.

***

It was just the two of them at Mickey's. They sat holding each other's hands and talked about what she couldn't remember, but what she could remember was her eyes. There was a sadness that she could not place, and she wanted more than anything to take that sadness away. She leaned in toward Alex, and as she lifted her hand to caress her face, Alex pulled back and ran out of the bar, leaving her there alone and confused.

"Alex, wait!" Jen screamed as she snapped awake and almost jumped off the couch. It took her a minute, but after looking around and taking in her surroundings, Jen slumped back, put her hands over her eyes, and, with a sense of disappointment, said, "Shit." She needed to get over this. It's not like they were dating or had even known each other. They were two strangers who just happened to meet up over a couple of drinks one night. End of story.

The clock read 4:02 a.m., and she was wide awake. She couldn't remember when the last time was that she slept more than five or six hours, let alone almost fourteen! Turning off the television, she got up, stretching out the tightness in her back from passing out on the couch, walked into the kitchen, and started to make her lunch and dinner for the day. She didn't remember seeing a refrigerator, but recalling how the "sarge" said that they would be eating on the fly, she decided that the quick and easy would be best. Four peanut butter and jelly sandwiches, a bag of bagel crisps, a bottle of apple juice, and a twenty-ounce Code Red later, she packed her food in with the rest of her gear into the duffel bag.

She needed to run. She couldn't shake the leftover feelings from the dream she had and she didn't like it. She changed into her workout clothes, grabbed her bag, and headed out the door. She remembered seeing exercise equipment at the warehouse and she was going to give the gear a tryout.

Jen walked through the door at just after 5:00 a.m., went to the bathroom, and put her gear into an empty locker, organizing it as best as possible. Once that was done, she headed to her other locker and made the conversion on her weapon, put it back up, and then headed to the free weights. She worked her abs, chest, biceps, triceps, shoulders, and back, and as soon as she was done her last rep, she jumped on the treadmill. Listening to her iPod and Pink's latest CD, Jen started at a comfortable jog. After ten minutes, though, her mind began to wander, and the more it wandered, the higher she turned the speed up. Running always helps her to clear her mind and solve whatever it was that was bothering her at the time, and today was no exception. By the time Jen was done running, she had adopted the song "Hell Wit Ya" by Pink and was feeling better.

She got her towel and other necessities for her shower, got undressed, and turned the water on. It was a gang shower, all right. One pole with five heads on it in the middle of a "shower area" that was maybe eight-by-eight tiled room, how did the military do it? If there was one thing she liked, it was her privacy. There were times, of course, when you couldn't help but have to shower with others, but at least you were not two feet away from each other and looking in each other's eyes while trying to wash your ass. Oh well, she closed her eyes and just let the water beat on her back, enjoying the heat and peace that she was still feeling while she could.

***

At 0600, Alex walked into the warehouse, pulled out her lunch, and left her bag at the bottom of the stairs. She went into her office and, after putting her lunch in a drawer, looked around and took a deep breath. It was time to begin again, a new team, a new mission, and sense of unease about it all. There was something that she wasn't being told, and she didn't like it. Alex knew that there was always going to be times when information does not trickle down for some reason or another, but usually they were given enough info to at least properly prepare for what they were heading into.

With thoughts of different possible scenarios running through her mind, she didn't pick up on the clothes sitting on the bench or the water running; she just went to her locker and started to unpack her gear. The last of the items to go into her locker was an old picture of two little girls at the beach. One was center front with her arms crossed in front of her and making an "It's too cold and I am too scared" face. The second girl was in the background just to the top left, up to her knees in the water already, looking out at the ocean and wanting more. The girls were five years old in that picture, and whenever and wherever Alex went, that picture went with her. Tina gave it to her the first time she deployed and on the back she wrote, "Just a reminder that at an early age, you were always willing to go where others would not. Hurry home, Love, Tina." The second was another picture of her and Tina, only it was taken when they were twenty-three and Alex had just got back home from another deployment. They were at a club wanting nothing more than to be able to have a few drinks and catch up, but for some reason, no one would leave them alone. It seemed like every five minutes, someone was asking one of them to dance or using some pathetic one-liners on them, and finally she got tired of it. Alex went to the DJ and asked him if he would play a song for her and her new wife. When the song came up, the DJ shouted a big congratulations at them and, handing her phone to someone walking by, asked if they would take their picture. No one bothered them for the rest of the night. Tina had her arms wrapped around Alex's neck, and Alex had hers around Tina's waist. They looked like the happiest couple. Tina would yell at her about that later because for some reason, her dating life all but stopped for a while, and to this day, Alex still laughed about it.

Smiling at the memories, she closed her locker, turned around, and walked right into Miceli. Still wet from the shower, Jen slipped and began to fall backward. She threw out her arms to try and break her fall, but before she could hit the ground, Alex had her arms around her. Instinctively, Jen's arms went around Alex's neck, subsequently dropping the towel that she was holding around her body. It looked like they were in the middle of a dance—Alex dipping Jen, their lips only an inch from each other, and their eyes locked. Alex could feel the heat from Jen's body, smell the scent of the shampoo she had just used, and feel the softness of her skin beneath her hands. Realizing what just happened and what was happening, Alex stood Jen up, avoided looking at her naked body, and turned away. Jen bent over, picked up her towel, wrapped herself back up in it, and looked at Alex, who seemed frozen in place with her back to her, looking intently at the lockers.

"I am sorry. I should have watched where I was going," Alex said, speaking to her locker.

"No, it's okay. Sometimes an accident is just an accident." As she went to open her locker, she looked over at Alex and saw how red she was. "Are you okay? I hope I wasn't too heavy for you. I didn't hurt you, did I?" She was genuinely concerned.

"What?" Alex asked, true question on her face as she turned around to face her. "Why would you think you hurt me?"

"Sorry, I was just making sure." With that, Jen watched Alex turn and all but run out.

Quickly Jen got dressed and headed out of the bathroom, trying to focus on what was in store today, but instead, she kept thinking about how good those arms felt around her. "Damn it!"

***

"I don't know how you all run things on your side of the house, but it doesn't matter to me. What matters is that we do things my way with no exceptions, no questions, and no hesitations. From my experiences with every facet of investigations from drugs to personnel movement, there is one thing that I have come to understand. You don't have time." She looked at the five officers standing in front of her and wondered if any of them was going to believe or understand what she was telling them. "Once you start to question people, the time clock is running. People talk, people see, and people hear. No matter how quick, how silent, and how perfect you plan everything out, eventually the wrong people are going to find out, catch on, and your whole op becomes ineffective. Now why am I saying this? What does it mean?"

O'Malley answered first. "Sarge, once the bad guys know that we are looking for them, they hide, change routines, and sometimes stop what they are doing altogether until we back off."

"Exactly. Since our mission seems to track and apprehend the top contributors, I can guarantee that we have five shots or less before they become aware that something is going on, and they either go into hiding or on the offensive." Taking a deep breath, the sarge walked up and down the line, hands behind her back, taking each one in. When she got to Miceli, she showed no signs of distress or acknowledgment as to what happened earlier, just the cold stare she shared with everyone else.

"Information collection is key. Typically you all grab a dealer, question him, wait for him to flip or not, lock him up, and go to the next in line." She paused long enough to let them silently agree with what she said before continuing on. "The way it is done on your end of the house is ineffective and mediocre at best." Eyes opened and chests started to puff out. Yup, she insulted them. "The way I have tracked down and questioned supposed suspects are not authorized or legal in situations like this, so that leaves us straddling a fence, so to speak."

She waited for Douglas to finish deflating and come off the defensive before continuing. She had their attention, and now she had to get their understanding and support. As much as they might believe that she was in charge, and she was, she completely depended on them. They would decide whether this team and operation worked or not. They held all of the cards, while she held none, but the difference between this group and herself was that she had the poker face.

"We are going to merge tactics in hopes that the combination of the two will prove effective. You might not agree with everything I order you to do and you might have severe issues with my methods. If you do, wait until we are clear of the suspect. Do not question me in front of the—as you put it—bad guy. It undermines authority and proves a weakness within the ranks when what is needed most is a show of unity and force. We only get one shot at this and we can't blow it." Just as she finished her statement, the front door slammed open.

In an instant, Sergeant Thomas had her berretta drawn and set on the door. The team, seeing the sarge's reaction, ran for the lockers before hearing a commanding voice. "Stand down, Sergeant."

Just as quickly as she had pulled her weapon, it was returned, and she was at the position of attention. "Sirs," she said.

The team looked on and watched as their sergeant stood stock-still on the spot until the general and the chief stopped directly in front of her. She rendered a proper salute and waited until she was told, "As you were, Sergeant," by the general before mildly relaxing her position. General Scott could have been a poster child for the military. He had the standard high and tight and chiseled features that most people have come to expect from pilots, but the look on his face was that of a man who knew how to get things done. He was the type of person that if you were standing face-to-face with in a bar, you knew that you had better be the one to back down.

The team regrouped on their own and took up position behind Master Sergeant Thomas, waiting to find out what was going on.

TRUST

The chief joined General Scott on his left-hand side and, looking at his officers, seemed to noticeably relax.

"I see you have successfully chosen your team, Sergeant." General Scott said with a hint of a question in his tone.

"Yes, sir, I have."

"And do you have complete faith in them?"

"Sir, yes, sir."

"So you are willing to personally vouch for each one and accept any and all responsibilities as their team lead?" The general asked, studying her reaction.

"Sir, I have the utmost respect and confidence that this team will accomplish whatever tasks are assigned both now and upon completion of training." *This can't be good*, she thought to herself.

The chief looked at the general and, once given a nod, addressed the group. "Good then, Master Sergeant Thomas. This is your new team. You are now lead not only for training but field work as well. At this point, you are an experimental unit. No real guidelines or instructions have been set forth as of yet with the exception of one. As of right now, you are not bound by jurisdictional lines. You are authorized to conduct your investigations wherever they take you within the continental US, although I doubt very much if you will be traveling outside of Massachusetts. You will not report to your divisions nor will you answer any questions as to what your assignment is. Your respective captains have all been instructed that you are on loan for a joint agency training seminar, followed by training instructor's certification school. They are under the impression that you will be training the new recruits when all is said and done."

"I want every one of you to understand that although you know very little as to what you are training for, you have my best NCO leading you," General Scott stated as he looked at the newly formed team. "She has done more than most could ever dream of. She is highly capable and proficient in every facet of her job and will be an asset to you. You made her cut, and to be honest, I didn't know if any of you would, which means that you all have the ability to work as an effective and cohesive unit, ensuring mission success." He took a minute to look around the warehouse before continuing.

"We came here today so that you could see my face and the chief could verify the fact that the only person outside of your group to be informed of anything is me."

The chief picked up and continued, "As unorthodox as this all seems, please believe me when I say that there are good reasons for the precautions that are being taken right now. I will get updates as needed, but other than that, you are assigned to Master Sergeant Thomas." Looking at his officers as if saying goodbye, the chief finished by saying, "Good luck."

Addressing Master Sergeant Thomas, the general continued, "Thomas, you have done amazing things in the past, and although I know you may feel that this is beneath your level of expertise and experience, I feel that you are the only one that I can *trust* to accomplish this mission. Be safe." And with that, the chief and the general left without saying another word.

Chapter 7

"Sarge, what the—"

"What's going on?"

"Why did—"

"Enough," Alex said to the group as a whole.

"Sarge, why did the general say that you are the only one he can trust?" Antonelli asked. It was a comment that struck him as odd.

"When we were overseas, he decided to tag along with myself and my team. I told him that he was not going on a mission with my team until he completed a tasking that I required from all of my troops and do it right." And to herself, she thought, *Among other things.*

Shocked, James couldn't help but ask, "What did he say, Sarge?"

"He did it."

"What did you have him do, Sarge?" Miceli asked.

Bringing herself back to the matter at hand, she looked at Miceli and smiled. "Upstairs, everybody, into the conference room and I'll show you." And as they ran up the stairs to the offices, all she could think was, *This is where reality sets in.*

In the conference room, Sergeant Thomas put twenty pieces of paper in front of each one of them as well as one pen and one envelope and then stood back at the head of the table. "Each one of us in this room is aware of the risks we take every day going to work. There is no day that is safe. When something happens to one of us, some general, or in your situation the chief, pulls up the standard 'Sorry for your loss, your son/daughter was brave and yada yada yada' form. We have people in our lives that love us for some reason or another, and they deserve better than that."

She stood straight up and, out of the left pocket of her cargo pants, pulled out an addressed letter. "This is the letter I wrote explaining everything that was important enough for me to do what I do, why, and things that need to be said. These are things only you know and only you should say. You will write your final letter to whomever it is that you need to say something to. You will write it and address it but do not seal the envelope. When you are done, come to my office individually. I am not going to read it, but I do have a justifiable reason for this to be accomplished. You have all the time that it takes to complete." Slipping the letter back into her pocket, she walked out.

"Isn't this kind of morbid? I mean shit, I don't want to go and jinx myself," O'Malley said, looking around, hoping for support.

"Did anyone see who her letter was to?" Antonelli asked.

Miceli saw only a first name, but something told her that she knew who it was. "No," she said, "but do you really think she is going to let us out of it? Hell, she made a general do it."

Realizing she was right, the team looked at the paper in front of them and, with deep breaths all around, began to write. At first, the room was silent with the exception of scratching on paper, but after about ten minutes, small sniffs could be heard coming from different people.

O'Malley stood up, smiled, and said to the others, "See you guys in a few," and then walked out the door to see the sarge.

"In," was the only response he got after knocking on the Sarge's office door, so opening the door, he went and stood in front of her desk.

"What is it, O'Malley?" Sarge asked without looking up from whatever it was that she was writing.

"I am finished with my letter, Sarge," he said as he tried to hand the letter and envelope to her. Looking up first at the envelope and then to him, she said, "No, you are not. Did you give any thought to what you wrote? Are the words you put on that paper the last words you want someone to remember you by?" She paused. "No, they aren't. Don't come back to me until you did exactly what I asked."

With a look of incredulity, O'Malley walked out of her office and back to the conference room. "There is always one," she said with a sigh, looking at the door O'Malley had just left out of, before going back to her paperwork.

Forty-five minutes later, Douglas walked into the sarge's office and held the envelope out to her. She looked up at him.

"Good, hold on to that and go clean your weapon while you wait for the rest of your team." As he walked out of her office, she saw him wipe his eyes.

Over the next twenty minutes, the rest of the team trickled into her office and received the same response given to Douglas. Finally O'Malley was the last to knock on her door.

"In."

"Sarge, I am done," he said, eyes red-rimmed.

"Go downstairs and clean your weapon with the rest of your team."

Confused, he turned around and walked out to join the rest of his team but only after taking a minute outside of her office to try and collect himself.

Fifteen minutes later, she came down the stairs and observed as the team cleaned their weapons in absolute silence. Always happens like this, and she was not surprised at the effect it had on them. "Are you all done yet?"

James stood up. "Yes, Sarge. Just finished."

"O'Malley, do you know why I turned you away when you first came into my office?"

"No, Sarge, I don't." He couldn't look at her.

Addressing them all, she began, "O'Malley came into my office with his first letter, and I sent him away, as I am sure you are all aware of. I did this because he did not truly consider what I had asked you all to do. Composing my letter was the second hardest thing that I had ever had to write. Writing these letters make you admit to yourselves that you are not indestructible, you are not invincible, and that you are, in fact, just human. You can be hurt and you can die." Looking around at the solemn faces in the group, she knew that what she was saying was sinking in.

"From here on out, that letter stays in your left front cargo pocket. This is so that, should anything happen to you, I know where it is and I can get it to the appropriate person." She heard the exhales and saw the conflict each had within themselves, and that was a good thing. Anyone who could walk away without having felt the effect of writing that letter was someone that you didn't want on your team.

"Sarge?" Miceli asked.

"What is it, Miceli?"

"Forgive me for asking, but you said that it was the second hardest thing you ever had to write. What was the hardest?"

She was quiet up until now, and leave it to Miceli to pick up on the little comments that most would let slip by. Standing up straighter, shoulders back, chest out, and clearing her face of all emotion, she said, "A letter to the mother of one of my men that died in combat. Now it's time to get to work." She turned on her heels and walked to the workout area.

Why did she answer that? Miceli asked herself as they followed the sarge to begin their training.

***

"From this point on, you need to be prepared for anything. You will be drilled over and over again on everything that we go over and things that we haven't. You are going to be put in situations that are impossible to get out of, but the reason for that is because I need to see what you will do. Will you give up? Will you quit? Will you take a stand knowing that you may not come out of it alive? I know that you think that I am going over the top, but let me ask you this, what if I am not?"

They had positioned themselves around the exercise mats and watched as the sarge pulled out a medical bag.

"Um, Sarge?" Douglas said.

"What is it, Douglas?"

"We have all been through first aid and CPR. It is an annual requirement," he said, and a round of nods went around the group.

"Well, I am glad to hear that, Douglas, but since we are not doing any of that just yet, why don't you go ahead and empty the bag out for me?"

He did what he was told. He emptied the bag out one piece at a time and laid each one in a neat line across the mat. Although he recognized most of the equipment, there were a few items that he had never seen in a first aid kit before.

When all of the items from the bag were removed, the sarge stepped up. "How long does it take for an ambulance to arrive on scene when an officer goes down, Antonelli?"

"That depends on where they are, time of day, and how volatile the situation is, Sarge. Anywhere from ten to thirty minutes would be my guess."

"Douglas, how often do victims die due to the delay of medical treatment?"

"I don't know, Sarge, but I personally have witnessed two," he replied, paying closer attention now.

"James, why is it important to know combat lifesaver skills?" She knew he could answer this because as a sniper, he had gone through this training rigorously.

"Because CLS provides us with enough knowledge to treat extreme casualties while waiting for medical personnel to arrive on scene. We provide immediate care from stopping severe bleeding to providing needle chest decompression to casualties with tension pneumothorax. Since we are on scene already, we are their best hope for survival. However, the first rule under fire is to return fire and then tend to the casualty when it will not endanger the mission or you." He spoke without even thinking about what he was saying. This was a subject he studied intensely when he was in the Army because he never knew when a buddy might need help.

"That would be correct. Now let me break it down to blonde terms here… If you get shot, you may not have enough time to wait for an ambulance. The difference between you living and you dying will be whether or not your team knows enough CLS to maintain you until we can get you the help you need. Now let's get started."

With the help of James, Sarge went through the basics beginning with how to properly apply a dressing, the difference between a dressing and a bandage, how to determine if a tourniquet is required, and the uses and applications of quick clot powder and bandages. They demonstrated how to properly lubricate the nasopharyngeal airway tube to ensure that the airway is maintained and the tongue does not fall to the back of the mouth, blocking the airway. They moved on to the immediate action treatment for sucking chest wounds and how to identify and treat tension pneumothorax. She then pointed out the pressure points for the brachial artery and the femoral artery and how to effectively isolate blood flow using these four spots and finally went over the various methods used to move casualties.

"You have to remember that when an individual is shot or otherwise wounded, they are going to be in pain. When a person is in pain, they don't always cooperate. They scream and sometimes they even try to assault you. It is different with every case. However, there is one thing that remains constant…you. You need to maintain your focus at all times and remove all emotion from the situation. Otherwise, you are useless. Sometimes when the world goes to hell, you are the only one there to help." She knew all too well how true this statement was.

"This bag goes with us everywhere, and Douglas will verify that its contents are up to date and there are no shortages. You never know when you will need it, and I hope that we never will, but bring it just in case." Looking at the group, she moved and stood in front of Antonelli. "Drop. You've just been shot in the chest. You have an open chest wound that went through and through."

Antonelli dropped, and the group went to work. At times, she would remove two of them and tell them that they are returning fire or just not in the area. She gave scenarios of them coming under fire and watched as they positioned themselves to treat the wounded, usually taking their cue from James.

At times, she would drop more than one of them if something was done wrong or if they put themselves in a bad or dangerous position, but surprisingly enough, it didn't happen often. They were surprised when, in the middle of their lunch, the sarge dropped James due to an airway obstruction. As they went to insert the nasopharyngeal airway tube, she stopped them just before they could actually insert it into his nose and then allowed them to finish their lunch, much to James's relief, as she went up to her office.

"Hey, James, what did you do in the Army anyway?" O'Malley asked just after the sarge walked away.

"I was a sniper attached with the 101st Infantry Division."

"And now you are in SWAT. I totally understand the need for the career change!" Douglas said, and they all, for the first time that day, laughed and enjoyed each other's company. That was until Sarge yelled from the stairs.

"Defensive positions inside the house and scatter throughout! Move!"

They ran to the "house" and took cover. They spread out through the house but always had eyes on each other. They held their positions while Sarge casually walked down the stairs and toward the building. She didn't know who went where; it didn't matter to her so long as they followed orders at this point. She stopped in their one blind spot just outside the "front door."

Pop-pop-pop-pop-pop! Five shots rang out. Within the house, they were yelling back and forth to each other, trying to get information on what just happened. Miceli, fanning out in an attempt to see what was going on outside, saw her first. Sarge was lying on her stomach just outside of the door and was unresponsive. After relaying the situation, Douglas acted as lookout, while Miceli ran out to retrieve the sarge and get her to cover.

Douglas opened the med kit, and as Miceli rolled the sarge over, she saw a note taped on her chest: "Hit twice, one in right leg three inches above the knee and one at the right side chest, sucking chest wound. James hit in left shoulder and losing consciousness."

"James, you are down with a shot to the left shoulder and going into shock. Sarge is down with multiple injuries," Miceli relayed to the team.

"I have James, but I need supplies," O'Malley reported. Miceli barked out orders without hesitation, taking control of the moment.

"Douglas, you need to take some gear to O'Malley but leave the kit here. Antonelli, move forward and give me a hand." Douglas passed Antonelli in the hallway on his way to the back while Antonelli came running from the first bedroom to help Miceli.

Moving quickly, Douglas and O'Malley assessed the "wound," applied dressings and bandages, covered him up, and elevated his feet in hopes to minimize the effects of the shock. Shock could be worse than the injury sometimes, and they were not going to take any chances.

Miceli assessed the sarge while Antonelli posted as security since the threat had not yet been identified. Upon removing the outer coat the sarge was wearing, she found another note: "Unresponsive, no breathing, pulse is weak, mimic the actual procedures."

Immediately she got herself in position to perform CPR. After performing the head tilt chin lift, successfully opening a clear airway, she leaned down to within an inch of the sarge's mouth. Jen felt Alex's body stiffen slightly as their lips got close, and she sat back up and stated that she had given the two initial rescue breaths and then moved herself into position over the sarge for chest compressions. Putting one hand on top of the other and placing them in the middle of the sarge's chest, she leaned forward on her knees so that her shoulders where directly over her hands and began to count out loud, moving her torso up and down slightly so that the chest compressions were properly mimicked. With every move, she felt the heat beneath her hands and the beating of Alex's heart—it was racing. All she could think about was the way their bodies fit so perfectly against each other that night, a night that now seemed so long ago. Regaining her focus, she was continuing to the second round of thirty compressions when the sarge slipped a note from her hand that read, "Breathing and pulse good."

Douglas returned to the front room to get a status check. "I need two pieces of plastic and tape," Miceli barked at Douglas. She needed to close off the chest wound. She taped all four sides of the first piece of plastic at the exit point and then rolled the sarge over so that she was on her back again. Taking the second piece of plastic, she placed it over the entry point, taping three sides and allowing air to be able to escape, and then moved to the leg wound.

"Get me a dressing and bandage. I am going to apply direct pressure," Miceli said as Douglas began to hand her the supplies.

While she was wrapping the wounded leg, Douglas said, "Direct pressure not working." He read from a piece of paper that the sarge had slipped to him.

"Find me the tourniquet," she told Douglas as she slid her hand up the sarge's thigh and put pressure on her femoral artery.

Alex couldn't think. She had the whole scenario planned out, but at no point did she think that Jen would be the one working on her. It was bad enough that she brought her lips so close to hers that she could feel Jen's breath cascade over her lips, causing her stomach to tighten. Then as she went to perform chest compressions, she could feel the energy radiating from Jen's hands and flow throughout her entire body and she could have sworn that she felt Jen's finger brush against her nipple as she pulled away. But now, as she felt Jen's hand slide up her thigh, her body betrayed her. She became instantly wet and had to fight back the moan that wanted to escape. When Jen leaned down to put pressure on her leg, her body went into overdrive. She couldn't take anymore.

"Exercise is over!" the sarge all but shouted as she sprang up off the floor, almost kicking Douglas in the head. "Clean up and meet me at the mats," was all she said before leaving out of the "house" in an attempt to collect herself. Silently she condemned herself for her lack of control. She needed to shut down her body; she didn't need these distractions. She was throbbing and needed to calm herself down. She had rules for a reason, she reminded herself and, with a lot of effort, had her composure back as the group circled the mat once more, but seeing the look in Miceli eyes, Alex wondered if she was aware of what had just happened. *This is going to be long two months*, she thought to herself for the millionth time.

"Not bad for starters, but I expect perfection. There was too much talking and not enough doing. You need to be able to anticipate each other's needs in order to function under pressure. Go change into PT gear and meet back here in three minutes." With that, she turned and headed to the stairs.

***

When everyone had returned from changing, the sarge had sent them to the treadmills and instructed them to put the speed control to 6 with an elevation of 4.5 before walking away.

When the door to the offices closed behind her, Antonelli said, "Well, you have to admit, that scenario wasn't all that bad. I mean, hell, it could have been a lot worse, you know?"

James, looking straight ahead, said in his baritone voice, "I hope you don't think that this is over." Everyone turned their heads to look at him.

"What do you mean, James?" O'Malley asked, a hint of concern in his voice.

James turned his head and looked at O'Malley. "Think about all the training we go through. You start off slow and easy and then pick up the pace as you go."

"I thought we did pick up the pace," Douglas said as his breathing started to come more rapidly.

"No, he's right," Miceli interjected. "I mean, think about it, she is hard core, and that little exercise was anything but."

"Are you serious? When have you ever been through a class that went that far?" O'Malley asked.

"Never," Miceli and James answered at the same time; they both knew there was more to come.

After sitting in her office, calming herself down, and getting her mind back in the game, the sarge went to the stairs and looked down at her trainees. They were sweating, and Douglas and Antonelli were breathing hard. "Off the machines and do ten laps around the inside of the building and do it fast!" she shouted down. *They are going to separate, they always do*, she thought as she walked over to get herself into position.

By lap five, Antonelli was falling behind, and by lap seven, Douglas was, too, effectively separating themselves from the pack.

TRUST

Two calming breaths later, she fired off two shots in rapid succession. The first hit Douglas in the back just below his right shoulder with red paint, and the second hit Antonelli in the left leg on the back of his thigh.

"You've been hit, so you should be down and screaming." She didn't move; she waited to see how they were going to respond.

Antonelli was down by the workout equipment, Douglas was down by the house, O'Malley and James took cover behind the six-foot wall, and Miceli took cover in the restroom. With no weapons available to them, the sarge wondered how they would get out of this one.

Cracking the door to the bathroom, Miceli tried to assess the situation. None of them had weapons, and everyone was pinned down. She took note of everyone's position, and James was the closest to her. She was able to gain good visual contact, and while maintaining her cover, she and James, through hand signals, worked out a plan. After a brief disagreement, James relayed it to the others, including the wounded. With a small nod of the head, everyone counted to ten.

James and O'Malley screamed in unison as loud as they could. When they started to scream, Douglas and Antonelli crawled to the closest cover available as Miceli came running out of the bathroom at full speed, heading for the three-foot wall that stood twenty feet away. *Pop!* As soon as the shot was fired, James ran to the lockers to retrieve his weapon while Miceli drew the fire. She wanted to run from the wall that she was behind toward the "house" but never made it. *Pop-pop!* She felt both hits. One shot got her in the ribs on her left side and the other on her ass. She went to yell to inform the rest of the team as to the extent of her injuries, but the sarge interrupted.

"Miceli! What in the hell was that? What in God's name were you thinking? You had the perfect cover and you left it. Why?" the sarge screamed as she came down the stairs. She was furious. Standing up, Miceli put her hands on the wall. "I had to draw fire, Sarge. It was the only logical solution."

"How is making yourself a target a logical solution, and how could you all agree to it?" What was wrong with them! Would they really be willing to sacrifice each other if it was real bullets flying?

Standing up, O'Malley looked at Sarge. "I agree with Miceli, Sarge. It made sense."

Coming from the lockers with his weapon in hand, the sarge turned to James and asked, "How in the hell could you agree to what just happened?"

"Sarge, at first, I didn't agree. Why sacrifice when there is no need to? We couldn't send anyone to go and get Antonelli and Douglas because they would be sitting ducks if they did and we didn't have our weapons available to provide cover fire for a rescue attempt," James answered as if stating the obvious.

"The two of you argued about something. What was it? And you did not answer my question," the sarge replied with a voice that was as cold as ice.

"Sarge, may I answer your question?" Miceli asked.

"Somebody better give me an answer." *Why did she do that to herself?*

"Sarge, we had two wounded and stuck out in the open. No further shots were taken at them, so it was obvious that the "gunman" was waiting for us to come get them so that they could take us out one by one. The positioning of everyone, scattered around, made it possible for a distraction. The two wounded may have been wounded, but they were conscious. They were capable of moving themselves out of danger. The yelling would only do so much, but we knew it would not be enough to distract you from noticing the injured making an attempt to get to cover. We had no weapons, so even if they had made it to cover, we still would have been pinned down. We needed to get to a weapon, and there was no way around it. I am the fastest and James was the closest, so it only made sense to use myself to distract you in order to get the team to a point where we could at least defend ourselves." Her ribs and ass hurt, but she would be damned if she was going to let the sarge know it.

Maintaining a stillness that a statue would not even be able to compete with, the sarge looked at Miceli. "And that makes it all right for you to sacrifice yourself?"

Without so much as a blink, Miceli responded, "Sarge, the good of the team sometimes outweighs the good of the one."

"Would you have done the same thing if those had been real bullets?"

"Yes."

"Do you want to be a hero? Is that what it is?" Her voice was as hard as stone.

"No, Sarge."

"Then why did you do it?" Sarge asked through gritted teeth.

"Because, Sarge, it had to be done." There was finality in her voice that told her she was done with the topic.

Turning to look at the rest of the team, she asked them all, "Do you all agree with Miceli?"

As one, they answered, "Yes, Sarge."

"Fine. Then let's continue," was all she said, but she was furious. The decision Miceli made was one that she herself had made in the past, and Miceli was right, it was a logical move and the only option that they had. She just could not grasp why it bothered her so much that Miceli was willing to take the chance and to make the sacrifice.

"Can someone please tell me why two of your teammates who were struggling with the run were left behind? A team is a team at all times and cannot function properly and effectively if they are separated." She gave each one of them the time to try to think up a good excuse for this one, but not one word was said. "There is no reason, and I mean absolutely no reason in the world, to leave a team member behind. I may accept your decision for the distraction tactic Miceli pulled, but I will never accept you leaving a team member behind. Laps! Now!"

Alex, still furious, went to her office and stowed her rifle but loaded her 9mm and put three extra magazines in her pocket. Grabbing a can of Mountain Dew, she walked out of her office and downstairs to begin round two.

Pop! Miceli was down again, this time she was hit in the back. "Get down!" O'Malley yelled. *The sarge is really trying to prove a point to Miceli*, he thought. *God, I hope she shuts up long enough to get out of here alive tonight.*

It was 2135, and they handled the last three scenarios perfectly. The sarge had made sure to target everyone on the team, but she had to admit that Miceli had gotten the brunt of it. One way or the other, she would conform. She was prepared for the hate that was sure to come and was willing to accept it so long as she could get her to understand that she was not going to be the "hero." She watched as they emergency-evacuated her to cover, performed CLS, and maintained their security and perimeter.

"Outstanding," she said. "You are finally learning. Now go home," Sarge ordered as she turned and headed back to her office.

They went to their lockers, switched out the hardware on their weapons, and left. Everyone was worn out and resembled the walking dead. By the time Jen got home, she managed to draw just enough energy to take a shower before finally passing out.

Chapter 8

When her alarm sounded off at 0500 the next morning, Jen slapped it off and sat up. "Ouch! What the hell?" She got up, turned on the light, and walked to the long mirror she had on her closet door. "Son of a bitch!" She looked at her body and the small bruises and welts that covered it. Every shot she took left its mark on her, and they were not pretty. The longer she stood there, the more furious she became. "Okay, Sarge, it's on!" She got dressed, made her lunch and dinner, and headed out the door.

Miceli walked into the building with a sense of purpose and headed straight for her locker in the bathroom. She put her food up, wet her hair down, and put it into a tight bun. Then just as she was headed to her other locker to switch out the hardware on her weapon, she ran into the Sarge.

"It's 0610, Miceli. Why are you here so early?" She was expecting to be alone and for everyone to be too tired to show up early, especially Miceli.

"Well, Master Sergeant Thomas, I wanted to be sure that my weapon was clean and ready to go for today, and I was under the impression that if you are on time, then you are late." And as an afterthought (and stab), she added, "Ma'am." *You are not going to scare me off*, was all she could think. Knowing that she was the main target yesterday had her seeing red.

"Good," was all she said before heading upstairs to her office. Miceli was mad, and she knew it. The anger in her eyes was evident, and there was no mistaking the line that she was drawing. Miceli wanted confrontation, and more than that, she wanted payback. The question was how hard could she be pushed before she finally pushed back?

At exactly 0700, shots were fired, and the team ran for cover. It was the first time today, but it wasn't going to be the last. She gave them a late lunch, allotting them three minutes before opening fire yet again. Today there was no mercy shown, and every one of them felt it, but none more than Miceli. They didn't know when she was going to fire or with what weapon or who she was going to fire at, but what they did know was to watch for her because it was going to come fast and hard.

By 1834, Sarge noticed that regardless of what the team was doing or what was happening, they were sticking closer to cover, allowing only minimal points of contact. "Take five and get yourselves something to eat," she said to the group and watched as they ran to their lockers to get their food.

After she inhaled her ham sandwich, the sarge put in a set of earplugs, turned on her stereo, and hit Play. After everyone left the night before, she had mounted her speakers (four of them) in the rafters and against the walls. The noise was almost deafening between the sounds of sirens, city noises, and ship horns sounding off; not another sound could be heard. Walking out to the catwalk, she put on her NVGs and proceeded to cut the lights off.

The team covered their ears when the sarge hit Play and noise filled the warehouse. The acoustics must have been phenomenal because there was no way that any speakers could be that loud. They looked at each other, trying to figure out what was happening when they were thrown into darkness. "She must have cut the circuit breaker to the lights off," O'Malley screamed so the group could hear him over the noise.

"Damn, I've been hit!" Douglas screamed, "Find cover!" and with that, they scattered to the wind.

For the next hour, the sarge walked around the building, picking them off one by one, and stopped only when she ran out of ammunition. Calmly she walked back up the stairs into the office area, turned off the music, or noise as some would describe it, removed her NVGs, and tuned the lights back on. Giving them a minute to regroup, she sat down, placed her empty magazines in her top desk drawer, locked her weapon in the built-in safe in the bottom drawer, and drank a can of Mountain Dew. Ten minutes later, the sarge slowly got up and went to see the damage.

The five of them looked like hell. They were sitting on the floor against the wall by the bathrooms, and all of them were covered in paint. Each one of them acquired at least six shots a piece with the exception of Douglas and Miceli, who earned twelve and fifteen respectively. The sarge walked up to them, crossed her arms over her chest, and looked down. "It's easy to protect yourselves and the team when you can see and hear each other, but it is a whole other ball game when you end up in the dark. Think about today and go home." She got halfway to the door before turning back and informing them, "The paint will wash out." Smiling to herself, she left them there on the floor as she left for the night.

Everyone looked at Miceli. "Miceli, what does the sarge have against you?" Antonelli asked after realizing how many times she had been hit today.

"Not enough to stop me but enough to piss me off. I have a plan if you guys are game." The guys looked at each other and agreed to go in with Miceli. She was being targeted, and sometimes you just have to cross a line to prove a point.

***

At 0545, the entire team stood waiting for the sarge. Today was a new day and today the tables were going to turn. At 0559, the sarge walked in and, seeing them all gathered and waiting, asked, "Are we wanting to begin early today?" with the hint of a smile creeping up on her lips.

"We are ready whenever you are, Sarge," Miceli responded with a wide smile that was unsettling to the sarge, though she refused to show it.

"I will be down in a minute. In the meantime, form up in the center of the room and stand by," she instructed them before heading to her office. She dropped her bag, removed her 9mm from the safe, loaded the empty magazines, and tried to figure out what was going on. They were up to something, and Miceli was the ring leader.

Did yesterday finally break her? Doubtful with the smile she flashed her when she said that they were ready. Looks like today was going to be an interesting day. This group of officers was impressing her. Normally it would take a month for a group to start acting like a functional unit, but this group was already there. They had a common enemy and they had a plan. Maybe it was time to allow them to win one…if they could.

She walked the line, taking in how everyone was wearing baggy clothes instead of the form-fitting ones from yesterday. If they thought that a small change like that would lessen the strength of the impact of each shot, then they were in for a surprise. "I will tell you what, let's make a deal. If you as a group can get in nine clean shots at me, then not only will I inform you as to what you will be training on for the remainder of the next two months but, I will also let you have a full half hour to eat your lunch and dinner for the next week. There will, however, be a time limit to this game of forty-five minutes, but if I get two clean shots in on each one of you, then you fail, and the next two weeks will be hell on earth for you." Looking at each one of them and then stopping at Miceli, she asked with an air of confidence and a smile on her face, "Deal or no deal?"

Without hesitation, Miceli said, "Deal, Sarge. When do we begin?"

"Now!" as soon as she said it, she began to fire and then headed toward the women's bathroom. Diving through the door, she knew that she had hit three of them square in the chest, but what bothered her was that they showed no signs of even feeling the impact. She caught one in the back as she dived through the door, but it was of no consequence. Posting herself by the door and opening it just a crack, she was able to see through the opening between the door and the hinges. They had spread out, which was good. Miceli was standing almost straight up behind the three-foot wall. *What is she doing?* Letting the door close fully again, she took a step back and got into position to make her next push but was stopped short just as she was about to make her move.

Miceli kicked the door open and fired all of her fifteen rounds at the sarge's chest. Twelve hit dead center, and three hit right mid-thigh. Alex was dumbstruck. Her weapon had jammed on her. If it hadn't jammed and had she not been frozen to the spot with the sight of Miceli and the absolute power that radiated from her—she was breathtaking—then she might have been able to stop her in mid form.

"Sarge, for future reference, always verify the serviceability of your weapon and all its accessories." Miceli smiled and walked out of the bathroom.

When Sergeant Thomas came out, after taking a minute to catch her breath, the team was lined up with their weapons on their hips and their vests at their feet. She gave nothing away as to what she was thinking as she looked them up and down. The victory in their eyes was awesome, and she was proud of them, but there was no way that she could let them know just yet. Things were moving along faster than she had anticipated, and she was ecstatic with how well they came together. "So who planned this, and what did you do to pull it off?"

They all looked at Miceli just before she responded, "I planned it, Sarge. After you left, I went into your office and took your magazines. I brought them downstairs where, after cleaning our weapons, we adjusted the spring settings so that they would only fire three rounds before losing their loading abilities. Realizing that on duty we would all be wearing our vests, we decided that it would be in our best interests and personal comfort to wear them here during training, and I must say that these dragon skin vests are light and pleasantly form-fitting." Miceli smiled at the sarge with such malice that she almost took a step back to keep clear of the daggers that showed in her eyes. "I assumed that you would attempt to fire on us early on and that if you did it on the ground level, you would take cover in the restroom because that is what I would do. We positioned ourselves accordingly when you dived in, and the rest you know." And with a small laugh, she said, "The deal you made was just an added bonus."

"Well, a deal is a deal. Change into your cargo pants and T-shirts and then meet back here."

Miceli and the sarge both walked to the bathroom to change, both making sure to keep a good distance from each other. Miceli couldn't help but look when the sarge opened her locker, and when she saw the pictures, she stopped what she was doing.

"I'm sorry," Miceli said and looked down after realizing that the sarge was looking at her. "I didn't mean to intrude."

"No worries. If I didn't want anyone to see them, I would have kept them at home," she said as she took one last lingering glance at the pictures hanging on the door.

"Was that your sister you were with at the beach?" She didn't know why, but she wanted to know.

"No, that was Tina. Take a look." Alex took the picture down and showed the back of it to Jen.

"You two have known each other forever then. Have you always been tight?" Jen asked as she returned the picture and then pulled her shirt off, exposing her bruised skin.

Alex caught her breath when she looked over at Jen. She had painful-looking bruises all over her back and legs. Knowing that she had put each one of them there intentionally made her cringe inside. She never once complained. She stood there with her shirt off and her foot on the bench, untying her shoe, while Alex just stared. She couldn't help it. Jen's body was magnificent, and she had been trying to destroy it. With a look of complete sorrow, she spoke in a whisper. "I'm so sorry."

Looking up with confusion on her face, she asked, "What? What are you sorry for?" Hearing the pain in Alex's voice made her forget how furious she was with her.

"I never realized…," she replied, pointing to Jen's back, and then she stood up, determined to regain her composure. She attempted to take her shirt off, flinched for a second, and then positioned herself so that her back was to Jen, and finally removed it—with effort.

Jen was not going to let this go, not after all of this; she was due some answers, and Alex was not going to turn her back to her. She walked around to position herself in front of her and stopped short. "Oh my god! Is that from me? Are you okay?" Alex turned her body at an angle away from Jen's line of sight when she stepped closer, so she went to reach for Alex's arm and then thought better of it. Alex's chest was turning black from where she had shot her at almost point-blank range. She knew that getting hit hurt, but she didn't realize the damage it could do at close range. Sarge was never closer than twenty feet to them when she opened fire, and now Jen knew why. "Sarge, you could have small tissue damage. You need to get checked out."

"I'm fine. It doesn't hurt. Now get dressed because we have a lot of work to do." She threw her paint-stained T-shirt into her locker and slammed it shut. "Get the led out, Miceli," she said and walked out the door.

"What is her problem?" Jen said as she stormed out of the bathroom to fall in line with the rest of her team.

"Your training will be on several areas of both law enforcement and military tactics. Most of what I am going to be showing you will be completely dependent upon either prior training or future training. Everything relates to everything else. Miss one thing and everything fails." She paced back and forth with her hands behind her back, trying to gather her thoughts before continuing. "We began with CLS. I want to live, and because of that, I feel that it is the most important area of study. We all hope that we never need it, but we need to be prepared. I will be training you on information gathering, hand-to-hand combat, weapons handling, human takedowns, verbal and silent communications, stealth surveillance, silent entry techniques, building clearing and searching, and interrogation techniques." Looking up, she called out, "What is it, Douglas?"

"Sarge, most of this stuff we already know. Why beat a dead horse?"

"Like you knew first aid? I am not going to simply instruct, give you a test, and then call it good. I believe in reinforcing your training with exercises. We will run through scenarios that will incorporate every aspect of what you have learned over and over again until you are doing them without thinking." Walking up to O'Malley, she said, "Gunshot to the chest, shows signs of tension pneumothorax, what do you do?"

Without hesitation, he replied, "Insert needle between second and third rib and then—"

She cut him off with a wave of her hand. "There was no hesitation. He was confident of his answer and sure of himself. Were any of you this confident prior to this week? How many of you, with the exception of James, even knew what tension pneumothorax was?" No one raised their hands. "Now you can save someone's life because I grilled you on it nonstop and it has become muscle memory." She stopped in front of the group and, with a voice completely devoid of emotion and cold as ice, said, "You may not like the way I do things, but I don't care. I always get results, and as long as what I do works, I am going to keep doing it." She looked directly at Miceli. "If you don't like it, then leave." She waited a few seconds so that what she was saying could sink in. "Good. You have thirty minutes before we begin. I suggest you get ready."

***

End of week 2

"Do you think she will ever give us a day off?" Douglas asked as he was putting a tourniquet on James's leg.

"God, I hope so. I can't take much more if she doesn't. How many days have we been at this now?" O'Malley asked as he was writing the time of the tourniquet placement on James's head.

"Twelve days now. I don't have any food left in my house and I need to do laundry bad. I guess she was serious when she said that she didn't have a life."

Walking onto the catwalk, Alex looked down at her team. They had progressed well; not only had they mastered CLS, but they were also on point when it came to maintaining the appropriate amount of cover at all times. They weren't even thinking about it anymore; it was second nature.

"It's 2047," she yelled down to the team working on James. "Go home and get some rest. Monday we begin again." She turned and went back into her office to work on her writing some more. She didn't know what had come over her in the past few days, but she had the indescribable need to write, so that was what she had been doing. It began with poems, but now she was writing a couple of songs and she wanted to finish them—she had to finish them.

"Are you coming, Miceli?" James asked as he held the door waiting for her. They had cut the lights in the main part of the building, so now the only lights remaining were the two bathrooms and the offices.

"No you guys go on ahead and enjoy your weekend. I am going to shower first. I need to get the dust off before I go anywhere."

"See you Monday then."

Chapter 9

Jen walked into the bathroom. She was covered with dust, dirt, sweat, and, of course, paint. The sarge definitely had it out for her. The battle lines were clearly drawn, but if the sarge thought she was going to back down, she had another thing coming. One thing was for sure, the woman that she met in the bar was a fake. As she washed her hair and the paint off her body and saw the new bruises that were forming, she became even more infuriated. The look on the sarge's face every time she took a shot at her was that of pure spite.

After twenty minutes of hot water pounding on her back and shoulders, she finally turned the water off and went to her locker. Drying off, she ran a quick brush through her hair and started to get dressed. When she reached for her sneakers, she thought that she heard music playing. It was faint, but the more she listened, the more she thought it sounded like Jennifer Nettles from Sugarland; but when she came around to the door, she stopped short. Alex was standing in the center of the floor with a piece of paper in her hand, the remaining lights casting faint shadows across her face, and was singing.

> I'm not as strong as I may seem
> I'm just trembling inside
> A little girl with hopes and dreams
> And from you I will not hide
> My love I give and heart I share
> Just hold me in your arms
> Say you'll always want to be with me
> And keep me from harm

TRUST

Jen was awestruck with the power and emotion that she had heard. The song itself was a "quiet" tone, but the way Alex was singing and the look on her face froze her to her spot. Alex looked like she was suffering emotional pain with each word she sang.

> Please stand by me
> When the rain begins to fall
> And please stand by me
> When there is no sun at all
> When the road ahead is dark and cold
> And there is no end in sight
> Just please stand by me
> And make it all seem right.

At the last line of the song, a tear slipped down Alex's cheek. She stood still there for a minute, hands shaking at her sides. A couple of deep breaths later, she began a new song; it had almost the same slow pace, but it had an air of hope to it.

> The first day I met you
> I felt it in my heart
> And I knew in that moment
> We'd never be apart
> You captured my heart and my soul
> With one gentile kiss
> Now if you'll only grant me
> This one simple wish

"Shit," Alex said with so much pain in her voice that it broke Jen's heart hearing it. Walking toward the door, Alex balled the paper up, threw it into the trash, and left the building.

It took a moment for Jen to get her bearings. Her voice was the most beautiful thing she had ever heard. The way the shadows played across her face and the emotion that came to the surface were phenomenal. Watching her sing like that was like watching someone bare their soul; everything about it was raw—the power of the words, the emotions playing across her face, and the passion in her voice. It was breathtaking. She walked over to the trash can, retrieved the paper, unballed it, and took it with her when she left.

She wasn't paying attention to anything around her when she got into her car, so when there was a knock on her window while she was reading the paper that she had taken out of the garbage with the lyrics to the songs Alex was singing, she almost jumped out of her skin. Rolling down her window and at the same time stashing the paper behind her back, she looked up. "I thought everyone left, Sarge."

"How much did you hear?" The look on her face was one of someone pretending to not care, but the fear in her eyes gave her away.

She didn't know what to say. She wanted to tell her that she heard it all and wanted her to keep going, that her voice left her in awe. "I was in the bathroom, so all I heard was muffled sounds, Sarge." But she couldn't look her in the eyes.

"You are a terrible liar, Miceli." Alex said and walked away.

***

"I'm telling you it is getting ridiculous! How in the hell do they always know we are coming? I swear sometimes I think that someone is tipping them off." Chris shook his head as he paced back and forth in the living room. "I don't know. What do you think, Jen?"

"I have been thinking that for two years now. Think about it, whenever we think we are getting close to something, it just disappears. The only time we came close to a bust was when Sullivan went on his own to do some checking on an anonymous tip. And look where that got him."

"Yeah, I don't know what I would have done if it was you. Tommy still refuses to take another partner. I can't believe we still haven't caught the guy." They were both lost in thought when Melissa came into the room.

"Okay, you two, enough shop talk," Melissa said as she handed Megan off to Jen. "Chris, I am hungry and I need coffee. How much do you love me?" She gave him a smile and batted her eyes at him.

Laughing, he grabbed his wallet. "Jen, what do you want from Dunkin' Donuts?" Five minutes later, he was out the door with the coffee and doughnut list, and as soon as the door closed behind Chris, Melissa rounded on Jen.

"Okay, Chris may believe the story you told him, but I sure as hell don't," Melissa said with a smile. "When are you going to realize that you will never be able to hide anything from me?"

"Megan, your momma is either hearing voices or having delusions again. If this keeps up, I am going to have to commit her and keep you all to myself." Jen spoke to her goddaughter while she stood next to the couch rocking her and smiling.

It was a beautiful Saturday, and since she had had zero time lately to see Megan, Jen made sure that this was her first stop of the day before running long overdue errands. Chris was ecstatic when Jen called asking if she could stop by, thinking that she would give up information as to what she had been doing the past couple of weeks. When she told him that she was in training to become a trainer, he seemed disappointed. According to Melissa, Chris thought she was going on some undercover sting operation or something along those lines.

"Jen, if you don't fess up, I'll tell Chris that you are lying to him and then you can deal with the fallout."

Faking a look of shock, she replied, "You wouldn't... I have a baby here! Do you realize the damage that could be done to her tiny little ears? There are some things that she should not hear at this young of an age."

Crossing her arms over her chest, Melissa smiled. "He will be back in fifteen minutes. Dunkin' Donuts is not that far from here."

Knowing defeat when faced with it, Jen took a deep breath. "You can't tell Chris a thing, got it?"

"Got it."

"Did Chris tell you about the girl we met at Mickey's?"

"Yeah, he said that it looked like the two of you were hitting it off real well, but then she just up and left. He said that you looked hurt. He was really worried about you."

"Overreactor as always, well, kind of. Anyway, she ran out of there because she figured out that she was going to be my instructor and she has a rule of not dating anyone she works with." Taking a deep breath, she continued, "So there I am in this woman's class who the night before kissed me in a way that rocked my world. She acted like we didn't know each other, and I tried to be good with it, but then as the days went by, I noticed that she was singling me out every chance she got. I have been shot so many times that it's not even funny. She and I drew the line in the proverbial sand, and it has been on ever since. I thought that she hated me, and to be honest, I was starting to hate her, too, but then last night, when she thought that everyone was gone, she sang. Melissa, she has the most beautiful voice that I have ever heard, but on top of that, she was singing songs that I think she had just written. You could feel the raw emotion in her words, and when she finished, I think that she was mad about something because she threw the paper with the words on it away and walked out."

"Okay, and…"

"Well, I took it back out of the trash and have been trying to figure out what the story was behind them and also what she meant by them." She was blushing and she knew it. "I know it looks bad, but…"

"Do you have it on you now?"

"It's in my back pocket," Jen said, feeling really embarrassed but admitting to the truth. Melissa was always good to her, and when she and Chris got married, she took Jen as a sister. Melissa was the only person whom she felt she could trust sharing her feelings with; Chris was like her brother, but Melissa understood.

Reading over the words, Melissa looked at Jen. "Did she make the first move at the bar?"

"Yeah."

"Did you think that she was *really* into you?"

"Yeah, I did," she said with a disappointed sigh.

"Honey, I think that the first one is her saying that she has to put on a front but wants to admit that she needs someone. She wants someone to see her for who she really is. The second…do you really not know what it means?" She was shocked at Jen's ignorance as to the meaning of the songs; they were so simple.

"I told you that I didn't."

"You captured my heart and my soul with one gentile kiss? Seriously, Jen, you can be dense. The song is about you." Smiling, she handed her the paper back and enjoyed the utter shock written across Jen's face.

"No way, it could be anyone. I mean, really, we only talked for a few hours."

"Think about it, Jen. Does she ever look at you differently than the others, tell you things she wouldn't normally tell the others, and does she single you out? Trust me, honey, it's about you. If you really don't think that she could feel that way, then why don't you go look in the mirror? Because it's written all over your face. Like it or not, honey, you have it bad for her, and from the looks of these lyrics, so does she."

Jen looked at Megan like she held all of the answers. *It couldn't be true. I don't like her, I am pissed at her. We are at war, so to speak. Oh man, was she right?* "So what am I going to do, Melissa?" She moaned, closing her eyes and tucking her head into Megan as she rocked back and forth.

She felt so bad for Jen. "Sweetie, you have been hiding for years. She will come around. You have to be patient but you can't lie to yourself."

Walking through the door, Chris boasted, "I have braved the streets of Boston to bring coffee and doughnuts to the ladies of the house!"

Rolling their eyes and laughing, Melissa and Jen retrieved their coffee and doughnuts, leaving the topic of Alex behind them.

***

Alex was on her fifth screwdriver in an hour and a half and was about as drunk as she ever got. When Tina couldn't get her best friend to open up and tell her what was bothering her, she decided on a secondary plan of attack. Using the excuse that they had not gone out dancing in over a year and, figuratively speaking, let their hair down, she dragged Alex to one of the nicer clubs in Boston. "I am so proud of you, Tina," she said as she leaned across the table to get her friend's attention. "You are doing something you love, have a place you are proud of, and for the first time in years, you look happy," she said with a sloppy smile.

Smiling at how damn cute Alex could be when she let her walls down and just how vulnerable she truly was, Tina nodded her thanks. "So are you writing yet, or are you still blocked?"

"I wrote two songs and then threw them away!" she said with an air of pride and almost slipped off her seat.

"Why would you do that? You never throw your writing away. Even when you think it is crap, you have always kept it."

"First," she said as she took another sip of her drink, "I know them by heart. Second, they pissed me off. So I got rid of them." She looked around the dance floor that they were mere inches away from. Four people had already asked her to dance, and four times she had refused. She was not in the mood to dance with anyone but Tina. The music was going at a steady beat and had been good so far, and Tina was not one to waste an opportunity to dance. "Come on, it's time to dance." She pulled Alex up, and they wound their way onto the dance floor, finally stopping in the center. Surrounded by people, Alex let go and freed herself to move with the rhythm of the music. Tina leaned forward and was almost yelling to be heard. "What were the songs about?"

"The songs?" Alex looked at her quizzically, and then she smiled and asked, "Will you keep it a secret?"

Tina saw a familiar face in the crowd of people moving toward them. The music was fading, and the timing was perfect; it was now or never. "Definitely."

She stopped where she was, a look of pain on her face that she had not been aware she wore. "They were about Jen. Tina, I want to touch her, I want to hold her, but, Tina...I want her to hold me. When she is near me, I feel like my blood is on fire. It takes everything inside of me to keep from going up and wrapping my arms around her. I want her so much, Tina." And as the music faded from the upbeat tempo to a smooth slow song, she closed her eyes and swayed on her feet, wanting.

Tina slowly backed away from her friend, hoping against all hope that Alex would forgive her for what she was about to do.

The look on Jen's face as she stood behind Alex was that of complete shock. At the same time, her chest filled with a happiness that made her feel like she was going to explode. What was it about this woman that had her wrapped so tight? She didn't know what she was doing until she had pressed her body against Alex's back, wrapped her arms around her front, and began to sway with the music. Alex crossed her arms over Jen's, holding them in place, and leaned her head back against her chest. Feeling the heat, Jen's body began to form itself around Alex; there was no space between them, and it was as if they were one body swaying to the music that surrounded them. She bent her head into Alex's neck, smelling a hint of a sweet perfume before touching her lips to Alex's soft skin.

Alex swung around so fast that Jen was almost knocked to the floor. Swaying slightly, she looked at Jen in utter confusion, her blue eyes a sea of want and pain. Jen stepped up to her again and slowly wrapped her arms around Alex's waist. Letting out a shuddered sigh, Alex leaned her body completely against her, wrapped her arms around her neck, and took in her strength. For the first time in years, she felt safe, she felt protected, and the realization of that was overwhelming. She looked up into Jen's emerald green eyes, eyes that looked at her with such tenderness that she had to catch her breath. Gently pulling on her neck, Alex pulled her face closer and pressed her lips to Jen's. Fire exploded within her chest and tore its way down and through her entire body. Shaking slightly, Alex parted Jen's lips with her tongue, savoring the softness of her lips, the taste of her mouth, and the soft moan that she had pulled from within her. She pressed her body harder against Jen, the kiss deepened, the hold she had tightened, and she felt her body slipping away on a wave of desire.

Reluctantly Jen pulled back but held onto Alex's arms as if for dear life. Then she leaned her forehead against Alex's and said, "Let's go."

Jen led Alex to her car, and once situated, her voice deep with want, she asked for directions and put the car in gear and drove. Jen pulled up in front of Alex's apartment, jumped out of the car, ran around the front, opened the passenger door, and offered her hand. She held Alex tight against her as they walked up the stairs to the second floor and guided her into the apartment. Jen closed the door, and when she turned around, Alex was there, inches from her, with a fire in her eyes that made her stomach turn in knots. In the next moment, she was pinned up against the door, Alex's body pressed against hers, thigh pressed firmly between her legs, and hands around her neck; she was pulled deeper into a fevered kiss. Her hips rocked down onto Alex's thigh of their own accord, causing a deep groan to escape and her body to tremble with a want she had never known before. Stepping back with her hands on Jen's chest, Alex smiled, basking in the knowledge that she was the reason for the want in her eyes, eyes that had turned such a deep shade of green they were almost black. Taking Jen's hand, she led her to the bedroom, wanting to release the pressure that had been building between her legs and within her body, which was now shaking uncontrollably with want. Once inside the bedroom, Jen turned and stepped into her, guiding her backward until her legs touched the back of the mattress, put her hands on either side of her face, and kissed her so softly that Alex lost herself completely within it. She gently laid Alex on the bed, leaned over, and kissed her, first on the temple and down to her cheek, to the tip of her chin, and finally to the base of her neck where her teeth nipped at the soft skin and then replaced them with her lips. Pulling back, Jen looked down at Alex and smiled before standing up.

"Don't move," she said before she left the room.

Alex walked out through the living room and into the kitchen where she poured a glass of water. Bracing herself against the sink, she took deep breaths, trying to calm the radiating heat that was running throughout her body and slow the pulse she felt throbbing between her legs. Ten minutes later, she returned to Alex's room, placed the glass of water on the end table, walked into the bathroom, retrieving two aspirins, placed them next to the water, and covered the now sleeping Alex with the comforter that was lying at the foot of her bed. She looked so vulnerable and innocent that she was having a hard time associating the sarge with the woman lying here in front of her. *Which person is she?* Jen wondered as she turned and walked out of the apartment.

"Leaving so soon?" Tina said as she stood in the hallway watching Jen come out of Alex's apartment, almost eliciting a scream from her.

"I just wanted to make sure she got home okay. Why did you leave her there? Jesus, she was toasted!" Jen was furious. "How can you call yourself her friend?"

"Number one, I knew you would get her home. Number two, I knew you wouldn't take advantage of her. And number three, she needs you. That's how I could leave her there." Tina was so calm that it was disturbing, but her eyes were sure.

"You don't know me Tina. For all you know, I could have taken advantage of her, and in the state that she was in, it wouldn't have been hard." Dropping her gaze, she added, "And she doesn't need anyone," surprised at the pain she felt inside when she said it.

"Jen, I don't care what side of her you see at work. I have known that woman for over thirty-two years and I am here to tell you that you got to her in a way that she doesn't understand, and it thrills me to know that she might have a chance at being happy again." Taking a deep calming breath, she added, "That woman wears her heart on her sleeve, and it has been broken so many times that I can't even count the women that were wrong for her in every way imaginable. She has done more and seen more than she will ever tell anyone. She has been to places that no one should have to go, and she has done more for me than anyone ever has. She deserves to be happy, and I know she doesn't agree. Otherwise, she wouldn't set all of these goddamn rules that keep people out. I have heard people talk about you at the precinct, and from what I saw at the bar, tonight at the club, and what she has told me about you, you just might be the person to finally give her what she deserves. I saw the way you looked at her. Well, let me tell you something, she wants you just as bad."

"She will never let me in, Tina." Her voice was flat and eyes full of emptiness. "It doesn't matter, anyway." She took a deep cleansing breath and continued, "Look, she passed out, but I made sure she got to bed and I left some water for her, so…"

"Already? Damn it!"

"What?"

"She won't remember anything that happened tonight."

"That might be a good thing then. Tina, you can't force her into something that she doesn't want."

With a deep sigh, Tina looked at Jen. "She wants it, Jen. She's just afraid."

Chapter 10

Week 3

Walking into the warehouse an hour early on Monday morning, Jen's mind was wandering. "What is going to happen today? Does she remember what happened? And if so, is she upset that it did? Is this going to be awkward?" Heading to the bathroom and with her mind reeling, she didn't notice the sarge getting off the treadmill.

She went directly to her locker, opened it, and sat down on the bench, her mind still wandering on what Tina had said, on what Melissa had said, and what had happened in the apartment.

"Good morning, Miceli. You're here early. Did you enjoy your weekend?" Sarge said as she walked to the showers.

All she could do was to stare after her. Hearing the water turn on, she turned back to her locker and started to unpack her bag and slowly replace the clothes she knew were going to soon be trashed with paint and sweat. The only thing that she could think about for the remainder of her weekend was how good it felt to have Alex in her arms, the smell of her perfume, the softness of her skin, and the warmth of her kiss. When she replayed what happened, two things continuously ran through her mind. First was hearing Alex say to Tina that she wanted for Jen to hold her, and the second was Tina saying that Alex needed her. She couldn't remember the last time anyone had kissed her like Alex had. "You can tell everything from a kiss" is what she had always said because in a kiss, you are sharing the essence of your feelings with that person, and that's what it felt like. *Alex shared everything in her with me.* Leaning forward, resting her elbows on her knees, and threading her fingers behind her neck, she tried to get her composure.

"Miceli, are you all right?" Alex asked. Seeing her like this was unusual; she looked like she was fighting some sort of internal battle.

She jumped up, startled at the sound of Alex's voice so close to her. "Yeah, Sarge, I'm fine," she said before running out of the bathroom.

Alex watched Jen leave out like she was running from something and couldn't help but wonder if she was the one that she was running from.

"So far, we have covered CLS, silent communication, and…" She looked at her phone. "Stand by," she told them as she turned and began to walk away.

They watched the sarge walk toward the stairs, her back rigid. "Who do you think she is talking to?" Antonelli asked.

"Doesn't look good," James said. They watched her back as she finished her conversation and slapped the phone shut with an almost imperceptible sigh.

Turning back toward the team, she said, "Douglas, you drive a Suburban, is that correct?"

"Yes, Sarge."

"Can we use it." She wasn't asking.

"Yes, Sarge."

"Leave your weapons and grab some water and your IDs. I will be down in a minute. Douglas, go and get your vehicle and bring it to the door."

The sarge came out of her office in her dress blues ten minutes later carrying a sports bag, much to the shock of the team. Miceli was awestruck. Her eyes had turned the same shade of blue as her coat, her makeup was on but natural-looking, her hair was in a tight bun, and the ribbons and medals that she had on her chest were amazing. Alex was beyond anything that Jen had ever seen before. She could not take her eyes off her.

Aware that she was being stared at by every member of the team, Alex decided to explain. "Colonel Jacobson called. He is the CO at my unit and he wants me in his office ASAP. So we need to get a move on it." She walked out the door, leaving everyone staring after her in shock.

TRUST

They drove in silence to Hanscom AFB, with the sarge in the passenger's seat staring out the side window. When they arrived at the base, the guard at the gate approached the Suburban and was about to ask for IDs when he saw the sarge. "Hey, Sarge, when did you get back?"

Alex leaned over Douglas to get a good look at the guard. "A few weeks ago. How are you doing, Peters?"

"Great, can't wait till you are back in the rotation, though. Hey, why are you here? Aren't you supposed to be on reconstitution time, Sarge?"

She smiled at Peters' excitement. "New assignment. I'll get with you later. Let everyone know that I am back, will you?"

"You got it, Sarge!" Peters stepped back and waved them onto the base.

She directed them around the base until they reached the colonel's building and parked in the back. Once everyone filed out, she turned to them.

"Stand by the vehicle until I am done. Don't go anywhere, don't do anything, and for God's sake, don't embarras me," she said as she turned and went into the small brick building.

"Sir, Sergeant Thomas reporting as ordered," Alex stated as she stopped in front of the colonel's desk and rendered the proper salute.

"What is it exactly that they have you doing, Sergeant Thomas? Because every time I try to find out, I get stonewalled and I don't like it. You are my troop, and I want to know what the hell you are up to and why I am being told to issue you equipment without questions!" He was furious. Sergeant Thomas worked for him, and having to give her unquestioned support like he was working for her was not acceptable to the colonel.

"Sir, I am not at liberty to say at this time."

"So I am just supposed to sign over this equipment to you with no explanation? That is not how I work, Sergeant." Colonel Jacobson was irate. Thomas already had an ego on her, and now some general up top was feeding it too.

"Yes, sir, that is what I was told." She knew that she had to play this cool. The colonel had it in for her, and she didn't need any complications.

"Sergeant Thomas, I don't like this situation at all. I want you to remember that sooner or later, you will be coming back here and under my command, and at that point, I will expect full cooperation at all times."

"Understood, sir."

Madder than he had been in years, he walked past Sergeant Thomas and opened the door. "Come on."

Senior Airman Miller pulled into the parking lot just as he saw Sergeant Thomas walk into the building. He didn't know why the colonel wanted to see him, but if the sarge was here, he knew that it couldn't be good. Curious, he approached the small group of people standing beside a Suburban, watching the sarge walk in and who seemed to be aggravated about something.

"I don't think she could handle a stressful situation. I mean, teaching it and living it are two different things," O'Malley said.

"I will say this, she is a bitch!" Antonelli chimed in.

"Excuse me," Miller said as he addressed the group. "Do you all know Sergeant Thomas?" he asked, noting that the biggest one of the group and the female were trying to stay as far from the conversation as possible.

"Oh yeah, we were just talking about her," Antonelli said with a half smile. "Have you had the unfortunate opportunity of working with her?"

James and Miceli flinched, Douglas and O'Malley snickered, and Miller lost it. "Who do you think you are talking about the sarge like *that*? That woman…" Two more cars pulled into the lot next to Miller. Both occupants, Staff Sergeant Williams and Senior Airman Johnson, got out and went to stand by their friend, noting the anger emanating from him.

"What's going on?" Williams asked, watching the group in front of them and putting a hand on Miller's shoulder in hopes of calming him down.

The rage in his voice was obvious. "They were putting the sarge down."

Looking at the group in front of him, Williams said in a low and calm voice, "That woman is the only reason that we are alive today. She is the most loyal friend and competent soldier I have ever had the pleasure of knowing. I suggest that you get in your vehicle and leave now."

Stepping up before the situation could get any worse, Miceli chimed in, "I am sorry for my friend's ignorant statements. I do respect her, and we are actually working with her now, which is why we are here. We were just waiting for her to come out." Miceli looked at the men who appeared to be two seconds from killing Antonelli. "Please forgive me for asking, but did you say that she saved your lives?"

Appraising Miceli to determine if she was wanting to know the answer or just trying to save her friend's asses, Williams took a moment to gain control of himself.

"When we were in Afghanistan a few months ago, we—"

"What is going on here?" Sarge asked from just a few feet away. No one noticed her come up on them. Looking back and forth between her old team and new, a fire lit in her eyes with the knowledge that Williams was about to tell her team details of what had happened overseas. "What were you about to tell them, Williams?"

If he could have, Williams would have collapsed in on himself under the weight of her stare. "Sarge, we were just about to tell them what happened overseas because—"

"You are to repeat none of that to anyone. Is that clear? They have no reason to know what happened, so let's keep it to a need-to-know basis. Got it?" She was furious. The team would never follow her if they knew what had happened.

"Yes, Sarge," the three of them responded at once.

"What are you three doing here?"

Miller stood up straight. "Sarge, the colonel sent for us."

What was he going after? "You all know what is authorized and what is not. He is fishing for something and he is going to throw his rank in your faces to try and scare you into talking. You need to remember that he is not authorized to know anything, with the exception of the basics. Don't slip. If you think that he is pushing too hard or that he is crossing a line, I want you to call me immediately. Understood?"

"Got it, Sarge." Williams felt a weight that he didn't know he was carrying lifted. "Thanks, Sarge."

"Hey, Williams, do me a favor, would you? Find out why Peters is working gate duty instead of armory detail, would you?"

"Yes, Sarge, consider it done."

Turning to the officers, she said, "You five, in the vehicle. Now."

With a final nod to her old team, she drove off with her new one, wondering what was going to happen next. They pulled into a spot right in front of the armory, and when the ignition was turned off, Sarge turned and looked at the team.

"Obviously I can't leave any of you unattended, so everyone follow me and do not—I repeat—do not embarrass me."

"Hey, Lieutenant, what are you doing here?" Antonelli asked as they walked into the armory. "Everyone, this is Lieutenant O'Brien from the narcotics division."

O'Brien was an Irishman, if ever you saw one. At five feet and ten inches tall, he was average in height, he wore his extremely red hair in a high and tight, his freckles took up most of his face and arms, and he had that air of defiance that first- and second-generation Irishmen tended to hold.

"I am on my two-week tour. You knew that I was in the guard, Antonelli. Harris from IA is too. What the hell are you doing in here?" Stepping up to the counter, Alex looked at O'Brien. She knew of him; he was supposed to be one of the best gunsmiths in the Air Force.

"We are here to pick up some comm links," she said as she handed him the hand receipt signed by the colonel authorizing her to assume custody of the equipment.

"Oh yeah, the colonel told me that you would be coming in to get these today. Sarge, you need to know that the colonel already pulled the equipment that he wanted you to have, and ma'am, it's not the best." He had heard about her and was shocked at how little she was. She had a reputation for perfection and, from what he was told, never questioned. He shifted his attention back to Antonelli.

"What the hell are you doing here? I thought that you were in some type of training class."

"Well, Lieutenant," he started before looking at the sarge and quickly reverting to what the cover story was, "we are learning different training techniques so that we can put them to use on the job." He hated lying to the lieutenant; he had always respected him. "I didn't know that you guys were in the military."

Rolling his eyes at Antonelli and his ignorance, Technical Sergeant O'Brien looked at Sergeant Thomas. "I will be right out, Master Sergeant Thomas, so if you would just stand by." He walked to the back in search of the sarge's equipment.

Looking at the case that was earmarked for Master Sergeant Thomas, O'Brien paused as curiosity got the better of him. Why would the colonel intentionally issue crap equipment to one of the "best" search and recovery NCOs, and why in the hell were Antonelli and the other officers from the various precincts here with her? Something wasn't adding up.

"Sarge, who outranks who?" Douglas asked. He never liked O'Brien.

"I do, why?"

A smile lit his face up. "Just curious, Sarge." It seemed like everyone was afraid of her, suffered hero worship, or tried to keep their distance; watching the lieutenant treading lightly around the sarge made his week.

O'Brien came around from wherever he was in the back with a metal briefcase in his hand and put it on the counter for the sarge to inspect. She opened it and saw its contents, and the look she gave O'Brien made him take two steps back.

"Sarge, I am sorry, but the colonel wouldn't let me give you anything else. I told him that this stuff was ancient, and one of the comms was always transmitting but he didn't care."

Nodding and smiling to herself, she thanked him and left without another word, the team fast on her heels. "We have two more stops to make."

O'Brien watched Master Sergeant Thomas and the officers from the Boston PD leave. After a few moments of silent debate with himself, he picked up the phone.

"Harris? It's O'Brien. Meet me at the base for lunch. I just saw the 'pulled' officers with Master Sergeant Thomas. I think that we need to do some digging." He hung up with Harris and made one more phone call before getting back to work on the damaged weapons that had just come in from Afghanistan.

The next stop was at supply where she was issued six black tactical hats, six pairs of black tactical gloves, six flashlights, and six sets of black kneepads. She gave them to James who stored them with the comm equipment in the back of the Suburban before heading to their final stop. It wasn't until after they arrived and she was speaking with the airman behind the counter that her calm demeanor began to crack.

"You have got to be kidding me. This is not acceptable. I was supposed to be given a Suburban or a vehicle equivalent to it."

Not knowing what to do, the young airman looked at the sarge like she was going to bite his head off. "Sarge, I don't know what to say… Colonel Jacobson said…"

"Stop right there," she said, holding her hand up. "Did you just tell me that he is the reason you are trying to give me something other than what was requested?"

Seeing the lost look on his face, she flipped open her phone and was making the call to the colonel when, imagine the coincidence, he came walking in the door.

"Is my car ready yet, airman?" Jacobson said with a smile on his face. He wanted to be here to see her reaction to the vehicle that he arranged for her to be issued compared to the one that she had requested. With any luck, she would lose her composure and go off on him, and then it would be game on.

"Sir, is there a reason that the vehicle that was requested is being denied?" She was so calm, and the room was silently waiting for an answer.

"I will give you what is available, and unfortunately for you, the other vehicles have been reserved. If you don't like it, then don't sign for it." The smile on his face was that of triumph.

"No, sir, I just wanted to verify. Thank you for your assistance." She turned back to the airman and held out her hand for the keys. When he placed them in her hand, she thanked him and walked out without a backward glance.

Miceli didn't know what was going on, but she was glad when they got to the parking lot. Although everyone had walked back to the Suburban, Sarge had walked around to the side of the building. Curious and knowing that she should probably stay with the group, she instead went to find the sarge. She turned the corner and, when she did, watched the sarge punch one of the doors on the side of the building and immediately begin shaking her hand out. She was pacing when Miceli came up on her.

"Sarge, what's going on? I'm sorry, but it looked like that colonel had a hard-on for you, like he was baiting you or something." Looking down at the sarge's hand, Miceli lost it. Taking Alex's hand into her own, she looked it over. "Jesus, Alex, what the hell did you hit the door for? You can't let assholes like him get to you, and damn it, we need to get your hand looked at."

She enjoyed the contact more than she wanted to admit, which explained why, when Jen used her first name, she didn't immediately pull her hand back. She was being so gentle with her that she felt herself begin to relax and enjoy the heat that seemed to be coming from her touch. It was the concern in Jen's eyes that snapped her out of it. She pulled her hand away with more force than was necessary.

"My hand is fine. We need to go." She turned, but when she tried to open the door to the box van that the colonel was kind enough to issue her, a pain shot through to her wrist so sharp that she actually flinched. In a heartbeat, Miceli was at her side, taking the keys and blocking the door.

"Sarge, I know that you are tough and nothing gets to you, but for once, will you admit that you are hurt? I won't tell anyone. Just let me drive, and it will stay between us. Please."

She didn't know why she gave in to Miceli's request, but she did just the same. She got in on the passenger's side and put her seat belt on.

"Do not tell anyone, understood? I am not hurt that bad, but at the moment, I don't feel like arguing." With a nod, Miceli got in, backed up the van, and, when she came around the corner, told the others to follow.

"Can I ask you a question, off the record?" Miceli asked, thinking how dangerous this could be and ignoring the warning bells going off in her mind as they drove off the base and headed back to the warehouse.

"Yeah, go ahead."

"Why do you feel like you have to always be so strong in front of everyone? Why can't you admit when you are hurt or pissed?"

"First, I am not hurt. Second, I have a responsibility to my team to give everything I can. If I can push through pain, I will and I can't let my emotions drive my actions. If I did, people could get hurt." She put her head back against the headrest and closed her eyes, hoping that the throbbing in her hand would at least ease up.

Jen took a quick look at Alex. With her head back like it was and the way she was trying to shield her hand, she looked vulnerable. Jen felt a pain inside her chest for the pain that Alex pushed herself through. "I wanted to tell you thank you."

Opening her eyes, she turned her body enough so that she was facing Miceli. The look on her face was that of confusion and extreme thought or concentration. "Why?"

"Off the record?"

"Yes." What was it with this woman?

Tightening her grip on the steering wheel until her knuckles were white, she braced herself for the truth. "I locked myself up for so long that I forgot what it was like to *feel* anything, and talking with you that night at the bar, well, let's just say that you helped me to come back to myself and to the world."

Alex didn't know what to say. All at once, her chest filled, her stomach did a flip, and she felt...good. "Well, I am glad that I could help you and I apologize for any pain I might have caused you." It was the right thing to say, but it left her feeling empty.

"Thanks," was the last word that they spoke to each other for the remainder of the drive.

***

When they got back to the warehouse, they found that four more cases had been left at the bottom of the stairs for them inside. Alex hoped that this gear was in better shape than the rest of it. She had them store all of the gear from the base and what was left for them in the first office upstairs. "Laps, go!" She needed to assess the damage she did to her hand without anyone watching. When they left, she went to her office and, after closing the door, started flexing her fingers and rotating her wrist. It hurt, but there was no real damage to anything, just a little swelling. With her hand in the condition that it was in, she decided that today would be a good day to PT. After changing out of her uniform and back into PT gear, she headed downstairs.

She ran them from the docks to Malden and back, did calisthenics, and, when they got back, conducted a weapons inspection. Finally at 2013, she dismissed them for the day and sent them home. Her hand was feeling better, and her mind was beginning to clear; it was time to get to work, and in order to do that, she was going to need rest. Hand-to-hand combat begins in the morning, and she was looking forward to it.

For the rest of the week, she showed them how to take a fall, how to hit without being hit, how to drop someone with a single strike, leg sweeps, throws, and so much more. On Friday, when they came in, their day began with getting shot at and was full out until 1800. They were tired, sore, and overall worn out, perfect time to go into one-on-one hand-to-hand combat mat training.

"We never fight when we are rested, so we don't train to fight when we are rested. Pair up, one as the aggressor, one as the defender. I don't want to see anyone 'being nice.' We train in the same manner as we would really fight." She had been avoiding any physical contact with Miceli since coming back from the base no matter how small, but now, looking at her, the sarge realized that she couldn't avoid it anymore. "Miceli, you're with me. I will be the aggressor to begin with."

The guys looked at each other, knowing that Miceli was going to get hurt again but knew that there was nothing they could do or say about it. Miceli saw the looks that she was getting from the guys, and it pissed her off. They automatically thought that she was going to get her ass kicked. Well, she was going to show the sarge and the rest of them what she was made of.

For the next two hours, the six of them took turns being the aggressor, and they were all so tired they looked like they would drop at any moment, except for Miceli and the sarge. The guys began to circle the two of them and watched as Miceli would flip the sarge and then watch as the sarge would bounce and drop Miceli. The two of them were going for broke, wrapped so tight in the moment; neither realized that they were being watched. When the sarge got Miceli into a half nelson, everyone thought that she would tap out, but somehow Miceli slid out of the sarge's grip and flipped her, dropping her hard on the mat. Lying on top of Alex, Jen's right leg between hers, she had both of her hands pinned over her head and her forearm pressed against her throat. For a minute, they just stared at each other, Jen wanting to lean down and kiss her right where she was and Alex pointedly aware of the unbelievable throbbing and heat that was pulsing between her legs. With every breath Jen took, her leg moved just enough to send a jolt of utter excitement through Alex's body. The intense look in Jen's eyes was driving Alex mad; she could feel every inch of Jen's body that was touching hers. Alex couldn't take it any longer; she thrust her hips in the air and at the same time rolled to the right. She jumped up, realizing only then that they had an audience, and addressed the group, trying to regain her composure.

"Good job this week. See you Monday morning in your cargo pants. Dismissed."

It took every ounce of willpower she had left in her not to sprint up the stairs and away from Jen's watchful eyes, eyes that she knew were watching her even now as she walked away.

"Damn, Miceli, you really had her there for a minute. That was awesome." Douglas couldn't control his excitement. "I thought she was going to tap out for sure. How in the hell did she pull out of that hold?"

Trying to control her racing heart, she looked at the guys and smiled. "Next time she isn't going to get away." She headed to the showers as the guys left, talking about who would pin who next time.

Jen felt the heat between Alex's legs and saw the fire behind her eyes every time she took a breath. She didn't know what happened, but the more they fought, the harder they fought, and the harder they fought, the more excited she got. *Damn it, Jen! Get yourself together*, she told herself as she threw her dirty clothes into her bag and sat down on the bench.

"What the hell is wrong with you?"

"Excuse me?" Sarge said, feeling a bit defensive and not liking it.

"Oh, sorry, I wasn't talking to you." She could feel her face heat up, and all she wanted to do was get away from her.

Alex reached out and put her hand on Jen's shoulder, feeling that current of electricity run from Jen directly into her. "I just wanted to tell you that you did a good job today." After a small chuckle, she added, "I must admit that I am impressed with your takedown skills and defensive tactics." Why couldn't she stop talking, let alone touching her?

Standing up, Jen stepped in front of Alex, stopping only inches from her, her eyes boring into Alex's. "Thank you, Sarge. Have a good weekend." With a shuddering breath, she broke eye contact and left, grateful to be able to put distance between the two of them.

***

Week 4

"Let's recap," the sarge said as she walked the line Monday morning. "So far, we have covered CLS, hand-to-hand combat, silent communication skills, defensive posturing, and takedowns. There are things that you need to know to be effective when in a fight. One, expect to get hurt. Two, always expect your opponent to be better than you. And three, trust that your team will save your ass, if needed." She looked at them standing there, listening, hanging on her every word, and she knew they were beginning to trust her. She reminded herself of that every day so that she knew why she did what she did, why when she hurt someone intentionally she could still sleep at night. "James and Douglas, go upstairs and bring down all the gear that we got from the base last week."

They took off up the stairs and into the office. "What is going on with the sarge and Miceli do you think?" Douglas asked as he was picking up the kneepads. "They go at each other like they have a history or something. I am just waiting for one of them to kill the other. I mean, shit, do you see the way they look at each other?" He looked expectantly at James, who was squaring himself off and not happy about being asked things that he considered to be personal about his team members.

"You have two people that want to get everything that they can out of the training. They are both alphas, so they are going to knock heads. But all that I see is two people that are in this for the long run." James didn't believe what he was saying. He watched the two of them go at it and saw the fire in their eyes and the fight to push each other away. They had something going on, but whatever it was, he hoped that they figured it out soon because Douglas was right, they were going to kill each other if they didn't.

After laying all of the equipment out on the table by the lockers, the sarge issued each one of them kneepads, gloves, flashlights, and masks. "James, would you come over here, please." She pointed to the briefcase when he came to stand by her. "Open it up and tell me what you think."

While James was inspecting the equipment, she addressed the group, "As you all know, we have been issued a box van. It is big, ugly, and obvious. Unfortunately that will be our team's mode of transportation from now on. So in the future, if I tell you to get in the van, you know what I am talking about. Got it?"

"Yes, Sarge."

TRUST

James looked at the communications equipment and pulled each piece out one at a time. Shaking his head, he looked at the sarge. "Sarge, what we have here is an ancient version of the E1675-7R VOX DUCER two-way throat microphones. We have six comms, so there is no backup if one breaks. This one looks like it has been messed with, so I don't know the status, but I have doubts as to its operational capabilities."

"Set up the base and show them how to operate the system. Leave the broken one for me." As James handed out the comm lines and explained to the group how they worked, Sarge watched with anticipation. They were good, but were they good enough?

Taking her earpiece and mic, she said, "Let's do a functions check." All of the comms were good, with the exception of the sarge's. "It looks like the mic is stuck on transmit. James, do you know how to fix it?"

"I'm sorry, Sarge, but I don't."

"Doesn't matter. I think that I can manage. The key with voice communication is to talk as little as possible. The last thing that we need is to have everyone in a panic and trying to talk over each other. Dawn your equipment and then, everyone, go outside. Get whatever you can and furnish my house from what you can find from around the building." As they walked out the door, she spoke to them over the comm line.

"From here on out, this comm link is your only means of verbal communication, understood?" After getting acknowledgment from the team, she headed to her office, shutting off the lights as she went.

"This is Antonelli. We have no lights in the building, standing by outside the door waiting for instructions."

"This is James. Be advised from here on out Sarge is Blue One, O'Malley is Blue Two, Douglas is Blue Three, Antonelli is Blue Four, I am Blue Five, and Miceli you are Blue Six. Does everyone copy? Sound off in order."

The sarge acknowledged, and the rest followed suit. "Blue One to Blue team, I am unable to assist. Proceed with caution with the setup of the house as previously discussed." She settled back in her chair, made a few phone calls, and began the task of finishing the song that she started a couple of weeks ago as she listened to the team shuffle around the house and on high alert, thinking that she was going to ambush them.

***

"Blue One, this is Blue Two. Do you copy?"

"Go ahead, Blue Two."

"Requested tasking has been completed, awaiting further instructions."

"Stand by." She walked out of the office with a backpack over her shoulder and turned the lights back on. As she walked through the "house," she noted how well they did. There was a refrigerator, beds, what appeared to be tables, leftovers of a couch, and various other pieces and parts that they fabricated to look like furniture to include a front door. The team was filthy, covered with dirt and who knows what else from their search and find mission.

"Everyone, go shower and change. Eat your lunch over by the workout equipment, and I will see you back here in an hour."

"Yes, Sarge," was all she got, but every one of them had a complete look of puzzlement on their faces. She couldn't help but laugh as she walked into the house.

An hour later, they were formed up and waiting, curious as to what was in store for them next.

"I have hidden 'drugs' and other items of contraband in the house. Your tasking is to enter undetected, search the house, and retrieve all the items that I hid." She looked them over before continuing. "I am going to show you techniques for entering a building undetected, from opening a door to entering through a window. Stealth is the key. Once you have correctly entered the building, I would suggest that you look everywhere but maintain your cover. We enter buildings and areas thinking that we have good intel or that we know what to expect, but going in with that mindset will get you killed, and that is not acceptable. Regardless of what you are told, you will always clear a building before searching. There will *never* be a time when you don't. Do I make myself clear?"

"Yes, Sarge."

After reviewing procedures and tactics for the next hour, she released them to search. Over and over again, they first cleared the house, verifying that there were no unexpected obstacles or situations, and then went through the house looking for the items the sarge had hidden. As the hours passed by, the team slowed, fatigue winning out until at 2201, she called everyone in.

"See you tomorrow in your cargos, vests, weapons at the ready, and all additional gear that you were issued today. Dismissed."

***

At 0700, Sarge, in all her gear, stood in front of the house, anticipation clearly evident. "Today we continue with everything that we have learned. Blue Two, you have the team. Conduct an outside perimeter check and then a building clearing and search." She stepped back and went to the catwalk for a bird's-eye view of the events that were about to unfold.

After clearing the outside perimeter, O'Malley called the team over the comm and gave the first of many directions. "Go," Blue Two said as they entered the house. Two broke left, Three broke right, and Four, Five, and Six continued forward to the hallway.

Pop-pop! "Blue Four, Blue Two, and Three are down and unresponsive."

"I have rear. Six, can you get a fix on the target?" Antonelli called.

"Two men down, Two is in the middle of the kitchen, Three is by the couch in the living room. Advise of two possible hostile targets. How do you want to proceed?"

Antonelli was trying to figure out where the sarge was firing from and how she was able to get both of them in rapid succession, but he couldn't.

"I repeat, Blue Four, this is Blue Six. How do you want to proceed?" Miceli asked again, but when she got no response from him, she got on the comm. "Blue team members, this is Blue Six. I have lead. Blue Two and Three, if you can hear me, stay down. Blue Five, stand fast in the hallway but keep eyes and coverage on the living room. Blue Four, cover the rear. I am going to clear the kitchen."

She edged out slowly from the hall; she had a good view of half the kitchen, and there was nothing there. Nodding to Blue Five, she punched around the corner as Five took up position at the living room door. Within a matter of two seconds, she saw Blue Two face-down on the floor, an overturned table, and someone jumping up from behind it firing two rounds off, and she immediately returned fire. While Miceli was taking and returning fire, Five fired off three shots, and Four fired off two while taking one himself.

"Cease fire, cease fire," Sarge called through the comm. "Everyone, out for debriefing."

"What the hell? What are you doing here?" Antonelli asked as Miller, whom he recognized from the base, came around the corner.

Walking up to the assembled group, Sarge began with introductions.

"I am sure that you all remember Sergeant Williams, Senior Airman Miller, and Senior Airman Johnson." There were nods all around. "They were kind enough to volunteer their time this week to help you properly train. They are going to be your targets, victims, and instructors. They will be treated with the utmost and proper respect." Smiling because she couldn't help herself, she looked at her old team. "I want to thank you guys again for helping me with this, but with that being said, I think that it is time to get to work."

For the rest of the week, Sergeant Thomas took on the role of Blue One, assimilating herself with her new team. She showed them how to act as a full and cohesive team and as two separate coordinating groups. She assisted in performing CLS, building clearing, weapons handling, and searching. By the end of the week, they were fluid in their movements, anticipating each other's thoughts and acting like a well-oiled machine.

"Sarge, can I have a word?" Williams asked.

"What's up?" she asked as she joined him while walking away from the group.

"Why haven't you gone over personnel searches yet? They have been taking detainees for three days now, but not once have they had to search them."

She was hoping to avoid this until next week, but Williams was right. They needed to do this while they still could with the extra bodies that they had.

"You're right, let's get on it. Will you grab the gear, please?"

Williams watched as the sarge walked away. You didn't work with someone for a year straight without getting to know them. She was hesitant. Sarge never hesitated. *So what is going on?* he asked himself.

"Personnel searches you have done many times throughout the course of your careers, and although I know that you probably feel like you know what you are doing in this regard, I want to evaluate your proficiency." She walked over to Williams and was joined by Miller and Johnson.

"I love this part. How much do you want to bet they don't find everything?" Johnson asked. Johnson was always easily pleased, she thought.

Smiling, she said, "Are you guys ready?"

"Let's do it, Sarge," Miller said. "Oh, hey, Sarge?"

"What?"

"I just thought I would remind you that I am not going to let you renege on your promise." Eyebrows going up and down with his mischievous smile always got to her, and he knew it.

"I know, Miller. I am buying for the first hour, but after that, you are on your own." She laughed, and her three old team members went to load up on contraband.

Williams demonstrated the proper techniques for searching, adding in the fact that although most people prefer to wear gloves during a search, they are the best way to miss items during a search. "Sometimes we have to do things that we don't like, but if it's going to save your or someone else's life, then you had better suck it up and be willing to press on. Just remember, dirt washes off, but blood stains forever. I would rather get my hands dirty than have to sew up my buddy because I missed something."

The team broke off into pairs and began searching, but Miceli, looking at the sarge, had to mentally prepare herself. She knew that she would have a lot of contraband on her, and she was bound and determined to find it all the first time around.

Miceli put the sarge's hands on the wall, directed her to step back until she was almost ready to fall over, and had her spread her legs. She placed her left forearm and hand on Sarge's back, placed one leg between the sarge's to keep her from moving, and began patting her down with her right hand. Miceli was systematic with her searches. She always began searching the right side of the subject and, once completed, moved to the left. Nothing ever got past her, and she didn't plan on letting that change.

She went down the sarge's right arm, touching a spot and then pulling slightly on it, making sure that not one inch was missed. Continuing down her right side, she patted her ribs and moved her hand to check under the sarge's bra and then hesitated. Sensing her hesitation, Sarge turned her head slightly and whispered, "You have a job to do, Miceli, and if you can't do it, then you might as well walk now."

The sarge was right, but as she thumbed under her bra and brushed against her breast, Jen felt Alex stiffen slightly, causing Jen's heart rate to triple. Continuing on, she searched the waistband of her pants, legs, and feet. Stepping back one step, she continued her search, moving her hand up the inside of Alex's leg, and when she came to the point where she had to pat down her crotch and ass, she paused only for a moment before continuing on.

The moment that she felt Jen's hand slip between her legs, feeling for contraband, she felt her legs begin to shake and her stomach tighten, and moisture began to flow from her. She tried holding her breath and closing her eyes, but nothing helped. Even when Jen's hand moved away, she could still feel the exact spots that she had touched still pulsing with heat. She broke out into a sweat.

Jen could hear her own heart beating; her breathing was shallow at best, and her hands were beginning to shake from the want. She could feel when she brushed against Alex's breast how quickly her nipples hardened and how when her thumb was tracing the line of her waistband Alex's stomach began to quiver, and, most of all, the heat and instant moisture she felt when she had slid her hand between her legs. The reactions that Alex had to her touch caused equal reactions within her own body.

Finally stepping back, Miceli took a deep, if not ragged, breath and took inventory of what she had found. All told she found two bags of marijuana, one pipe, a twenty-two mini revolver, three knives, and four bags of cocaine. All simulated, of course.

"Did I get it all, Sarge?"

Trying to regain some amount of control, she took a deep breath before answering, "Good work. Yes, you found it all. Stand by and wait for the others to finish."

It was two hours before the guys were done searching, having to search two and three times each until every piece of contraband was found on the first pat down. The whole time, Miceli stood there watching. "Okay, everyone, we are done for today." It was 1900.

"Time to go to Shannon's!" Clapping his hands together, Miller looked at the sarge.

"Monday morning, cargo pants. Have a good weekend."

Everyone split up and headed in different directions, but just as Alex was heading to the shower, she heard her name called. Williams was behind her. "What's up?"

"I asked around about Peters, and it turns out that he found some discrepancies in the paperwork and up channeled it. I don't know what it was that he found, but the next day, Master Sergeant Pope had him assigned permanently to gate duty. My guess is that he jumped the gun, so to speak, and, instead of asking questions, went straight up without thinking. I doubt if the discrepancies were valid, especially if the paperwork was done by O'Brien. You know how through he is."

"I don't know, that just doesn't sound like him. Peters is meticulous about his paperwork and he is by the book. Thanks for checking into that for me, though."

He paused for a moment and looked around to make sure that no one else was in hearing distance. "Sarge, I want to talk to you about something else, but it has to be friend to friend. Can we do that?"

She always respected Williams; he was insightful and an all-around good man. "Yeah, what's up?"

"That's what I was going to ask you."

"What do you mean?"

He was looking at his feet but knew that he had to ask. "Are you seeing Miceli?"

Her face turned to stone. "You aren't allowed to ask those types of questions, Williams. That is crossing the line."

"I am asking as a friend, not as Sergeant Williams. Sarge, it is obvious in the way you look at her that you have a thing for her. I am not one to pry or tell you how to live your life, but I think you need to hear this. She is hot for you and you are hot for her, so what is the problem?"

"I don't see people I work with. Most people can't separate work and personal, and when you start seeing someone you work with, the chances of you making mistakes increase. Too many people count on me to—"

Waving his hands at the line of bull that she was trying to play off, he interrupted her midsentence. "Sarge, you need to stop. In a way, I agree with your logic, but there are times when your heart wins out. I think that this might be one of those times, and there is nothing wrong with it."

"It isn't my heart, it's my hormones—big difference. Now get dressed. We have some drinking to do." As she walked off, she tried to convince herself that what she said was true. *Hormones, not heart.* She kept repeating that over and over until she started to believe it.

Chapter 11

Week 5

She was shooting at them from the catwalk when the door opened and General Scott walked in, watching as the team scrambled to pull the injured to safety, perform CLS, take defensive postures, and use comm. to relay point information. *Impressive*, he thought to himself. Looking around, he spotted the sergeant on the catwalk, found the stairs, and went to join her.

Once she realized that she had company on the catwalk, the sarge looked up. "Sir." She jumped up, rendering a salute.

"Sergeant Thomas," he said as he returned her salute. "We need to talk. You might want to bring your team up as well, and this is something that you are going to need to hear."

"Yes, sir." She turned and called down, "Conference room now!"

Two minutes later, the team was gathered at the conference table, Sarge at one end, sitting down, and General Scott standing at the other. "Sergeant Thomas, I need a status report."

"Training is progressing well, sir, and the expected completion timeline is three and a half weeks. No significant alibis to report, sir."

"Have you received all the equipment that you requested?"

"In a roundabout way, sir, yes. We were given outdated comm. links and a box van instead of the Suburban, but we will make it work, sir."

"Is the colonel aware of the substandard equipment?"

"Yes, sir, he is the one who ordered it." Raising an eyebrow a fraction of an inch was the only indication she got of annoyance from the general.

"Your orders are as follows—find the key suppliers of drugs to Hanscom Air Force Base, apprehend, and turn over to federal agents. The only arrests authorized are the top suppliers. However, you are authorized to gather information however you see fit." Looking directly at Sergeant Thomas, he said, "Are we understood?"

"Yes, sir."

Looking around the table at the officers seated before him, General Scott paused, choosing his words carefully before leaning forward and addressing the group. "The standard rules no longer apply to you. Sergeant Thomas is going to show and teach you things that you may not agree with, but what you need to understand is that Sergeant Thomas knows where the line is and she has never crossed it." He straightened up, took one last appraising look around, and walked out without another word.

"Shit." Alex was not happy, and for the first time, it showed.

Looking at the sarge, it was obvious to the team that something the general said got to her, and if it got to her, then it had to be bad. "Sarge, what did he mean when he said that the rules no longer apply?" Douglas asked what everyone at the table was thinking.

Alex took a moment to collect her thoughts before answering; she needed to calm her own nerves. "That I will have to explain to you later. Who here is good with computers?"

Douglas raised his hand. "Sarge, I can find anything you want or need."

She already knew that Douglas had a way with computers; his jacket stated that there was nothing that he couldn't do with one.

"Sarge?" Miceli said.

"What, Miceli?" She didn't have time for a Q&A session.

Miceli leaned forward, locking eyes with her. "The general is holding something back. There is more to this assignment than he is letting on, and I would like to know if you can think of any reason as to why he would withhold information from us."

"There are a million reasons why a general and the chief of police would hold information back, Miceli, so don't waste your time trying to figure it out. All that you need to worry about is doing the job that you are training for. Got it?"

Surprised at how short and uninformative the sarge was, Miceli didn't know what to say. "Yes, Sarge."

Nodding her head, she pulled an envelope out of her pocket, opened it, and handed it to Douglas. "I want you to go home and get your laptop now. Bring it back here, and then we will talk about what is on that paper." She looked around the table, contemplating her next move. "I want everyone else to build me three tables, three foot by six foot with the leftover lumber. When you are done, get chairs out of the unused offices and bring them downstairs. Go." The second they stood up, and Sergeant Thomas was on the phone, making the necessary arrangements to comply with the general's orders.

When Douglas got back, the tables had been built and the chairs were set up. "Douglas, look at the name on that piece of paper. I want you to get me every single bit of information that you can on him. I want to know what he does, thinks, knows, and who his friends and family are. I want you to explain to everyone around you how and why you are doing what you are doing. Am I clear?"

"Crystal, Sarge." He turned with a smile on his face and began to teach his team how to do the not-so-legal searches.

Five hours later, Alex came downstairs and looked at the team who was huddled around Douglas and his laptop. In the last five hours, Douglas showed them various sites and search engines that could be used to access information as well as how to access "back doors" when the need arose. Diligently they took notes and asked questions as they stumbled through the training. They had reconfigured one of the tables to act as an information board, strategically placing any and all information that they had gathered on their suspect on it. She looked at her watch—1800; it was early according to her standards, but she also knew that she had a long night ahead of her. "Wrap it up, everyone. Leave all of the information that you found on the tables. We can review it tomorrow. Dismissed."

They watched as the sarge walked up the stairs and back into her office before any of them spoke a word. "Holy shit! She let us out early. I don't know what to do with myself," O'Malley said with mock surprise, grabbing at his chest.

"Oh, shut up, O'Malley. We better get out of here before she comes back and changes her mind." Antonelli was watching the offices, expecting to see the sarge come out and put them back to work.

As was becoming her routine, Jen took a shower before leaving, making her the last one out with the exception of the sarge. She couldn't stop thinking about how quiet Sarge was after the general left, and since when does she release them early? "Screw this," she said, shaking her head. She shut her locker, grabbed her bag, and left, smiling and thinking about what she would do with her unanticipated free time.

Chapter 12

Just as Jen was about to unlock her car to leave, someone came at her from behind, slammed her body against the door, covered her eyes, put tape over her mouth, pushed a bag down over her head, and wrapped her hands with duct tape in front of her. She tried everything that she could think of to stop the attack, but not only was she pinned, whoever this was had friends. She was picked up and thrown in the back of a vehicle facedown by two of the kidnappers. One climbed in the back of what she assumed to be a van with her, and the other, she guessed, went around to the front to join the driver. As soon as the front passenger door slammed shut, they sped off.

She rolled over, hoping to find something she could use to cut the tape holding her hands together, and when she couldn't, she began kicking. Her goal was to either kick whoever is back there with her or kick out a window, either way, something would happen. The moment she made contact with the side of the vehicle, her legs were pinned down and taped together. Trying to keep herself from panicking, she made mental notes of left and right turns and any noises or smells she happened to sense in hopes of getting some kind of idea as to where they were taking her.

After the ninth left turn and at least an hour later, or so it felt, the vehicle began to slow, and when it finally stopped, she could feel movement around her. *The least I can do is hurt as many as I can before I go down*, she told herself. The front two doors opened and then closed, and she listened to the footsteps of her kidnappers as they came around to the back and opened the door. Before she could prepare herself to attempt some type of fight or even resistance, she felt a knee come down on her legs while her arms were lifted and pinned over her head. Whoever these people were, there was one thing that she was sure of—they were professionals. The attackers were perfectly in sync with each other, and as soon as she felt hands grab her feet, the knee on her legs was removed. The hold on her hands remained tight and never loosened even when she was thrown over someone's shoulder and carried into some type of building where she was finally dropped on the floor, hard. She tried to sit up, but just as she rolled over to her right side and began to push up, she felt the barrel of a gun press into her temple and a voice, soft and calm, say, "Try to get up again and you will die." She lay down on her stomach and waited.

***

As she lay there waiting for whatever it was that was going to happen, she took note of what she could. *Come on, Miceli, you're a cop. Think…what is there to know. Okay, from the bottom up, floor is made of concrete and is coarse, not smooth like you would find in someone's home. It was slightly humid, and there was a smell of fresh cut wood and seaweed. Damn, I am at the docks. What the hell did I get into?*

She didn't know how long she was on the floor for, but she never passed out or relaxed, she couldn't; she was continuously nudged by a boot, the back of her head grabbed and lifted up, or some part of her body was stepped on. She was tired and getting scared, but she was damned if she would let them know. After what seemed like forever, she was picked up and put on what felt like a folding chair about a foot from where she had been lying.

Her kidnappers grabbed her hair, pulled her head back, and lifted the bag off her face just far enough to take the tape off her mouth. "Yell and you will get hurt, cooperate and you will be let go." The same voice that held the gun to her head earlier spoke into her ear. She couldn't pick up an accent indicating where her attackers might be from, and all that she knew at this point was that they were silent, specific, and cold. Every move they made so far was deliberate, and she had no doubt that these people would follow through on any threat they made. She was getting scared. She mentally evaluated her situation—she could not feel her hands, her legs were tied together, she didn't know where she was, and she was outnumbered at least three to one. *If they would just take this damn hood off, I might be able to figure a way out of this.*

"What is your name?"

"Jennifer O'Malley."

"So you like to tell lies, do you?" the unknown voice asked with a hint of anticipation. "Do it."

The chair was pulled out from under her, and the moment she hit the floor, she felt three punches, all landing in the gut. She was coughing and still trying to suck in air when she was lifted back up and on to the chair.

"What is your name?" Her captor's voice was like the calm before a storm.

She took a minute to catch her breath and then sat straight up. "You already know, so why don't you cut the crap and tell me what you want." She spat out her words with as much venom and calm restraint as she could find.

"It looks like we have a lively one here." He laughed a controlled laugh before continuing. "Okay then, what is your new sergeant up to these days?"

They are after the sarge? Not a chance in hell am I saying anything. "Who?"

"Sergeant Thomas, the woman who has been training you. What is she teaching you and why?"

She smiled. "I don't know who or what you are talking about, asshole."

"You will, little girl, you will. That you can trust me on." The tape was put back over her mouth, and she was thrown back onto the floor before he even stopped speaking.

What felt like hours later, the only things that had changed were the number of times she was prodded in the ribs by someone's boot and her temper. Fury replaced fear, and determination replaced doubt. *They are not getting anything on the sarge no matter what.* The "or what" was the part that she was trying to prepare herself for when she was grabbed again.

Tossed on the chair and tape ripped off again, she was asked, "What is your teacher teaching you?"

This time, she laughed. "Don't know, I'm not a good student."

After a short moment's pause, her captor said, "Drink," just before what tasted like water was forced into her mouth. "I am not going to poison you. I just want information, and how can I get that if you die of dehydration?" her captor said with a hint of humor in his voice. "Drink."

She did her best to try and spit it out, but a hand pressed against her mouth, preventing her from being able to. For the next hour, she was made to drink water and asked the same question. "What is she teaching you?" Jen changed her answers from simple laughter to blatant insults. "Well, I think I will just have to come back to her. Are her friends still upstairs?"

In a voice she didn't recognize as her own, she said, "Who the fuck do you have?"

"Oh, don't worry, little girl. We'll take good care of them." Footsteps walking away was all she could hear.

They kept her on the chair and awake for what seemed like forever. Every time she thought that she was going to pass out from exhaustion, she was nudged or questioned again. Always the same question. Finally, as she began to slip into unconsciousness, or so she hoped, she asked herself, *How long are they going to do this for before they decide they don't want to deal with me anymore?*

"Wake up, little girl, you can't fall asleep on me. That would be rude," her captor said as he grabbed a handful of her hair and lifted her head up. "You have been here for two days now, and I am afraid that I am running out of patience with you. Stand her up." Hands grabbed her from under her arms, lifting her to her feet. She swayed with fatigue but refused to fall. "What is Shannon Thomas teaching you?"

She couldn't help herself. She began to laugh so hard that she was sure she would end up crying. "Do you really think that that pathetic attempt at screwing up her name is going to change anything? Go to hell, you sorry son of a bitch. Just do what you are going to do because I am tired of your shit." Taking a chance, she sat down, luckily finding the chair without falling to the ground. She held her head up high, chin up and shoulders out. "I said do whatever you are going to do, asshole."

There was a moment where everything was silent. "Miceli, are you hungry?"

That's when she smelled it, cheeseburger and fries. She had not had anything to eat since noon on Monday, and if it had, in fact, been two days, then that would explain why her stomach was twisting in knots from the smell of it. "No, shove it up your ass…please," she said with an angelic smile.

Hearing the footsteps come closer to her, she decided that it was now or never. Clenching her hands into fists, she positioned her tied feet to the best location that she could and bowed her head. She waited, hoping beyond hope that they would make a mistake, and to her satisfaction, they did. Someone stopped in front of her, and after counting to three, she jumped up, fists punching out while at the same time propelling her head straight up. She caught the bastard in the stomach with a forward thrust punch, and when his head reflexively came down, she caught him under the chin with her head. She jumped forward, hoping to connect her shoulder with the man in front of her, and was elated when it did. She and her captor went crashing head over heels as they hit the ground, hard. "Bring it on, assholes!" she screamed with everything that she had left in her.

Jen didn't know what to expect, but it wasn't laughter. As she tried to get her feet under her, the bag was lifted off her head, and once her eyes adjusted, she sat there in shock. Standing in front of her was Williams, Miller, and Johnson. The sarge was rubbing her jaw and trying to get back on her feet. She was in the warehouse on the first floor in front of the "house."

"What the fuck is this? Where are the guys?" was all she said as Miller cut the tape off of her wrists and Johnson cut the tape off of her legs.

"Here, I think you should eat something," the sarge said as she handed her the food that she had smelled earlier. She was smiling, shaking her head, and rubbing her jaw as she walked up to the catwalk and back into the office area. A minute later, the rest of the team was walking down the stairs, looking tired and worn out.

"Hey, Miceli, how did you do?" Douglas asked, but when he got close enough to see her more clearly, fury washed over his face. "What the fuck! What did you do to her! You're going down, assholes."

Just as Douglas, O'Malley, James, and Antonelli were about to jump on Miller, Williams, and Johnson, Miceli stepped in between them, screaming, "Wait, they didn't hit me." Although it wasn't true, Miceli didn't want to see them fight over her.

"Then how did you get the bloody lip?" James was seeing red.

"I hit the sarge and split my lip when I landed on her."

Shock rippled through her team as they tried to process what she just said. "Way to go, Miceli!" Antonelli screamed as he picked her up and spun her around.

"Let me down, Antonelli," Miceli said, laughing. "Hey, what day and time is it?" she asked Williams.

"It's four Thursday morning."

"Shit! My wife is going to kill me!" Douglas said in a panic. "Someone give me a phone!"

"Don't worry about it, Douglas. I called your wife and told her you were sent on an op and would not be home for a few days. She was good with it," Sarge said, smiling as she came back down the stairs. "Welcome to your introduction to interrogation techniques. I will see you all back here at 1300. Have a good sleep."

Alex left the team behind, knowing that they were staring at her like she had completely lost her mind.

**

"Interrogation is about patience, practice, and calmness. If you continuously change your questions, you are going to do one of two things—give your suspect time to think of a lie or two or give him time to steer you off course. Intimidation is grossly underrated and can be accomplished by sheer presence. Assaulting your suspect is not required or condoned when you can use force of presence. Most people will give up information when confronted with multiple figures and one calm interrogator." She walked around, looking at nothing and trying to avoid Miceli's stare before continuing. "For example, out of the five of you, three started to break after fifteen hours, and you had nothing to be scared of. In most cases, an interrogation such as the one you all were subjected to yields results within a matter of a few hours, and that is with the known terrorists and corrupt individuals that are out there. Today you will be watching a series of different interrogation techniques in the conference room that had been previously conducted in the field. Pay close attention to the positioning of the various individuals as well as the types of questions asked, and when they are over, I will be standing by down here, waiting."

"Sarge," Miceli said, her voice so cold that she felt chills go up her back.

"Yes, Miceli."

"Did you record our interrogations?" Her eyes locked with Sarge's; she was going to answer this one.

"Yes, I did."

"Can we see them?"

"Why?" *This can't be good.*

"Can we see our own then?"

Alex thought about all of the pros and cons to letting them watch their own interrogations and finally relented. "Yes, I'll get them to you if you want them by the end of the day. Now go."

She worked them hard until 2300 Thursday and 2251 on Friday. By the time Jen got home, she had forgotten all about the interrogation video sitting on top of her DVD player. Instead, she went straight to her room and passed out. She did not leave her apartment for the rest of the weekend.

Chapter 13

Week 6

The first two days were spent learning how to find information on suspects, search engines that you can use to access files that were difficult to find, how to sort out the necessary information from the useless, and how to organize everything so that it forms the perfect picture. Wednesday and Thursday, they went over building clearing, searches, CLS, weapons handling, verbal and silent communications, takedowns, silent entry techniques, and interrogations.

Sarge instructed everyone to report in business casual clothes on Friday morning for training. When 0700 came around and the sarge stepped into the warehouse, the team drew a collective breath. She was wearing black pumps, black dress slacks, with a burgundy silk shirt. Her strawberry blond hair was down, showing off its full body and slight wave, stopping right between her shoulder blades. Miceli was the quickest to pull her eyes away from her.

Jen had finally watched her interrogation video the night before and was shocked at what she saw. Watching herself being carried in, dropped, and constantly messed with for more than forty-eight hours without food, all the while trying to protect the same person who stood over her a majority of the time, pissed her off. She watched it over and over until she thought that she had it memorized, but as she was about to turn it off and finally crash for the night, something caught her eye. She rewound the tape and played it again. How could she have missed it? Every time she was nudged, picked up, slammed down, or in general touched, Sarge had turned her head away. Fast-forwarding to the last few minutes of her "captivity," Jen watched the TV intently. The sarge could have stopped herself from being knocked to the ground, but she didn't. If she had stepped out of the way like anyone else would have, she would have gone headfirst into one of the support posts for the house; instead, the sarge took the hit in order to deflect her. Jen didn't know what to think.

"James, I need you to grab the comm. equipment. Douglas, I acquired a laptop for our use, if you would grab it out of my office. Antonelli, get the CLS kit. And, O'Malley, here are the keys to the van, go get it."

With the exception of the sarge and Miceli, everyone scattered. When the sarge was sure that they were alone, she addressed Miceli. "Miceli, is everything okay with you?" She had been a bit distant since her interrogation.

"I am fine, Sarge. I am just ready to get started."

***

"The key to invisible or stealth surveillance is to be one step ahead of the person that you are watching." Putting her comm. link in, she began. "Radio check, this is Blue One."

In order, they all responded, "Blue Two, Blue Three, Blue Four, Blue Five, Blue Six." Taking a deep breath, she continued on, "Every person on a team has a job. Be it a specialty or joint, each person is instrumental in attaining success. Today we are going to Faneuil Hall to practice the art of surveillance under stealth conditions. I am going to float, observing hand movements, body placement, and facial gestures. All these are key factors to a successful mission. Douglas, you will stay back in the van. I need you to run checks on whoever and whatever we request as fast as possible. We will need pertinent information only, so be mindful of that. In addition, you are responsible for pickup or evacuation. Prior to any surveillance, you will study road maps, draw out one main route and two secondary, and know where to stage this beast of a vehicle so as not to draw attention."

As they pulled into a parking spot around the corner from their destination, the sarge continued, "O'Malley, you will stay here, while Miceli, Antonelli, and James, go and mingle in the crowd. You need to blend in and relax while maintaining contact with your team and keeping within eyeshot of the target. Although it sounds easy, when you are in a crowded place, targets can disappear in the blink of an eye, so position yourselves accordingly. Remember to maintain radio discipline. Be mindful of alleyways, doorways, shops, vendors, large groups, and anything that can cause distraction or obstruction. Go."

After five minutes, Sarge grabbed O'Malley and walked away from the van toward some flower vendors. As Sarge leaned over to smell a bouquet of lilies, she said, "Douglas, mass plate number XVE 5276, female, run it." O'Malley was watching the sarge the whole time she spoke, and if he had not been on a comm. link with her, he never would have known she was doing anything other than smelling flowers.

"Victoria King, 1321 Redwood Lane, Cambridge. She is an accountant, married, one child."

Leaning into O'Malley, Sarge wrapped her arms around his waist, put her head against his chest, and said, "O'Malley, you are running the show. Tail her. I want info." She stepped back, waved goodbye to him, and walked away, blending perfectly into the crowds of Boston.

O'Malley bent over to tie his shoe. "This is Blue Two. Target is a white female, approximately early thirties, blue jeans, white sneakers, and yellow T-shirt. Copy?"

"Copy" was heard from each member, and the hunt was on.

Alex walked around, weaving in and out of different groups and different shops, going in whatever direction would give her the best view of one of her team members. Occasionally, she would correct someone because they would be noticeably staring, talking into the comm. too loudly, talking too much, not enough, or too obviously. For the most part, however, they were doing an outstanding job. They had picked it up and were running with it with so much excitement and vigor that Alex couldn't help but smile. It was always amazing to watch a new team spread their wings and show what they were made of.

Stopping in front of a candy shop to get a quick scan of the area, she looked at her watch: 1137. *She just might let them sit down and eat out.*

"Alexandra! Oh my goodness, it is you. You are even more beautiful than the pictures I have seen!"

Confused and wanting to get away and back to work, she said, "I'm sorry, ma'am, do I know you?" Alex didn't know who this woman was, but the fact that she knew her name and was calling her out in the middle of a training session did not make her feel comfortable.

As she stepped up closer to Alex and took her hands, the woman's voice cracked as she explained. "I am Jeremy's mother," she said as she pulled Alex into a hug and began to cry. Trying to get herself together, the woman stepped back but still held on tightly to Alex's arms, as if she was afraid that she might disappear if she let her go. "He always said how much you treated him like he was your own family, how much you taught him, and how much he looked up to you."

With tears streaming down her cheeks, Alex couldn't help but step back up to Mrs. Brooks and hug her again while at the same time trying to regain her composure.

"I got the letter you sent after he died," Mrs. Brooks said solemnly. "I appreciated it so much… You will never know."

Fighting the tears, Alex pulled herself back and held Mrs. Brooks at arm's length, trying to gather the strength that she needed to be able to say what she had been wanting to say to this woman since the day her son died. "I am so sorry that I let him down and I am sorry that I wasn't there in time." As the tears began free-falling down her cheeks, she added, "It was my fault that he died, and I accept that, but I truly hope that one day you will be able to forgive me for failing both you and your son." Before Mrs. Brooks could say another word, Alex was gone, hidden within the crowd.

Forgetting that her microphone was stuck in constant transmit mode, Alex keyed her mic. "Outstanding work, team, meet back at the rally point."

She was silent the entire ride back to the warehouse. No one spoke about what they heard, and no one wanted to bring it up. When they got back into the building and all of the equipment was returned to the proper cases, Sarge rounded on them.

"You have all been working your asses off, and it shows. It is now 1258, go home, enjoy your weekend, and relax. You have all earned it." She put on a fake smile, nodded to them, and walked out the door.

"What in the hell was that all about? Who was that? Does anyone know?" Antonelli asked, confused.

"Who had eyes on her? Anyone?" James asked, and when no one replied, he added, "Look, whatever that was, whatever happened today, we need to forget we heard it. That was private, and I think Sarge deserves to think that we were ignorant to that conversation, agreed?"

There were nods all around before Douglas spoke up. "I don't know about you fools, but it is one o'clock on a Friday, which means that there are a lot of beers waiting for me."

"You mean a lot of chores your wife left for you," Miceli shouted as she ran for the door and out to her car.

***

As Jen was walking into Dunkin' Donuts to treat herself to an iced coffee and a chocolate cruller, she saw Tina, who just happened to be on her way out. "Hey, Jen, how's training going?" Tina asked with an air of ease about her as she took a sip of her coffee.

"Fine. The sarge cut us out early today and gave us the weekend off. Now I just have to figure out what I am going to do with all of this free time." She laughed weakly as she turned around and walked with Tina to her squad car.

"Yeah, I heard her come in around two, but I was getting ready for work. I guess I'll get with her tomorrow. God, these double shifts are a killer. I don't know how anyone could willingly do them," she said as she leaned on the door.

Knowing how Alex and Tina were close, Jen took a chance. "Hey, it might not be any of my business, but do you know of a Mrs. Brooks or a Jeremy?"

Instantly Tina lost all of the color from her face, and her body went rigid. "Why, what happened? How did you hear about them?"

"We were out on a training exercise at Faunal Hall, and a Mrs. Brooks walked up to Alex. They talked to each other for a few minutes, she said something about a Jeremy, they parted ways, and that's it. She rounded us up, gave us the weekend off, and left pretty quickly. The only reason I ask is because she seemed kind of off."

"Oh my god!" Tina pulled out her phone and called Alex's cell. "Come on, come on, pick up." Panic was beginning to take hold. "Damn!" She ended the call, and as she was dialing in Alex's home number, Jen grabbed her arm.

"What's wrong, Tina? What's going on?" She was scared now. Why didn't she see that something wasn't right when they were cut out early?

Tina held up her hand, indicating that Jen would have to wait, and then spoke rapidly into the phone. "Alex, it's me, honey. Please call me ASAP. I need to talk to you." She slapped her phone shut, cussing.

"What the hell is going on and what the hell is wrong with her, Tina!" Jen said, grabbing Tina's shoulders. She was afraid now.

Looking at Jen, Tina saw the confusion and fear building in her face; her body was tight, and it was obvious that she was worried. "I'm not the one who can tell you that. I wish that I could, but there are some things that are not for me to say." Realizing that she had no alternative and believing this to be a true emergency, she took a chance. "Can you do me a favor?"

"Yeah, what?"

"Go by her place. If she doesn't answer the door, there is a spare key behind the fire extinguisher. Use it to get in and make sure that she is okay."

"What the hell is going on, Tina!"

Handing Jen a card with her cell number on it, she said, "Call me as soon as you find her and let me know if she is okay."

She didn't need telling twice; the look on Tina's face was near to panic, and Jen took off running. Alex lived only a few blocks from where she was. She wanted to know what was going on, but after seeing the trepidation and fear in Tina's eyes, she knew that she needed to get there as fast as possible and that there was nothing that could have slowed her down. She ran at a full sprint down the street, swerving around cars and pushing people out of her way, until she came to Alex's apartment building. She took the steps two at a time and, when she finally got to the door, knocked. No answer. "Shit, where is it!" Jen turned, looking for the fire extinguisher. Alarm had gripped her, and her heart felt as if it was going to pound right out of her chest. She was covered in a cold sweat, and her hands were shaking so badly that it took her three attempts at sliding the key into the lock before she could get the door to open.

"Alex, are you here?" she said as she quietly shut the door behind her. She was running on pure adrenaline, and her senses were piqued, which was why when she walked toward the living room she was able to hear Alex before actually seeing her. Jen didn't know what she expected to see when she walked into the apartment, but it wasn't this. Sitting in the corner of the living room with an empty wine glass on the floor next to her, knees pulled up to her chest, head in her arms, and wearing nothing more than an old gray T-shirt and a pair of running shorts, Alex was in a ball, crying. The pain at seeing her like this was like a clamp on her heart. She ran over to Alex, knelt down in front of her, and gently placed her hands on her arms. Softly she said, "Alex, Alex honey, it's me, Jen. What's wrong? Talk to me, please?"

It wasn't until Jen had touched her that Alex realized someone was in her apartment. Still crying but trying to get herself under control, she willed the tears back and took a shuddering breath. *Why did she call me honey? Why did she even care what was wrong with me?* Taking another deep breath, she steadied herself. She refused to let Jen see her like this any more than she already had. Slowly she stood up and, looking away from Jen, which was harder to do than she had thought it would be, said in a strong, self-controlled, and professional voice, "I am fine. There is nothing wrong. Now if you will please excuse me, I would like to be alone." *I don't deserve her*, was all that she could think about as she tried to get by Jen in an attempt to escape the penetrating gaze that she was under.

Jen watched as Alex tried to steady herself, and when she asked her to leave with the same tone she had heard every day for the past month as she refused to look her in the face, the pain inside doubled. Jen stopped her from escaping with her body and put one hand on each wall, effectively boxing her in. She had no doubt in her mind that if Alex wanted to get away from her, she could, but when Alex looked up and met her eyes, seeing the pain that was radiating within them, Jen lost the last shred of control that she had. She wrapped her arms instinctively around Alex, pulling her in tight. "It's okay, I'm here. You can talk to me." She wasn't prepared for what happened next. Slowly Alex's arms circled around her neck, holding onto her like she was a life preserver. Her body began to shake, and when Jen felt the first tear hit her shoulder, all that she could think to do was protect her.

Picking her up, Jen carried Alex over to the couch, sat down, and cradled her in her lap like she was a child, gently rocking her back and forth. Kissing her softly on her temple, she whispered, "Alex, I am not going anywhere. I am not going to leave you and I am not letting you go. I have you, baby. It's okay." She held her until Alex's crying stopped. Her breathing slowed and became even, her body relaxed, and she fell asleep.

Listening to the rhythmic patterns of her breathing, Jen waited another fifteen minutes before she decided to move her to the bed. Getting up slowly, she held Alex tight to her body as she walked down the hall to the bedroom. The door was open, and when she saw the condition that the room was in, she froze in place; it looked as if a tornado had hit. Carefully working her way over discarded boxes, uniforms, and other odds-and-ends items on the floor, she found the only debris-clear spot on the bed and gently laid Alex down and pulled the blanket over her. She picked up the uniforms and other clothes off the floor, putting them into one of the discarded boxes and sliding it into a corner. In another box, she cleared the remainder of the clutter off the floor and placed that box on top of the first. Looking over to the bed, a piece of her melted. Alex had rolled onto her side and curled herself into a ball; the look on her face, even while she slept, was pained. All Jen wanted to do was to crawl into the bed and hold her and hope that she would feel safe, even while she slept. Instead, she walked to the opposite side and began to clear away the clutter strewn across the bed. She cleared away uniform belts, a couple of hats, and a few shirts as quietly as she could so as not to wake her. Finally she came upon two blue folders lying open and a clear plastic baggie that looked like a letter covered with blood in it. Carefully she sat on the end of the bed and looked at the three items in front of her. The first folder was a Bronze Star with Valor. The award read, "For outstanding professionalism, courage, and bravery while under fire." The second was an award for the Purple Heart. "Holy shit," she whispered to herself. Turning to look at Alex and seeing the way she looked lying there, she never would have thought…she looked so vulnerable. "Jesus, what happened over there?"

Jen froze when she began to hear Alex mumble in her sleep, "Stop, I'm sorry, please," were the only words that Jen could make out, but the pain was radiating from her, and the look on her face could only be described as fear. When Alex was quiet again, Jen turned her attention to the plastic baggie that was sitting in front of her now. Without opening the bag, she took in what she could see. The paper was six by nine inches, the kind you would get from a writing tablet. Two pages with writing on the front and back and she was right—the letter was covered in blood. She turned it over, and on the back, she found a signature: "Your loving son, Jeremy."

Alex jumped up, screaming, "Get down!" and tackled Jen off the bed and onto the floor, covering Jen's body with her own. After loosening the death grip that she had on Jen, Alex pushed up on her arms and looked around the room frantically before finally realizing that she was in her own apartment and safe. Before she knew what she was doing, she let out a pain-filled moan and lay back on top of Jen.

Instinctually, Jen wrapped her arms around Alex. "Shh, it's okay. I've got you."

That brought her back. Alex, realizing for the first time that Jen was holding her and seeing her like this—weak—sent her jumping back and up against the wall. "What are you doing here? Why are you in my apartment, and why in the hell are you in my room?" Quickly she looked down, making sure she still had clothes on and trying to remember how Jen got in there and what the hell happened.

She was trying to calm herself down, taking deep breaths, when she looked at the bed. With utter fear in her eyes and with a shaky voice that she didn't recognize as her own, she looked at Jen. "You know, don't you?"

Walking slowly over to Alex and confused as to why she was so upset about her seeing the awards, she said, "According to those, Alex, you're a hero." She placed her hands gently on Alex's hips. "What's wrong, baby?"

For the first time in her life, Alex not only needed to be held, but she realized that she wanted to be held too. Alex slowly stepped into Jen, pressing her body against hers and wrapping her arms around Jen's waist, and cried. "I'm not a hero. Jeremy is dead because of me. No matter what those pieces of paper say, I will always know that it is my fault that he died. I tried to get there, but before I could knock him down, he got hit." She pushed Jen back a couple of steps and pulled the sleeve of her T-shirt up to show a scar. "It went through my arm and into his chest." With pleading in her eyes, she silently begged Jen to understand. "If I had known that he was going to stand up, I could have stopped him, but I didn't...I didn't know."

Jen stepped up to Alex and wrapped her in her arms again. "Come here," she whispered in her ear and pulled her over to the bed. After positioning themselves so that they sat face-to-face and hand in hand, Jen looked at Alex. "Tell me everything that happened." And for the first time in her life, regardless of secrecy and protocol, Alex told her everything.

Alex told her about the recovery mission, how they were shot down, Jeremy getting hit, the hike back to the border, the feel and smell of Jeremy's blood as it ran down her back the more they walked, coming under fire again, and being picked up by the convoy. Shaking and staring off as if seeing everything again, she said, "When we got back to the base, I took the letter out of his pocket. When I saw what it looked like, I knew that I could not send it to his mom, not like this." She held the baggie up. "I rewrote the letter and sent it off before sitting down to write his mother a letter from me. I couldn't let her get some generic letter from some general who didn't even know him, telling her how sorry he was for her loss. Jeremy talked about his mother all of the time, and I wanted his mother to know what kind of a man he turned out to be and how much he spoke of and respected her." She sighed. "It took me three days." She looked down at their joined hands and wondered how long it would be before Jen confirmed to her that she was right, that it was her fault, and that she had failed him.

Jen pulled her hands away and rested them on either side of Alex's cheeks, tilting her face so that she could look in her eyes. "Alex, you didn't do anything wrong. He made a rookie mistake, and like it or not, it happens. You can't keep blaming yourself for what happened, or it will consume you."

Alex stood up, ran her fingers through her hair, and paced for a minute. "I know, I know you're right, but…" She let out a deep sigh. "What are you doing here?"

"I had a bad feeling when you released us early, but I didn't know what to make of it, and then when I saw Tina… Oh damn! Hold on just one minute." She dialed Tina's phone number and, when she picked up, said, "No, she is okay. Yeah, she's fine. I am going to be here. Okay. Bye."

"What the hell was that about? And was that Tina?" Alex was getting agitated now. She was not a kid to be handled.

"As I was saying" Jen said, taking a deep breath, knowing that she was on borrowed time. "I saw Tina at Dunkin' Donuts, and we got to talking." She paused for a moment and then continued, "I asked her if she knew a Mrs. Brooks."

"How did you know about her?" And then realization dawned on her. "The comm. line was open. How much did you guys hear?"

Wanting to shield her but knowing that she needed the truth, she replied, "All of it."

"So you thought it would be okay to ask my friends about it!" She was furious. How dare she pry into her private life. She had no right.

Jen stood up in front of Alex and raised her voice to match hers. "Alex, I was worried about you. When I asked her about Mrs. Brooks, Tina almost lost it. She tried calling both your phones, and when you didn't answer, she was scared, and damn it, so was I. She was on duty, so she asked me if I would come over and check on you, which I was going to do anyway after seeing the look on her face." Looking down and speaking in almost a whisper, she continued, "When I saw you on the floor, I thought I was going to die. I didn't know what to do, so I held you until you fell asleep and then I carried you in here." She shook her head. "Like it or not, I don't want to see you in pain. I..."

"What? You what?"

Jen looked up and grabbed Alex around her waist with one hand and the back of her neck with the other. Pressing her lips to Alex's roughly, she rode a wave of desire that had been steadily burning inside of her since the first day they met.

Alex was so shocked she couldn't move for a moment, but feeling the need as Jen parted her lips with her tongue desperately searching for her own, she gave in to what she had been fighting since the day she walked out on her in the bar so long ago. She wrapped her arms around Jen's neck, pulling herself harder against her and entwining their legs, desperate to feel every inch of her.

Jen tried to control the primal need that was driving her flesh, but with a trembling voice, she captured Alex's hungry eyes with her own. "I want you," she whispered before burying her face into Alex's neck, kissing and biting it as if it could provide her with life.

Moaning, Alex tilted her head back, as if offering herself to this woman who was causing her flesh to burn. Every nerve in her body was vibrating; she felt the heat that was now traveling throughout her body, adding to the intensity of the pulse that she could feel throbbing between her thighs.

Jen pinned Alex against the wall, her tongue exploring the heat and softness of her mouth, while her hands slipped under Alex's shirt, need escalating and driving her every move. Her fingers lightly skimmed over Alex's abdomen, causing the muscles to tighten and flex, up her sides until finally finding her breasts. Brushing her fingers over her hard nipples caused Alex to release a shuddering groan that sent Jen into overdrive, and she couldn't think; all she knew was the need. Pushing her thigh harder between Alex's legs, Jen pulled Alex's shirt off and took one hard nipple between her teeth and gently bit down. Alex's back arched, and her fingers threaded their way into Jen's hair, holding her mouth and searching tongue to her breast as she gasped for air, and a soft moan escaped her lips. With her mouth on one breast and then the other, Jen's hands explored the soft skin of Alex's back, ribs, and abdomen until both of their bodies were trembling with need. With every gasp and moan that passed over Alex's lips, Jen found it harder to control herself. When Jen's name softly fell from Alex's lips, the last shred of control was lost. Jen slipped her fingers into the waistband of Alex's shorts and, with one quick movement, removed them.

Alex was gasping for air, and her voice was hoarse with desire as she said, "We can't." *But I want to so much it hurts*, was all that she could think.

"Oh yes, we can." She dropped to her knees and without hesitation took Alex into her mouth, drinking in her lover's heat.

"Oh my god!" Alex's head flew back, and her body went rigid. Her heart was racing, and her body was screaming for release. Jen's hand slowly traveled up Alex's body, stopping between her breasts and holding her against the wall where she stood.

Smelling her, feeling how swollen she was, and tasting her sweetness sent Jen's body right to the edge. She felt her clit throbbing, her own wetness soaking through the thin cotton of her panties, and her thighs tightening and shaking as she engrossed herself in Alex's excitement.

When Alex felt Jen's lips on her, all conscious thought was lost. Short quick gasps were all Alex could manage as she felt her entire body begin to tingle, her legs shake, and tiny spasms of ecstasy overtake her almost instantaneously. "I'm…going…to…"

Jen stood straight up, picking Alex up with her and wrapping Alex's legs around her waist. She found Alex's mouth and kissed her with an uncontrollable passion as she walked them over to the bed and laid her down. Taking her shirt and bra off in a whirlwind of movement, Jen slid her burning body on top of her, whispering in her ear, "Not yet."

Alex couldn't think; it felt like her body was on fire. She wanted to come, she needed to come, and when she felt Jen's weight press down on her, skin against skin, breast against breast, and Jen's teeth biting on her neck, she flew to the edge. She wrapped her arms around Jen's back, pulling her hard against her oversensitive body and relishing the weight of her body, the soft groans, and the rapid breathing that were escaping from Jen's lips. "God, I need to feel all of you," she breathed into Jen's ear.

In less than a heartbeat, Jen had removed her remaining clothes and slid back on top of Alex, painting Alex's leg with the heat of her desire. Alex scissored her legs around Jen's, thrusting her hips against the firm muscles of Jen's leg and rocking back and forth, bringing herself back to the edge. Jen couldn't take it anymore; in one fluid movement, she pushed herself up and down, coming to rest between Alex's legs. She let her fingers find their way through Jen's wetness, grazing her clit once, twice, before slowly sliding inside of her. Alex's hips roared up as she let out a small scream, gripping the sheets in her hands as if they were the only things keeping her from flying away. Feeling Alex's muscles close around her fingers and the rippling tremors that were growing in strength brought Jen to the edge of orgasm as well. She closed her eyes, concentration on the woman that she was holding, making love to, and brought her lips down to once again taste her. She knew as soon as her tongue touched Alex's swollen, hard clit it would send her over the edge, and she was right.

"Oh god, baby! Oh god, Jen!" She moved her fingers in and out faster and faster as her tongue circled Alex's clit with increasing pressure and speed until Alex's whole body began to shake, sending her into full body convulsions. Tasting the sweet release and hearing Alex scream her name sent Jen over the edge, riding the wave of ecstasy that Alex had led her to. For a moment, Jen just lay where she was between Alex's legs with her head resting on her thigh before she began to pull herself up the length of Alex's body, letting her tongue trace a line from one spot of ecstasy to another and finally settling her lips on Alex's. With a softness she had never felt before, Jen kissed Alex, long and lingering, until finally lying on her back. She took Alex into her arms and allowed sleep to take them both away.

***

It was just before dawn when Alex woke up in Jen's arms. She had her right arm and leg over Jen's body and was resting her head on Jen's breast. Looking at the woman that was holding onto her so tightly, she realized how utterly happy and content she was. For the first time in years, she felt safe and warm and did not want for anything else. She stared at Jen in wonder, appreciating everything there was about her.

She moved her hand slowly across Jen's chest, tracing the outline of her breasts, down her sides, over her hips until she came to her thighs. She was breathtaking. Brushing her lips across Jen's breast, she lifted herself up enough to straddle her hips, pulling the blanket that half-covered them off and allowing her eyes to take in the beautiful sight that was Jen's body. Slowly and deliberately, she leaned down and allowed her lips to guide her along the rise and fall of Jen's breasts, over the delicate pink nipple, and down her ribs. As her lips moved, so did her hands, lightly tracing the outline of her body with only the tips of her fingers; she felt her skin react. Small goose bumps rose from the places she touched, and the more she kissed and touched this beautiful body, the more ragged Jen's breathing became while she still slept.

With each passing moment, each kiss, and every touch, Alex's heart sped a little more. Heat from her body moved itself to join the throbbing pulse that was already pounding between her legs. With her lips moving to Jen's perfectly flat stomach, she took the weight of her body onto her arms, allowing her legs to slide in between Jen's and slowly part them. Carefully she continued moving down her body until finally she could slide her arms under her hips and kiss her way from one thigh to the other. When she let her tongue slide momentarily over Jen's clit, she heard her gasp.

Waking up to find Alex between her legs, lips and tongue teasing, and arms wrapped around her hips excited her body into a rigid yet quivering state of pleasure. "Oh my god."

Looking up to meet Jen's eyes, Alex smiled. She angled her mouth just enough so that her breath warmed Jen's already wet epicenter when she spoke. "Good morning. Sleep well?" Before Jen could answer, Alex had taken her into her mouth; heat flooded her body, her hips tilted up, and her back arched. She reflexively grabbed the sheets on the bed and wrapped her fists in them. She heard and felt Alex moan against her clit, sending a surge of excitement shooting through her body, bringing her to the edge.

Alex felt her swell in her mouth, and she pulled herself back until her tongue could only brush the tip of her. Enjoying the trembling in Jen's legs, the way her breathing had sped up, and how magnificently wet she was, Alex was in heaven, lost in Jen's pleasure. Pushing down the excitement she was feeling between her own legs, she skimmed her lips against Jen again, and each time her lips touched, she felt Jen jerk as if being shocked. "Look at me."

Jen looked down and was overcome by the intensity of Alex's gaze. Her eyes had turned a deep royal blue and were searching; they were searching for her. "Alex..." But before she could say anything else, she was taken away. Alex slid her fingers deep inside of her while her mouth pressed down simultaneously on her clit, completely engulfing her in a wave of heat and tremors of desire.

She slid her fingers slowly in and out while at the same time circling her clit at the same almost painfully slow pace. As Jen's muscles tightened more and more around her fingers, her body began to tremble and her legs went rigid. Alex increased the speed at which she entered her and the pressure her tongue put on Jen's clit. Bringing her to the peak, Alex waited until just the moment before she knew that Jen would not be able to stop herself from coming. In one fluid motion, she slid her fingers deeper into her and let her thumb take over for her tongue while sliding on top of her, pressing her lips to Jen's mouth and claiming her at the same moment that she climaxed.

Alex kissed Jen, holding her in her arms until the last of the tremors faded away, and then laid her head back on Jen's chest, listening to the beating of her heart. She closed her eyes when Jen wrapped her in her arms, enjoying the softness of her skin and strength in her arms. As she listened to her breathing fall back into the same soft rhythmic pattern, Alex began to fade away to sleep with the realization that for the first time, she felt like she was home.

***

The bedroom door slammed open as Tina pushed herself through. "Alex, what the hell!" She stopped dead in her tracks when her eyes came across Jen and Alex in the bed together. "Oh, I am so sorry. I'll wait in the living room." She looked from Alex to Jen, smiled, and then walked out.

"I have to admit," Jen said, smiling as Alex sat up, "the way you wake me up is much more satisfying."

Alex moved and turned herself so that she was straddling Jen and lowered herself until she was within an inch of kissing her lips. "I like the way that I wake you up better too." Before Jen could wrap her arms around her waist and claim the awaiting kiss, Alex jumped up and out of the bed, laughing with a teasing smile in her eyes.

Before Alex could even pull a shirt over her head, Jen was on her. "I can't believe you just did that. How am I going to go out there and talk to her if I can't get the image of you straddling me out of my head?" Leaning down, she took Alex's ass in her hands, pulled Alex's body against her own, and kissed her—a long, deep, and deliberate kiss.

When Jen's tongue entered her mouth, searching for her own, Alex's body reacted. Her pulse began to race and her hands wrapped around Jen's neck and wound their way into her hair. Her stomach tightened with anticipation, and she became instantly wet. Drawing on the last bit of control that she had in her, Alex put her hands on Jen's chest and backed up two steps. "I want you so bad right now I can taste it. But"—she put her hand up when Jen tried to take a step forward—"if we don't get out there soon, she is going to come back in here." Bending over, she picked up a pair of pants, slipped into them, quickly threw a shirt on, and headed to the door, smiling. "Are you coming?"

"Not yet, but I am sure we can take care of that later." She stood there confident, enjoying the want in Alex's eyes as she watched her run her eyes up and down her naked body. "But only after I play a little catch-up with you."

Alex resisted the urge to step back into Jen's arms and kiss her one last time before leaving out of the room. She took one last lingering look. "I think that can be arranged," she said in a deep melodious voice before walking out of the room, leaving Jen to stare open-mouthed after her.

***

When Jen came out into the living room, Tina was sitting on the chair, almost bouncing out of her skin. Alex was sitting on the couch, four shades of red but smiling. "Good morning, Tina," Jen said, smiling as she sat next to Alex and draped an arm over her shoulders. "So how are you?" Watching Tina was like watching a kid who was about to open her presents on Christmas morning.

"I'm fine, thank you." Trying to control her excitement and failing, she continued, "Well, it's about time you finally got out of your own way, Alex. And, Jen…thank you!" *Thank you, thank you, thank you.* Looking back and forth between the two, she took in how comfortable they looked. Alex was leaning against Jen, and the way that Jen was holding her gave Tina the impression that she would always be there to protect her.

"Tina! Seriously! I don't know why I put up with you sometimes. What was so important that you just had to walk in to my bedroom to get me?" As serious as she tried to sound, she heard the laughter in her own voice.

Tina tried feigning innocence. "Me? You are the one who doesn't answer her phone, return messages, or answer the door when I knock. I was worried about you all night, and I am sorry, Jen. I know you called, but how was I to know that you were going to stay all night?"

"Uh-huh." She laughed and shook her head. "So why are we talking now if you know that I am fine instead of later then?" All she could think about was the way Jen's finger was absently tracing up and down her arm.

"Hun, I was worried, and that was why I came charging in, but since I don't keep anything from you and we are all here, anyway, I think that Jen and I need to talk about some things that I feel need to be addressed. Feel free to stay if you would like."

"Oh no, you don't! Wipe that smile off your face. You are not doing this, Tina. We are not kids anymore! Stop laughing, this is not funny!" Alex was furious.

Watching Alex and Tina go back and forth allowed for Jen to see just how close they were. Alex loved this woman, and she loved her back. She was glad that Alex had someone that knew her so well that she could throw her off guard and make her crazy like Tina was doing right now. "What shouldn't she do, hun?" She smiled down at Alex, who was now quickly getting past the fury stage and moving to scared and concerned.

"Tina, don't."

"Go ahead, Tina. I am definitely curious now."

Alex was almost to the point of begging. "Tina, please"

Tina was laughing in spite of herself. "Well, what happened to 'I don't screw around with people I work with'?"

"You are the one who told me that sometimes we have to break our own rules!"

"My my my, a bit defensive, aren't we? Would you like to leave while Jen and I talk?"

"There is no way in hell that I am leaving, but damn it, T. Please don't embarrass me."

Tina snickered. "Sorry, hun, it's too late for that. If you only knew how red you are right now!" With an extreme effort, Tina pulled herself together, put a serious look on her face, and then turned her full attention to Jen. "Are you going to hurt my best friend?"

"No."

"Will you be able to separate your work and personal lives when it comes to my best friend?"

"Yes."

"Are you aware that since we are both cops, if you hurt my friend, I will make sure that you are blackballed on every assignment for the rest of your career and that no one will ever want to partner with you again?"

"Jesus, T! Knock it off!"

Jen pulled Alex closer and looked down into her eyes. "It's okay, Alex." Then she addressed Tina once again. "I would expect nothing less."

Tina leaned forward, elbows on her knees, smile on the corner of her mouth, and mischief in her eyes. "Do you love my best friend?"

Alex jumped straight up and stepped in front of Tina. "That's it, it's time to go. I love you, hun, and I will call you later."

"What? What did I say?" she asked, laughing at how completely out of sorts Alex was, but when she looked over her head, Jen looked her in the eyes and nodded.

"Bye, hun. I can't believe you just did that to me," Alex said, smiling as she walked Tina to the door.

She gave Alex a hug and, before turning to leave, whispered in her ear, "She loves you. Don't run from this one." She let her go, gave a quick wave to Jen, and left.

Alex pressed her back to the door, her face as red as an apple. "I am so sorry. Sometimes she just—"

Jen walked up to her and interrupted Alex in midsentence. "She loves you and wants to make sure that you are happy and that no one hurts you. Friends like her are hard to come by." Then she took Alex's face in her hands and kissed her softly before picking her up and carrying her back to the bedroom. "I believe we have a little matter of you teasing me and then walking out the door to address," she said as she closed the bedroom door and picked up where Alex had left off.

Chapter 14

Week 7

Alex and Jen had agreed the night before to stay at their respective apartments during the week in hopes that it would make it easier to separate their work and personal lives. Now sitting in the women's bathroom and getting ready for another week's worth of training, Alex and Jen put their gear up and began to get dressed for the day. After a moment of internal debate, Alex turned to Jen. "Nothing is going to change when it comes to training, you know that, don't you?" It was the first time that subject was brought up, and Alex wasn't sure how Jen was going to react to the fact that she was not going to go easy on her.

"Sarge, I don't know what you are talking about, but if you don't mind, I have to get ready. I have a feeling that it is going to be a long week." Jen stood up, kissed Alex, and walked out of the door smiling, leaving Alex to stare after her.

"We are going to be working nights from here on out, so you need to get yourselves prepared to make the transition," Alex said as she walked the line, stopping to look at Jen a fraction of a second longer than the rest. "Most of all, viable information is acquired at night, which means that we must be capable of surveillance in less than ideal conditions. Douglas, what information did you acquire for me on the name I gave you?"

"Nothing much, Sarge. He is a low-level drug dealer, been a Blood for five years, arrested for small drug charges, lives in a blue multifamily three-story house at 83 Blue Hill Avenue on the first floor alone, no family, been known to carry a concealed 9mm, but no violent charges or history. Word on the street is that he carries the nine just to intimidate or impress, but that is neither here nor there." Douglas informed the sarge with a hint of disappointment at the lack of information that he was able to recover.

"Good. We will come back to him later." She walked over to the "house" and looked at it intently. After a minute, the sarge turned back to the team. "Douglas and Antonelli, get the gear from upstairs to include the cases that were left, bring it all down here, lay it out on the table, and perform a function and serviceability check on the comm. equipment. O'Malley, pull the van up to the front door and load up the vests. Miceli, go upstairs to my office and get six hundred Simunition rounds, separate them out to one-hundred-round groupings on the table, and then stand by to have some fun. Go."

As James watched everyone scatter, the sarge approached him. "James, I am going to need your help explaining and teaching them how to use the equipment they're pulling. As it stands, besides myself, you are the most qualified individual on the team. Should anything happen to me, you need to be prepared to assume responsibility. They already trust you and have shown that they are willing to follow your lead, but I need you to assimilate yourself into more of a leadership role within the team."

He did not take his eyes from the sarge's nor did he show any sign of emotion, just determination. "Sarge, I will do what you tell me to do and I will do what needs doing, but what is going on? Where is this coming from? I have been patient in waiting for some sort of explanation for the secrecy because I understand the need for 'need to know,' but I also know the nature of the training that you have been giving us. How bad is the situation and what shit are we about to get thrown into?"

"Walk with me." She turned and led him out behind the building and just stood there, leaning against the wall for a moment, looking out at the ocean. "James, I don't know. The general isn't telling me anything. He gave me that name that I had Douglas check into, and aside from that, you guys have been given the same information that I have. I don't like it, something big is going on, and I don't know what it is. I will say this, whatever it is, I guarantee that our bosses don't want it getting out. Regardless, I will not chance anyone on the team getting hurt or killed because they were not prepared. I hope like hell that I am going overboard on the training, but if I'm not…I hope that I can do a good enough job in preparing the team for whatever it is that is coming."

James crossed his arms over his chest and looked out at the ocean with the sarge in silence. A horn sounding off in the distance seemed to break him from his reverie. "Sarge, I know that you had some serious shit happen to you overseas, but you need to remember that we are not there. I hope like hell that it isn't as bad as you think that it might get, but that is all it is…hope. I agree with you, this looks like it is going to be messy, and having no intel to go on is not a good way to start anything. I will have your back and the teams as well, but you need to know that nothing had better happen to you. If you go down, the team will fall apart, whether I step in or not."

"No, it won't, not if you are there, and I don't plan on going down, but I won't rule out anything either." She took a deep breath and turned to face him. "This can't only be about drugs getting onto a base, but I do think that the drug trail will lead us to whatever the real issue is, and I don't think this lead that the general gave us is going to get us far. Call it a hunch."

He looked down at the sarge, and for the first time since all this began, he saw concern and fear in her eyes. "Nothing is going to happen except us nailing whatever it is that the general is leading us to. I have never backed down from anything, and neither has anyone that is in there." He tipped his head to indicate the team waiting for them inside. "I will take care of them should the need arise, but it had better not. Sarge, you need to remember that everyone in there, myself included, is personally invested in this. You swore an oath just like we did, so if and when the shit hits the fan, don't go thinking about becoming a hero. Got it?" Looking at the sarge, he knew that without a doubt she would sacrifice herself for the good of the team, and he did not know how to get her to understand that she didn't have to.

TRUST

She looked at him without actually seeing him and let out a hollow laugh. "Got it, Big Guy. Now let's go and teach them how to do the fun stuff."

***

Everybody loaded their weapons and extra magazines, grabbed their gear, loaded themselves and the mystery cases into the van, and headed to Hanscom. "Sarge, how are we going to get the weapons and ammo on base? Don't we need permission from the instillation commander or the Security Forces commander?" James did not want to have to deal with any unneeded problems.

"I'll make a call if I have to."

As they approached the gate, Airman Peters looked in the window and, upon seeing the sarge, gave an award-winning grin and waved them through. "That was easier than I thought it would be," James said with disdain.

"Too easy, I have to remember to have a little talk with him later about that. Complacency is what gets people hurt or killed. Home station or not, he was in the wrong," she told the group as they proceeded through the gate.

She drove them to the far end of the base, so far, in fact, that the team was beginning to think that they were lost before the trees that were surrounding them gave way to an open area resembling a city street. There were houses complete with fences, mailboxes, cars, and even yard decorations.

After everyone filed out of the van, Sergeant Thomas addressed the group. "This is a simulator, if you will. If we are going to train for searches and extractions, I figured that it would be more beneficial to us if we trained in an environment that was as close to the real thing as possible. Sergeant Williams cleared the calendar for us to be able to use it for the week, and that was no easy task, so let's not waste any time." She went to the van, pulled out the mystery cases, and laid them on the ground. "Although we will not be using these today, I wanted you all to see what equipment we have and will be using. James, step forward, will you."

He opened the first case and pulled out two GPS beacons. "Tracking beacons, looks like they are good to within three feet. Good to have." Impressed, he put the first case aside and opened the second, and when he did, his face lit up. "Outstanding! Now we are going to have fun!" James could not contain his excitement; Miceli thought he looked like a kid in a candy shop.

Smiling despite herself, she turned back to the rest of the team. "What Officer James means is that we will be training at night using the aid of night vision goggles or NVGs. They are not easy to come by and they cost more than you make in a month, so you will handle them with the utmost care."

"Sarge, where did you get these? They are brand-new!" James was still staring in the case and all but drooling. There were collective chuckles throughout the group as they watched the normally calm and cool James get so excited that he cut off the sarge without even realizing it.

"General Scott saw a possible need for the GPS tracking beacons and NVGs and, as such, felt that it would be in our best interests to have them readily available. Now everyone gather around James and listen to what he tells you when it comes to the NVGs because tomorrow if you don't wear them correctly, you will regret it," she said with a devious smile that told the team how serious she was. "We will worry about the GPSs later." The sarge stepped back and made room for them to come forward.

They gathered around James and listened intently to everything that he was telling them. By the time James was through explaining how to system check, wear, and operate the NVGs, as well as their capabilities and benefits, the excitement of using the new equipment had rippled through the rest of the team.

"Here is what is going to happen. Douglas, you are going to get in the van, do a ride around, and get a feel for the area. Note all possible drop-off, pickup, and egress routes that are available. Also assess the buildings and surrounding area and note possible emergency extraction locations. The rest of you are going to learn the art of observation, building infiltration, and extraction techniques. Stealth is going to be the key, so be aware. If I can see you, then the 'people' who live here can see you, and that is not acceptable. We are now going to put into play everything that we have learned and see how well you have not only retained the information and training but how well you can also put it all together in real-life scenarios." She looked around the training site before continuing. "This setup forms a complete two-city block, so you will need to be mindful of the surrounding buildings and possible civilians that may be in the vicinity. You will have two hours to get a feel for the area, so I suggest that you not waste any time. Gather as much information on what you see as possible and meet me back here. Go."

Douglas jumped in the van and began driving slowly around the block, stopping at times to get a closer look at something that he found interesting, driving down alleyways, and backing up into different types of driveways. The rest of the team stayed together as they walked around the simulated city. She could see them pointing out fire escapes, side doors, porches with crawl spaces, and flat top roofs. Although James was doing a majority of the pointing and talking, everyone, at some point, noted or brought some type of observation to the group. Without having to be directed, they swapped out van driving duties, ensuring that each one was up to speed with all aspects of this new training. What surprised her the most was that at no point did any one of them drop their guard. There were eyes to the front, back, and sides of the team at all times, and they always stayed as close to cover as they could.

With fifteen minutes left before the team was due back, Alex picked up her phone. "Sir, it is Master Sergeant Thomas. I need my old team for the next two weeks beginning today. I know that it is short notice, sir, however, they are the only other people that I trust and I guarantee that they will not reveal the nature of this team or its mission." She waited, listening to the general chastise her for the lack of notice, but ultimately granted her the request.

"They will be yours as of tomorrow. Will your team be ready to go by the end of next week, Sergeant.?" General Scott asked. Although he sounded like he was asking her a question, what he was really saying was that they had better be ready to go and that she was running out of time.

"Yes, sir. Sir, will Colonel Jacobson know who the team will be assigned to or any other details?"

"No, Sergeant Thomas. All that he will be told is that they are being sent for training. If he should give you or any members of your team any problems, I want a call immediately. Do I make myself clear?"

"Crystal clear, sir. Thank you, sir. I will report back to you at the end of next week." She hung up the phone and let out a deep sigh of relief. With any luck, she could get them ready by then, and now that she knew she would have help, she felt a weight lift and a twinge of excitement for the first time since this assignment began. Now if only she could figure out what they were really supposed to accomplish with this mission.

The team gathered around the sarge at the back of the van. "Every one of these buildings has been equipped with furniture so as to give you the most realistic and accurate training as possible. Today we will work solely on building clearing as a team and also as two separate entry type teams. There will be times that we will get separated and we need to know how to enter a building from two entrance points without killing each other in the process. We will practice communication techniques, silent entry, stealth entry and exit techniques, and expedient egress maneuvers. I want no mistakes. You all know what you need to do, and now is the time to prove that you can do it."

They went over and practiced their tailing/surveillance techniques with the sarge acting as the person of interest, building entry, room searching, interrogations, and personal searches. Sarge posted herself and James at different locations posing as the aggressors giving and returning fire and resisting detainment whenever possible. She placed the GPS tracking beacons on herself and James, giving everyone the opportunity to become familiar with the operation and field knowledge of tracking. The team was at the top of their game, and everyone was thorough and detailed in every aspect of the training. The sarge noted that Miceli was even more thorough with the personal search this time than she was before, so much more so that she had to hold her breath to keep herself from jumping a couple of times during the pat down.

***

"Yes, sir, I understand completely," Colonel Jacobson said as he paced back and forth in his office while talking to General Scott over the speaker phone. "Yes, sir, I will have them report to you immediately. Sir, are you reestablishing Master Sergeant Thomas's team?"

"Colonel Jacobson, if it was a requirement for you to know the nature of Master Sergeant Thomas's assignment, then I would have told you, but since it is obviously a matter of interest to you, no, I am not reestablishing Master Sergeant Thomas's team. Miller, Williams, and Stiller have been selected for specialty training due to their accomplishments while stationed in Afghanistan. You should be grateful to have them under your command, Colonel."

Colonel Jacobson stopped pacing and looked at the phone. He knew that he had pushed as far as he could for information and that if he pushed any harder, he would pay for it. "Yes, sir, I am lucky to have the compliment of airmen, that I do. Is there anything else that I can do for you, sir?"

"No, Colonel. I think you have done enough already. Send me the men ASAP. Good day."

Colonel Jacobson looked down at his phone and the now disconnected line. "What the hell is going on?" General or not, he was going to find out what was happening with his people and why the general was all of a sudden taking such a keen interest. These were his men, and as such, he had not only a duty but also an obligation to know what it was that his men were doing.

***

What the hell? Master Sergeant Pope asked himself as he was driving around the base, checking up on his men and the different posts they were assigned to. *Why are there gunshots coming from the training grounds?* When he had checked the schedule on Friday, it was showing clear for the week. He picked up his radio. "Base, this is Raven 1. Do we have anyone scheduled to be on the training grounds today?"

Sergeant Williams answered the radio, "Yes, sir, that would be Master Sergeant Thomas, and it looks like she has it reserved for the next two weeks, sir."

"What times does she have the range blocked out for, Sergeant?"

"Until 1,800 today and 1,500 to 2,300 for the remainder, sir." This wasn't good, although he was trying to keep the use of the training grounds quiet as per Sergeant Thomas's request, there was no way that he could keep it that way now, not with Pope nosing around. Quickly he grabbed the schedule and wrote in Master Sergeant Thomas's name and blocked out the two weeks that he had just told Pope about.

Pope drove out to the training grounds and parked his vehicle so that it could not be seen from where the group was actively training. He knew that the grounds were not reserved prior to today and he also knew that Williams was Thomas's pet. From what he had been told, Thomas was detailed out on another assignment, and if that was the case, then what was she doing here? Picking up his phone, he called the colonel. "Sir, this is Master Sergeant Pope. Did you clear Master Sergeant Thomas to use the training grounds?"

"No. Are you telling me that she is there?"

"Yes, sir, with five other individuals. It looks like she might have a new team that she is training, but I don't recognize any of them. Sir, is there anything that I should know about? I know that she is the senior ranking, but if I am going to be running things while she is gone, I would like to know if there is anything going on that I should be made aware of."

"That does it! Did she reserve the range for today only?" Colonel Jacobson was furious.

"No, sir, she has it blocked out for the next two weeks for night training."

"Call O'Brien and Harris and tell them they need to get here. I am cutting them orders for the next two weeks starting tomorrow. I want the three of you to report to me in my office at 1200 tomorrow.

And by the way, Sergeant, you are losing Senior Airman Johnson, Senior Airman Miller, and Staff Sergeant Williams."

"What? Sir, are you serious? I just got them back! Where are they going, and for how long this time?"

"They will be tasked out for the next two weeks to training, and before you ask, Sergeant, I don't know what kind of training they are being tasked for. This is coming from higher. I will see you in my office at 1200 tomorrow."

"Yes, sir." He hung up the phone and watched Thomas and her new team enter, clear, and egress a couple of times before calling O'Brien and Harris. *What is she training for now?*

***

The training went well, and spirits were up on the drive back to the warehouse. They were complimenting each other on shots taken, calls that were made, and Douglas's driving skills. "Sarge, what's up with all the planes coming in and out of the base?" Antonelli asked, thinking about how often their conversations would be interrupted because of how loud the planes were and how they must have been right under the flight path.

She was so used to hearing the planes coming and going both overseas and at home that she didn't even notice them anymore. "The missions vary depending on requirements and priorities. Some are used for troop transports, but primarily they are used to transport cargo, everything from standard base supplies that are needed for everyday operation here or at other bases within the US and overseas. They also transport damaged or destroyed equipment and weapons that are being sent back from forward deployed locations overseas for repairs or destruction. As it stands, sixty percent of all damaged weapons come to Hanscom because we have one of the best gunsmiths in the Air Force assigned to our armory. Staff Sergeant O'Brien can proficiently fix weapons that other units would just write off as non-repairable in less time than it would take most others to conduct the initial evaluation. In fact, he has been the lead gunsmith for going on ten years now," she told him as they pulled into the parking lot of the warehouse.

After unloading, storing the gear, and cleaning their weapons, the sarge addressed the group. "Okay, tomorrow I want everybody in their cargos and ready to go at 1200. We are going to be working late every night for the next couple of weeks, so if you need to make any arrangements, I suggest you do it now. Have a good night, everyone. Dismissed."

As the guys left, Jen and Alex headed to the women's bathroom. "Umm, question," Jen said as she opened up her locker, avoiding eye contact with Alex.

"Yeah, what is it?" she asked, throwing her T-shirt into the bottom of her locker and pulling a new one out.

"Are we off duty?"

"Yes…wh—"

Before Alex could finish her sentence, Jen was on her. She pinned her up against the adjoining wall and kissed her hard, bruising her lips with an entire day's worth of longing behind it. Alex's arms instinctively went around her neck as Jen pressed her body against hers, the want and need that had been held back all day finally able to reveal itself. Eventually the kiss softened, and Jen slowly pulled herself back far enough so that she could look Alex in the eyes without separating their bodies. "My god, you are beautiful."

Smiling at the compliment, Alex made to lean forward and steal another kiss but was stopped short when Jen pulled back just enough to put her out of range.

She closed her eyes in an attempt to maintain what little bit of control she had left over herself. "If you kiss me again, I am going to take you home with me and make love to you all night long. I want you in so many ways right now you can't even begin to imagine, but we agreed that during the week, we would keep it as professional as we could, remember?"

"Oh my god, how can you stand there and be so calm?"

"Oh, baby, I am far from calm, which is why"—Jen took a step backward, keeping her hands on Alex's hips to keep her from following—"I am going home now." With a crooked smile, Jen looked at

Alex one last time. "I will see you tomorrow, Sarge." With a forced calm, she took one more step back and turned, closed her locker, and walked out the door, leaving Alex in a state of shock, excitement, and bewilderment.

"This is going to be harder than I thought," Alex said as she put her shirt on, shut her locker, and closed up the building for the night before leaving.

Week 7
Tuesday, 1200

Colonel Jacobson was sitting behind his desk when O'Brien, Harris, and Pope came in. He didn't wait for the door to close before beginning. "Master Sergeant Pope, get a team together and get out to the training range. O'Brien, you will be in charge of the assembled team. I want you there because it sounds to me like your people are going to be there with Thomas and I want them to see someone that they know. It might help to relax them. Harris, I want you at the gate conducting random vehicle checks. Make sure that her vehicle is searched thoroughly. We know that she will have weapons and ammunition. When you find it, make sure that she knows that the next time she comes, she will need authorization. Don't give her a hard time, just be professional and then call me as soon as you clear her to leave."

"Not a problem, sir, but I ask again, what is going on here?" Pope did not like being kept in the dark.

"Like I told you yesterday, Master Sergeant Pope, I don't know but I will find out. I will be damned if Master Sergeant Thomas thinks that she can come back and start doing whatever it is that she wants like she is in charge. This is my command, not hers, and I will find out what is going on here. I assume that if she has the BPD with her again today, it might be beneficial to the two of you"—the colonel nodded to Harris and O'Brien—"to know what they are up to since nobody seems to know anything on your end either."

There were collective nods in all directions, and then Harris, Pope, and O'Brien left the colonel's office to get themselves started on what they thought was going to be an interesting day.

***

Sergeant Thomas and Sergeant Williams stood back by the stairs in the warehouse and watched as the old team and new team talked. There was a lot of laughing and chest beating as to who did what and how much better who was at what. As happy as she was to see the camaraderie forming between her two teams, there was work to be done. "All right, everyone, gather around the tables." She walked with Williams to face the group as a whole. "For the next two weeks, we are going to be getting our rhythm, so to speak. In front of you on the table is a map of the training area laid out in the form of a typical street map. I want you all to become familiar with it and study it the same as you would if you were going out on a real operation. Douglas, when we leave here, I want you to make sure that it comes with us. That map is your life and the lives of your team. Memorize it and make sure that you plan out every scenario accordingly. Johnson, Miller, and Williams here have been assigned to assist in our training for the next two weeks. They are not going to be nice. They know what the enemy tends to do and where they like to hide. They are familiar with every aspect of the training that you have been receiving because they lived through the real thing, doing it over and over again for the past year during active missions. As always, you will show them the utmost respect and take everything that you can get from them. This is your last chance to hone in your training, skills, and abilities before they are put to use in the field. Now is the time to ask questions and make mistakes, not when we get out there in the real world."

Pausing for a moment to look around the group and let the weight of her words sink in, she continued, "Miller, Johnson, and Williams"—a mischievous smile formed on her lips—"give us your best, nothing less, understood?"

Miller leaned forward, hands on the table, and a challenging smile tugged at him.

"Not a problem, Sarge. I just hope you can take getting your ass handed to you."

She leaned forward, bringing herself within an inch of Millers face. "Bring it on, little man."

"Let's go!" Williams said from behind Sarge. "It's time to kick some ass!"

***

They pulled up to the front gate and were greeted by Technical Sergeant Harris. "Good afternoon, Sergeant Thomas. Welcome back."

"Thanks, Harris. How have you been?" She never liked him. From her experiences with him in the past, she labeled Harris as the type of NCO who cared more about making himself look good and less about the welfare of his troops.

"Just fine, Sergeant." He looked over at Douglas. "What are you doing here?"

IA rat squad, he thought with a smile. "Just doing a little training with the sarge, seeing how she does things."

"No one better to learn from. Okay, I need you to pull the van into that spot over there, if you don't mind. We are conducting random vehicle checks today."

"Not a problem, Harris," Douglas said as he drove to the spot just past the gate on the right-hand shoulder.

He pulled up, and as he was putting the van in park, Sarge turned to face everyone in the back. "Leave your weapons on the benches clearly visible and get out."

Sergeant Harris came up to the van with a young airman that Sergeant Thomas did not know. "Technical Sergeant Harris, I am informing you now that there are nine 9mm weapons in the van and two thousand Simunition rounds. We are heading to the training range to conduct some standard drills, and all of the weapons have been converted over for that purpose."

"Understood, Sarge. Thank you for the heads-up." He turned and began searching the undercarriage of the van with a mirror and flashlight while he had the airman search the inside. When they were finally done with their search, Harris sent the young airman to begin searching the next vehicle in line while he went to speak with Thomas. "Sergeant Thomas, do you have authorization to bring those weapons and ammunition on base?"

"Only verbal, Harris, but if you would like, I could make a call and get the paperwork sent down here while we wait." She had to remind herself that he was only doing his job.

"That won't be necessary, Sergeant Thomas. I trust your word, and it's not as if the Boston PD is going to try to take over the base." He let out a small laugh. "Sarge, are you going to be training today only or on a regular basis?"

"We are scheduled to come here to conduct training for the next two weeks."

"In that case, I would appreciate it if you would have Colonel Jacobson send down an authorization letter so that the guys here at the gate are covered."

"I didn't get authorization from the colonel. It came from higher-up, but I will have the paperwork sent down." Damn, she didn't want it known that they were going to be here.

Harris smiled. "Sarge, you know how the colonel is. If he doesn't get a heads-up, he is going to kick my ass. Would you mind if I pass the information on to him?" He wanted her to feel like he was asking for her permission.

"I understand, go ahead and let him know, and I'll get the letter to you by the end of today. Are we good to go?"

"Yes, ma'am, have a good one." With a small wave, he walked back into the gate shack, watched as she and her team got back into their van, and left before calling the colonel. "Sir, she just went through."

"Any problems?" the colonel asked.

"None to report, sir. However, just to inform you, she has quite an interesting assortment of gear with her."

"What gear are you talking about? What does she have, Harris?"

"Sir, she and her team all have M-9s with approximately two thousand rounds of ammunition, NVGs, and GPS tracking equipment. In addition to that, I think you should know that Williams, Johnson, and Miller are with them."

What the hell is she doing with all of that gear, and why is she training BPD on it? Why in the hell do I have to give up three of my men to train these people? "Thank you, Harris." Colonel Jacobson hung up the phone, and as he grabbed his hat and walked out of his office, he confirmed to himself that Master Sergeant Thomas was overstepping her bounds. "She is going overboard in the BPD's training. It's time to shake things up a little bit, I think."

***

"What the hell is this?" Williams said as he looked and saw a team conducting training on the range that he had reserved for them. He was furious. "I cleared the range until next Friday. No one is supposed to be here, Sarge. I don't know what happened."

"Everyone, get your gear on and get yourselves ready. Williams, come with me." They walked over to the assembled group together, trying to figure out what had happened.

O'Brien removed his helmet as he walked over to the new arrivals. "Afternoon, Sergeant Thomas, Sergeant Williams. Is there something that I can do for you?" he asked, looking annoyed that he had to stop his group's training in order to talk to them.

Williams stepped up. "The range was reserved for our group. Why are you here?"

"I think what Sergeant Williams meant to say is that he reserved the range for us from 1500 to 2300, Sergeant O'Brien," Master Sergeant Thomas said, clearly annoyed.

O'Brien looked at his watch and then back at Williams. "It is 1430 now, and the way I see it, you are not due to have the site for another half hour. We will be done here before 1500, so why don't you just relax, Williams." He looked at the sarge and smiled. "Good afternoon, Sergeant Thomas. How are my guys doing? I hope they are presenting a positive image of the BPD."

"They are doing just fine, Sergeant." She looked over to O'Brien's group. "Let me know when you guys are done, will you?"

"Sergeant O'Brien!" the colonel called from just behind the parked van; no one had heard him pull up.

Just as he thought, Sergeant Thomas had her old team back. As he walked up to the group, he made sure to make eye contact with Williams, Johnson, and Miller and was pleased when all three of them looked down or away. "O'Brien, how are things coming along?"

"Sir, the team is looking good. In fact—" He was cut off when the colonel's phone rang.

"This is Colonel Jacobson." After a moment, his back went rigid, and his face showed signs of concern. "What do you mean today? That aircraft wasn't due in until Friday." He listened for a minute longer. "No, I will sign for and pick them up. Just stand fast and I will be there in fifteen minutes." He hung up the phone and looked at O'Brien. "O'Brien, I am going to need you to come with me. It looks like the cargo that was due to come in on Friday just arrived."

O'Brien's face shifted from smugness to that of concern. "What? Yes, sir." Without hesitation, he stripped off his gear as he walked to the colonel's car, clearly ready to go.

He didn't have much time, lucky for him the flight line was close to the range. He nodded once to Sergeant Thomas, aggravated at the fact that he couldn't stay to find out what type of training she was trying to conduct. He flipped open his phone. "Sergeant Pope, this is Colonel Jacobson. Meet me on the cargo ramp," he said as he walked back to his car.

Williams looked at the sarge. "What the hell was that?"

"I don't know but I honestly don't care. At least they are gone. Let's get everyone moving."

***

Week 8
Friday, 1800

"John, are you sure that it is a good idea to not tell them what we are really trying to do here?" Chief Collins asked General Scott as they entered the warehouse.

"Mike, if we do, it could compromise everything. Sometimes the best information is no information, or don't you remember that from back in the day?" The general looked at his friend, understanding his concern but knowing what had to be done.

"We are not in Syria, John," Mike said, but he knew what his friend was getting at. Thinking back, he remembered issuing out orders to his troops, giving as little information as possible so as to keep his men alert and shielded from the truth of what they were doing. If his men had known the big picture, they would have taken shortcuts, and he doubted if the end result would have been the same. In all, five men were lost, a number that was well below the projected casuality numbers. When he reported back the results of the "successful" mission to his commander, who at the time happened to be the man standing next to him, he realized that in the long run, he had done the right thing. Had any of his men known that they were walking into what was expected to be, and by all rights was a cluster fuck, the causality rate may very well have been higher. Sometimes ignorance of a situation is the best way to protect your men.

Understanding his friend's concern, the general reminded him of a harsh but simple truth. "Mike, it is not about the person, and it is not about the people. It is about the mission."

They shared a look of resignation and understanding between the two of them and, without another word, sat in the chairs at the planning table and waited for Master Sergeant Thomas and her team to return in silent contemplation.

***

Training had progressed well, and every once and a while, Pope or Harris would show up to the range and watch them during their training and compliment a judgment call or tactical procedure from time to time before leaving as quietly as they had come. When Friday finally came, the team broke off from training early and headed back to the warehouse.

Spirits were up, and the satisfaction that they felt as a whole radiated throughout them as they grabbed the gear out of the back of the van and headed inside. It wasn't until the doors closed behind them and were halfway to the stairs that they realized the general and the chief were waiting for them. All conversation stopped, Sergeant Thomas rendered a salute, and the team as a whole locked up. "Sir," she said to the general.

"Is your team's training complete? Are they ready to accept an assignment?" the general asked without preamble.

"Yes, sir."

"Master Sergeant Thomas, we would like to speak with you and your team," General Scott said as he turned his back to them and went with the chief back upstairs and into the conference room. The team followed the general and the chief and took their seats at the conference table, hoping to finally find out what it was that that they had been training for.

"Three months ago, an incident occurred that caught my attention. I will not go into details as to the circumstances surrounding the incident, but it was clear to me that it was necessary to keep the situation as quiet as possible," the chief began. "I assigned IA to investigate the incident primarily because Sergeant Harris is one of the best investigators I have, and by assigning IA to the case, I knew that no information would be leaked. However, IA has not been able to come up with any viable leads or pertinent information with the exception of the name that has already been given over to you. Michael Bullard is the only lead we have in this case." The chief stepped aside and made room for the general to take over.

"I detected an upsurge in drug-related incidents on the base, and rather than standing idly by and waiting for the local PD to do all of the work for a matter that involves and directly effects the base and ultimately the mission, I contacted the chief here and discussed a joint operation of sorts to try and stop, or at least minimize, the drug trafficking on base. Once we agreed on how we wanted to work it, I went to Washington and approached the DoD, requesting that we be allowed to assist the local authorities in matters that directly affected operations and mission effectiveness. They agreed to a one-time trial run, completely off the books, and if it worked, they would consider expanding the program, but if it failed, then all of the backlash will fall on the chief and myself… We agreed." The general looked at the chief and handed the floor back to him once again.

"We believe that Mr. Bullard is dealing opium on the base as well as in the streets of Boston. He is our only lead, and so far during this investigation, we have not been able to pin anything to him. He has been able to shake the surveillance team assigned to him at every turn, and we have yet to be able to witness any unlawful acts being committed. There is no doubt in my mind that this individual is a low man, but he is all that we have and ultimately he is all that you have to go on."

He stopped, taking in the eyes watching him for a minute, and silently cursed himself for withholding information from them. These people sitting in front of him were his people, and they trusted him, yet he wasn't telling them what they really needed to know.

"Do what you need to do to get information on who is at the top of all of this. He is an ant in the big scheme of things, and I couldn't care less about him. Get what you can, find out who the top dealer is, and take him down."

General Scott stepped up to his side, put his hand momentarily on his friend's shoulder, and looked at the team. "Master Sergeant Thomas, I know that this is not new information to you or your team, but understand this, there is a lot riding on this assignment. Get it done, make me proud, and be safe. I want weekly updates of which I will relay to the chief so that we are all on the same page. If there are any important developments that arise, call me immediately. Are we understood?"

"Yes, sir."

"Good." He and the chief walked out of the conference room, leaving the team in silent contemplation.

***

James was the first to break the silence. "Sarge, forgive me for saying this, but they are full of shit. I think there is a hell of a lot more to this than what we are being told. Do you have any idea as to what the hell is going on, because I think that we both know that DoD wouldn't authorize something like this for your standard drug ring. I mean, really, Sarge, how many times are they going to try and feed us this line of bullshit?"

They all looked at her expectantly, some with complete trust and some with avid curiosity, but it was James who stared her down. She knew that he knew how the military and DoD worked, and she also knew that he was looking out for the team. He was strong, smart, and, most of all, honor-bound. He was a natural leader, and because of that, because she respected him, she answered in complete truth.

"I haven't been told anything more than you all have been told. I agree, there is a hell of a lot more to this than they are telling us, and that is never good. No matter what is going on, though, I know that this team is more than capable of handling it, whatever it is." She paused before continuing, "You know the absolute silence that you feel throughout your entire body, the moment that every nerve in your body vibrates and every one of your senses becomes hyper aware because you know that the target is about to come into view and you know that you have only one chance at it? That is what I feel like right now."

"Shit," James said, shaking his head.

The rest of the team sat there waiting in complete silence. They were tired, sore, and filthy from the day's training, but with the visit they just received, on top of the sarge's and James's reactions, every single one of them was jolted with a second wind. This was it—training was over, and it was time to go to work.

After a minute of silent contemplation, Alex looked up. "Douglas, that name I gave you, Michael Bullard, were you able to come up with any new information on him?"

He looked defeated. "No, Sarge."

"Sarge." Antonelli spoke up. "I was going to bring this up later, but things were off the hook, so I never got the chance, but I called a friend of mine in narcotics."

"You didn't call O'Malley, did you? I don't want anyone knowing anything about what we are doing." She was not happy, and it showed.

"No, Sarge. I called one of the guys I went to the academy with and told him that I saw Bullard dealing and wanted to know what his deal was."

"And?"

"And he said that this guy was 'promoted' within his faction recently and that lately his sect has been taking over more and more territory. He said that they are still dealing the typical marijuana and crack but that they now have the corner market on the opium trade in the area and it is the good stuff. They are trying to figure out where it is coming in from because it is top quality."

"If IA was put in charge of the investigation, then why didn't we get any information from their end of the investigation?" O'Malley asked. "Something seems off with that, doesn't it?"

"I don't want to speculate, but sometimes it is better to go in blind. If they are hitting dead ends, then a fresh perspective is what is needed." Looking at the team, she could see the fatigue and excitement on each of their faces.

"Okay, here is how this is going to go down. We are not going to have a lot of time or chances at figuring this out. This might be a street gang we are dealing with, but they are organized, and once we get started, red flags are going to go up. We don't need or want to be noticed. My goal is going to be five or less individuals investigated/interrogated. Anything more and we will be noticed, and if we are noticed, then we can consider this whole thing dead in the water because they will lock up tight. No more than two weeks, folks. Just two weeks at most is what we have to figure out who is the responsible individual or individuals."

She looked at them for a minute before continuing. "We are going to do this my way, interrogations included, so be prepared." She paused, taking a breath and collecting her thoughts. "Douglas and Antonelli, I want you to watch him tomorrow night, I want to know when he heads back to his house, if he is alone, and what time it is when he gets there. I want you to get me info on entrance points, egress routes, building plans, as well as a good idea on street activity at all times. Clear?"

"Crystal, Sarge," Douglas said.

"Yes, Sarge," said Antonelli.

They looked at each other with clear smiles on their faces. Time to play.

"Sarge?"

"What is it, Miceli?"

"If we do the interrogations your way, then how in the hell are we going to be able to go to court? The interrogation techniques that you taught us are not legal in the civilian world."

"Not everything goes to court, Miceli, and call it a hunch, this is one of those times that the suspects will quietly agree to whatever it is that is offered."

Looking around her, the sarge knew that they either didn't fully understand or didn't fully agree with what she had just told them. She knew the conflict that some of them were silently struggling with; she had felt it herself the first time that she ran a "silent" mission, but she pressed on just as she knew that they all would as well. "The rest of you will be here 1800 Sunday. We will form the game plan, get our gear, and get this thing started then."

Agreement all around, and when she finally dismissed them, she watched as each one of them left. Douglas and Antonelli were talking and gesturing with each other, trying to figure out the best course of action for the next day, while the others were walking tall while the excitement they were feeling was plastered all over their faces. The simple fact that they were finally able to get started changed each and every one of their attitudes and personal perceptions about themselves. She understood how they were feeling, she had once felt it herself, but she had a bad feeling about this whole mission that she just couldn't shake.

Sliding her arms around Alex's waist from behind, Jen leaned into her ear and whispered, "Baby, you can't protect everyone. What happens happens, but we have a job to do. For now, you need to take a break and get yourself rested because we are all counting on you."

Alex turned and wrapped her arms around Jen's neck, enjoying the warmth she felt in her arms. "I know, I know, but it is easier to say it than it is to believe. They are my responsibility, Jen. I have to worry." She stepped in closer to Jen, basking in the safety of her embrace.

How does she do it? she thought to herself. *Two completely separate personalities, I wonder if anyone else knows how fragile she really is.*

"Come on, baby, let's make an exception to our rule tonight. Go back to your place and get some rest and some cuddle time in. I have a feeling that we are not going to have much time for anything but work once we get started."

Agreeing, Alex gave Jen a quick but soft kiss, took her hand, turned, and led them out of the building and to their cars, looking forward to the peace that the night would bring.

Chapter 15

Sunday night, 1800

"Okay, what have you got for us?" the sarge asked Douglas and Antonelli.

Antonelli began, "The subject is approximately six feet tall, black hair, medium build, and has a scar running from his left cheek down to the base of his jaw. His residence…"

Sunday night, 2000

"Are we clear as to the game plan?"

Collectively, they said, "Yes, Sarge."

"Okay, Douglas, I want you to review your extraction and egress routes again. James and O'Malley, conduct another equipment check. I want verification that all of the equipment is operational and grab a duffel bag so that we have a way of removing anything illegal that we might find. Antonelli and Miceli, I want you two to review the site layout and verify that there isn't anything that we might have missed. Douglas, make sure that we have the med kit in the van and hope that we don't need it. At 2300, we will reconvene and go over the plan again. We head out at 2345. Any questions?"

No one moved; they all just looked back at her. "Let's get to it then."

***

It was raining when they pulled up in front of the suspect's house. The few lights that actually worked on the street shed an ominous orange glow on the empty lot three houses down and on the pizza shop across the street from it but nothing else. Normally the street would be crawling with dealers, junkies, drunken bar patrons, and prostitutes, but because of the rain, the street was deserted. Douglas parked the van directly in front of the dilapidated house, turned off the engine, and then climbed in back with the rest of the team. "Comm. check, this is Blue One." Alex initiated the final check.

"Blue Two copy," James responded.

"Blue Three copies," Antonelli confirmed.

"Blue Four copies," Douglas replied.

"Blue Five copies," O'Malley stated.

"Blue Six copies," Miceli acknowledged.

"Let's do this," the sarge said as she opened the back door to the van, and she and her team headed to the house.

The sarge was wearing the same gear as the rest of the team: black cargo pants, kneepads, vest under a black shirt, and black mask but with one exception—she was wearing a bulky black hoodie. She waited for the team to position themselves on either side of the front door, the only entry and exit point in the house, before she approached. As she climbed the steps, she made sure to stomp her feet so that if there was anyone inside, they would know that she was coming. When she knocked on the door, the only thing Michael Bullard could see from the eyehole was someone rocking back and forth, hands in the front pocket and hood pulled over their head, covering their face. The moment she heard the deadbolt disengage and the doorknob start to turn, she took one step back, effectively signaling for her team to go. Before Bullard had even opened the door an inch, James had slammed through it and, in one fluent move, pinned him against the wall and handcuffed him. Antonelli, Douglas, and O'Malley, who followed directly behind, moved past James and began silently clearing the house, while Miceli, who followed behind O'Malley, put tape over Bullard's mouth and a black hood over his head. Sarge was the last to enter, closing the door quietly behind her.

"Clear," Antonelli reported through the comm. link from the back of the house.

"Begin," the sarge ordered quietly into her microphone, and as the team began to systematically search the house, she went back to the kitchen, looked through the cabinets, pulled out a large mixing bowl and two glasses that she had then filled with water, and then went back to the front room.

The house was a typical drug dealer's house, the walls were covered with various posters of rap artists and *Maxim* poster girls, the furniture was used and battered, to say the least, and the only things of value were the stereo system and the sixty-inch plasma TV that was mounted on the wall. There were holes and dents scattered in the walls throughout the entire house, several windows had cracked and were being held together with duct tape, and half of the doors had been damaged or knocked off the hinges.

When the team had completed their search of the house, they reassembled in the living room and gathered around their suspect, who was currently kneeling on the floor and struggling to get up. The sarge held the bowl out for the team, and they filled it with everything that they had found, including a Beretta 9mm. She took the gun, removed the magazine, and put both pieces in her pocket. Finally, she stepped in front of Bullard and nodded to James, signaling for him to remove the bag.

As soon as Bullard could see again, he looked around, and what he saw scared the crap out of him. Six people stood around him in black clothes with ski masks on, and right in front of his face, in a bowl, was his stash—dime bags, pills, tabs, shrooms, and tar.

The sarge squatted down so that she was at eye level with him. "Speak only when spoken to. Scream and you will pay. Do you understand?"

He looked around him. *I am so fucked!* he thought and, realizing that he had no choice, nodded.

The sarge ripped the tape from his mouth. "Who is your boss?"

"What? Get the fuck outa here, bitch."

Sarge took four of the pills out of one of the baggies from the bowl that she was holding, lifted a glass of water up, and, one at a time, dropped them into the glass. "I don't want your drugs. I want a name."

"I don't talk to the cops, bitch!" he spat out.

She put the tape back over his mouth. "Have no doubts, I am not a cop. They have rules, I don't," she said as she began to pour the remainder of the pills into the cup.

"And if you don't answer my question, you are going to find out what happens when you drink down the same drugs that you have been pushing," she said as the last pill entered the cup, turning it light blue in color. "When I take this tape off your mouth, you will answer my question, or you will drink." She looked over to Douglas and nodded. He forced Bullard's head back and held it there while Sarge ripped the tape off his mouth again. "Who is your boss?"

"Fuck you...," he began but was stopped short when water was splashed into his mouth. Before he could spit it out, his jaw was forced closed and the tape was put back on. Being forced to swallow the water scared him so bad that he tried to scream through the tape and struggle out of his bonds, but to no avail.

She was like the calm before the storm as she sat patiently waiting for him to stop struggling. "I don't want your drugs. I just want to know who your boss is. I am not leaving until you tell me who he is. But understand this—if you lie to me, I will be back, and if I do have to come back, you will regret ever having been born."

These ain't no cops. If I don't get this shit out, I am going to OD. Fuck! He looked around at the people surrounding him again, at the people in his house, and realized that someone pissed the wrong people off. His heart was racing, and he was sweating like there was no tomorrow. It was "give up a name or die," so he nodded to the person questioning him, and the tape was ripped off his mouth again. "All I know is the cat who passes me the shit to sell off. Ace."

"And where can I find Ace?"

"He lives over on Ruffles Street. Big white house with a porch, and he has those Christmas lights still hanging on the porch. It's the only one on the street with those lights still on."

The sarge stood up. "Follow me." James stood Bullard up in one quick motion and then followed her through the house and into the bathroom. "I said I didn't want your drugs, and I don't," she said as she started to dump the contents of the bowl into the toilet. "But I don't want you to have them either." She flushed the drugs down the toilet while Bullard, too scared to do much, stood by with a look of horror on his face. "If you tell anyone that you had visitors here tonight, I will make sure that they also know that you ratted one of your own out to save your own skin. As for the drugs," she paused for a moment as if she was trying to think up an explanation, "tell your friends that you were robbed."

"What the…"

The duct tape was put back over his mouth, effectively cutting him off again. "Tape him to the radiator in the living room."

He was led back into the living room where he was taped, hands and feet, to the radiator, and it wasn't until the intruders left that he saw the two glasses. The one with the drugs looked just like it did when the pills were poured in, but the glass next to it was only half full.

Three more dealers were tracked down, searched, and questioned but to no avail. As with Bullard, any drugs found were flushed, and all of the weapons that they had come across, all 9mm Berettas, were removed and turned over directly to Chief Collins for destruction. As far as they could tell, the scare tactic was working, but none of them knew or would give up any real names. The only names they would get were other low-level dealers like themselves, and since there were so many different sects throughout Boston, trying to find the people in charge was proving to be more difficult than they had initially thought. There was no way to go in undercover, and although each low man gave up someone slightly higher in rank than they themselves were, the team was still a long way from where they needed to be. Morale was getting low.

Chapter 16

It was Friday night, and the team sat gathered around one of the corner tables at Mickey's, each one silent and lost in thought with beer in hand, trying to figure out what the next move was going to be. The bar was empty with the exception of the bartender and themselves.

"We need to keep pushing until someone gives us something." Antonelli was frustrated.

Leaning forward on the table, the sarge tried to make eye contact with each one of them, projecting a sense of confidence that she herself didn't have, but they were all staring at their drinks, frustration mounting and morale low.

"No, word will get around, if it hasn't already. We need the element of surprise, and at this rate, we are going to lose it soon. O'Malley, I need you to find a connection between everyone we have interviewed. There has to be something that links them all together. No matter how small it is, you need to find it. The rest of us will just have to keep up standard surveillance and tailing." She looked up, pausing for a moment, as she watched as a man wearing blue jeans, a white polo T-shirt, and carrying a backpack approached them. He stopped directly behind Jen.

"Can I help you?" Alex said, not only annoyed at the fact that this individual interrupted her but also noticing that there was something about the way he was looking down at Jen that made her uneasy. The moment he walked into the bar, it was as if he was honed in on her, his eyes never leaving Jen, and she didn't like it. Everyone looked up from their bottles at the same time.

"Oh shit!" Douglas said, clearly surprised. He stood up so fast that he knocked over his chair. James looked at the newcomer with a deadly stare. "You have a lot of nerve coming in here!"

Having her back to the door, Jen never saw who it was that was now standing behind her, but seeing the instant shock, anger, and physical reactions of the team, Jen went into alert mode. Slowly she turned around, and the moment her eyes met his, she jumped.

Once Jen saw Tyrell Williams, her reaction was instantaneous—she jumped up, hit him with a perfect upper cut to his jaw, and then tackled him to the floor. She moved so fast that it took her team a minute to realize what was happening before they could react. Four punches to the face were all that she was able to get in before James grabbed her from behind, pulling her off him. Slipping free from his grip, she ran back at the man who was still lying on the floor, getting one solid kick to his ribs in before the rest of the team descended upon her, pulling her back and away from Tyrell. She fought her team, jerking, sliding, jumping, and pulling, trying to break the hold they had on her. Alex positioned herself directly in front of Jen, trying to block her line of sight to the unknown man. The look in Jen's eyes was murderous, nothing but pure rage. If they let her go, she was going to kill him, of that she had no doubt.

"Stand down, Miceli! Miceli, I said stand down!" Alex got right into her face. "I said stand down!"

Jen wasn't listening, nor did she register the fact that Alex was speaking to her. He was here, he came up to her, in her place and in front of her friends. He took Emily away from her; he wasn't getting anything else.

"LET. GO. OF. ME," she growled.

Alex grabbed Jen's face and positioned it so she had no other choice than to look at her. "Jen! Jen! Baby, you have to stop!" She forced eye contact and said in a calm and soft voice, "Baby. Stop." Jen blinked, stopped struggling against the restraining hands, and looked at Alex. Her eyes were still murderous, but the pain that was surfacing within them rocked Alex to the core. *What was going on, and who the hell is this guy?*

Through gritted teeth, Jen looked over Alex's head at Tyrell, who had just stood back up, holding his jaw and wiping blood from his lip. He asked in a voice so calm that it sent chills up Alex's spine, "What are you doing here?" *All I need is for them to loosen their grip just a little and I can finish him off.*

Looking at the group of officers that were holding Officer Miceli and then back to Miceli herself, Tyrell said in a soft clear voice, "Officer Miceli, I know that you want to hurt or kill me right now, and I don't blame you, but please I need to say something to you."

"I'd leave if I were you," O'Malley said with a growl.

"If you don't get the fuck out of here, I am going to let her go and turn my back so she can finish what she started!" James said.

Looking back and forth at the exchange that was going on between the officers and this man, Alex realized that it was going to get bad in here real soon. She was getting nervous.

"What makes you think that I want to hear anything that you have to say to me?" Jen's voice was quiet, but the hate, fury, and rage behind the words were clear and deadly.

Putting his bag on the floor, Tyrell put his hands up in front of him in a gesture, showing that he meant no harm, and looked directly at Jen. "Ma'am, I did the unforgivable, I took a person's life. To you she meant the world, and at the time to me, she meant nothing."

"No shit!" Jen screamed out.

Waving his hands, Tyrell said, "No no no, ma'am. Please hear me out."

"She doesn't have to do anything you say," Douglas barked.

"Finish fast or I am going to do what I wanted to do six years ago." Her entire body was trembling with rage.

Alex slowly turned so that the right side of her body was against Jen's front, her right hand holding tight to the front of Jen's pants. She tried to position herself so she could see everyone involved.

"When I got locked up, I bragged about what I did. I was trying to earn points and respect and with some people I did. No one messed with me, which was what I wanted, and it went on like that for more than a year." He took a breath as if preparing himself for what was coming next. "Then one day, I got a new cellmate. We got along fine, which was okay by me, but what was most important to me at the time was that he had my back and I had his, which in jail is the most important thing to have, ya know, backup. We talked about a lot of different things, family, friends, girls, and whatever else came up. We became tight like real friends, not just someone to have your back, and it was cool. Then one night, about six months after he got there, he asked me what I did to land myself in jail. I told him the story like I had told it a hundred times before, with pride." He paused, shame filling his face. "He was furious. It turns out that he knew her. He said that she was the only teacher who gave a damn about him. He told me what she looked like, the things that she had done for him and some of the other guys, and he told me what kind of a person she was. He said that he couldn't believe that I could brag about killing someone as nice as her."

Tyrell paused to take a few calming breaths, trying to pull the tears that were forming in his eyes back to keep them from spilling over. "Officer Miceli, every day for the next year, he told me and reminded me of the kind of person that she was. He told me what she was like and the things that she did for people. He told me that she was more of a mother to him and his friends than anyone had ever been. Ma'am, one night, while I was lying on my bed, I started to cry. It had finally hit me what I had done, and I couldn't handle it. I talked to the shrink and I talked to the chaplain and I prayed a lot. I realized that I hated who I was and what I had done. I wanted to make up for what I did, but I didn't know how. I thought about what Bean, that was my cellmate's name, had told me about her. He remembered her with such vivid detail I couldn't believe it. I knew what she looked like, how she laughed, what her smile was like, what she did, and I started to understand why she wanted to teach. I got released a year early for good behavior. I got my GED while I was locked up, and now thanks to my GED teachers writing letters of recommendation and the support that they gave me, I am enrolled at UMass. I am studying child psychology and high school education. I want to give back what I took from others, but I know that no matter what I do, I can never erase what I did." Tears were pouring down his cheeks, and his voice cracked as he continued. "Officer Miceli, I took your partner, your lover, away from you, and for that I am eternally sorry."

"Oh sweet Jesus!" Alex breathed. *Why didn't she say anything?* She could feel Jen behind her, her whole body shaking. And when she turned her head to look at Jen, her heart broke. The tears that were falling down her cheeks made her want to hold her in her arms; she wanted to take away the pain.

"Officer Miceli, I can't change the past. God knows that I would if I could, but I want to help you to maybe change the future. I want to give back and make amends to you, and I think I know how to start doing that."

"And just how do you plan on doing that?" Jen's voice was cold and calculated, but still it cracked with pain.

"My brother is still in with the Bloods, and he told me the other night how they had the major hookup. They are getting opium and other stuff from some military guy. My brother just transports the stuff, but he has to meet with one of the guys running it tomorrow night. They are going to meet at his place. I love my brother, but he doesn't care who he hurts, and I have this bad feeling that he is in over his head." He opened his bag, took out a piece of paper, and handed it to Alex, who was the closest to him. "I was wrong for what I did, ma'am, and I swear to you that whenever I find something out that can help you stop people from doing what I did, I will come to you. Your partner helped a friend, who in turn helped me. Now I want to pay it forward to you." Taking a deep breath, he looked at each member of the group one at a time, finally stopping back at Jen, and then sighed, "They meet at 1100 tomorrow night." And with that, he picked up his bag and left.

"Let me go," Jen said flatly after watching Tyrell walk out. She sat back down, the rest of her team slowly returning to their chairs and joining her as she downed the rest of her beer. After taking a moment to get herself together, she looked around the table and took a deep breath. "Thanks guys." There were nods around the table, and although she felt like she was in the spotlight, everyone's eyes kept going back to the sarge.

Work is work, she told herself. "What do you guys think, should we check it out? It's something, at least."

"Why are you even listening to that loser, Sarge?" O'Malley was shocked.

"Sarge, you can't trust a word he says," Douglas growled.

"He's nothing but trash!" Antonelli yelled.

"He's probably just trying to set her up, Sarge," James tried to sound logical and falling just short.

Void of all emotion and with eyes as cold as the ocean, Jen looked at everyone around her and said, "We need to check it out."

Silence.

Cautiously Alex asked her, "Why? Is there anything to be gained, or is it personal?" *Oh, baby, I am so sorry.*

Jen locked eyes with Alex as the team watched, not knowing what to expect. "First, personal feelings cannot drive a decision. Second, he cried and didn't fight back when I nailed him. Sometimes people do change. And third, his brother is a Blood. Everyone we have tagged so far has been a Blood. If he thinks that his brother got in over his head then he probably did. We are at a dead end right now, and his brother is in with a "military guy," so why not take the chance. It is the best we have, and the fact the "military" was dropped…well, I say that it is a viable lead."

Alex studied Jen. She couldn't imagine the level of control that she was exerting, but she doubted if she would be able to maintain it for long. With an air of confidence and calm that she didn't feel like she truly possessed, Alex looked at everyone at the table. "I agree with Miceli. Does anyone else?"

They all looked back and forth between the sarge and Miceli before tentatively voicing their agreement.

"Fine, O'Malley, get me everything you can on that address to include staging area and egress routes. James, I want you to verify comm. and ammo. Douglas and Antonelli, get me a background check on this guy, I want everything. Rally at 1800 tomorrow. Let's go."

As everyone got up, they made sure to touch Miceli on the shoulder, silently letting her know that they were there for her. Jen didn't move; she just sat there trying to get her composure back.

"Why didn't you tell me?" Alex asked quietly after everyone else had left, not knowing how to express how much she felt her pain and wished more than anything that she could take it away.

Fighting back the tears threatening to fall, Jen stood up. "I was out of line, Sarge. For my outburst and lack of professionalism, I apologize." Then she walked out without looking back.

What the hell just happened? "Jen, wait!" Alex jumped up and ran out the door, trying to catch her, but she was too late; she was already gone.

***

It was after 3:00 a.m., and Alex was pacing back and forth across her living room on the phone while Tina sat there watching her. "No, Chris, I haven't found her yet, and her cell is still off. Where else could she have gone?"

"I don't know, but she will turn up, Alex. When she came over earlier, she said that she just wanted to spend time with Megan. Melissa and I knew better, but we figured that after spending a little time with the baby, she would cheer up like she usually does. By the time I realized that not even Megan could snap her out of whatever it was that was bothering her, it was too late, and she was walking out the door. I don't know what to say, Alex, except that I am worried too. Look, I am on duty tonight, so I will keep an eye out. If I see her, I will call you. If she should call or contact you, though, please call me and tell her that Melissa and I are worried and to please call."

"I will. Thanks, Chris." Slapping the phone shut, she looked at Tina. "Please tell me that she is all right."

"Honey, her past just came back and slapped her in the face… She just needs time."

"She called me Sarge before she left. Tina, I can't lose her, I just can't." The tears streamed down her cheeks. "Tina, I…oh god." She dropped down on the couch next to Tina, her legs not capable of holding her up anymore, and allowed the tears she had been holding back to finally fall.

Tina wrapped her arms around Alex, not knowing what else to do. Watching Alex, seeing her in this much pain, she was at a loss. "Talk to me, Alex."

"I..." The door opened, and they both turned at the sound.

"I'm sorry," Jen said, looking down at her feet. "Do you want me to leave?"

She didn't know what to make from the shocked expressions on their faces. "I'm sorry, I'll just go."

Tina jumped up. "No, Jen, I think that I am going to go. You two need to talk." She looked at Alex with what she hoped was encouragement. "I'll call Chris. Give me a call later, will you?" A few seconds later, she was walking past Jen and out the door.

She couldn't look Alex in the eyes. *What if she is still upset about what had happened?* Who was she kidding? Just looking at her, you could tell that she was.

"I saw your light on, so I figured you were up, but if you want me to leave, I'll understand."

Alex was dumbstruck. *Why would she think that I didn't want her here?* For the first time in her life, she couldn't speak, and all that she could do was look at her.

Looking down at her feet, Jen felt all of the color run out of her face, and her stomach twisted in knots. "I understand, I'm sorry. I guess I'll see you tomorrow night."

Jen turned to leave, but the second that her hand touched the doorknob, Alex called.

"Jen, wait!" Alex was across the room and behind her within seconds, taking her hand from the door and turning her so that they were facing each other. "Why would you think that I wanted you to leave?"

She didn't see it before, but now that Alex was mere inches from her, she felt like a knife had just been shoved through her heart. Alex had been crying, and Tina was there trying to comfort her, all because she lost control. "Because I lost control, lost perspective, hurt my team, almost hit you, because of all that, you had to out us just to get me under control, and I walked out on you." She leaned back against the door and rubbed her hands over her face hard, trying to do the right thing. "I just wanted to tell you that I am sorry."

Taking a chance, Alex stepped into Jen, putting her hands on her hips and head on Jen's chest. "Do you remember the first night we made love?"

Hoping that she still had a chance, Jen slowly brought her hands up and wrapped them around Alex. She felt it when Alex softened against her. "Yeah, every minute of it."

"You said I'm not going anywhere. I am not going to leave you, and I'm not letting you go."

"I didn't think that you would want me anymore considering the way…"

"I'm not done, Jen." Alex captured Jen's now light green eyes with her own. "I don't want you to let me go. For the first time in my life, I feel safe and protected and I feel that way because of you. I know that you are going through a lot right now, but please don't shut me out because I won't be able to take it if you do." Softly she brushed her lips against Jen's and put everything that she had on the line. "I love you, Jen. I've fallen in love with you and I don't want to lose you. Please."

How could she say that? "I hurt you when I got upset with him for killing Emily. Hell, just for bringing her up." Her voice was less than a whisper, her world was in chaos.

"Jen, baby, you loved her and that will never go away, nor should it."

With her voice trembling, she replied, "I thought that—"

Before Jen could even finish, Alex wrapped her arms around her neck and pulled her down, kissing her with everything that she had and everything that she was. The moment that their lips met, every barrier that Jen had ever built over the years disintegrated, and she was left exposed and vulnerable. She had never wanted anything more.

***

The team was there waiting for them when the sarge and Miceli walked in; all eyes were on Miceli.

"Are we ready to do this guys?" Jen asked, trying to sound amped up like she had a thousand times before.

"Ready if you are," Antonelli said as Miceli walked up to the group and began reviewing the intel.

"Sarge, we decided that given the fact that we now have a strong prospect, we thought this would be a good time to use the GPS tracker on the 'contacts' vehicle. If it turns out that this group is not involved, we can always get it back at a later time."

"Agreed," she said and then joined the rest of the team to review for the night's mission.

Three hours later, they were in the van and headed out to Tyrell's brother's, aka Black's, house.

"Final review," the sarge ordered as they drove.

O'Malley briefed as he secured his vest. "Antonelli, O'Malley, and you, Sarge, will enter the backyard from the opposite street. There is a six-foot wooden fence in the back that you will have to climb, but the house adjoining the back fence is vacant, so you should be able to enter undetected. Post in the backyard behind the house and wait for the all clear. In the meantime, James will post in the bushes at the northeast corner of the front yard. Miceli will stand by in the van with Douglas and wait until the 'meeting' starts. Once it is clear, Douglas will drive up, Miceli will jump out and place the GPS tracker on the unknown contacts vehicle. Once the tracker is in place, she will post with James and stand by. When the meeting is over, on the sarge's command, we will enter the building and do what we do."

Douglas slowed the van to a crawl but never fully stopped. "First stop, Blue One, time to go!"

As soon as O'Malley opened the back door to the van, he, Antonelli, and the sarge jumped out and took off into the backyard of the vacant house. The fence posed no problems to any of them, and in no time at all, they were in position at the back of the house to the right of the back door. With the exception of a barking dog somewhere off in the distance, it was silent and the night was overcast, blanketing the house in darkness. Sarge looked around the yard, trying to get a feel for the area. There were no security lights, just the dim yellow glow from what appeared to be the kitchen window. The house, which at one time must have been a good size and beautiful two-story home, appeared to be from the outside, at least, unkempt and trashed. Subconsciously she noted the overgrown grass and weeds, discarded beer cans, and various other forms of trash scattered throughout the yard, paint peeling off the house, and a piece of tape, like a Band-Aid, stretched across a crack on one of the upper windows. The back door looked to be solid; however, she was betting that the lock was as old as the house itself and doubted if the doorjamb would pose much of a problem getting through. "This is Blue One, we are in position," she stated into the comm. Now all they could do was wait.

Coming in through the neighbor's yard, James posted himself in the Yarrow bushes, which completely concealed him but also provided him with an uninterrupted view of the front yard and house. There was almost no street traffic and even fewer pedestrians passing by on the sidewalk. James took in all that he could from what he could see. What little there was of a lawn didn't look as if it had been mowed in a few weeks and was bare in some spots. There were small bits of trash scattered about, two strips of cracked and broken concrete marked the driveway, and the porch looked as if it had hosted more than its fair share of parties. There were slats missing sporadically along the railing, the wooden steps and deck were worn from foot traffic and weather, the gutters were dented and sagging in places, and the peeling paint made the house look as if it was battle-scarred. There was no porch light on, which made James uneasy. Although it would make it difficult for any passerby to see him go in, it also made it impossible for him to see if Black had any weapons on him when the time came to go in. "Blue Two is in position. Miceli, there is a driveway in the front, so be prepared."

At the end of the street, she and Douglas waited in the van. "Got it."

At exactly 2259, a car pulled into Black's driveway. "Black Lincoln Town car just pulled into the driveway," James relayed to the team. "I can't see the plates." A moment passed before he continued, "The suspect is approximately six feet in height, medium build, blue jeans, black boots, black hooded sweater, and black ball cap. I can't see his face, but he appears to be Caucasian." James watched the suspect walk to the front door, hands in the front pocket of his sweater and head down, but he had a feeling that whoever this person was, he was completely and acutely aware of his surroundings. Just as the unknown suspect got to the front door, Black stepped out and closed the door behind him.

"Black and the unknown suspect are not going in the house."

"Damn it!" Douglas yelled as he slammed his fist against the steering wheel.

Thinking fast, Miceli came up with an idea. "Douglas, drive up the street slow," she told him as she disconnected the cabin light.

He drove slow down the street, and just as the van passed in front of Black's house, Miceli opened the door and jumped out using the van for cover, ran a few steps to keep from falling, and then, in a crouch and only a few feet away, ran to the passenger's side of the car parked in Black's driveway. She placed the magnetic GPS to the underside of the vehicle's frame and waited until James gave her the all clear signal. She ran in a half crouch to join him and take up position. "Blue Six is in position with Blue Two."

"Blue One copies. When the opportunity presents itself, proceed."

"Copy that."

Fifteen minutes later, the unknown suspect and Black walked back to the car. Black walked between the mystery individual and their staging position, preventing Miceli and James from getting a good look at his face. Black waited until the car pulled away before heading back to his house, and the moment he opened the door, James was on him, pushing him inside with Miceli right on his heels. The sarge, seeing Miceli and James moving toward the house, gave the order to go and was coming in the back door just as the front closed.

While O'Malley, the sarge, and Douglas cleared the house, Antonelli searched the downstairs bathroom while James and Miceli taped Black's mouth shut, placed a hood over his head, and handcuffed and searched him. Once Antonelli had completed his search, Black was placed on his knees on the floor of the bathroom, and Antonelli stood guard while everyone else began searching the house. Five minutes into the search, James called the sarge over the comm. "Sarge, I need you down here in the basement."

"En route."

When she arrived in the basement, the sight laid out in front of her caused her to stop short and catch her breath. She looked around, a whole cache of military grade weapons and ammunition was lined up against the wall and floor. While the rest of the team continued the search of the house, oblivious as to what was found in the basement, James and the sarge took a quick inventory of the weapons and ammunition and loaded everything into some duffel bags that they had found stashed in one of the corners. "Douglas, pull the van into the driveway."

"Copy that."

As they loaded the bags into the back of the van, Sarge called to the team over the comm. "After you have completed your search, grab our dealer friend. We are taking him with us."

The trip back to base was silent. James kept his eyes on the duffel bags, while the sarge seemed completely removed from her surroundings, a void look in her eyes. Tension mounted until they pulled up to the warehouse, and Sarge finally spoke. "Lock his ass up upstairs." Antonelli and O'Malley moved with a quickness, sliding Black out of the van, and all but carried him up to the office area. The rest of the team unloaded the equipment and duffel bags and stood by waiting on the sarge, who was now standing at the head of the table and looking down at the bags scattered on the table before her, arms crossed in front of her chest. She took a deep breath and then turned around. "The game has changed. I don't know where it is headed, but it won't be pretty." She stared each and every one of them down, driving her point home.

Not one of them blinked, looked around, or said a word. Five pairs of eyes stared back at her, waiting, five pairs of eyes that said, "We are in this till the end, Sarge."

They opened the bags and boxes and laid everything out on the floor as they re-inventoried each and every item, and when they were done, the team stood there in shock as they realized the enormity of the situation. Twenty M-4s, six M-240s, thirty-eight M-16s, fifty 9mm Berettas, a thousand rounds of 9mm ammo, two thousand 7.62mm rounds, two thousand rounds of 5.56mm, and what appeared to be two logbooks. Sarge looked up and asked the group, "Was anything else found?"

Douglas turned ghost white as he looked up at the sarge. He pulled out a single piece of paper, unfolded it, and handed it over to her.

"What is it, Douglas?"

"Sarge, I didn't think much about it at the time, but something told me to grab it."

She looked down at the paper that Douglas had handed her; it was a blueprint of the armory at Hanscom. On the back, she recognized the numbers and letters for what they were…shift schedules and key codes for the door locks.

"What in the hell did we just fall into?" O'Malley said. Everyone turned their eyes to the sarge.

"Masks on everybody. James, go and get our friend from upstairs and bring him down here, please." When James left, the sarge turned to O'Malley. "O'Malley, I need you to grab the logbooks and blueprint and figure out what there is to know. There is something in there that will help us, I guarantee it, so find it."

"I'm on it, Sarge!" He grabbed the paper and logbooks and went upstairs to the conference room, determined to uncover whatever information there was to find in the books that he now held in his hands.

Alex placed a chair five feet from the recovered cache of weapons and ammo, and James came down with Black and placed him on the chair.

Sarge nodded to Antonelli, indicating that he was to be the one conducting the interrogation.

James pulled the hood off Black's head, and Antonelli began his interrogation, with the rest of the team providing presents of force. "Who are you getting these weapons from?" Antonelli asked.

***

O'Malley poured himself over the logbooks. The sarge entrusted him with this portion of the investigation, and he wanted to make her proud; he wanted to earn her respect. Going back and forth between the two books, he tried to find hidden codes and tie together half pieces of information from one book to the other; he lost himself within the contents of the journals. The blueprint sat in front of him, pushed as far away as he could get it, while the logbooks lay open just below. Scrap paper lay scattered over the table, arrows and lines pointing to timelines, people, and places while he tried to discern some form of logic to tie it all together. He wanted more than anything else to be able to find a connection somewhere hidden within the books sitting in front of him. He wanted to be able to give the sarge something to go on, something that she could use. Finally, after three hours of constant scanning, he took a moment to run his fingers through his hair, leaned back in his chair, and looked at his watch, trying to clear his mind, just as his phone rang.

"O'Malley."

"Status report."

"Sarge, I have been over and over this stuff." He pulled two of the papers that were sitting off to the side and placed them in front of him, just below the two ledgers. "What I have been able to figure out so far is that some guy, I assume that he is the supplier called Mr. J., gets payment from Black and then directs him as to where to pick up the drugs, ammo, and weapons. Black then picks them up and delivers most of them to someone named Lucy, while the rest stays with him." He took a breath before continuing, wishing that he had more to tell her. "There are a whole bunch of alpha numeric codes here, but I haven't been able to make heads or tails of them either. On top of all that, twice a month, he drops off cash to some guy that he calls Lieutenant but makes no pickup. I think that this last one, Lieutenant, is a payoff, but I am not sure.

Things were starting to come together. "Good job. Keep working on it and see if there is anything else that you can find," the sarge said, and just as she was about to hang up, O'Malley spoke.

He had been flipping through the second ledger while the sarge was talking, and it was when he got to the last page that he found it. A picture of Lieutenant O'Brien and Sergeant Harris was tucked into a little cutout in the back of the book. It showed Black handing O'Brien an envelope with Harris standing by his side. They appeared to be at the docks at night during this little exchange, and it was easy to tell what was going on from the picture. Looks like Black wasn't taking any chances. "Sarge, we have a problem."

***

Alex listened intently as O'Malley relayed the information that he was able to discern from what he had found in the ledgers, but when he told her about the picture, everything fell into place.

Black was still sitting on the chair, staring blankly out at nothing. He was your typical gangbanger in his baggie red sweatshirt, jeans that were ten sizes too big, red sneakers, bad attitude, and misplaced loyalties. Antonelli was the designated questioner, so it was he and his voice that acted as the sole interrogator, while the others remained positioned around in a semicircle in front of Black. Antonelli had been going easy on him, following the same methods they had been trained in and asking him only who his supplier was over and over again. Black never once looked at him, answered him, or indicated that he was aware of his presence. He had the air of indifference, as if nothing in the world could bother him and no one would ever get to him.

They were out of time, and she had to do something about it, so after hanging up the phone, she went to her office, pulled out some additional supplies, made a phone call, and then returned to the main floor and to the rest of her team. As she approached Black, she listened as Antonelli asked him once again who his supplier was, and when Black remained silent, Master Sergeant Thomas drew her weapon, pointed it at Antonelli, and said, "You had three hours and failed." She shot him twice in the chest. Antonelli dropped where he stood without ever having been able to protest. She looked at James while wiping red droplets from her face. "Move him."

James stepped forward, grabbed the back of Antonelli's collar, dragged him over, and dropped him at the foot of the stairs.

She turned and put the barrel of the gun to Black's forehead. "When and where do you meet them? I am not playing games and I don't have time for your shit. Make a decision right now. I am not a cop, so I don't play by their rules and I could give two shits about dropping you right here right now…after I kill your brother. We cracked your ledger, and I am out of patience, so you had better start talking fast, you piece of shit."

Alex's voice was cold as ice, and as she spoke, the malice in her tone sent shivers up Jen's spine. *What is this woman capable of?* Maybe it was the ice in her voice, but Jen thought that more than anything else, it was the look in her eyes. Absolute nothingness. Her eyes lost all resemblance of ever having anything human in them; she looked like a wild and crazy animal about to feast on the prey that it has just cornered. She had become a monster.

She cocked back her weapon, tired of waiting. "Get his brother down here. He can watch him die first." As Miceli turned to head up the stairs, Black screamed.

"No, wait! I'll tell you everything I know. I ain't going down for those assholes! My bro has nothing to do with any of this, just leave him out of it. He's a good kid." For the first time that night, Black was realizing the enormity of the situation. Sweat covered his face instantly, and for the first time in as long as he could remember, he was scared.

The sarge put her weapon on safe and returned it to its holster without taking her eyes off him. "Tell me everything, or you and your brother die."

Black did as he was told.

Chapter 17

When Black was finally done telling all that he knew, the sarge looked at Douglas. "Take him upstairs and secure him and then get back down here."

As he was being led away, Black called out, "Leave my brother out of this. I told you what you wanted, now let him go! I said let him go!" His screams continued until he was back upstairs and secured in the office once again.

When Black and Douglas were finally out of hearing range, Antonelli got up and joined the team. "Are you okay?" the sarge asked.

"Yes, Sarge," he said, even though it felt like he had been hit square in the chest with a sledgehammer. *Simunition rounds hurt even with a vest on*, he thought to himself.

"Thank you for going along with that, and I am sorry that I couldn't give the rest of you a heads-up, but time was running short. Good job on keeping your positions," she said as a footnote. She wished that she could have warned them, but there was just no way to do it effectively. She flipped open her phone. "O'Malley, I need you down here now and bring what you have." She ended the call and walked toward the back of the building and out the back door as she punched in a new number.

The night was perfect, the moon was full, the breeze was light, and the air was fresh. Alex paced back and forth on the concrete walkway as the phone on the other line rang. She was furious, and it was time that she got answers. The only thing that she could think about was the fact that they were lucky tonight. She could have lost her entire team had Black known that they were coming. They had been set up from the beginning, and although she had a feeling from the start that there was more to this whole situation than what she was being told, she still felt betrayed.

Finally, an answer. "Master Sergeant Thomas, it is 0515 on a Sunday morning. This had better be good or your ass—"

"You set me and my team up, sir. I want to know what is really going on." Alex was clear and cool. She didn't care if he was a one-star general; she could have lost her team because of the lack of information that he had given her.

General Scott woke up instantly with her statement. "What have you found out?"

Alex relayed all the information that Black had given up, what O'Malley was able to find, and what she had been able to piece together.

"Master Sergeant Thomas, are you alone?"

"Yes, sir."

"Are you aware as to what percentages of damaged weapons are considered repairable?"

"Approximately two out of every three, sir," Alex said without even thinking about it. Hanscom is a top-notch repair facility, and everyone on the base was aware of the fact that seven out of every ten damaged weapons were sent there for repairs.

He took a deep breath, and as he walked into the kitchen to start a pot of coffee, he began, "I noticed Colonel Jacobson and Master Sergeant Pope assisting in the unloading of an aircraft one day when I flew into the base about twelve months ago unannounced, and I found it odd. I asked the loadmaster if this was a normal occurrence, Colonel Jacobson unloading an aircraft, and he told me that the colonel only showed up if the aircraft came from the AOR. The fact that a loadmaster, who was not stationed at the base, knew this about the colonel got me to wondering, why would a full bird colonel be unloading an aircraft, especially Colonel Jacobson of all people? Later that day, I made an inquiry as to the contents of the cargo that was being off-loaded. I was told that the cargo was damaged and destroyed weapons and the additional hardware that went with."

General Scott paused for a moment as he poured himself a cup and took a sip of his coffee, leaning against his breakfast bar and trying to decide how much more information he should give her.

Alex was pissed off, tired, and out of patience. Employing the last bit of restraint she had within herself, she took a calming breath before continuing. "Sir, with all due respect, I want and need it all. My team and I are going to find out what is going on one way or the other, but I don't want them going on with this assignment completely blind. They have trained hard for this, and every one of them is trustworthy and will follow orders without question, sir, but I respectfully request that you don't leave them in the dark when they don't have to be." She held her breath, knowing that it was entirely up to the general as to the amount of information he would allow them to have and knowing that no matter what he did or didn't tell them, they were going to have finish this.

"Approximately six months ago, I happened to be in the armory when an Airman Peters informed Sergeant O'Brien about having found excessive parts requests as well as inconsistencies in ammunition usage. Two days later, I saw him working the front gate. Finally, and this is how the BPD is connected, I received a phone call from the chief of police a month before you returned." He took a breath before continuing. "The chief and I served in Syria back when things were just getting bad, and we went through hell and back together. From what he told me, there was a drug bust that had gone bad, and as a result, there were several injured and two killed. The weapons used by the suspects were military stamped M-4s as well as the ammunition. He immediately ordered the investigation to be taken over by Internal Affairs and ordered all those involved to not talk about what was found or any details associated with the incident. However, two days later, it was reported that the weapons, four of them, and ammunition had been either misplaced or stolen from the evidence room. He also informed me that along with the weapons and ammo, four kilos of pure opium was found, and that, too, was gone. I went to meet him for lunch the following afternoon, wanting to talk in person, and as I was waiting in the parking lot for him to come out, I saw Sergeant O'Brien and Sergeant Harris walk into the building together, and that is when I made the tie-in. I put one and one together, talked to the chief about my theory, and together we decided that we needed verification so that the situation could be dealt with. The rest is just details."

Alex stood there, looking out at the ocean without actually seeing it and wondering how much time could have been saved had she had this information to begin with. She was furious at the thought of how much time had gone by since the general had begun to have suspicions as to what was going on.

"Master Sergeant Thomas." The general interrupted her silent contemplation on the timeline of events. "There is a reason for the information blackout that I imposed on you and your team."

"And that would be, sir?"

"Ultimately these individuals will be prosecuted by the court system. There needed to be a proper investigation that led you to where you are at, not speculation by myself and an outside agency who were sharing information that should never have been shared. I know how you are, Thomas. You are thorough and detail-oriented. I have never seen you do anything half-assed, and you are the only one whom I thought could actually get to this point, which is why I chose you." He was relieved that Thomas had gotten herself and her team to this point, and until now, he never realized how much he was counting on her to be able to do it. "Master Sergeant Thomas, I am going to send two Security Forces individuals to you from Otis AFB with at mobile vault. Secure all that you confiscated tonight in it, along with all of the applicable paperwork and then sign it over to them for transportation and holding at Otis until this is over so that the chain of evidence is not tainted. Before I call them, is there anything else that you are going to need?"

She thought about it for a minute before responding. "I need surveillance cameras and all associated equipment as well as additional ammunition, sir."

"I will have the Otis boys bring it with them. Is there anything else, Thomas?"

"Just one more thing, sir. I am going to need them to detain the individual that we were able to acquire the information from."

"Understood. They will pick him up when they bring the vault. Is that all?"

"Yes, sir. Thank you."

As she hung up the phone, she leaned her back against the cold bricks of the building, listening to the sound of the water lapping against the concrete ledge of the walkway, the screaming of the seagulls as they searched for food, and the horns of the boats as they came in and out of dock. Once she felt herself centered and in control again, she took one last look around at the water before turning back inside to prepare her team.

***

When the team was reassembled, they took off their masks and vests and stood in a semicircle around the tables, looking down at the weapons and ammo until the sarge returned. They were shocked and pissed off and, more than anything else, wanted heads to roll. Every one of them felt betrayed, and they wanted nothing more than to nail the sorry individuals that were behind all of this.

"I have had it with this bullshit," O'Malley said. "We need to get out of here and nail their asses to the wall. I mean, really, we have enough on them right now to do it, so what in the hell are we waiting for?"

"Man, I looked up to Sergeant Harris, that sorry son of a bitch! I want to be the one who takes his ass down," Antonelli chimed in.

"Guys, we need to be careful. I know that we are all pissed off and feel like we have been betrayed," James began.

"You think we haven't?" Douglas was dumbfounded.

"But…if we don't go after them the right way, all the I's dotted and the T's crossed, then they are going to get away with it all. Right now, all we have is the word of a gangbanger and a questionable picture, and we all know that isn't enough."

"James is right guys." Miceli chimed in "We are close but you all know that if anyone finds out that we are checking into one of our own, not only will we be hard pressed to prove what we found, but the blue line will close up around the two of them quicker than anything, and you know that once that happens, we won't be able to get close enough to them to even see the color of their hair. We have to play this right."

O'Malley looked around the group, sat on the corner of the table, and let out a sigh of frustration. "These two have friends everywhere. I hope that all of you realize that once this goes down, there are going to be people who will consider us rats. We are about to walk into the middle of a serious shit storm."

James looked at O'Malley and added, "Let's not forget the fact that there is the US military involved in this as well. You think that we will hit walls when we go after O'Brien and Harris on the cop side of things? Well, I can tell you this…the military has ways of hiding everything and anything when they think that it might look bad. This is not going to be easy."

There were nods of agreement from all around.

The sarge came in the back door, and as she approached, the team began. "I want everything that you can get me on Colonel Jacobson, Harris, and O'Brien. Pull property taxes, service records, properties owned, and pull all requested time off…leave chits. Set up an evidence board so that we can see what it is that we are looking at. I'll be back." As quick as she came in, the sarge was gone.

Antonelli looked around at the team. "Hey guys, how are we going to get information on them when it comes to the military side of the house?"

"I think that is what she is going for now," Miceli said, concern flooding her face.

***

Five hours later, Sergeant Thomas walked back into the warehouse carrying a manila envelope. The Security Forces team had picked up all of the evidence that was collected as well as Black, dropped off the surveillance equipment that had been requested, and were en route to Otis Air Force Base.

"What do you have?"

Douglas looked over from the evidence board.

"Sarge, I pulled everything that I could, and this is what we were able to find. Colonel Jacobson has an old farm house in Concord out in the middle of nowhere, but that was all I could find on him. Lieutenant O'Brien has been with the Boston PD for twelve years and Sergeant Harris ten years respectively. Both have impeccable records as well as various citations that they have earned throughout their careers. I dug into their financial records, and there are no red flags. In fact, everything looks perfectly normal, nothing indicating any type of illegal activities anywhere. They both rent apartments in Quincy, and neither one of them own land or property anywhere. Other than the fact that they are both BPD cops, they never worked in the same division or precinct. The only tie the two of them have to each other is that they were both assigned to the 557th military police squadron out of Hanscom AFB. I wasn't able to get anything on their military service..."

She dropped an envelope on the table in front of Douglas. "I did."

Douglas opened the envelope while the sarge took a step back as he skimmed over the papers that he pulled out and then handed them off to Antonelli to be placed on the evidence board. Finally, when the last of the papers had been added to the board, they all stood around looking at it, trying to put the whole story together from all of the bits and pieces of information that they had managed to gather together. Finally Miceli spoke up. "Sarge, would you walk us through what we have here, please?"

Just then, Alex's phone rang. "Thomas." Her posture stiffened, and for just a moment, her eyes flashed over to Jen. She turned her back and walked a few feet away while the team stared after her.

Although the conversation lasted less than a couple of minutes, the team picked up on every movement the sarge made from the stiffness in her posture to the hand brushing through her hair to the sudden stillness, and they knew that it could only mean one thing: bad news.

Closing her phone, she had to take a moment to collect herself before turning and facing the group. *Hold it together, Alex.*

"There was an interdepartmental joint takedown planned last night at the docks with the fourth, fifth, and eighth precincts." She had their complete attention. "They were going in on an anonymous tip that said there was to be a massive drug deal playing out, and it looks like someone tipped off the dealers because they were able to get away before it actually went down but not before a firefight ensued."

"What happened?" Douglas asked, his voice shaking while he leaned against the table.

"They shot and killed one suspect."

"What else, Sarge?" James asked this time.

"Officer Thomas Amos was shot and killed at the scene, and four other officers are currently at Boston General, all with gunshot wounds." A rogue tear slid down Alex's cheek.

Seeing the hurt on Alex's face, Jen knew instantly. "Oh god, not Tina?"

"Why did they call you?" O'Malley asked at the same time.

"I was notified because I am listed as her emergency contact and as her next of kin." She looked at the rest of the team before continuing as she absently wiped the rogue tear from her cheek. "Officers Michael Williams, Alicia Gomez, Tina Savage, and Christopher Lee are all in surgery, no status yet. I need to go to the hospital…"

Every one of them had begun to pack up their gear before she had a chance to complete her sentence. Douglas stated that he would bring the van around, and before she knew what had happened, Alex and the rest of the team were on their way to Boston General.

***

Not a word was spoken during the short drive to Boston General. When they pulled around back to the emergency entrance of the hospital, the sight was unnerving. With the threat of a thunderstorm looming overhead, the lights flashing from ambulances, fire trucks, and police cars added to the sense of foreboding. If there was one constant in life, it was that when an officer is wounded or killed, the blue line shows up in force and nothing will stop them from seeking out justice or providing a display of unity. There was every news agency in the Boston area camped out in the parking lot and along the emergency entrance to the building, waiting for updated information about the wounded officers and reporting on the fallen. As the team filed out of the van and walked to the emergency room door, they were met by the chief of police.

"Sir, what happened?" Antonelli asked, concern and fear shadowing his eyes.

"I will bring you up to speed in the conference room inside. Sergeant Harris from IA is heading the investigation and is waiting for us. Follow me." The chief turned and walked through the doors, but the team did not follow.

The sarge looked at all of them. "Say nothing, give nothing up, and follow my lead, understood?"

Tension, anger, fury, and rage radiated from each one of them, but they all knew that what the sarge said was right. They needed answers and the only way to get them was through Sergeant Harris, the man they all knew was a traitor.

"James, with me, please," she said as she walked back toward the van. When James joined her, the two of them spoke only for a moment before she walked back to join the rest of the team.

"James will be back in a minute. In the meantime, just stand by here for him."

Although James was gone for no more than two minutes, to the team it seemed like an eternity. When he finally rejoined them, they followed the sarge's lead and went into the hospital and right into every officer's worst nightmare.

The emergency room and halls were packed with firefighters, paramedics, nurses running back and forth, and police officers from all over the Boston area. As they walked through the hall, each one of the officers they passed gave them small nods or disparaging looks; absolute fear had gripped them all.

"Jen!"

Jen turned just in time to see Melissa come running to her.

"Oh god, Jen, oh god, I don't know what happened. They said he was shot, but they won't tell me anything else."

It was then that the enormity of the situation hit. Up until that point, she was in a daze; everything around her had seemed surreal, and she felt like an observer. The moment she saw Melissa holding Megan, Jen realized that that beautiful child, her goddaughter, might never see her father again or know what a wonderful and good man he was. Jen was paralyzed, gripped with a fear that she hadn't felt since she had received the call seven years ago telling her that she had lost Emily.

"Melissa?" James said from beside her.

"James? I don't know what's going on. They won't tell me anything!"

Leaning down, he put his hands on Melissa's shoulders, trying to calm and steady her. "We are going to nail the bastards that did this, but right now, you need to calm down. The best doctors in Boston are with him, and he is a strong man, so the best thing that you can do right now is to calm down and pray. We need to get brought up to speed, but then we will be back, okay?"

Tears were cascading down her cheeks, but finally she looked up at James and his dark brown eyes and said in a whisper, "I can't live without him, James" She looked down at Megan. "She needs her father."

"I know." He turned and took Jen by the arm and continued down the hall with the rest of the team.

The conference room was surrounded in dark wood paneling, generic pictures hung at regular intervals, thread bare burgundy carpet, oval oak table, and black leather chairs. On the wall to the right of the door stood a bookcase filled with medical journals and reference books, and standing in front of it was Sergeant Harris, looking solid with his best professional face on.

As they filed in and each took their seats, Harris remained where he was, trying to figure out what in the hell was going on. The chief had requested that he come here and fill him in on what they had so far, but there was no reason for the sarge and her team to be here. "Chief, this briefing is sensitive. No one is supposed to know the details of the investigation except IA and yourself."

Sitting at the head of the table, the chief sat ramrod straight in his chair. "Sergeant Harris, this team is being established and trained to act as IA's foot soldiers. They will go in and do the dirty work conducting stakeouts, searches, and making arrests for whatever and whenever your investigations deem necessary. Although their training won't be complete for another two weeks, I think that it is time they get brought up to speed."

No one on the team moved; they all saw what the chief was trying to do.

Sergeant Harris walked to the opposite end of the table from the chief, the slightest signs of concern flashing across his face. "Chief, this is highly unorthodox. I don't know…"

The chief stood up so fast that his chair went flying backward. "I don't give a flying rat's ass as to what you think or know about your fellow officers here. We have officers upstairs right now fighting for their lives, and the bastards who put them in here are probably celebrating out there on the street! Now either you give me the briefing I requested or turn in your goddamned badge and send me someone to me who will!"

Harris stood stock-still for a moment, looked over the assembled group, and began his briefing. "Yes, sir, I apologize. What we know so far is this. At 0100, undercover officers with the eighth precinct's narcotics division were supposed to buy a kilo of opium from Darius Riddick, aka Puma, a one-star general in the Prospect Street Bloods and his main supplier. Approximately twenty patrol officers were standing by in an abandoned warehouse at pier 29, waiting for confirmation of the exchange, at which time they were to surround the individuals and apprehend them as well as the opium. Puma and his supplier never showed, however. At 0115, the officers who had been waiting in the warehouse came under fire. It is obvious that the suspects were tipped off, so the question is, who tipped them off. We have no leads as of yet. However, all available officers are canvassing the area and all possible informants are being questioned."

When it was clear that Harris had completed his briefing, the chief looked at him. "And?"

"And what, sir? Unfortunately that is all the information that we have so far."

"Have you recovered any shell casings yet?"

"Yes, sir, but I think that—"

"Do you have any of the crime scene photos?"

"Yes, sir, but—"

"What part of bring them up to speed do you not understand?"

"Sir, are you sure?"

"Now, Sergeant Harris. Waste any more of my time on this, and I will relieve you of your duties."

"Yes, Chief." Harris paused, looking the team over before proceeding. The fact that the sarge was here was unnerving. She was smart and knew how to put things together. He just hoped that this small bit of information wouldn't set her into motion. He pulled his laptop out of its bag, inserted a SIM card into a slot on the side, and turned the monitor so everyone could see the crime scene photos as he talked his way through the slides. "We recovered .556mm casings and we are assuming that they were fired from M-4 rifles, but it will take time to verify." As he spoke, pictures of shell casings individually tagged showed on the monitor as well as pools of blood from where the officers had fallen. "This is not the first time shells from this caliber weapon have been found, and there is currently an open investigation as to the whereabouts of these weapons, but so far nothing has come up."

Harris clicked through the photos of the casings and warehouse interior at a relatively fast speed, but when pictures of the outside came up, Sarge quickly spoke and, with an almost imperceptible movement from her eyes, got the team's attention. All eyes memorized the computer screen before Harris could close the lid.

"Sergeant Harris"—Alex leaned forward, her arms resting on the table—"would you like for me to see if I might be able to link the casings to a weapon from our data base at the base?"

"Not as of yet, Sergeant Thomas, though I do appreciate it. We believe that the weapons used may have been purchased from a local gun show using an alias." *Shit!*

With a detached indifference, she shrugged her shoulders. "The offer remains open should you change your mind. If there is nothing else, and with your permission, Chief, I would like to check on the status of the officers and then get back to work. I understand that you wanted them briefed in on the case. However, their training is not complete yet, and we have a long week ahead of us."

The chief began, "If any of you need time off, I will understand and—"

Alex stood up. "Not possible, Chief. They have training to do, and I am running out of time. As you are well aware, my orders for this training end in two weeks, and if I am going to get your people where they need to be, I will need every bit of the time that I have left. If they take time off, I will be forced to remove them from the program." She looked at her team. "Time to go. You have four hours to do what you need to do, and then it is back to work." Alex walked out without looking back.

They waited in the family waiting room for the doctors to come and let them know the status of their friends and loved ones. The room was filled with the wounded officers' families who were huddling close to each other, some in shock while others silently crying. Antonelli, O'Malley, and Douglas sat in the far corner of the room like statues, occasionally getting up to bring coffee or whatever food they could scrounge from the vending machines while they waited for what seemed like forever. James sat next to Melissa, quietly talking and reassuring her as she rested her head on his shoulder, while Jen paced back and forth, gently rocking Megan in her arms and telling her that her daddy would be all right. Alex sat alone in a chair next to the door. Her face was shut down, void of all emotions, but inside she felt as if she was dying. Tina was her only family and everything in the world to her; if she lost her, she didn't know what she would do.

Over the next hour, three different doctors came in—the first to inform Mrs. Williams that her son was pronounced dead at 1257, the second to inform Jonathan Gomez that his wife, Alicia, made it through surgery but was in critical care and they were only giving her a 50/50 chance of survival, and the last to inform Mrs. Lee that her husband, Christopher, received a gunshot wound to the left shoulder and lost a considerable amount of blood but should make a full recovery.

Half an hour later, Melissa, still shaking but relieved, left to bring Megan to her mother's house, leaving Jen sitting in a chair beside Chris in his room. "The doctors said that you are going to be fine Chris." Jen said while looking at him. He was ghost white with wires and tubes hooked up all over his body monitoring him as he slept. She needed to talk, or the fear from the night would take over. "Why were you there? Why didn't you tell me you were going to be there, and why in the hell did you have to get shot?"

"I didn't mean to," he whispered as he slowly began to open his eyes. "Damn, I feel like I got run over by a truck."

"You think you are hurting now? Just wait until Melissa gets back. You have some serious ass kissing to do, my friend."

"Oh hell," he groaned as he turned to look at Jen.

Jen leaned in closer to Chris. He looked like he was an inch from death. "You look like shit."

"Thanks for the reassurance, partner."

Standing up, Jen took Chris's hand; hearing him talk had made her feel so much better. "Chris, did you see anything? Do you know what happened?"

He tried to sit himself up, but the moment he tried to move his arm, he felt like a red-hot knife had been jabbed into his shoulder and was slowly being twisted. His head snapped back, and he hissed in pain.

Putting her hand on his good shoulder, Jen held him where he was. "Buddy, you took one to the shoulder, so I wouldn't recommend moving all that much just yet. Chris, I need to know if you saw anything."

"It was dark in there. All I saw was the flash from the barrels when they shot at us. Everyone hit the deck or looked for cover and started to return fire, but by then, I had already been hit. All I know is that it was loud and confusing."

"You didn't see any faces?"

"No, but I will say this, the guns they used on us had to have been modified to automatics because whatever it was that they were shooting at us with, they unloaded a lot of ammo. They had to be waiting for us because I never heard them come in. I mean seriously, Jen, how could they have known that we would be in there and waiting?"

I'll tell you how, Harris and O'Brien set you guys up. "I don't know, partner, but I will find out." She looked him right in the eyes and squeezed his hand to drive her point home.

Chris's eyes widened. "You know who it was, don't you?"

"What? No, Chris, how could I know that? I was out on a training op of my own."

As much pain as he was in and still feeling the effects of the anesthesia, his eyes were still full of an intensity that bore a hole into Jen. "You know, Jen, don't lie to me. You never could keep shit from me. Who was it? Did you nail them yet? What's going to happen now?"

"Chris, stop. I don't know…"

"Tell him."

Jen turned to see Alex framed in the door to the room. She stepped in, closing the door behind her, and stopped on the opposite side of the bed from Jen.

"But I thought…"

"Chris, Jen has been investigating the whereabouts of missing weapons for the past couple of weeks. Tonight we finally caught a break on the location of said weapons and were about to start conducting recon when we were informed of what happened, so naturally we came here right away. We are close to nailing the bastards."

He looked back and forth between the two women who stood flanking his bed. "This is going to be bad, isn't it?" he asked Alex.

"Yeah, it is, but we are going to get them." The way she stood and the cold surety in her voice left no room for doubt.

Chris took a moment to clear the fog in his head and collect his thoughts before asking his next question. "I heard about everyone except for Tina. How is she?"

Alex had just come from Tina's room. The bullet hit her in the head just above her temple and followed along the outside of her skull before exiting out the back. She had a severe skull fracture and concussion; unfortunately she went into shock at the scene, and as a result, she slipped into a coma. The doctors said that she could wake up in an hour or never. Looking down at Tina, the only person that Alex considered to be family, was more painful than any physical pain she had ever felt in her life. Her hair was crusted with blood, and she had a broken nose from when she fell. Where the doctors had shaved the areas at the entrance and exit points were the stitches, standing out as if accusing her for her inability to protect her friend. "She is in a coma, but the doctors are optimistic. She will be fine."

Not completely believing Alex, Chris turned and looked at Jen. "Jen, watch yourself with these guys. They know what they are doing. I don't want to see you in the bed next to me, you got it?"

"They aren't the only ones who know what they are doing, Chris. I'll come around and check on you later, okay?" She leaned down and gave him a kiss on the cheek and then walked out the door with nothing but payback on her mind.

As Alex made to follow Jen out of the room, Chris grabbed her arm. "Don't let her do anything stupid, okay? She can put up a good front, but don't believe it. I don't want her in here next to me or worse. Got it?"

She took one appraising look at him before answering.

"Got it."

***

When Harris was finally back in his car, he flipped open his phone and called Colonel Jacobson. "Sir, I think that we might have a problem."

"What happened?"

Harris told the colonel about what had happened at the docks and finished with his conversation with the chief and Master Sergeant Thomas's team. "Sir, what if she figures it out?"

Colonel Jacobson paused for a moment, thinking through the information that Harris had just relayed to him. "I don't think that there are going to be any problems. Harris, think about it, when Thomas has a feeling about something or someone, she doesn't stall or delay. She goes right in and handles the situation. When something strikes her as odd, she questions all aspects of whatever it is that is bothering her until she is satisfied. It's in her nature. She can't let anything go until she has satisfied all probabilities. She obviously found nothing questionable and is too preoccupied with training her team to care about what is going on with the BPD."

"Sir, I would have questioned it."

"We are not talking about you, Harris. We are talking about Thomas here, and I am telling you now she doesn't suspect a thing. Now go do whatever it is that you are supposed to be doing, and I will see you on Tuesday." Jacobson hung up the phone and laughed. "And they said that she was the best."

***

No one spoke until they were back in the warehouse.

"Well, at least we know who Lucy is now," O'Malley said as he sat down next to the evidence board and opened his computer, the rest of the team right behind him. He began a search on the cargo ship named Lucy, the ship that they had seen in the background of the pictures Harris took from the docks, with the rest of the team packed in tight behind him, watching everything that he was doing. Finally, after an hour, O'Malley turned around and looked at the sarge.

Taking a deep breath, he began, "Sarge, the *Lucy* is a cargo ship that primarily travels up and down the East Coast, delivering freight to different ports. I tracked down the ship's manifest and found that Boston, for this trip, is the first port of dock, meaning that it was empty when it arrived. It is currently being loaded up for follow-on destinations of New York City and then Miami. The alpha numeric codes that were found in the logs we confiscated were actually two container identifiers that are scheduled to be delivered to New York.

The containers are supposed to be carrying coffee and scrap metal respectively. It was due to sail out tomorrow at 1200. However, it looks like there is an engine problem with the ship and will be stuck here until a week from Wednesday because they have to wait on a couple of parts to fix the problem."

Antonelli looked at the sarge, absolute malice in his eyes. "Sarge, I say we go hit them where it hurts. Let's get the stuff off that ship."

"No." Looking at the team, she knew immediately that it would be a suicide mission. "Not one of you has been to sleep in over twenty-four hours. Every one of you has been pushed to your limits, and as it stands now, any operation that we attempted would fail. I want each one of you to go home and get some sleep. Do not go for a drink, do not call your friends or family, and do not stop to check up on anyone." At the first sign of protest, she held up her hand. "I know how you all feel. Believe me I do, but at this point, we are all useless. We need to recoup and process the past few days' events if we are going to have any chance at doing this right. We are not after the pawns in this. We are after the ring leaders, and I guarantee that they are going to be well rested and ready to play. We will meet back here at 0600 on Tuesday morning to go over what is next, and in case you don't know, it is Sunday, so that means stay home tomorrow, sleep in, watch TV, eat, talk to your spouses, and do anything, but think about this. I know I am asking for a lot, but trust me, I know what I am talking about."

It wasn't until the sarge started talking about sleeping and rest that every member of her team started to really feel the fatigue set in. It was as if a wave was crashing over them and washing away what little energy they had left. By the time the sarge had finished speaking, they were all either sitting on the table or leaning against each other. Although none of them wanted to admit defeat, they all realized how right the sarge was and, one by one, started to head out.

Just as James reached the door, he stopped and looked back to see Miceli talking to the sarge. Knowing how the sarge was, James knew that Miceli was probably trying to get her to leave, too, instead of staying behind and coming up with a plan. It was obvious to James that Miceli and the sarge had some type of romantic relationship, and he hoped that it was strong enough to offer the support that the sarge was going to need. "Miceli, get the sarge out of here and make her take her own advice, please."

Alex looked up at James and then to Jen before finally giving in to the both of them. Smiling, she watched James leave and then took Jen's hand in her own and left. Where they were going, she didn't know, but so long as Jen was there with her, nothing mattered except crawling into the bed and holding each other.

***

Tuesday, 0600

Alex stood on the catwalk, watching her team sort through and place all of the information that had been gathered onto the board and around the table in a way that would allow them to tie in all aspects of the investigation. They started to arrive shortly after five, and by five fifteen, they were all there and discussing all of the little bits and pieces of the investigation and trying to see how it all tied in. When they got to the information from manila envelope that she had brought, just before getting the phone call from the chief of police, it was obvious that James was the only one who understood how to read the contents properly. After reviewing each page that he had previously pulled off the board, he would hand it to one of the others to be placed as he directed.

They all looked like hell, and although she knew that they did not get much sleep, she felt better knowing that they were capable of focusing on the task at hand and not on vengeance. She herself did not sleep more than a couple of hours. She spent her day off pacing back and forth, waiting for some kind of news from the hospital, and finally at 3:00 p.m., she gave up waiting and called. All the nurse in the ICU would tell her was that Tina's vitals were strong but ultimately no change and to be patient. Several hours later, Jen was finally able to convince her to go to bed, and when Alex felt Jen's arms wrap around her, she finally gave in to the exhaustion.

She came down the stairs and joined her team at the situation table as she called it. "Okay, although I know that Officer James has probably informed you as to the information that I was able to dig up, I am going to recap. Lieutenant O'Brien and Sergeant Harris deployed with the colonel seven years ago when the colonel was still attached to the 192nd Military Police Squadron out of Langley Virginia. They served a year together in Iraq, and two years later, Colonel Jacobson was transferred and assigned to be the Deputy Commander of the 557th Military Police Squadron at Hanscom AFB and last year, he was promoted to commander. He must be pulling some serious strings because officers never stay at any one base this long. I went through the manning documents and bumped them with the deployment from seven years ago, and twelve names repeatedly came up. I then looked at all subsequent deployments and found that six out of the original twelve names, including Lieutenant O'Brien and Sergeant Harris, popped up, but what was unusual was that they all deployed at times when they were not scheduled to be rotated. Now out of the six, one is always deployed. Three years ago, the armory began ordering increased numbers of parts for weapon repairs, butt stocks, firing pins, barrels, etc. And a steady rise since, not enough to raise any red flags to outside agencies but enough so that someone at the base should have questioned. Unknown fact, forty percent of all weapons damaged or destroyed overseas go to Hanscom for repair or destruction. Out of those, one out of every three are currently being destroyed. However, that doesn't add up when you consider the amount of repair parts that are being ordered.

"In addition, the Air Force authorizes nine hundred rounds per person for training and qualifications. Airman Peters, the one that was standing gate guard duty, used to work in the armory until the day his inventory report showed a shortage of ammunition. He forwarded it up the chain of command, and the next day, he was working the gates. That was a year ago, and at the time, his superior was your Lieutenant O'Brien. I called Airman Peters after finding out all of this, and he informed me that on average, only two hundred to four hundred rounds of ammunition are typically used for each training session, but according to his numbers, every round of the nine hundred allotted had been used. Williams and Miller have been working flight line duty and have since informed me that the colonel personally signs for specific cargo off specific flights, namely flights from Afghanistan. Looking at the manifest, I backtracked the cargo to determine who the senders were for the past four years. Every crate that the colonel signed for was sent from one of the six individuals that I mentioned earlier."

James looked confused. "Wait a minute, Sarge, how was the colonel working with them? I mean the colonel is active duty and they are guardsmen?

"Guardsmen do deploy with their own units, but they can also be used as backfill for the active duty components. They fill in when active duty has holes due to shortages on the manning document, medical issues that prevent a member from deploying, or any number of other scenarios. As it stands, since the colonel is commander of the active duty component and although the guard has its own chain of command, the colonel can pull, or to be more politically correct, request backfill from the guard. The guard component is only at the base one weekend a month and two weeks a year, and although they have full-time members, their commander is not one of them, so he has no problem with Colonel Jacobson handing out base assignments."

Miceli was flabbergasted. "Wait a minute here, Sarge, let me see if I have this right. For years, Colonel Jacobson has had these six guys"—she held up the paper with the names on it—"sending weapons from Iraq and Afghanistan that had been tagged as destroyed, but in reality, he and his crew were fixing them and selling them to the highest gangbanger drug dealer that came along? I mean, really, how can an operation like this slip through the cracks without anyone noticing?"

With the slightest hint of a smile, the sarge answered, "There are ways around everything, and who really watches the police? Think about it. They have kept this little operation small and within themselves. People do what they can to avoid the colonel. O'Brien is the only one who knows what happens to the weapons, and Harris and O'Brien have the means to push the sales on the street and to cover it up if needed, but you forgot one other aspect of this whole situation." She paused and looked around the group positioned in front of her. "The drugs. Afghanistan is overflowing with opium."

"So the drugs and weapons are smuggled into the country on military aircraft, pushed through the armory, and sold to the local gangbangers who then ship them off to New York and to who?" Douglas asked.

O'Malley was first to answer. "The Bloods. It was the Blood gangs from New York that set up the sects up here. They keep in contact and sell guns, ammo, and drugs to each other. Narcotics said that there has been a major upsurge of opium-based drugs being circulated on the streets both here and in New York."

"So why hasn't anyone picked up on the weapons then? You know how the gangs are. If they have guns, they are going to use them," Antonelli chimed in.

"Who says that they haven't? Think about it for a minute, do you really think that people don't get paid off, blackmailed, or killed when people get on their trail?" Alex knew as soon as she said it just how right she was. "So here is the question, where are they keeping all of the guns, ammo, and drugs while they are waiting for the next sale because they can't keep all of that in the armory without someone noticing?"

"Sarge, I think we will be finding that out sooner rather than later," James said. "I know that you said to rest and take the day off, but I just couldn't, so I went down to the docks. By the time I got there, the majority of everyone had gone, but I did run into one of my buddies from the range that is now one of the uniforms guarding the crime scene. While I was talking to him, I realized that the cargo ship *Lucy* was still there and that there was a container still waiting to be loaded right where the exchange was supposed to have been made, so I took a peek inside." He paused long enough to pull photographs out of his bag before continuing. "It was a scrap metal container, and as I walked through, I noticed that there were spaces, little holes if you will, between the metals that had been separated out. Just big enough to slide a gun into, and to add to that, on top of each bale of metal was a loose round piece of scrap just big enough to cover over the spaces and hide the holes. This morning, I was able to confirm that the shipping container that I was looking in had the same shipping label as the one in the logbook, and if the second container is transporting coffee, then my bet is that the opium is being sent in that one because coffee hides the scent, for the most part, from the drug-sniffing dogs. My point is that the weapons were never delivered, and my guess is that the same can be said for the drugs, so someone still has them, and I doubt if they are going to sit on them for too long. We have GPS trackers on both Harris and O'Brien's cars, so I say let's see where they have gone and do go."

"Is that what you were doing when we were waiting for you at the hospital, putting the tracker on Harris's car?" Miceli asked.

"Yeah, the sarge had me tag his vehicle as soon as she realized that he was there and that he was the one investigating the crime scene."

Clearly happy, O'Malley clapped his hands together. "Way to go, Sarge! Let's find out where they have been." With that, O'Malley turned, sat in front of his laptop, and started pulling up the information that would tell the team where O'Brien and Harris have been since the GPSs had been installed.

"Let's be clear about a few things before any of you get going on anything else," the sarge said to the team. This is the point where even the slightest mistake could end in disaster, and she wanted to make sure that nothing was overlooked. "First, let's be clear on the primary players and their state of mind. The point man in the gang will be easy to take down at a later time, so let's not concentrate on dealing with him just yet. However, I do want his name and all information that we can get on him and his most trusted associates. In the event that they show up or we have to deal with them, I don't want any surprises. Second, our primary targets are going to be Colonel Jacobson, Harris, and O'Brien. Harris and O'Brien are tied in not only to the military side but to the PD side of the house as well. We can assume that they are using their departmental resources as well as their street contacts to keep an eye out for anything that seems out of the ordinary. That being said, we need to assume that we are now being watched. With the chief insisting that Harris brief us, he now knows that we are in the loop, and Harris knows that he gave out a lot of information to us. I can guarantee you that he called the colonel and probably O'Brien as well and informed them as to what information he had to feed us. Colonel Jacobson is about power, and at this point, he has convinced himself that nothing can touch him, but that doesn't mean that he will take any unnecessary chances. Finally, you need to understand that the three of them together have unlimited resources and, if caught, stand to lose everything. When the time comes to take them down, they will do anything, and I do mean anything, to avoid being arrested. The risk here is not finding the drugs and weapons. It's going against people who will do *anything* to keep from being caught."

"Sarge."

"Yes, O'Malley?"

"If we have Black and he is the courier, don't you think that it will send out a red flag?"

Not a hundred percent sure of what she was going to say, Miceli interjected, "Well, maybe we can use him."

O'Malley was right, keeping Black in custody would send up warnings to anyone watching. "Use him how?" the sarge asked, curious as to where she was going with this.

Doing what she does best, Miceli started talking, shooting from the hip as she so often was told she did. "Well, Sarge, if there is one thing that holds true, it's that there is no honor among thieves. This whole operation could be damaging to a lot of people, both civilian and military. When we brought up his brother to Black, he spilled everything. He would have done anything that we asked so long as his brother didn't get hurt, right?"

The sarge was trying to see where she was going with this but couldn't. "Right."

Gaining momentum, she continued, "So let's use our resources. We have a chief of police and a general that we might be able to use to get something that Black wants. He cares about his brother more than anything else, so let's use him as a bargaining chip. Let's see if our bosses can get the US marshals to offer witness protection for the both of them in return for Black's cooperation. We get him to do the pickup, like we know he will have to and testify against the Bloods on everything that happened, and in return, he and his brother get a fresh start, new identities, and everything."

Shaking her head, the sarge looked at Miceli and the team. "As much sense as that makes, I don't think that they would go for it. If you remember correctly, they wanted to keep all of this hush-hush. Involving the marshals would blow everything out into the open, and testifying against the Bloods would mean court and media. That is opposite of what our mission is and what they want."

Everyone stood still for a moment, looking at both sides and trying to come up with a solution to the pending problem of Black. Finally Antonelli stepped forward. "Actually, Sarge, this might work to everyone's benefit. It's true that no one wants the embarrassment of the situation being made public knowledge, but if we look at the big picture, this could make the chief and the general look like heroes."

"How do you figure that, Antonelli?"

"Well, with the government trying to crack down on gangs and corruption, the laws have changed, and with the introduction of the Patriot Act, wide-scale arrests and detentions are now possible. Anyone having knowledge of and/or partaking in the illegal activities of an organization can be grouped and detained under the Patriot Act. According to the provisions, any activities that are 'dangerous to human life that are a violation of the criminal laws of the United States or of any State' and are intended to 'intimidate or coerce a civilian population' is punishable under the Act. We can take a lot of people down in one move if we do it right, Sarge."

"I'll think about it. In the meantime, O'Malley, get me what you can on the top Blood members from Black's sect and the GPS records of Harris and O'Brien's movements. Antonelli, help him with that. Miceli and Douglas, put all this information the sarge motioned over the top of the desk and toward the board in order. Get another board if you have to, but start it from the first deployment seven years ago, showing how everyone and everything ties in. In addition to that, make sure that you include the shooting from the other night." It did not escape her observation how the entire team both flinched and stiffened with her last comment. "I want pictures and hard facts and finally I want to know what is on that board that we won't be able to use if this does, in fact, go to court. Not everything that we have done was exactly 'legal,' so you need to take that into consideration as well." She looked at her watch, 0730. They were all itching to get started but were waiting for her say so, which means that she still had some sort of positive control over them. "James, come with me, please. The rest of you get to work." When she turned her back to them and walked away, she could hear the rapid ticking of keys on the keyboard, the shuffling of papers, and James right on her heel.

***

Before they could reach the stairs, Alex's phone rang. Flipping it open as she walked, she answered, "Thomas." She only took two more steps before stopping dead in her tracks. "I'll be right there." She turned to James, confusion filling her face for a split second before regaining her composure. "That was the hospital. They said that I should get over there now, but they wouldn't tell me anything more. If you don't mind, we can talk on the way to the hospital."

As much as the sarge tried to hide it, James saw the fear in her eyes. "Would it be okay if I drive?"

With a nod, they left the warehouse without speaking another word until James had put his Ford Taurus in drive and pulled out of the parking lot. "James, you have worked both the military side and police side of things. You know how the politics work and the roadblocks we might hit, but that's neither here nor there. Fact is that neither the chief nor the general will want to go along with what the team wants to do, so I want to put that aside for now."

James was shocked. "So you are saying that you are not even going to present it as an option?"

She stared intently out of the front window but didn't register anything she was seeing. "Let's stay on point here. My concern is that everyone wants payback, and that is dangerous. I don't want anyone taking any unnecessary risks, going off half-cocked or trying to take justice into their own hands when things go down. I hope that they all will be able to do their jobs, but I refuse to not be prepared for the possibility of it happening. I need you to help me watch them, and if you think that any one of them might be a risk I want to know immediately."

James thought a minute before forming his response and decided for the direct approach. "Does that include you, Sarge?"

That snapped her out of her zone; she turned and looked at James for the first time since leaving the warehouse, but before snapping at him and putting him in his place like she wanted to, she took an internal step back. She knew that James would do the right thing whether she asked him to or not, and for him to say what he just did reaffirmed her initial opinion of the man. Slowly she turned her head to look out the window again before replying. "I won't do anything stupid, but yes."

James nodded his head, knowing that there really was nothing more to talk about. When they finally reached Boston General, he pulled into a spot close to the visitors' entrance and told the sarge that he would wait for her in the car, but if she heard him, he did not know because before the last words were out of his mouth, she had already slammed the door and was sprinting through the entrance. "Good luck," he said to her retreating form.

By the time Alex got to Tina's room, she was covered in sweat and tearing each breath from her chest. She had run from James's car through half of the first floor of the hospital and up six flights of stairs because the thought of waiting on an elevator was more than she could handle. She came to a screeching halt just inside the door of Tina's room. She didn't know what she had been expecting, but it wasn't this. There in front of her was Tina, sitting up with a pillow propped up behind her, television on, and talking with a nurse.

When Tina looked past the nurse and saw Alex standing just inside of the doorway, fear engulfed her. The look on her face, her pale complication, heavy breathing, and being covered in sweat made her fear for the worst. "Oh my god, Alex, what's wrong? What happened? Are you all right?"

In three steps, Alex had crossed the room and was standing beside the bed. Tears filled her eyes as relief flowed through her.

"Everything is fine, sweetie," she said as she wiped away the falling tears from her cheeks. "How are you feeling?"

"I have a splitting headache, but other than that, I feel fine."

The nurse smiled at both of them, turned to check the IV bags hanging on the pole next to the bed, and then quickly and silently left. As the door closed behind her, Tina whispered, "Do you think I could get her to go out on a date with me?"

"Are you serious? Tina, you got shot in the head. You almost died and you just woke up from a coma and you want to go out on a date?"

"Well, why not? After all, I didn't die and a girl does have needs," she said with a sly smile on her face.

The emotional and mental rollercoaster that she had been riding for the past few days had taken its toll, and she didn't have it in her to laugh. Alex took Tina's hand. "T, I am so sorry. It's all my fault. If I was just a little faster, you wouldn't be in here."

"Alex, you have nothing to do with this. It was a drug bust gone bad, that's all. There is no way you could have known or stopped it from happening. Just like always, they knew we were there, and because of that, they were able to get the drop on us."

Alex began to shake. She was staring down and looking at Tina's hand in hers and realizing just how close she had come to losing her. Rage was beginning to take over. Watching all of it unfold in front of her, Tina slowly began to get scared for her friend. "Alex, what's going on?"

When Alex finally looked up, the look on her face was nothing less than pure unadulterated rage. "I am going to nail their asses to the wall."

"You know who did it." It was a statement, not a question. "Have they caught the assholes yet? What are they going to do?"

"Yes, I know who did it, and no, the department isn't looking for them. Like I said, I am going to nail their asses."

Tina had never seen Alex like this before, and for the first time, she was almost afraid of her friend. At this point, Alex was capable of anything, of that she had no doubt. "This is what you have been doing, isn't it? You know who did it because it has something to do with your current assignment, doesn't it?" When she got no response, Tina grabbed Alex's face in her hands and, fighting the wave of dizziness that suddenly threatened to overtake her, tried to get through to her friend. "Alex, I want those bastards just as bad as you do, maybe even more, but you have to keep your head on. I want those assholes behind bars for the rest of their lives, living in a cell with a big guy named Bubba for a cellmate. The best punishment they can get is losing their freedom and knowing that for the rest of their pathetic lives we won, not them. We have to do this right."

Alex all but screamed, "We nothing! You are not getting out of this bed until the doctor tells you that it is okay and then you are going to sit your ass on my couch and take time off to heal. I'll get the bastards that did this!"

There was only one way to keep Alex safe, and Tina knew it. "Fine then. I want you to promise me something."

"Name it."

"Promise me that you will do this right. I want those bastards to have to answer for what they did in court. Promise me that you will make sure that it happens. Promise me that you will let a judge decide what they deserve…not you."

"Tina."

"Promise me."

Alex looked at her friend. She was pale and tired. There was blood crusted in her hair, and the bruises on her face stood out as if accusing her for failing to protect her friend. Looking at her reminded Alex just how fragile Tina really was. "Fine, I'll see what I can do. In the meantime, I want you to relax and get some rest."

Ten minutes later, just as Tina finally gave in to sleep, Alex leaned over her friend, kissed her on her head, and silently left the room.

She was already on the phone when she slid into James's car. "Sir, I need to talk with you and the chief now." There was a brief pause. "Yes, sir, that would be fine. I will meet you there in one hour." She hung up and told James where they needed to go. While James drove, Alex called O'Malley. "Do you have their current locations?"

"Yes, Sarge, Harris is at the fifth precinct, and O'Brien is out on Freemont Street."

"Thanks, O'Malley. Call me if they head anywhere near the chief's office." She shut the phone and looked at James as they pulled into the parking lot. "This should be fun."

Chapter 18

The moment the receptionist, a middle-aged woman who reminded Alex of Sally Field, saw Master Sergeant Thomas and Officer James, she stood, knocked once on the door to the chief's office, and opened it, motioning for them to go in. The chief's office was impressive in a way that afforded a full bird's-eye view overlooking the city. The walls were covered in dark-grained wood and decorated with diplomas, certificates, and awards, all of which complemented the large mahogany desk sitting just to the left of the door. To the right were two chairs, coffee table, and small couch meant for more personal meetings, but Alex barely took notice. Instead, she and James went directly to where the chief and the general were, standing in front of the windows with their backs to them and looking out over the city.

Before she could say anything, General Scott spoke as he turned to face her. "This had better be good, Master Sergeant Thomas. Meeting here like this could compromise the entire mission if the wrong people found out."

She met his stare with that of her own. "We need some strings pulled."

The chief could see the tension radiating in the air around Thomas and James. *This is not going to be good.* "Let's take this over to the couch, shall we?"

The general and the chief took the chairs, leaving the couch for her and James. When everyone was finally seated, the chief looked at Thomas. "Well?"

"Things have changed, and although you may not initially agree to my request, I ask that you hear me out completely before making your decision as to whether or not we can proceed in the manner we are requesting."

Both men looked at each other for a minute before coming to some sort of silent agreement. They sat back, and with a nod from the general, she proceeded to present her plan and request.

Two hours later, she and James were heading back to the warehouse with a passenger, silently contemplating what was to come next.

***

The sarge walked into the warehouse to find a mobile vault, her team, Black, and two US marshals waiting inside for her.

"What the fuck more do you assholes want from me now?" Black snarled at her.

"You three follow me, please." She motioned for the marshals and Black to follow her upstairs and into her office.

As soon as the sarge's door closed, James walked in with Tyrell Williams. The look on everyone's face was that of shock, but none more than Miceli. Without so much as a word, he escorted Tyrell upstairs to the sarge's office and then returned to wait with the rest of the team.

"Before all of you start jumping me, let me just say this, it looks like the game might be changing."

"The Feds are going to take over, aren't they?" O'Malley chimed in.

"What the hell is going on?" Miceli asked.

Looking at the group before him, James fought back the desire to fill them in with what he knew. "The sarge will brief us all when she is done, and until then, I don't know what is going to happen."

Thirty minutes later, Tyrell walked out of the building with the marshals, head down and not speaking a single word to any of them. Finally, after another long five minutes of waiting, Black and the sarge emerged from her upstairs office.

As they reached the door, Black stopped, turned around, and positioned himself right in the sarge's face and pointed his finger at her. "If you don't follow through on our deal, I will find you."

With a minute wave of her hand, Sergeant Thomas stopped her team from advancing on them. "I never go back on my word. I don't like you and I sure as hell don't trust you, but unfortunately we need each other, so like it or not, we are stuck together."

"Yeah, that may be so, but I have a feeling that as soon as one of your people gets the chance, I am gonna end up with a bullet in my chest," Black said as he looked at her team, eyes stopping on Miceli.

"You have my word that my people will do their jobs, and as of right now, their job is to protect you."

Black saw the confusion flash across all of the faces, except for one. Miceli's face was an open book—she was filled with hate. "So you think, but I'll tell you what I think… That bitch right there is gonna cap me the first chance she gets." He left before Alex could respond.

Turning to face the group, she began, "All right, everyone, listen up. A federal surveillance and federal search warrant have been issued for the colonel's house, land, and all other properties. We have been given the go-ahead to take the colonel and all known associates, including the gang members down under the Patriot Act, so we have to do this by the book. Everything is going to be timed, planned, and coordinated so that nothing and no one can slip out of this. By the time we are done, we are looking at taking down almost every Blood gang member in Boston and, if we are lucky, a few from New York as well."

"But, Sarge, how? I mean, what is going on?" Antonelli asked, confusion written on his face.

"Black gave us the names and addresses of several of the top- and middle-ranking Blood members and will have more by tomorrow. In addition to that, once this mission is complete, he is going to testify in court on how the guns and drugs were obtained, how they were distributed, and how the process of shipping worked on his end. As the courier and driver for the top-level bangers, he knows where and when things happen as well as what is being transported and to whom. He can not only tie the colonel, Harris, and O'Brien to the Boston Bloods but also tie all of them with the New York sect. By the time all of this is over and everyone has flipped on everyone else, we have the potential for hundreds of arrests within a matter of days."

Miceli couldn't hold back. "And just what is it that makes you all of a sudden trust a gangbanging, drug-selling, and most likely murdering loser like him?"

James turned to face her. "Because, like you said, he loves his brother. If he does what he agreed to do, then he and his brother go into witness protection and ultimately get a new start. He may not care what happens to him, but he does care about his brother."

She took three calming breaths before continuing. "I thought that the general and the chief wanted this kept quiet. This is anything but."

The sarge looked at the team and smiled. "When James and I explained to them that while keeping this quiet would, in fact, save a lot of embarrassment for both sides, exposing it on the largest scale possible, with extraordinary results, would make them political heroes. They found it hard to argue. Miceli, you were right earlier, so we presented the idea to the general and the chief, and they agreed."

"Damn, this is going to be big," Douglas thought out loud.

Alex looked at Jen. "Miceli, come with me."

Jen followed her out the back door and stood with her back against the building, looking out at the water, waiting.

"Miceli, what happened?"

"What do you mean, Sarge?"

"You were the one to come up with the idea of recruiting Black into this whole thing. The look on your face when I informed everyone about the plan was nothing less than pure rage."

Patiently Alex waited for Jen to explain her reaction and hoped to God that she would not have to pull her from the team. Finally, still looking out over the water, she answered, "First, I was caught off guard, and it threw me for a loop, but I know that it is not a good excuse. Second, I don't trust him or his brother, and the thought of having to put any of our lives, especially yours, in his hands does not make me happy." She paused before turning to look Alex in the eyes. "I give you my word that I will not do anything to jeopardize me, my team, or anyone working with my team. This is not about me and my issues. It's about stopping bad guys from doing bad things. I know that I have to let go of the past and I swear to you that I am slowly doing that. Maybe this will help me."

"Answer me this… Will you do whatever it takes to protect Black? If you are the only one that can, will you risk your life to save his?"

With absolute conviction in her voice, Jen responded, "Yes."

Then give me your word that you will not allow him to be hurt in any way if it is within your means to prevent it."

"I give you my word."

With a nod, Alex turned, opened the door, and the both of them stepped in, leaving the past and all doubts behind them.

As she approached the team, the sarge dug into her pocket, pulled out her keys, and tossed them to Antonelli. "Grab my car and pull it up to the door here so that we can load the cameras and gear in the trunk." Antonelli left without a word. "Douglas and Miceli, continue to correlate the information that we have. I want it perfect so that there is a clear picture as to the sequence of events for the past seven years. James, call Williams and see if you can get him to pull the shipping manifests for any cargo shipped by any of the six individuals on our list and signed for by the colonel. Be careful. I trust Williams but I also don't want him accidentally falling into the middle of all of this, nor do I want his digging raising any red flags. Once you are done with that, get to work on what we discussed earlier and then get Black the weapons we took from him back. We don't need to raise any red flags for him either. O'Malley, can you pull a recent satellite image of Colonel Jacobson's property for me?"

***

"Sarge, how do you know that the colonel won't be there?" O'Malley asked from the back seat as they approached Colonel Jacobson's private driveway.

"There is a transport coming in at 1730 from the AOR, and one of the packages on it is from Calloway. He is one of the colonel's six that is currently deployed, so I am counting on him needing to be there to sign for it. If you figure the amount of time it will take for the aircraft to taxi in, doors open, package found, and then to sign for and move it, I figure we have him occupied for at least two hours."

The quarter-mile winding road that acted as the colonel's driveway was well kept, wide enough for only one car to navigate at a time. It would have been easy to miss from the main road if you didn't know it was there. Trees, bushes, and shrubs flourished on both sides of the narrow drive, casting dark looming shadows, effectively isolating it and anyone on it from the outside world. Halfway down, they found a place to pull off and parked the car behind a large set of bushes about 150 feet from the main house.

"O'Malley, where are Harris and O'Brien?"

"Looks like they are still at the base, Sarge," he said from the back seat as he stared at the laptop sitting on his lap.

"Okay, stay here. Keep watch on them and let us know if anyone comes in via comm. We are going to start at the barn that we saw from the satellite photos and go on from there. We will keep you posted so you can map the area as we go along."

"Got it, Sarge."

She and Antonelli grabbed the cameras and all the associated gear out of the trunk and headed through the trees, bushes, and scrub, noting how unkempt the land was. Finally they reached the clearing. "Blue Three, this is Blue One. Do you copy?"

"Copy."

"We are at the back side of the barn, no entrance or exit possible from here."

"Copy."

"No windows or entry points on either side, approximately ten foot clearance from tree line to sides and back."

"Copy," he said as he jotted down notes on a copy of the satellite image of the colonel's property that he had printed out before they left.

They paused for a moment as they assessed the surrounding area. Side by side, they sat squatting down just inside of the tree line. "Driveway leads to a square clearing approximately a hundred feet long and wide. To the left of the clearing is the primary residence, one story brick ranch, front door facing east and away from the driveway with a gun-clearing barrel to the left side of the door. To the right is the barn approximately 80 feet wide and 150 feet long. The main entry has a door built into a sliding door. The sliding door is approximately twelve feet in length and fifteen feet high. No signs of movement in the home or barn," she reported.

"Copy, still no movement from the suspect's vehicles."

"Antonelli, go check the house."

He moved through the surrounding foliage until he was as close to the house as his cover would allow. After a brief moment, he quickly ran from where he was to the back of the house, staying low, and conducted a window-by-window check. When he finally returned to where the sarge was positioned, he reported to her and over the comm. to O'Malley. "Primary house visually inspected from outside appears to be all clear."

"Copy that, Blue Two."

"Blue Three, this is Blue One. We are going into the barn."

Antonelli and the sarge took one last look at the surrounding area and then headed to the barn's front door.

"Shit, Sarge, it's locked."

"Move aside."

Antonelli took a step back and watched as the sarge expertly picked the lock and slid through the now open door.

"Where did you learn to do that, Sarge?" Antonelli asked once they were inside, flashlights on, looking for a light switch.

She found the switch and turned on the lights. Smiling, she turned off her flashlight. "I wasn't always a cop in the military."

They looked around the barn, trying to get a feel for it, and relayed all pertinent information to O'Malley. There were support beams running the length of the barn ten feet apart on the right and left side. To their immediate left was a lawnmower and various other yard equipment, and to the right was a set of stairs leading to what she assumed was a hayloft directly over their heads, approximately thirty feet long. The back half was filled with old furniture, discarded appliances, and old car parts. There were bales of hay stacked three high across the width of the barn down the center, effectively separating the two sides. Standing against the hay in the center was a workbench with rugged plastic shelves to the right and an old footlocker to the left. "Let's start in the loft," the sarge said as she began to climb the stairs.

There was nothing but dirt and dust on the loft floor. The access door that was once used to move hay in and out was padlocked shut. "Let's set one up here and angle it so that it covers as much of the area in front of and behind the workbench as possible."

"I'm on it, Sarge," Antonelli said and, with speed and proficiency, extracted a camera from the bag, angled it, and zip-tied it to one of the support posts. Following that, he attached a portable battery pack to the back and turned the camera on.

"Blue Three, this is Blue Two. Are you getting a signal?"

"Stand by." O'Malley opened the second laptop that he had brought and searched for a signal feed from the camera. Once he located it and verified the image's clarity, he confirmed. The cameras were motion-activated and would only turn on if there was activity and would turn off after two minutes of inactivity. The sarge would have to set up the remote recorder in a spot that had access to a power supply, but so long as she was within one hundred meters of the cameras, the receiver would pick up the videos that were sent on its specific frequency.

Just as they were about to head back down the stairs, O'Malley came over the comm. "Blue One, this is Blue Three. I have two vehicles heading your way, and one appears to have government tags. O'Brien and Harris's cars are still showing as being on the base, so I don't know for sure who it is!"

"Shit, they took the Suburban!" She ran down the stairs, locked the door, and cut the lights just as she heard the vehicles pull up outside the door. Turning, she sprinted silently up the stairs, taking them two at a time, and just as she dropped down next to Antonelli, the door opened.

***

Colonel Jacobson unlocked the door to the barn, turned on the lights, and waited while Harris and O'Brien carried two duffel bags each inside. Harris and O'Brien went directly to the workbench and started to unload the bags on and around the workbench, while Jacobson grabbed what looked like gallon-sized baggies off the shelf next to them. Once all four bags had been emptied, Jacobson asked, "So what do we have?"

O'Brien took a step back and, with a smile, turned to the colonel. "Nine kilos of pure opium, eleven M-4s, three Berettas, and three thousand rounds of .556 ammunition."

"Well, this ought to make our friends happy," Jacobson said as the three of them got to work, evenly distributing the opium into the baggies he had put on the workbench in front of them. "What's the going street rate for what we have here in these bags, anyway, O'Brien?"

"Give or take $200,000 to $225,000, depending on quality and where you are." He smiled. "I do believe our friends are going to be pleased. With what we have here"—he motioned to the table—"and what we have downstairs, I figure they will have about $750,000 worth of quality product. Add that to the hardware and ammunition, and they will be sitting pretty."

"Well, boys," Jacobson said with a smile, "I spoke with our associates and agreed to $400,000 for everything. I hope that is acceptable to you."

"Five-way split?" Harris asked.

"Five-way split, the three of us, Calloway, and Pope."

Harris and O'Brien nodded their agreement, clearly pleased with their soon-to-be payday. Once they had evenly redistributed the drugs into the baggies, Harris turned, walked to a spot approximately fifteen feet from the workbench, leaned down, and lifted open a trapdoor that was hidden in the center of the floor, but before he could go down, Jacobson stopped him with a question. "Did you get the shell casings out of evidence?"

Harris turned and looked at him. "Yes, I got all thirty of them, but there is no way that they can just go missing. I have stalled for as long as I can, but they are supposed to be running tests on them tomorrow. If they trace them back to the base…"

"They won't." Jacobson went to the footlocker sitting just to the left of the table and opened it. Reaching in, he pulled out an M-4 and fully loaded magazine. Harris and O'Brien watched as he locked and loaded the weapon, went outside, and fired off the entire magazine into the clearing barrel. When he came back in, he tossed the casings on the workbench. "Wipe these down and then you can switch them out." At the look of confusion on their faces, he laughed. "I procured this particular weapon from a distracted dealer at a gun show in Providence last year. Security at those types of events are not as good as people think."

Laughing, Harris and O'Brien quickly wiped down the casings, ensuring that there would be no fingerprints found by the lab techs and placed them in another plastic baggie for safekeeping until Harris could get to the evidence bag. Once he transferred the casings into a new evidence bag, he would then copy all the information on it and walk it to the tech himself, telling them that it was a priority and that they might just get something on the bastards who killed their brethren. Little did anyone know that it was Harris who had tipped off the assailants to the sting that was meant to catch him.

They took the weapons, ammunition, and drugs into the root cellar and, when they were done, closed the door. "Colonel, I am not going to be able to cover up our associates' little misgivings much longer. They were supposed to call it off, not go on a shooting spree," Harris said as he wiped sweat from his forehead.

"I agree, sir. They stepped over the line this time," O'Brien added. "Don't get me wrong, I am not sorry that we tipped them off, but I went through the academy with one of the guys they killed. Granted I never liked him, but still."

"So we tell them to lie low for a while, and if they screw up or decide not to listen, we can always send your new team on a wild goose chase until the matter can be addressed. If our clients don't want to listen, then we replace them. I am quite sure that the local Crips or any number of the other gangs out there would love to be given the opportunity to do business with us."

"Sounds good to me, sir," O'Brien said, "but I don't think that we should make the transaction at the docks. There are still a lot of patrols out and about in the area, and with recent events, every crackhead and homeless bum in the area is going to be quick to report anything suspicious to try to get into our good graces. There is a $100,000 reward posted to anyone who can provide information leading to an arrest of the individuals who shot at, wounded, and killed our fellow officers." He wiped away a fake tear.

Harris chimed in, "He is right, sir. We need to find a different exchange location."

Jacobson thought about it for a moment. They were right, of course, but the problem was that there was a lot to be transported. Finally, after some internal debate, he made his decision. "Make whatever arraignments you have to. We will make the swap here at 2200 Saturday night, and before you argue with me, think about this for a moment. I only use this house on weekends, and when I want to go hunting, during the week, I stay on base or with whatever woman I decided to play with that particular night. If they decide to cause problems, we will handle it. After all, it's not like we don't know where they live."

After a moment of agreement and laughter, they left, already making plans on what they were going to do with their soon-to-be payday.

***

"Blue One, this is Blue Three. Both vehicles have left. You are clear."

"Copy, Blue Three. Did you hear any of what happened?"

"I did, Blue One, and I think you might be pleased to know that I recorded most of the conversation—that is, at least as much as could be heard through your open comm.—and can play it against the video."

"You are now my favorite person, Blue Three."

They moved quickly, placing a camera and battery pack in each corner of the barn, one in the hay just behind the workbench with an optimal view of the trapdoor. When they finally came to the trapdoor, Antonelli stopped them. "Blue Three, this is Blue Two."

"Go ahead."

"I'm going to turn the final camera on. Once you get the signal, let me know. I want to record what is down there before we leave."

"Copy."

Antonelli hooked the battery pack up to the last camera and waited. "I have clear picture and I am recording Blue Two."

The sarge pulled the door to the root cellar up and, as she descended the stairs, found a chain for the light and pulled. What she saw stopped her in midstep. The cellar was approximately fourteen feet by twelve feet. In front of her and on the far wall, rifle racks had been set up, and on them were forty-seven M-4's and just below them were four footlockers full of ammunition. To the right, there were more gun racks, only these were holding forty-eight berretta 9mm handguns with their respective ammunition in another two footlockers below them. To her left was another twenty-three M-16s and, like the others, footlockers below with the ammunition required. Turning to look behind her, she knew that she had found the drugs. There was a shelving unit that ran the length of the entire back wall, and filling every available space were coffee cans. "Antonelli, are you getting all of this?"

"Yes, Sarge. Sarge, open the lid on the coffee. I just want to verify the contents."

Stepping forward, she took one of the cans off the shelf and opened the lid, coffee. Reaching into the can, she felt around for only a second before pulling out a plastic baggie filled with the opium that they had just watched the others fill. "Should we take it, Sarge?" Antonelli asked as he slowly panned the camera around the room one last time.

Carefully she replaced the baggie, covered it back up with the contents of the can, and placed it back on the shelf exactly as it was. "No, let's just find a place to put the camera and get out of here." After a couple of minutes, they finally decided on putting the camera on the right-side corner of the floor under the shelves that were holding the drugs. They turned out the light and secured the door.

After a few more moments of deliberation as to where to place the recorder, they found an electrical outlet in the far back corner of the barn hidden by an old dresser. She kicked out the back panel of it and placed the recorder inside and, after verifying operation, quickly made their way back to the car.

The three of them rode in silence for the hour and a half that it took to get back to the warehouse. It wasn't until they pulled into the parking lot that Master Sergeant Thomas finally spoke. "Say nothing about this to anyone. We will fill the rest of the team in in the morning, but for now, this stays between the three of us. Am I clear?"

They answered in unison, "Yes, Sarge."

When they entered the warehouse, the only one left was James. O'Malley and Antonelli went to stow all of the gear and were gone before James even looked up. It wasn't until she stood directly in front of the board that he realized they were even back. "How did it go, Sarge?"

"It was enlightening, but I will fill you in tomorrow. Is everyone else gone?"

"Yes, Sarge, I cut them out around 2100. They didn't want to go, but I figured they needed to get some rest while they could."

"Good call." She turned and studied the boards for a minute; there were four now instead of just the one that was there when she had left. They had done well. A timeline was set up, and a paperwork trail linking the colonel and his associates to shipments, leave chits, shipping manifests, deployment records, and a number of suspicious unsolved shooting reports filled the boards. Rubbing her face, she turned to look at James. "James, call it a night."

"I am almost done, Sarge. I just have a few more things to put up," he said as he stood bent over a large pile of paperwork.

Smiling, she took the papers that he was looking at. "I need you fresh in the morning too. It's time to call it a night."

Smothering the urge to take the papers back and finish putting the timeline together, he let out a deep sigh and then stood straight up and stretched his back. Finally he took his first real look at the sarge and saw the smile on her face. "You found something, didn't you?"

Crossing her arms over her chest, her smile widened. "We found the mother lode."

He was shocked but he waited for her to continue, and when he realized that she wasn't going to give him anything else, he asked, "What? What did you find?"

She smiled. "If I told you now, I would never get you out of here tonight. You will find out when everyone else does tomorrow. Now go home, James. That's an order."

Reluctantly he left, knowing that he would not get much sleep.

Alex followed him out, verified that the door was secure, and went to the one person in the world whom she knew would be able to empty her mind and allow her to rest.

***

Wednesday, 0800

The team stood looking from the timeline board to the multitude of papers on the tables and back to the board. There were discarded coffee cups and doughnuts scattered everywhere. On the way back from the colonel's house, the sarge had O'Malley copy the audio and video they had captured to a CD. "I need everyone in the conference room now." The team stopped what they were doing immediately and followed her upstairs in silence. Once everyone was seated, she began, "I see the timeline is coming along well. Have there been any new developments that need attention?"

James answered, "No, Sarge. We are putting copies of everything that we find in a separate file so that when we have to turn the information over, we can do it quick."

"Good." She had moved a TV and a DVD player into the room when she came in that morning, and now she stood next to it, arms crossed and with a smile on her face. "Last night was very informative for us. As you all know, Antonelli, O'Malley, and I went to place surveillance cameras in and around Colonel Jacobson's house and property. However, given the limited number of cameras and new information that we stumbled across, we decided to only set up in the barn."

Everyone sat at the table, waiting patiently, excitement in their eyes. Jen, however, showed nothing but confusion. Alex had told her nothing when she came in the previous night, except that things had gone well.

"Instead of telling all of you the reason for the change in plans, I thought that it would be easier and more interesting if I showed you instead." She turned the TV on and hit Play. "Antonelli and O'Malley, don't give the ending away," she said with a smile before she took a seat next to Miceli, and for the next fifteen minutes, every eye was glued to the TV.

When the video was over, everyone looked at the sarge. "James, you and Douglas get this timeline finished. O'Malley and Miceli, keep an eye on O'Brien and Harris. See if you can pinpoint where they have been since we started tracking them. I want to know if there is a place or area that they frequent more often than anywhere else because if there is, then we can hopefully add a little more circumstantial evidence to the pile. Antonelli, head back out to the colonel's house and do a perimeter check, look in the surrounding tree line and the remainder of the property, verify that we did not miss anything, and make note of anything that might complicate the takedown on Saturday night. Check in every hour but be back here by 1400 so that you can fill me in on anything that you did or didn't find. I am going to go over the satellite pictures and figure out how we are going to do this." She stood up, pulled the DVD out of the player, and handed it to James. "Put this with the rest of the evidence. Now let's get to work."

Jen stayed back after everyone else had left. "Why didn't you tell me about this last night? Don't you trust me?" The hurt in her eyes was obvious.

"That's not it. I didn't even tell James." She reached for Jen's hand and was surprised when Jen took a step back. "I told the others to keep quiet until we were all together so that everyone would be brought up to speed at the same time."

"I'm not everyone else, Alex. You can trust me."

"I know."

"Then why didn't you tell me?"

"Because when I got home, I wanted to be Alex, not Sarge. I wanted to forget work and enjoy us."

Jen looked at Alex with probing eyes. "Right. Well, I guess I had better get to it then, Sarge."

She watched as Jen left the room. For the first time in her life, Alex regretted a decision that she had made.

***

Miceli was staring at the laptop. It was noon, so it wouldn't surprise her if O'Brien was on his lunchbreak, but since when did he do lunch at Black's house? "Hey, O'Malley, check this out. Looks like our friend Black is having guests over for lunch."

"How much do you want to bet that Black is the go-between?"

"I never bet on a sure thing."

He leaned back in his chair. "How long do you think it will take him to let us know what is going on?"

"Who knows," Miceli said as she leaned back in her chair and waited.

Three hours later, the team gathered around the conference table, looking over pictures that Antonelli had taken of the barn and access road as well as the satellite images. "Antonelli, did you find anything of consequence during your sweep?"

"No, Sarge, but the main access door to the barn should be addressed. As you can see here"—he pointed to a picture of the barn door—"it is on a rail slide system. I think that if we are going to do this thing in the barn, then we should block the door from sliding open. It is easier to control the area if we only have to worry about a standard size door as means for escape, but it also means that the standard door will be our only access and only egress route as well."

"Understood. James, where are you with the timeline?"

"Everything has been mapped out and tied in. In addition, O'Malley, Miceli, and I mapped out the locations that Harris and O'Brien spend more time at than others. We traced Harris's car and can prove that he went directly to the forensics lab after he left the barn last night. The lab shows Harris signing in at 2311, the casings turned over for evaluation at 2315, and then he signed out at 2318. That timeline coincides with what you and Antonelli picked up on camera last night. O'Brien made a stop at Black's house this afternoon at 1203 and—"

The sarge's phone rang. She looked down and pressed the speaker button. "Yes."

"There is going to be a pickup on Saturday night," Black said without preamble.

"Where and when?" The team was staring at the phone; none of them had been confident that Black would hold up to his end of the deal, but now that he had called, they were all wondering how much he would actually tell them.

"Ten Saturday night at some farmhouse in Concord. We are supposed to meet in a barn of all places. One of the cops that we have been dealing with came by my place this afternoon to tell me. He didn't give me no address, just directions."

"How many people are going to be there?" Alex asked as she motioned for Douglas to write the information down.

"A lot. This is a big score, so they ain't takin no chances. Won't even tell me what we are supposed to be picking up. Puma, Big Mac, Slider, 8-Ball, T.J., and some bigwig from New York calls himself Diamond. Guess there is a lot to pick up because we are supposed to be showing up in three Escalades."

"Who are all these people?" she asked, not knowing if he would even know himself.

"Puma is the general here over all of the sects in Boston, Big Mac and Slider are his two top lieutenants, 8-Ball T.J. and me are just the transporters, and Diamond, like I said, is some big shot from New York."

"Anything else we should know?"

"I don't know but I can say this…this guy Diamond makes Puma nervous, so he's got to be someone important, if you know what I mean."

"I understand," Alex said, looking around at the team and seeing that they, too, knew the enormity of the situation that they were about to go headfirst into.

"Hey, one more thing."

"What?"

Black paused, and when he spoke again, the fear in his voice could not be mistaken. "I'm doing what you said that I had to do, but I need to know that if shit goes bad and something happens to me"—he paused before continuing—"does my brother still get protection? Will he still get out?"

"I give you my word that I will make sure that what was promised to you and your brother will happen. Your brother will be relocated and given a new identity and a new life, but only if you don't tip them off or try and back out of testifying."

"Yeah, I know." And with an audible click, he hung up.

She looked up. "O'Malley, get the laptop and pictures of the barn and bring them up here."

"Sarge," Antonelli was pulling his phone from his pocket, "my cousin is a cop for NYPD. I'm going to call and ask him what, if anything, he knows about this Diamond guy."

"Good, but don't."

"I know," he said, cutting her off as he walked out of the door to make the call.

James, after a moment of internal debate, spoke up. "Sarge, we are going to need help with this. Black just said that there will be seven of them and then you have the colonel, Harris, and O'Brien. They will all be armed, plus they are going to have access to the rest of the munitions that the colonel has in the barn."

Douglas was quick to add, "I have to agree with James on this one, Sarge. Is there any way that we could get your old team to back us up?"

She didn't like the idea of bringing anyone else into this. There was too much at stake already, and to bring in outside help at this point would be dangerous. "I…"

"Sarge?"

Alex looked at her. "What, Miceli?"

"Let's think about this for a second." Just then, O'Malley and Antonelli came back into the room.

"My cousin said that they know of a Diamond down there. If this guy is the one that he thinks, then he runs New York, New Jersey, and Boston. This guy is in charge of them all."

O'Malley was already in the BPD criminal database, checking to see if he could find any of the other names that Black had given them.

This might be bigger than we all thought. "Did you get anything else?"

"According to my cousin, this guy doesn't flash his position. In fact, if you were to meet him on the street, you would think that he was a lawyer or a business executive. Regardless of what he looks like, he leaves a trail of bodies wherever he goes, but he isn't stupid enough to get caught. The last time one of his lieutenants was stupid enough to openly disagree with Diamond, they found him and five of his closest and biggest supporters shot dead execution style out by the Hudson the next day."

"Good job, Antonelli," Alex said while her mind began racing a mile a minute.

"Sarge." O'Malley looked up as he closed the computer, having already found what he was looking for. "Everything that Black said was true according to what we have in the database."

"We need to come up with a plan." Douglas was starting to get concerned with the scope of the operation and the direction that it was taking.

"As I was saying," Miceli raised her voice a notch louder than the rest, "I have a feeling I know part of how we can work this without the need for outside help."

All eyes immediately focused on Miceli. She pulled the surveillance photo and placed it in front of her in the center of the table. "There are no outside security lights, so that will work to our advantage. In any other deal, someone is guarding the outside door to make sure that no one goes in and they can stop anyone from leaving if the need arises. With the number of people they are going to have and the amount of drugs, weapons, and ammo, my bet is that they are going to put two on the door and bring one in to do the heavy lifting." She paused for a minute as she tried to get her brain to catch up with her mouth. "Let's assume that Black is actually going to follow through on his end of this, and if that is the case, then we can leave him out for now. If they post two drivers at the door outside, then all we have to do is come up on each side of the barn and simultaneously taser them. Once they are down, we handcuff them and throw them into the back of the van, which will be pulling up the moment the door guys go down."

The team gave Miceli their full attention, but none more so than the sarge. "I think that you might be on to something, Miceli." She looked around the table before continuing. "Okay, we have had a lot of information dumped on us today, and I think that everything is looking good so far. James, I want you to find a secure location to store everything that we have collected so far and will be turning over for evidence. Douglas and Miceli, remove anything from the boards and table that shows anything that we found in the colonel's barn. O'Malley, I want to know where Harris and O'Brien are right now. Antonelli, get me five pairs of needle nose pliers and then meet me downstairs in fifteen minutes, and that goes for all of you. I need to make a call." The moment she stopped speaking, everyone went to do as the sarge directed.

When they had completed their individual taskings, Sarge joined the team downstairs at the boards. "General Scott and Chief Collins will be here at 0800 tomorrow morning for an update. I want everyone here at 0700 in tactical gear and ready to work, so get some rest tonight because we have a long few days ahead of us. Dismissed."

The team immediately collected their things and headed out, knowing that there was no point in trying to stay. Alex headed to her locker in the ladies' shower area and sat on the bench, head down in her hands, and after a minute nearly jumped out of her skin when Jen spoke from just inside the doorway.

"I understand."

Alex looked up, confusion written on her face. "What?"

Jen walked over and sat next to her. "I understand why you didn't tell me. I'm sorry about the way I acted earlier."

"It's okay."

"No, it's not. When you come home, you should be able to leave work behind, not bring it with you. I was wrong and I am sorry, but it is definitely not okay for me to be a bitch like that to you."

Alex turned to her and smiled. "Thank you." Leaning forward, she kissed Jen softly. "Can we go home?"

"Only if I can make it up to you."

"Deal." That night, neither one slept; instead, they gave themselves over to each other with a slow, soft, and lingering passion.

***

Thursday, 0800

The team was ready and waiting when General Scott and Chief Collins arrived in the conference room. After Master Sergeant Thomas had saluted the general, the meeting began with him asking for a situation report.

Sergeant Thomas proceeded to give them a rundown as to what was happening. She had the team move the timeline boards into the room prior to their arrival so that they could see for themselves all that had been uncovered. When Master Sergeant Thomas was done, the chief spoke up. "Will you be requesting backup?"

"No, sir."

"Master Sergeant Thomas, I don't want you taking any unnecessary risk. Is that understood?" General Scott stated.

"Yes, sir, agreed, sir."

"And you are positive that you will not be needing or requesting backup?" the chief asked again.

"Negative, sir. We have this."

"I hope you are right about this, Thomas."

"I am, sir."

General Scott and Chief Collins exchanged a brief look, nodded, and made to leave, but as the chief reached the door, he stopped and addressed the group. "I wish you all the best of luck." Then he turned and left.

Once they were sure that the two men were gone, O'Malley stood up. "Sarge, why didn't you tell them about what you and Antonelli found or at least show them the video?"

Miceli answered, "Because the general would have gone and snatched it all up along with the colonel, Harris, and O'Brien. Am I right, Sarge?"

"Exactly, no matter what has been agreed to, I can tell you this—with the amount of weapons sitting in that barn and for as long as this has been going on, questions are going to be asked. If this gets out, the general will be in the hot seat, so the quicker and quieter this ends, the better for him. Not to mention the embarrassment of the BPD when the press gets word that the head of IA and a narcotics officer were involved in drug smuggling, dealing, and weapons trading."

Antonelli was about to ask, "But—" when James cut him off. "No buts. If the general or the chief knew about what we found in the colonel's barn, they would act. This is a Homeland Security, National Defense, DEA, Central Air Force Command, and NSA jurisdictional nightmare. It's in their best interest to keep this whole thing quiet. No matter what they are telling us, you have to remember this…they are going to cover their asses before anything else."

"We have more important things to do right now, so let's get going," the sarge said as she headed out of the conference and to the van, the rest of the team fast on her heels. They drove to the colonel's farmhouse to determine their positioning and get a familiarization for the area, remove the firing pins from all of the weapons in the root cellar, and to rig the main sliding door, leaving the small door as the only one operational in preparation for Saturday night.

***

Six hours later, the sarge and her team were putting their gear up, and when the last pieces had finally been secured, she said, "Let's call it a day. We have everything that we need, and the last thing I want is for any of us to be burned out on Saturday when this all finally goes down. We will meet back here tomorrow at 1200 for an equipment check, and we will review the plans for the takedown again then." She looked at them one last time. "Go home, everyone, and get some rest."

They all left with smiles on their faces and a sense of anticipation. Jen and Alex were the last to leave, both seemingly lost in thought as they walked together side by side to their cars. As Alex reached her car, she turned to face Jen. "I'm going to drop by the hospital and visit for a little while with Tina tonight."

"Sounds good. I was wanting to go and check on Chris," Jen replied, but the she seemed distracted, distant.

"How about dinner? Around seven at my place?"

Jen turned to face Alex fully. "Sounds good," she said with a strained smile on her face.

Something inside her gut was throwing up warning flags, but Alex dismissed them, telling herself that Jen was just worried about Chris. She reminded herself that he was not only her ex-partner but her best friend as well. She opened the door to her car and had just sat down when she heard Jen say, "Shit, I forgot my bag inside." Shaking her head, she laughed at herself and then leaned down and kissed Alex softly on the lips. "See you tonight." She turned and took off at a jog back to the warehouse, leaving Alex to watch her retreating form.

***

Alex looked at her watch; it was 0830 and still no Jen. *This isn't like her.* She picked up her phone and called Jen's cell but was surprised when it went straight to voicemail. *Something is not right here. Am I overthinking things here, or should I be worried?* she asked herself before picking up her phone once again and dialing in another number. "Hey, Chris, I am sorry to bother you, but is Jen there?"

"Nope, I haven't seen her in a few days."

"Oh, okay, thanks." She quickly hung up the phone. "She lied to me and stood me up." Alex spoke to the empty room.

An hour later, Alex was just wiping down the table after having cleaned up from the dinner she had made when Jen walked in.

Seeing the anger in Alex's eyes when she closed the door, Jen paused. "I'm sorry I missed dinner."

With cleanup temporarily forgotten, Alex crossed her arms in front of her chest. "Where were you?"

Chris had left her a voicemail earlier, letting her know that Alex had called, so she was ready with her response. "I was so distracted when we left this afternoon thinking about Saturday that I decided against going over to see Chris. You know how he likes to ask questions," she said, trying to sound cute, but when Alex narrowed her eyes, she realized that she had better get to the point and quick. "I went for a drive instead to try and clear my mind. I was trying to figure out what it was that was getting to me so badly. I realized that I needed to come to terms with the fact that I had to work with Black. I mean, I know that my problem is with his brother, but still…," she said with an audible sigh before continuing. "It was harder than I thought. I had to fight off a lot of demons."

Alex studied Jen, taking in her words and overall demeanor, senses on full alert. "And now?"

With a smile that radiated throughout her entire being, she said, "I won. I came to terms with what I have to do and finally let go of the past." Slowly she stepped into Alex and wrapped her arms around her waist. Looking down into her eyes, she added, "I want to look to the future, and now for the first time in a long time, I can."

Chapter 19

Friday, 1200

The team moved like a well-oiled machine. Miceli lined up six of the dragon skin vests on the table, one for each member of the team, while Antonelli followed behind and placed a pair of NVGs on top of each vest. Once comm. checks were complete, the individual comm. sets were placed one on each vest. "I want each person to have five magazines on them when we go," the sarge ordered as she reviewed the satellite pictures again.

"Got it, Sarge," Douglas said as he and Antonelli pulled out several boxes of ammunition and began loading the thirty magazines and evenly distributed them to lay next to each vest. James followed behind, placing one Taser on each vest with the exception of sarge's. "Sorry, Sarge, but you are not certified to use one of these, are you?"

A small chuckle slipped from her. "No, James, I'm not." She looked at the gear sitting in front of her and then added to everyone, "Make sure that your tactical gear has identifiable police markers on it for tomorrow."

Finally the team had all of their gear laid out on the table and stood circling the sarge, waiting. "Update on O'Brien and Harris."

"Nothing out of the ordinary, Sarge," O'Malley answered quickly.

"James?"

"All of the recovered hardware as well as the video of us removing them are with the case file and under lock and key and in the agreed-to secure location, Sarge."

She paused for a moment, her hand slipping into the left cargo pocket of her pants and feeling for its contents. "I know that it has been a while since I made mention of this, but does everyone have their letter?" She pulled hers out of her pocket and held it up. When she looked around, she saw five hands go into five pockets and pull out five envelopes identical to the one she had in her hand. She looked each one of them in the eyes before continuing. "Thank you. Obviously the gravity of the situation has not eluded any of you." She slid her envelope, as did the rest of the team, back into her pocket, and she allowed for a moment of shared silence.

"Good, now let's review." For the next three hours, they constantly repeated every move they were going to make as well as went over contingency plans for the unexpected. Nonstop they practiced their entrance procedures, movements, and "shoot to wound, not kill" orders. They installed two bars inside of the van, one running down the length of each side, so as to be able to secure their prisoners when they were finally taken into custody. The sarge turned to her team as they finished their final run-through. "Everything looks good for now. I want you all to take your gear home with you tonight. Nothing is to be left here, and I will say this one more time, do not tell anyone anything. Okay, I want us set up and in position two hours prior to the start of their meeting. As with the plan, O'Malley, you will drop us off on the main road where we will…" Her phone rang, interrupting her, and after a quick look at the caller ID, she hit the speaker button and answered, "Hello."

"The meeting has been changed to tonight at eight," Black said in a hurried whisper.

"Why?"

"Diamond doesn't want to wait."

"Anything else change?"

"No, I gotta go," Black said in a rush, and then the line went dead.

James looked at his watch. "Sarge, it's 1715 now."

"Grab your gear. We will dress out on the way." As they pulled out of the parking lot, Sergeant Thomas made a phone call. "Sir, there has been a change."

***

Friday, 1900

"Everybody out!" Sergeant Thomas said as she jumped out of the back of the van. "O'Malley, get the van out of sight. I will let you know when we are ready for you."

O'Malley watched the team disappear into the woods from his rearview mirror as he drove away. "Good luck," he whispered to the disappearing figures in his mirror.

"Blue Five and Six, cross over now and position yourselves at the corner of the driveway closest to the house, and, everyone, dawn your NVGs," Sarge relayed over her comm.

"Copy Blue One." The team put on their night vision goggles, and then Douglas and Miceli crossed the driveway and continued through the woods toward the colonel's house concealed in relative darkness.

By 1923 hours, everyone was in position. "Keep your eyes open and nobody moves without my say so."

***

"What do you want up here, sir?" Pope asked as he pulled open the trapdoor.

O'Brien was standing next to Jacobson by the trapdoor, and Harris, who was at the workbench, looked at the colonel. "Sir, I haven't dealt with this new guy before. I say we only pull a couple of M-4s and 9mms, along with one box of ammunition for each."

"I agree, sir," Harris concurred.

Jacobson smiled more to himself than his associates. "No, bring it all up. I don't want them to know where we keep all of our products. We don't want our friends to think that they can come back whenever they want and help themselves. It's bad enough that they know of this place." He paused for a moment in thought. "In fact, I think that I should just put this place on the market tomorrow. I come up for retirement next year and I think now would be a good time to invest in a condo in the Bahamas." Jacobson and his crew shared a good laugh and then got to work.

TRUST

Once everything was up and organized neatly on the floor in front of the workbench, the colonel handed one of the M-4s and a loaded magazine to Pope. "Conduct a perimeter check and then wait outside for our business associates. Harris and O'Brien, grab your weapons and get ready."

Harris locked and loaded his weapon. "What about you, sir?"

Jacobson's smile was disturbing. "Already taken care of."

***

"Blue One, this is Blue Six. We have one suspect exiting the building, carrying an M-4," Miceli reported.

"Copy."

They watched as Pope conducted a perfunctory perimeter check around the tree line surrounding the barn and house passing within five feet of the sarge, James, and Antonelli. He circled around the three cars that had been parked behind the house until finally stopping in front of the barn door. After a minute, his posture relaxed, and he leaned his weapon against the wall, pulled out a cigarette, and lit it.

Sergeant Thomas watched Pope conduct and complete his rounds. "And he wonders why I don't like him. He conducts perimeter checks like he is out for a stroll and then just puts his weapon down on the ground like it doesn't matter…" Her silent thoughts were cut short by the sound of music. "Blue team, this is Blue One. Turn off your NVGs." One flash from the headlights would be enough to temporarily blind them.

"Blue One, this is Blue Five. We have three incoming vehicles," Douglas reported.

"Copy, Blue Three, this is Blue One."

O'Malley responded, "Go ahead, Blue One."

"What do I have inside the building?"

Looking at the laptop that he had set up on the passenger's seat of the van, he reported back, "Everything is out of the cellar and sitting halfway between the trapdoor and the workbench. Jacobson, Harris, and O'Brien are inside, talking."

"Copy that. You are clear to approach but stay out of visual range until you are given the go-ahead."

"Copy." O'Malley, who had been parked in a pull-off a half mile up the street, put the van in gear and headed out to join his team.

***

One after the other, the three black Escalades circled the drive until coming to a stop side by side next to the barn. Black was driving the third vehicle and had been tasked not only as courier but also as Diamond's personal bodyguard while he was there. As per Diamond's own instructions, he was to wait in the vehicle until they knew that it was safe. Under no circumstances was Diamond going to put himself in a situation where he could be caught. They waited, engine running, while the occupants of the first two vehicles exited, exchanged words with the guy at the door, and went inside, making sure that there were no surprises waiting for them. While Diamond waited for his men to check things over, he thought about how he came to be in the position that he was in.

Diamond had worked his way up in the ranks like everyone else. He took part in his first drive-by when he was thirteen, killing two Crips and some guy that just happened to be in the way at the time. When he got home that night, his old man clapped him on the shoulder and rewarded him with his first 9mm. Two weeks later, his dad, a lieutenant in the ninth street sect, was arrested and convicted on two counts of murder and a laundry list of other related charges, and from then on, he bounced from one OG's house to another. He watched his homeboys burn through their money on stupid shit like booze, gold, and bitches, but in the end, none of them ever had anything left of their money to show, so they always ended up back on the corner, pushing. By the time he turned eighteen, he had a good lawyer on retainer and he had figured out a very important lesson, which was that the cops didn't look for the guys in suits; they looked for the punks with bling. At twenty-three, he was a lieutenant, at twenty-seven a general, and now at thirty-eight he ran it all, everything from New York to Boston. *I got to where I am today because I*

TRUST

don't trust anyone, not even my own homeboys. That was after all why he changed the meeting time at the last minute.

Pulling himself from the past, he watched as Slider nodded to Black; all was clear. Black quickly turned the engine off, got out, and went to the back to open the door for him.

As they approached the barn door, Diamond looked at his men and smiled. "You two gentlemen, stay out here and let us know if anyone else comes." 8-Ball and T.J. stood on each side of the door like they were told to, 9mm in each of their waistbands and M-4's in their hands as Diamond and Black, the last in the group, went into the barn and closed the door behind them.

Chapter 20

As planned, O'Malley backed the van up the long and narrow driveway, stopping just short of the opening to the house and barn and ensuring that he would not be seen or heard. Opening the laptop, he took a quick assessment. "Blue One, this is Blue Three. I am in the first position and holding."

"Copy, Blue Three. What is the situation inside?"

"First group is standing in front of the contraband in a line, Jacobson in the middle, Harris and O'Brien to his left, and Pope to his right. The second group is fanning out as well. Looks like they are sizing each other up, no one is talking yet."

"Copy that, Blue Three. Advise us if there are any significant changes."

"Copy."

Game time, Alex told herself. "Blue Two and Blue Four, get into positions. Blue Five and six, stand by to go."

James and Antonelli moved silently along the sides of the barn, James on the right and Antonelli on the left with the sarge following right behind him. They posted at the corners. "Blue One, this is Blue Six. You are clear to go."

"Copy. On my mark…go." James and Antonelli punched around the corners at the same time and instantly fired their Taser. At the word *go*, Douglas and Miceli came, silently running out of the bushes toward the front door, duct tape in hand. Fifteen seconds was all it took to discharge the Taser, duct tape their mouths, put a hood over their faces, handcuff them, and carry them to the van, which had backed in closer to the barn while the sarge stayed back, guarding the door. Thirty seconds after that, they were all formed up behind her with the exception of O'Malley, waiting to go.

"Blue Three, once we go in, follow behind. Secure the door so that it stays open and then post yourself at the entrance. If anything goes wrong, you will be the only one who will be able to keep anyone from slipping out."

"Copy, Blue One." He watched as his team got set up and couldn't help but feel like he was being left behind.

"Blue Three, I need a situation report."

O'Malley was standing outside the driver's side door, laptop sitting open on the seat as he looked and listened. "Stand by."

***

Diamond approached the waiting group and took a courtesy look at what was laid out in front of him. He gave a slight nod to Puma, who then opened a black duffel bag and dropped it at Harris's feet. "Four hundred thousand dollars as agreed, gentlemen," Diamond said with a smile as Harris scooped up the money and put it behind the bales of hay. "I do feel the need, however, to inform you all as to the reason our little transaction had to be rescheduled to tonight on such short notice," Diamond said as he shook his head, looking disappointed.

"Blue One, hold your position. Something is going on."

"You see," he continued as he walked around his men, looking at each one and getting confused looks in return. "Although our business arrangements have been lucrative for all involved, business dealings on this scale tend to make me question everything and everyone." He stopped in front of Black, who was now sweating badly. He turned to look at the colonel's group. "You see, gentlemen, we have a small problem on our hands. Our associate here has been speaking with the police."

"Of course he has," Harris said as he looked between the two, shaking his head and a bit annoyed.

Diamond smiled. "No, gentlemen, I do not mean you." He turned and stood face-to-face with Black. "Why did you turn on your brothers?"

Black took a step back. "Diamond, I didn't, I wouldn't."

"Blue One, something is wrong. I think Diamond is onto Black," O'Malley said, eyes glued to the computer and the scene that was unfolding before him.

Diamond put his hand on the back of Black's neck, pulling him closer. "I took the gun off the first cop I ever killed, did you know that?"

"Get ready," Sarge told her team.

"No, Diamond, I didn't," Black answered, his voice less than a whisper.

"I only use it for special occasions like this one," he said as he pulled a Smith and Wesson 9mm from the waistband of his tailored pants.

"Sarge, you have to go now. Diamond is going to shoot Black!"

The sarge pushed through the door with her team right behind her. She went straight forward, and James and Antonelli fanned out to the right and Miceli and Douglas to the left just as Diamond pulled the trigger and shot Black once point-blank in the center of his chest.

"Police! Don't move! Everyone, drop your weapons!" she commanded as she watched Black fall to the ground in front of Diamond's feet.

"Ahh." Diamond lowered his weapon to his side but did not drop it. "Here is the officer that our traitorous associate was speaking to," he said as he looked directly at Miceli. "You do realize that you are the reason he is dead, don't you, Officer?"

"The way I see it, you evened an old score for me," Miceli said. "Now drop your weapons."

"I am going to kill you, Thomas," Jacobson growled, his body shaking with rage.

"No, sir, you are going to jail. Now for the last time, drop your weapons."

"My dear officers, that will never happen, look at us." Diamond motioned to the men he was standing with. "You are outnumbered and outgunned." With his last comment, his men stood up straighter, swelling with confidence. Harris and O'Brien had already begun to separate themselves from the group, moving together slowly toward the right side of the barn. Pope stayed where he was, less than a foot to Jacobson's right, while Jacobson stood planted in place, seeing nothing and no one around him except for Thomas.

Diamond had slowly inched his way to the left of his men in an attempt to get out of the direct line of fire. He knew how this would all play out; he had seen it before and he knew what to do.

"Kill them all!" he screamed as he dropped to the floor, knowing that the cops would be more concerned with the fools shooting at them and not with the one on the ground slowly making his way to the door.

All hell broke loose.

Everything happened at once. Puma, Big Mac and Slider pulled out their Berettas and pulled the triggers. Click. Jacobson dove behind the workbench and flipped it over, seemingly using it for cover. Harris and O'Brien opened fire with their department-issued weapons on Antonelli and James as they ran in an attempt to get out. Pope made an attempt at firing on the sarge and, when he realized that his weapon wasn't working, took aim and threw it at her. Alex ducked a second too late, and the butt stock caught her on the left side of her temple, causing her to stumble forward a step before she could regain her balance. Once Big Mac and Slider realized that their guns weren't firing, they hit the floor, screaming, "Don't shoot!" Puma went for broke, running straight for the sarge at the same moment that Pope's weapon made contact with her head. Seeing Puma charging the sarge, Miceli took aim and shot him once in the back of his right thigh, effectively dropping him in screaming pain. Douglas looked over to where Diamond was, just as he fired off two rounds while trying to low crawl away. Douglas saw it just in time to fire off two rounds in return while diving to put himself between Diamond and Miceli. The first round landed just over Diamond's head, and the other grazed the back of his left thigh.

O'Brien and Harris positioned themselves behind two of the support beams on the right-hand side, firing nondiscriminately in between attempts at running from one support beam to the other in hopes of getting to the door and out. After throwing his weapon, Pope turned and dove behind the upturned workbench with

Jacobson and took the M-4 that the colonel kept hidden from the underside of the table's surface. Once Alex got her footing back, she looked over just in time to see Diamond's bullet hit Douglas square in the chest, knocking him back and into Miceli, causing the both of them to hit the floor hard. "No!" As if waiting for the sarge to be distracted, Jacobson pulled out the two Berettas that he had kept hidden under the workbench next to the M-4 and opened fire on her. Miceli crawled for cover behind one of the support posts, pulling Douglas with her.

O'Brien and Harris were too busy laying suppression fire to notice James and Antonelli double back and around on them. Just as O'Brien reached the second-to-last support beam, James reached around, grabbed his outstretched wrist, and, with one punch, knocked him out. Harris looked over just in time to see James putting handcuffs on O'Brien. He lifted his weapon, took aim at James, and screamed, "Fuck you, James!" James looked up just before the shot was fired.

O'Malley had been trying to watch everything that was going on from the door when he felt a bullet graze by his head. An instant later, he saw the sarge go down, leaving a mist of blood in the air behind her. Diamond saw O'Malley's attention shift, momentarily distracted, and he took the opportunity to take aim.

Douglas felt the bullet hit, and although the vest stopped the bullet from penetrating his chest, he still felt the force when it impacted. It wasn't until Miceli had pulled him behind the support beam that he opened his eyes just in time to see the sarge go down and land on the floor right next to Black. He was deaf to the sound of Miceli discharging her weapon; all he saw was the blood as it began to pool out from under the sarge. O'Malley didn't have time to react to Diamond, who had been crawling on the floor out of sight before finally getting up to make a run for it. He looked up just in time to see Diamond point and aim his gun at his chest. A moment later, Diamond was flying through the air, arms spread out as if he were a bird in flight, and hit O'Malley full force. Screaming, they both went down in a twisting mass of arms and legs.

Harris took aim at James. "Fuck you, James!" Before he could pull the trigger, Antonelli fired, catching Harris in the right forearm. No sooner did Harris's gun hit the floor than Antonelli was on him. "No, man! Fuck you!"

Just as Antonelli was cuffing Harris, James looked up to see Slider and Big Mac get up and start running for the door with Miceli following close behind. James ran from where he was to try and intercept when more shots were fired; from where, he didn't know. Big Mac fell dead into James's arms, while Slider continued past them both only to be tackled by Miceli from behind just as he reached the door.

Jacobson and Pope watched the ensuing chaos. "Follow me," Jacobson told Pope as he pushed a bale of hay back and crawled toward the far end of the barn, Pope right on his heels.

Miceli's shot caught Diamond in his right shoulder, and after he and O'Malley untangled themselves from each other on the ground, Diamond didn't put up a fight; instead, he cried like a baby as he was being cuffed. O'Malley, once finished with Diamond, moved quickly to where Miceli was wrestling with Slider. "Miceli, get back!" O'Malley screamed and, once she was clear, Tasered Slider.

Even though he felt like he had been hit with a sledgehammer in the chest, Douglas still had enough sense to keep an eye on Pope and Jacobson. When he saw them disappear behind the hay, he forced himself to follow, passing by the sarge and looking down on her motionless form for only a moment before continuing on.

Through a series of hand signals, Jacobson instructed Pope to position himself behind an old tractor two-thirds back on the left side of the barn while he took off to the right, staging himself behind some old furniture and a refrigerator and giving both men ideal cover while at the same time still allowing them to see any oncoming assaults.

After Douglas passed by, Black took a quick look around. It looked like the cops had got almost everyone and were finishing up over by the door. Rolling over so that he could sit up, he looked down at the sarge. She was absolutely still, face pale, and lying in a small pool of her own blood. Just as he was about to check to see if she was dead, her eyes flew open.

***

She came too instantly, and the first thing she saw when she opened her eyes was Black staring down at her. She jumped to her knees fast, and just as fast, a wave of dizziness tried to overtake her. If it hadn't been for Black reaching out to steady her, she would have fallen back down. She wasn't aware of her blood-soaked shirt, only the pounding in her head both from where Pope's gun had hit and from where her head hit the ground. When her mind finally cleared enough to allow her to focus, she took in the scene.

"James, where is Jacobson and Pope?" she called over the comm as she and Black stood up.

Thank God! "I don't know, Sarge, but they didn't come this way, and neither did Douglas."

She knew exactly where they went. There were only two places with enough cover that afforded clear shots, and she remembered seeing them when they placed the camera equipment. She immediately squatted back down and pulled Black with her as she spoke into her comm again. "Blue Two, get everyone out of here and secure them in the van and then call the general. Blue Three, Four, and Six, begin CLS and call for paramedics. Blue Five, if you can hear me, stay where you are and wait for me there. You are walking into a trap." She turned and looked at Black. "You need to go with them and stay down," she said with a quick nod before turning in search of the others. Just as she reached the wall of hay, a shot was fired. "James, get them out of here now!"

"O'Malley, bring the van up here next to the other vehicles!" James directed as he pushed Harris through the door, bringing up the rear.

"We can't just leave them in there without backup, James!" Miceli argued as they dragged their suspects to the approaching van. "We need to get back in there!"

"Orders are orders even when we don't like them, Miceli," James replied, although he did agree with Miceli on this one. Before she could argue with him, he flipped open his phone and made the call.

"This is Officer O'Malley with the Boston PD. I need paramedics out to—"

"Miceli, I need a compression bandage!" Antonelli yelled, trying to be heard over the screaming of the suspects.

"Multiple GSWs," O'Malley continued on.

"General Scott, this is Officer James. We have a situation, sir."

"Oh, man, my leg!"

"We need a mobile vault, sir..."

"Shit, my shoulder!"

"ETA on the ambulances is fifteen minutes!" O'Malley reported to what was left of the team as he grabbed some bandages and dressings and got to work on Diamond.

"The general and the chief will be here in twenty via helicopter," James reported as he approached the van and began to help the others.

Black looked into the chaos that was in front of him. He had seen a lot of his homeboys get knifed or shot up and watched the cops do nothing but wait for the EMTs to show, but these cops were actually trying to help. For once in his life, he felt lucky, and although he didn't want to help the cops out of years of habit, he figured he owed Miceli one. "Yo, Miceli!" he yelled into the chaos.

Miceli looked up, as did the rest of her team and all of the guys that he once called his brothers.

"Fucking rat!"

"Traitor!"

"You gonna die!"

"Blood in, blood out, motherfucker!"

He paused for a moment, the realization of the consequences of his deal finally sinking in. "I just figured you would want to know that your sergeant lost a lot of blood and ain't lookin' too good," he told Miceli as the threats continued to be screamed at him.

Before Miceli could react, James grabbed her arm. "Antonelli, check Black out and find out how it is that he is still standing," he said before leading them both around to the front of the van.

"James, let me go. We need to get in there!" Miceli tried to pull away, but James had a vice grip on her arm that she could not escape.

Black pulled his shirt off to be checked, exposing the vest that she had given him the night before. "Miceli, did you give him this vest?" Antonelli called out to Miceli as she was being led away.

"She thought there might be trouble, so she came by last night and told me I would be a fool if I didn't wear it," Black answered for her, only now appreciating what she had done.

James turned and stood nose to nose with her. "Not until we know what is going on first. Miceli, these guys have training that you never will. If you go in there half-cocked, you will get everyone killed."

Miceli took a deep breath. "Then what are we going to do, James? We can't leave her in there alone with them. She is going to need help."

"Listen to me," James said as he turned to the computer sitting on the front seat. "O'Malley, I need you up here once you get everyone secured in the back."

"En route," O'Malley called from the back where he was putting the final dressing on Diamond just as he and everyone else heard more shots fired.

***

The sarge decided against following the same route that Douglas had taken; instead, she went to the left side of the barn, pushed the bales forward slowly, and painted herself against the wall. She wiped her left hand across her brow to clear the sweat from her face, not realizing that her hand was cold and shaking badly or that there was blood on it. If she was right on where she assumed Pope and Jacobson had posted, then this route would be her only shot at getting to them unseen.

She moved in a half crouch another ten feet and stopped behind a pile of old discarded crates. Her breathing was short and rapid, and she knew that she needed to get it under control before she either passed out or gave away her position. As she fought to get her breathing under control, she noticed movement eight feet ahead and at her two-o'clock position. Keeping herself low to the ground, she peered around the crates in an attempt to search for Douglas. It took her less than a minute before she spotted him leaning against one of the support posts on the right-hand side of the barn, weapon at the ready and a perfect target for both Jacobson and Pope. There was no debris or cover for him ten feet forward or aft, but as long as he did not move, the post would provide him cover, and it was possible that neither man on the opposite side of the room had spotted him just yet. And then he coughed.

His position compromised, Jacobson and Pope opened fire, shooting three rounds each at the post that Douglas was using for cover, sending splinters of wood flying in every direction. Sarge couldn't see from where she was whether Douglas had been hit or not; all she saw was him hitting the ground hard and landing on his back and blood spraying from his mouth on impact.

"Thomas, are you here?" Jacobson yelled out from behind the pile of furniture, trying to get a fix on her location, knowing that she would never leave a man behind.

"Blue One, are you okay?" James called over the comm line.

"Five is down. Do you have eyes?"

"Roger, we have you and Five in sight, and I think I know the positions of the two suspects."

"Copy," she whispered into her mic. *Think, Alex, think. What are you going to do?* She took one last look at Douglas and then turned and lay flat on the ground. With the way that the crates were stacked, she was provided decent cover, but there was one small gap four inches from the floor that gave her exactly what she needed. "Blue Two, did you recover the keys to the suspects' vehicles?"

"Yes, Sarge."

"Do you remember emergency convoy extractions?" she asked, praying to God that he did.

James looked at the monitor again, trying to see what the sarge was getting at before responding. "I do."

"What is she talking about?" Miceli was almost on top of James, trying to understand what was going on.

"Jacobson is on the right behind the refrigerator and furniture."

"Copy that." He and Miceli stared closer at the monitor when James finally began to understand what she was wanting him to do.

"You and one other, no more than that, and be prepared to provide suppressive fire cover."

"What about the second suspect?"

"I have that covered," she answered with a shaky smile. She was sweating badly now, and her whole body was beginning to shake. *Five more minutes, Alex, just hold it together five more minutes. You can do this*, she thought. "Let me know when you are in position and watch the beams."

"Copy that." Knowing that Miceli was going whether he agreed to it or not, he pulled her with him to the back of the van.

"What are we doing?" Miceli asked.

"What's going on?" O'Malley and Antonelli asked in unison.

Pulling the keys that he had taken from T.J. after they had Tasered him, James looked at Antonelli. "No time to explain, give Miceli your weapon." Antonelli handed over his weapon without a second's hesitation, and then he and O'Malley watched as they silently walked away.

James handed Miceli the keys. "Load new magazines. You are going to need every round you have," he said as he slid into the passenger's back seat.

Sitting behind the wheel, she swapped out the magazines on both weapons and then turned to look at James. "Okay, so what the hell are we doing?"

"We are going to go in and get Douglas. Now drive over there." She did she was told.

***

"Come on, Thomas, I thought you were the best," Pope called out, taunting her in hopes of getting her to give up her position. If there was one thing that he was sure of, it was that he wanted eyes on her first.

She looked over at Douglas. He was barely conscious and still coughing up blood. He was hurt bad, and if they didn't get him out of there soon, he wasn't going to make it.

"Thomas, we can stay here as long as it takes. I am not going to let someone put me in a cage just because I used my resources to make a little extra money on the side, but how much longer do you think your little puppet will last?" From his vantage point, he could see the officer and he didn't look too good. "I'll tell you what, Thomas, put your weapons down and walk to the center of the room. Then the three of us can go for a little walk, and your man can get the medical attention that he needs." He was not surprised when he got no response; in fact, he hadn't expected one...yet.

"Blue One, this is Blue Two. We are in position."

"Once you hear it, I want a clean in and out." Her voice was shaky, and her vision was beginning to blur again.

"Copy," James replied and then looked at Miceli's reflection in the rearview mirror. "Are you ready for this?"

The determination on her face was absolute. "You know it."

"I need you hundred percent on this. No matter what happens, Douglas is the priority, got it?"

"Got it," she answered, but she knew that if Alex needed her, she would have a hard time remembering that.

Sergeant Thomas took one last look at Douglas and then lined herself up. She lay flat on the floor, elbows planted, left leg straight out, right leg pulled up slightly for balance and support, every ounce of her being focused on her sight alignment/sight picture and her breathing. *Pop-pop!*

Jacobson looked over just in time to see Pope get shot, one hit to each of his shins. He watched as Pope dropped his weapon and slammed his head against the manifold of the tractor's engine before falling to the ground unconscious. No sooner did Pope hit the ground than a black Escalade drove through the side of the barn between himself and the fallen officer.

James had the door open and was out a second before the vehicle stopped. Miceli and Jacobson were exchanging fire, and the vehicle was becoming quickly riddled with bullets. James leaned down and grabbed Douglas by the arm holes of his vest and threw him in the back seat. As soon as he had him loaded, he screamed, "Go go go!" as he began firing out of the backseat window. Miceli dropped her weapons, threw the gearshift in reverse, and hit the gas. The last thing Miceli saw as the SUV barreled out was a figure in black streaking past the tractor toward the back of the barn, and in that one instant, she knew that Alex was okay.

***

"Give it up, Colonel!" Alex tried to yell, but her voice seemed like it was a mile away.

"Only when I am dead, you bitch!" he screamed as he tried to quickly brush away the debris that had been blown into his face and hair from the ricocheting bullets. Time was running out; he could hear the approaching sirens and he knew that if he didn't get out of there soon, he never would. *Where is she?*

"I am taking you alive, Colonel. Death would be too good of a sentence for you."

She was behind him; he turned around quickly, scanning the back half of the barn in hopes of spotting her, but to no avail. With all chances of escape slipping from him, Jacobson decided to search for her; if he was going to go down, at least he would go down fighting.

He looked left and right, up and down, and found nothing; it was as if she was a ghost. His heart was racing, and as the seconds passed by, he became more and more desperate. "Where are you!" he screamed after finally stopping his search and standing against the center part of the back wall. Panic, rage, and desperation finally overtook him as he stood there panting and looking around him as if he were a trapped animal.

Alex stepped out from behind the dresser where, only a few days prior, they had put the receiver for the surveillance cameras in. She didn't know if she would be able to hold herself up for much longer, so rather than taking any chances, she simply walked to the front side of the dresser and leaned back against it, as if she had no cares in the world. "I'm right here."

***

It took them less than fifteen seconds to pull out of the barn and stop in front of the van, but it felt like the longest fifteen seconds of their lives. Antonelli and O'Malley pulled Douglas out of the back seat fast, and as soon as he was on the ground, he began to take his shirt and vest off. "Where in the hell are the EMTs?" Miceli growled.

"Should be here any minute now!" O'Malley shouted, trying to be heard over the hoots and hollers and screaming that were coming from the inside of the van.

The movement from them removing his vest snapped Douglas back into full consciousness, and with it came the coughing and pain. Every breath was harder to take, and every cough was accompanied by a bloody mist until finally, with the last cough, a mouthful of blood came with it. "Turn him on his side." James ordered, trying to clear the airway of the mouthful of blood that remained.

"There are no open wounds, what the hell is going on?" Antonelli asked James as they assessed him for injuries.

James saw bruising on the left side of Douglas's chest. He traced his fingers along each rib and stopped quickly when he got halfway up, and he realized that one of Douglas's ribs was broken. He then leaned down and placed an ear on Douglas's chest and listened to him breathe. "His lung is filling up with blood."

"Where are the goddamned EMTs!" O'Malley screamed.

"Stay with me, pal, okay?" Miceli was holding his hand, trying to keep him awake.

"His pulse is getting rapid and weaker, James. We need to do something," Antonelli said as he handed the medical bag over to James.

He hesitated. "James, he is going to die if you don't do it." Miceli looked him directly in the eyes, trying to give him the support that she knew he needed.

After another moment's hesitation, he cast aside all of the doubts screaming at him from inside his head. "Antonelli, I need alcohol, a knife, and tubing. O'Malley, I am going to need you to hold him down, and, Miceli, watch for the EMTs and check the monitor. Make sure that the sarge is okay."

They moved with trained efficiency around Douglas. O'Malley threw one leg across Douglas's waist and positioned himself, hovering over his shoulders, while Antonelli handed the supplies to James. "Douglas," he said. As much as he knew what needed to be done, a part of him still needed permission. "Douglas man, this is going to hurt like a bitch, and I don't know if it is going to help you or hurt you. If you don't want me to do it, tell me now," he said while placing his hand on his friend's forehead.

Panic was beginning to overtake him. It felt as if a Mac truck was sitting on his chest; he couldn't get enough air no matter how hard he tried. He knew that he was close to passing out and he knew somewhere deep inside that if he did, he would die. Pulling the last remaining bit of strength that he had, Douglas looked up at James and, with a gurgling voice, croaked, "Do it."

It was then that he allowed his training to fully take over. "Alcohol," James called, and Antonelli handed him a soaked gauze pad.

"Knife." He held out his hand and never shifted his gaze. "O'Malley, hold him," he said as soon as he saw Douglas's body shift with the added pressure of being restrained. James used the surgical knife that was in the med kit to cut a one-inch incision between Douglas's fourth and fifth ribs. Once the incision was complete, he dropped the knife and reached out his hand. Immediately, Antonelli placed twelve inches of flexible plastic tubing into his hand.

"Get ready," James told those around him. "Three, two, one," he counted and then inserted the tube into Douglas's lung. His whole body went rigid when the tube was inserted, and the scream that came from his lips silenced everyone around him as well as all of those who had only moments before been cheering at him for being injured.

The instant that the tube penetrated the lung, blood started draining out, and Douglas's breathing became steadier while his pulse rate slowed and began to slowly strengthen. O'Malley backed away and went to join Miceli while Antonelli and James put a dressing around the tube and secured it in place with tape.

The second that O'Malley stepped up next to her, Miceli turned, grabbed him by the arm, and headed toward the barn. "Come on, we need to help her."

***

When Jacobson turned to find Thomas standing against his mother's old dresser like she didn't have a care in the world, he was infuriated. In that instant, he knew beyond the shadow of a doubt that if he was going to go down, one way or the other, he was going to take her with him. The rage that filled him blinded him to the obvious—that Thomas was close to dropping right where she stood.

Alex was pulling from the last of her reserves, and she knew it. Not only was she shaking and sweating profusely, but her vision was starting to blur. Her mission was almost complete, the suspects (all but two) were secured, and her team was safe and treating the wounded. *Now all I have to do is get him worked up. I don't have a chance if he is thinking clearly.*

"Aaaaaahhhhh!"

Jacobson tilted his head a fraction of an inch and smiled as the scream from one of her men—the one they came in to recover, he assumed—echoed throughout the barn. "Well, Thomas, it sounds like one of your men isn't doing too well. Obviously, and to no surprise, you are not the best," he said with a triumphant look on his face, trying to find a way to get under her skin.

She didn't have time to worry about Douglas; as far as she was concerned, he was being taken care of by the team, and they were trained as well as any other she had served with. "Yes, I am the best," she replied, trying to sound as casual as possible as she noted that one of his weapons was tucked into his belt while he held tight to the other.

"You are the reason for that man's screams, Thomas. He is probably going to die tonight, and it is because you failed him as a trainer and as a leader." He let out a bark of a laugh. "Women have no place in the military, and if the general wasn't bounded by all this equal opportunity and the kinder, gentler Air Force crap, he never would have backed you. You have no place in the military as far as I am concerned."

She paused for a moment as her earpiece crackled to life with a message. "Colonel, you are just saying that because you know that I am better than you ever were and ever will be."

Jacobson clenched his fists and began to turn red. "Fuck you, Thomas!"

Just a little more, Alex. "No thank you, sir. You are not my type. I have standards and you don't measure up," she baited, smiling the whole time.

"How dare you, Thomas!" He took a step forward, and his body swelled with rage; he was on the edge.

Alex knew it was time. She stood up straight, looked him in the eyes, and got ready. "No, sir, how dare you! You are a disgrace to the uniform and all that it stands for. And one other thing"—she paused long enough to make sure that everyone was listening as she knew they were—"I have the trust and respect of those serving both with and under me, and because of that, I know that when I say that you are to be taken alive, then that is exactly how you will go."

Jacobson was fast but not as fast as Alex. With one shot, she shot the gun from his hand before he could even get it halfway up. The bullet ricocheted off his gun and grazed his right cheek, and before he could draw his second weapon from the waistband of his pants, Miceli and O'Malley had come through the hole in the wall that the SUV had created, Tasered him, and dropped him to the ground.

As Miceli was putting the handcuffs on Jacobson, the distant sound of sirens could be heard. "We did it," she said, smiling at O'Malley as they both took an arm and stood Jacobson up. When he finally had his feet under him, O'Malley and Miceli turned to look at the sarge, but instead, all they saw was her weapon pointed at them.

"Get down!" she screamed.

Without hesitation, Miceli and O'Malley dropped to the floor, pulling Jacobson with them, and watched as the sarge fired off three shots in rapid succession in the exact direction in which they had been standing. Pope, who had regained consciousness, had recovered his weapon and was about to open fire when the sarge saw him. The shots hit their marks, two to the chest and one to the head, and Pope was no more.

As Jacobson was stood up once more, he took one last look at Thomas, and when he finally truly saw her, he laughed. Watching her stumble back a step made his failure to kill her seem less like a failure and more like a victory. "Well, Thomas, you might think that you beat me, but by the looks of you, it will be nothing more than a short victory," he snorted. "Looks like I did get you. How does that shoulder feel?"

Alex had been keeping herself in the shadows, but now that she was under one of the lights, Jen was finally able to see what Jacobson was talking about. She stood frozen in place, gripped with shock, anger, and fear at what she saw before her. Alex was covered in sweat, her entire body was shaking wildly, her breathing was rapid, left arm and hand soaked in blood, and the entire left side of her face looked as though she had painted it red. "Get him out of here and send help!" she told O'Malley as she ran toward Alex, catching her just as her legs gave out.

Oh god, not again! Jen scooped Alex into her arms and half-walked, half-ran for the door, fear and panic filling her, all the while talking to Alex. "Alex baby, stay with me. Come on, Alex, you can't do this to me. Wake up, Alex. Come on! Alex, you have to wake up!" Regardless of Jen's attempts, Alex remained limp and silent in her arms.

Chapter 21

The chaos that followed was more than any of them had imagined possible. Had James been any less than the leader that he was, pandemonium would have broken out, but in the hours that followed, he had proven that the sarge's choice in her second was just. Four ambulances arrived one after the other in rapid succession, and as they pulled up, he had Antonelli direct them as to where they should park, knowing that if there was going to be a helicopter arriving, there would have to be adequate space available to land. As the first EMTs exited the vehicle, pulling a stretcher, James began directing. "You two over here!" He waved. "Blunt force trauma to his right side breaking his rib. We inserted a chest tube to drain the blood from his lungs," James told the two men as they approached and began assessing Douglas, taking blood pressure, inserting IV tubes, and hooking him up to oxygen.

"We've got it," the taller of the two men told him, effectively dismissing him. Antonelli came running with the second and third EMT teams on his heels, stretchers and bags ready.

"Antonelli, take two teams with you to the van, but I need you two"—James pointed to the two EMTs that were closest to him—"to come with me." Antonelli took the EMTs to the wounded individuals and acted as security as they assessed the condition of everyone in the van while James led the way to the front door of the barn.

James heard everything that had happened, thanks to the sarge's broken mic, so he was ready when Miceli came through the door carrying the sarge in her arms. Quickly and gently, Miceli laid the sarge down on the stretcher and watched as the EMTs removed her shirt and vest and began hooking her up to monitor her vitals. "Get that IV line in, quick!" EMT 1 shouted.

"BP is 60/40. We are going to lose her if we don't get it up!" EMT 2 responded as he inserted the first of two IVs.

"Miceli, I need you over at the van now. Antonelli needs help," James told her.

Tears streaming down her face, she looked up at James, lost and confused. "What? James, I can't leave her!"

"Yes, you can and you will. Right now, we need you to let the EMTs do their job." He walked over and stood beside her. "You know she would kick your ass for worrying about her when we still have things to do. She is going to be fine, but right now, we need you more than she does."

Jen stood there watching as the EMTs frantically worked on Alex, and although she wanted nothing more than to be there for her, she knew that James was right; too bad her heart didn't agree. She wiped her face and nodded, but before she left, she looked at the two men working on her lover. "Don't you dare let her die." Neither men slowed or gave acknowledgment that they had heard her. She paused for a few more seconds and then headed to the van to help the rest of her team.

James waited until Miceli had turned her back to him, and then he reached into the sarge's left cargo pocket and pulled out the two envelopes that were inside. Just as he was tucking them into his pocket, he heard the helicopter approaching. "Cover the wounds, helicopter inbound. Prepare for prop wash!"

The UH-60 Blackhawk helicopter landed in the center of the parking area, and as soon as the skids made contact with the ground, six MPs exited and came running toward the team. James stepped out in front; it was his show, and he was not going to let the general or anyone else say any different.

"Sir, where is Sergeant Thomas?" the first man to approach, whom James assumed was the senior ranking, asked.

"Sergeant Thomas is down. I have the command."

"We are here to assist, sir."

"We have several suspects that will be going to the hospital via ambulance," James said as he pointed to the van. "They are going to need security escorts."

"Copy that, sir."

"We also need one man inside the barn to guard the weapons, ammunition, and drugs that are inside until the mobile vault gets here."

"Understood, sir." He turned to his team and relayed the orders to his men, and they headed out.

James keyed his mic as he waited for the general and the chief to get off the helicopter. It looked as if they were discussing something. "Blue team, this is Blue Two. Escorts are being provided by the military. Find out what hospitals they are going to. Blue Three, make sure we have all the video captured in case anything goes wrong."

"Copy that, Two. Video has already been captured and backed up. Good luck."

"Sirs, if you will follow me," James said as they approached.

"I want to speak with Thomas," General Scott said as he looked around at the chaos in front of him.

"Hey!" One of the EMTs that had been working on the Sarge came running up. "Look, we need to get her to Boston General now."

"So get in the ambulance and go," James retorted.

"She won't last the ride." He looked past James and to the helicopter that was idling just beyond him. "Look, I could call for a medevac chopper, but that could take thirty minutes to an hour, and she doesn't have that much time."

James turned to face the general. "Sir, we need to borrow your helicopter."

"I said I want to talk to Thomas!"

"Talk to her while we fly then because she is the one who needs it!" James turned back to the EMT. "Get her on the chopper and pack a bag because you are coming with." The EMT nodded his head and left to get his patient. "Chief, I can brief the both of you on the way." James headed to the helicopter and, when the EMTs approached, assisted them in loading and securing her in. "Blue Six, Black is our responsibility until the marshals arrive, so keep him under our personal watch. You are in charge until I relieve you. Send me updates as they come in."

TRUST

She was furious that James was going instead of her but, at the same time, knew and understood that James had a job to do and would do everything that he could to get her a relief as soon as he could. "Copy that."

Once the stretcher was secured, General Scott, who had followed James as well as the chief to the helicopter, gave the order to go, and like a bullet, they shot off into the night sky. With headsets on and flying like a bat out of hell, General Scott leaned forward in his jump seat. "Now tell me what happened, Officer James."

***

Miceli sent one MP with each ambulance. "Antonelli, go with them and keep me informed as to their conditions."

"Got it." And without another word, he headed to the ambulance that was now short one EMT.

"O'Malley, call for tow trucks. I want these vehicles brought to our garage for impound, and while you are doing that, tape off the area."

"Copy that," he said as he pulled out his phone and went to the front of the van in search of tape.

She pulled out her phone and began texting James.

> Pronounced dead: Big Mac, aka Tyrone Mitchell, and Pope, Coroner en route. Puma GSW to the right thigh, Diamond GSW to the right shoulder, flesh wound to the back of left thigh, Harris GSW to the right forearm, Douglas to be determined. All en route to Concord Hospital. Antonelli and military personnel accompanying. We are transporting 8-Ball, T.J., Slider, and Jacobson to be seen at Boston General to have the Tasered sites evaluated. Black will be checked out there as well for a poss. bruised sternum. All will be transported by myself and O'Malley. Will need backup upon arrival.

She was about to put her phone away when she realized that she had one more phone call to make. She dialed the number. "Tina, it's Jen... Something's happened."

Less than thirty minutes after the helicopter took off, three tow trucks, four security forces personnel from Hanscom, and the coroner arrived, and one hour after that, Miceli and Antonelli headed to Boston General with a van full of angry suspects and Black riding in the passenger's seat for his own safety, while O'Malley rode in the back with the suspects. It was the longest drive of her life. "Alex, please, you have to make it."

***

When they pulled the van up to the emergency room back entrance, they were immediately surrounded by reporters and medical staff. "We can't go out there with them, it's not secure," O'Malley called up to Miceli after having looked out of the back window. Before she could make a call for help, the doors opened again, and this time two rows of Boston Police officers came out and lined up shoulder to shoulder, forming a barrier between the press and the medical personnel. Following them were additional officers who, one by one, escorted the suspects into the ER to be evaluated. Finally, four federal marshals approached and formed a box around Black as he, too, was brought in for evaluation.

James was standing in the doorway, waiting as she and O'Malley, with his laptop, stepped out of the back of the van and made their way in while reporters tried to take pictures and shouted out questions. "Were you part of the team that... What happened? Were any officers killed? Were the military and local police working together?"

As they approached, O'Malley asked, "What the hell is going on?"

"How is she?" Miceli asked at the same time.

"Follow me," James said before turning and leading them to a private waiting area on the surgical floor.

When they walked into the small room, General Scott and Chief Collins stood up and motioned for them to take a seat on the small sofa across from them. Once seated, the chief began. "Are the both of you…"

Jen's phone rang. She looked down, held up her hand, stopping the chief in midsentence, and quickly flipped it open.

"Miceli." She listened for a minute while everyone in the room stared at her.

"Understood, see you soon." She closed the phone and addressed James. "That was Antonelli. Captain Raider has relieved him in Concord. They are going to medevac Douglas to be treated here because they said that Boston General has a better trauma center, but they said he is going to make it. Antonelli wanted me to relay a message to you. The ER doctor said that you saved his life," she finished with a smile.

The look of relief was momentary on James's face but disappeared just as quickly as it had appeared. "Well, that is good news," Chief Collins remarked. "Now, as I was saying, are the both of you okay? Do you need to be…" Shouting from outside the door interrupted him for a second time.

"Where in the hell is she!"

"Ma'am, you can't go in there!"

The door to the waiting room swung open, and through it in a hospital gown, face bruised and swollen, white bandage around her head, and pulling an IV tower behind her was a frantic Tina. "Jen, what's going on? No one will tell me anything!" She stopped when she saw the chief of police staring at her.

"Officer Savage, isn't it?" the chief asked, clearly agitated.

"Yes, sir."

"Where are they?" Another shout from just outside of the door was heard.

General Scott stood up. "This is ridiculous. We need—"

The door flew open again as Chris pushed his way in. "Are you hurt? I told Alex to make sure that you didn't do anything stupid! Where is she? I'm going to kill her," he shouted as he looked around.

The chief had had enough. "Will everyone shut up! Officer Lee, Officer Miceli is fine. Will you please escort Officer Savage back to her room and wait with her there until the status of her friend is known?" the chief boomed. "And shut the door on your way out!"

For the first time in both of their lives, neither Chris nor Tina argued; instead, they both turned and left from the same door in which they had come. After a minute, everyone remaining returned to their seats.

"Are the two of you okay?" the chief asked again.

"Yes, sir," they answered in unison.

"Good. Now as you know, there are reporters everywhere. You will not speak to them. If they come up to you, the only thing that you are authorized to say is 'No Comment.' Understood?"

"Yes, sir."

General Scott then spoke. "What happened tonight was the result of joint cooperation, excellent training, and professionalism. Tonight's results were better than the chief and I had hoped for, and for that, you are all to be commended for a job well done."

"Sir?" Miceli chimed in.

"Yes, Miceli."

"What is the status of Sergeant Thomas?" she asked, trying to sound less concerned than she was.

General Scott looked down at his hands and let out a deep sigh. "They don't know. She was in cardiac arrest when the helicopter landed. They brought her up to surgery immediately, and we haven't been given an update since."

"She lost a lot of blood, she needed a transfusion, and the shot to her shoulder nicked an artery. That's all they would tell me," James added, his voice hollow.

The general stood up. "We have a lot of phone calls to make, and statements have to be given to the press. James, I want updates as you get them, and we want to meet with your team at 0500 for an update and debriefing in the conference room."

James stood up. "Yes, sir."

The general and the chief left without looking back or another word spoken.

Over the next few hours, the small waiting room began to fill. Chris and Tina had returned minutes after they had originally left, followed shortly after by Antonelli, Airman Johnson, Airman Miller, O'Malley, and finally Sergeant Williams.

At 0312, one of the surgical nurses finally came into the waiting room. "Are you all here for Miss Thomas?"

There was a unanimous yes as everyone stood up.

"I just wanted to give you an update as to her condition," she said to the group. "She is still in surgery. The bullet nicked her artery, as I am sure that you are aware of, but the problem is the amount of blood that she has lost. It is not looking good, but we are doing everything possible to save her." She looked around and paused before continuing. "Is there anyone that we should contact?"

Tina, standing there looking like she herself was recovering from war, stepped forward and whispered, "That would be me. Her parents died. I am all that she has left." What little color that she had regained since being shot suddenly washed away, and had it not been for James holding her up, her legs would have given out on her.

"I understand, ma'am. We should know something within the hour, and as soon as we do, we will let you know." She took one last look around the room and then left.

"You were her second, right?" Williams turned to James as everyone went back to their seats and silent contemplations except for Jen, who was now pacing the room, unable to sit; Chris was walking beside her.

"Yes."

He tried to be quiet when he asked, but in a room as small as the one they were in now, there was no way to keep everyone from hearing.

"Did you get the letter from her?" It was a question that he never wanted to ask, and having to do so was the hardest thing that he had ever done in his life.

Everyone in the room looked up at the two of them, Tina and Chris with questioning looks and everyone else with fear, but it was Jen who looked James in the eyes when he answered.

"Yes."

As James made to reach in his pocket, Jen, who was now standing beside him, grabbed his arm.

"Not yet, do not pull it out unless it is absolutely necessary. Don't give up yet, do you understand me?" she said, looking over at Tina, who was now crying into her hands while O'Malley and Johnson sat on either side of her for support.

"She doesn't need to see it unless…"

"Yeah, Miceli, I got you," James said, hoping beyond hope that he didn't have to give the two different letters to the two women in this room.

At 0437, the door opened again, and this time, one of the doctors, still in his green surgical gown that was covered in blood, came in.

"Who is here for Miss Thomas?" Everyone stood up and came forward, leaving two spots open in front for Jen and Tina. When they stepped forward and filled in the gap, James answered, "We all are. How is she?"

"When she was brought in, she was in full cardiac arrest. We were able to stabilize her long enough to get her up to the OR. She lost a lot of blood and needed several transfusions due to the gunshot wound to her shoulder. The amount of blood loss is what caused the cardiac arrest, but we were able to patch that up. In addition, she sustained a concussion and skull fracture, but luckily neither should cause any lasting damage."

"What does all of that mean, Doctor? Is she going to be all right?" Tina asked.

For the first time since entering the room, the doctor noticeably relaxed. "She will be here for about a week, and then she will need a couple of months of physical therapy for her shoulder, but she should be just fine."

The cheers and shouts of excitement could be heard down the hall, high-fives were exchanged, and Jen and Tina hugged. "When can we see her, Doc?" Jen asked while she was still holding a crying Tina.

"She is in recovery right now, and then she is going to be moved to the ICU just until we can make sure that she is fully out of the woods. Come back tomorrow, but only one visitor at a time in her room. And don't stress her. She needs rest, so no talk about work."

"Ha!" O'Malley laughed. "I thought you didn't want her stressed, Doc. If we don't talk about work, then all she will do is stress!"

Everyone laughed as a confused but relieved doctor left the room.

James looked at his watch. "Guys, we need to go debrief."

***

They filed into the same conference room that they were in when they had received the officer-related shooting briefing from Harris. The events of the past twenty-four hours had taken a toll on all of them, and it showed as they slowly made their way to the chairs surrounding the conference table. The chief looked at his officers as they sat slumped in their seats, uniforms dirty and disheveled, dirt and blood smeared on their clothes, hands, and faces, circles under their eyes, and utter exhaustion in the air around them. "Chief, how is Douglas? Has there been any word?" James asked, trying to sit up a little straighter in his chair.

"Officer Douglas is going to be fine. They have him in the ICU for observation, but they expect to be able to move him to a regular room later today. His wife is with him now.

"I know that you are all exhausted, but the chief and I need to know what happened tonight. We need every detail," General Scott said as he and the chief each pulled out pens and paper.

"Sirs, I think it would be better if we just showed you," O'Malley said as he stood up and began to hook his laptop into the room's AV system. "James, do you want to fill them in as to what happened up until the point that we went in?"

For the next thirty minutes, General Scott and Chief Collins sat stock-still in their chairs as they listened to James recount the events of the evening and then watched everything play out on the projection screen. When the video was over, both men stared at each other before the chief finally stood up. "You have an evidence trail?"

"Yes, chief, we do. I will give it to you in your office in a couple of hours," James replied.

"What happened tonight was nothing short of amazing. You did your jobs with skill and professionalism and more than exceeded our expectations." He looked around the table before continuing. "I want you all to take the next two days off, get some rest, and meet me in my office Tuesday morning at 0900. We will fill out the reports then and will figure out where we will be going from there." He and the general stood to leave. "Remember, talk to no one about the events from tonight," General Scott said before he and the chief turned and left the room.

***

She lay there, eyes closed, quietly taking in her surroundings. She listened to the monotonous beep of the heart monitor and heard the muted sounds of shuffling feet across the floor that sounded like they were a million miles away, but still she was confused. *What happened?* She felt a presence near her, hovering over her, and she stayed still, trying to make sense of the confusion that plagued her mind—that was, until she felt a hand on her arm. "Get back!"

The nurse jumped back, letting out a small scream of her own and knocking a pitcher of water and cups off the side table and onto the floor. Jen, who had passed out from sheer exhaustion in the chair opposite of the nurse and next to the bed, jumped up. "Alex, it's okay. Shhhh, you need to relax. Baby, lie down."

The moment she heard Jen's voice and felt her hand in her own, the pain hit. "Ohhhh," she gasped. She felt as if someone had parked a cement truck on her chest, her shoulder felt as if there were a thousand red-hot knives being slowly turned inside, and her head felt like it was going to explode. As Jen helped her to lie back down, her body broke out in a sweat, instantly covering her body and soaking through her gown, heart monitor racing.

"I'll call the doctor," the now recovering nurse informed them after having picked up the water pitcher and cups that she had knocked over before quickly leaving the room.

"Are you okay?" she asked; the pain of just speaking was incredible.

"Yes, baby, I'm fine."

"I need to talk to General Scott and James," she said through clenched teeth.

Jen brushed the hair out of Alex's face. "No, you don't. You need to rest, and before you start to argue with me, I have a message for you." She paused for a minute and brushed her fingers through her hair, watching the heart monitor as Alex's heart rate began to slowly decrease again. "James did everything you asked and has been working with the chief and the general. He wanted me to tell you that General Scott will be here at 1400 Sunday." She looked at her watch. "That's twelve hours from now, to check on you. Baby, right now you need to rest."

"Douglas?" she asked, struggling to keep her eyes open.

"He's doing fine. He is going to make a full recovery."

Her eyes closed then, and when she opened them again, General Scott was standing at the foot of her bed. "Sergeant Thomas, how are you feeling?"

Every part of her body hurt. "Just fine, sir. I am ready for the debrief whenever you are."

General Scott smiled. "Not necessary, Thomas. Officer James has taken care of things, and I must say, you made a good choice in naming him your second."

"Thank you, sir."

"I just wanted to let you know that you and your team did a fine job. The skill and professionalism that you and your team exhibited is to be commended." Walking up to stand at the side of her bed, he continued, "Sergeant Thomas, I have ordered your team not to speak about the operation to anyone, and that extends to yourself as well. When you have had a little more time to recover, we need to sit down and discuss future operations for you and your team."

Alex was confused. "Sir? I thought that this was a one-time thing."

He smiled brighter this time. "Thomas, you of all people know that we in the military need to be fluid. Things change, and the success of this mission has brought a lot of attention to you and your team from the powers that be. When you get out of here, we will have a lot to discuss." With a curt nod, the general turned and walked out.

She lay in her bed, fighting off the sleep that was trying to reclaim her once again and trying to make sense of the conversation she had just had with the general, but her mind would not allow it. It wasn't until Jen came back into the room and took her hand that she allowed herself to drift into the painlessness of sleep.

***

The events of the days and weeks of the next month went by in a blur. No camera or news organization ever got the names of the members of the team that stopped the drug and weapons smugglers. Chief Collins was quoted as saying in one of the many news conferences, "The members of the elite team that was put together for the sole purpose of taking down the drug and weapons trade ring will be kept confidential so as to protect the individual members, their families, and future operations."

Diamond had cut a deal with the Feds and told them everything there was to know about the Blood organization—from the names of his top generals, major suppliers, and the connections linking the gang from New York to Boston and everything in-between; in return, he was entered into the witness protection program and relocated. The team spearheaded and organized the takedown and capture of every general and lieutenant in Boston. Every single one of them talked, giving up more names and details of the organization, in return for taking the death penalty off the table. Colonel Jacobson, Harris, O'Brien, and the five others involved on the military side were brought up on charges from both the military and civilian courts. All told, over one thousand arrests in five states of high-ranking Blood gang members were made in less than four weeks under the RICO and Patriot Act, and more were expected to come.

Alex and Douglas were released from the hospital. Alex wasn't home two days before she was chomping at the bit and wanting to get back to work. It took Jen, Tina, and Chris to take turns watching Alex around the clock the first week to keep her from doing too much. Jen, with no complaints, had moved herself in with Alex so as to take care of her for the first few weeks of her recovery.

Two months later, almost to the day of the operation, the team was called into the chief's office. After the initial roundup, all of the officers had been released back to their individual divisions until further notice. Alex had been released back to work on light duty and within her first month back had reorganized the entire base Military Police Squadron. The new Squadron commander was more than pleased with the changes that had been instituted and was already taking credit for the turnaround in the Squadron's effectiveness ratings.

As the officers walked in, they were greeted by the sight of Sergeant Thomas standing to General Scott's right and some stiff in a suit to his left. Before any of them could say a word, he addressed the group, "Officers, it is nice to see you all again. Please allow me to introduce you to Ken Matthews with the Office of Homeland Security." General Scott indicated to the man on his left. "Mr. Matthews has a proposition for you that he would like to discuss."

Matthews looked from the general to the chief and then took the floor. "Officers, the work you did in taking down the Blood organization and stopping a military-based drug trafficking ring was nothing short of amazing and has been noticed in high places. As a result, I was sent here to offer all of you positions with the Office of Homeland Security doing exactly what you did two months ago. You will be part of a team that investigates and apprehends threats to the United States on US soil. To be more specific, your team will investigate gangs, terrorist threats, and possible government corruption."

To no one's surprise, Miceli was the first one to speak. "Where would we be working?"

"We have a Boston-based office, so you would be working out of there."

The officers looked back and forth among one another, speaking to one another without saying a word. Finally James addressed the next question. "You said part of a team, how many will be on it?"

"Well, that really depends on how many of you—" Sergeant Thomas interrupted him by stepping forward.

"Let me explain so that we can get out of here today. The deal is they want a six-member team to do exactly what it was that we did, only this time the stakes are higher."

"Sarge, with all due respect, there is no way I am going into that kind of position with anyone other than you," Antonelli said. "And since you can't be part of the team…"

"Yeah, sorry, Matthews, but I don't feel right doing this without the sarge," O'Malley added.

"Sarge," James stepped forward, effectively silencing the remaining rejections, "the facts are simple. We all loved being a part of what we did, but without you, none of us would feel right doing this, and to be honest…I just don't trust anyone else to lead."

Alex stood there for a moment, staring at each individual member of her team, honored by the trust and respect that they were openly offering her. "Before any of you jump to any more conclusions without checking your facts first, I think that you should all be aware of the fact that Mr. Matthews spoke to me less than an hour ago, offering me the same position."

"But what about the military?" Miceli asked before her brain could filter her mouth.

"Master Sergeant Thomas has been granted an early retirement, conditional on her acceptance of this position," General Scott told them.

"Which I accepted."

"I'm in!" O'Malley shouted.

"So am I!" Jen added with a smile.

"Count me in," James chimed in.

"This is going to get interesting!" Antonelli said, laughing.

"My wife is going to kill me, but I am definitely in!" Douglas chimed in.

Matthews stood looking at Sergeant Thomas and the rest of her team, who had gathered around her. "Well then, we need to get you all over to headquarters and processed today because we have a situation that needs to be taken care of, and, Miss Thomas, your team is the most suited to handle it." Matthews turned to look at the chief and the general.

"Gentlemen, I am sure that I don't have to remind you that everything that was spoken in this room is classified and is not to be repeated." He turned and addressed the team again. "You will have until 1400 to turn in your weapons and uniforms and be at headquarters where I will meet you and get you set up and fully briefed in." Matthews walked out of the chief's office without another word.

The team filed out of the chief's office, and as always, Alex and Jen were the last ones out of the door. Before they caught up to the rest of the group at the elevators, Jen leaned into Alex.

"Just because we are working together doesn't mean that I am moving out, you know."

Alex stopped and looked at Jen. "Don't make me smile at work, it's unprofessional."

"Hey, Sarge, any idea as to what this first assignment is about?" James asked as they all began to file into the elevator.

Just as the doors were beginning to close, she smiled as she answered him. "Things that go boom."

About the Author

Aprille Canniff is a deputy sheriff and member of the Air National Guard. *Trust* is her first published novel, which she wrote while deployed to Afghanistan. She currently lives in Virginia with her wife and "ninja" cat. When she isn't writing or working, her passion is fishing and bragging about how big the one that got away was.

CPSIA information can be obtained
at www.ICGtesting.com
Printed in the USA
BVHW071005170221
600363BV00001B/18